The Past, the Present and the Loud, Loud Girl

A word of warning: never, *ever* try to cut your fringe when you're in a bad mood.

I gazed at my reflection in the toilet mirrors while a bunch of girls who were in the year below me charged about screaming and giggling about something or other in the background.

Hopefully, it wasn't my hair, but I couldn't have blamed them if it was. One single, solitary chunk of fringe was cut so high that a big, shiny patch of forehead positively *gleamed* at me in the mirror. My fringe would've looked better if I'd just let Tor's hamsters *gnaw* on it for a while...

Also available in this series:

The Past, the Present and the Loud, Loud Girl
Dates, Double Dates and Big, Big Trouble
Butterflies, Bullies and Bad, Bad Habits
Friends, Freak-Outs and Very Secret Secrets
Boys, Brothers and Jelly-Belly Dancing
Sisters, Super-Creeps and Slushy,
Gushy Love Songs
Parties, Predicaments and Undercover Pets
Tattoos, Telltales and Terrible, Terrible Twins
Angels, Arguments and a Furry Merry Christmas
Mates, Mysteries and Pretty Weird Weirdness
Daisy, Dad and the Huge, Small Surprise
Rainbows, Rowan and True, True Romance?

ALLY'S WORLD

the PAST, the PRESENT and the LOUD, LOUD GIRL

KAREN McCOMBIE

SCHOLASTIC

~~for LORNE sausage banana~~

~~for LORNE sausage Bonella~~

~~for Lauren Banana~~

for Lauren Bonella !

Scholastic Children's Books,
Commonwealth House, 1–19 New Oxford Street,
London WC1A 1NU, UK
A division of Scholastic Ltd
London ~ New York ~ Toronto ~ Sydney ~ Auckland
Mexico City ~ New Delhi ~ Hong Kong

First published in the UK by Scholastic Ltd, 2001

ISBN 0 439 99868 9

Printed by Cox & Wyman Ltd, Reading, Berks.

10 9 8

The right of Karen McCombie to be identified as the author
of this work has been asserted by her in accordance with the
Copyright, Designs and Patents Act, 1988.

Contents

PROLOGUE

Dear Mum,

I've decided to do something.

Don't panic: it's not like I'm about to pierce my lip, or enrol for the next Mars mission, or run away with the circus and juggle clowns or something. (Although you'd probably think all that was cool.)

It's just that, you know how I've been keeping a box with all our photos and school reports and stuff for you to see? Well, no you don't – which is the problem – but trust me, that's what I'm doing.

Well, anyway, apart from those bits and pieces, I've decided that I'm going to start writing down some of the things that happen to all of us; the things that matter, anyway. It's not going to be like a diary or anything – I don't exactly have the patience for that. (Though I did buy one a couple of Januarys ago; it was half-price in the stationery shop up on the Broadway. I started out OK, prattling on about *what* I'd done that day and *what* I was feeling and *what* we'd had for tea, but by

January 10th I was just doodling flowers on the page. And the entry for January 15th just said "BORED, BORED, BORED", so I kind of chucked it in after that.)

So this time, I think I'll do it like an essay... Only it might be a bit on the long side. You know what I'm like. Remember that last report you saw when I was at primary school? *"Ally is very bright and imaginative, but her mind does tend to wander..."* Hey, guess what? Nothing's changed. It's like Grandma says, I'd get twice as much done if I stopped wittering for five minutes. Which is sort of true, I know. And which is what I'm doing now, I suppose...

OK, so back to my plan.

I think I'll do it like I'm writing it for some stranger to read, 'cause – sorry, I don't mean to give you a hard time about this – it might make me too sad if I just set it all down for you. I suppose that's because I know it's not exactly likely that you're going to come walking through the door in the next two minutes or anything, and beg to read this...

But then, if – by some mind-blowing magic – you did, you'd have all our pictures and things to look at, *and* be able to read all my stories about what's been going on with me and Linn and Rowan and Tor. And, of course, Dad.

Speaking of Dad, I think I'll start with his fortieth birthday, 'cause that was when Kyra turned up, and when – don't panic – we nearly lost Tor...

Love you lots,

Ally

(your Love Child No. 3)

Chapter 1

WELCOME TO MY (WEIRD) WORLD...

Look at a map of the world, and find Britain (small, jaggedy, sort of in the middle).

Look at a map of Britain and find London (big blob, down in the south).

Look at a map of London and find Crouch End (weird name, nice place).

Look for Palace Heights Road (number 28, to be precise).

When you find number 28, stand on the pavement opposite and look at the terraced house with your eyes half-crossed (all fuzzy like that, it seems almost as posh as the ones on either side of it. *Un*cross your eyes and you'll see that it's actually pretty tatty round the edges).

I'm Ally Love, and this is where I live with my dad (Martin), a power-mad control freak (my seventeen-year-old sister, Linn), a complete airhead (my fifteen-year-old sister, Rowan) and a space cadet (my seven-year-old brother, Tor).

OK, so now look up, past the big bay living-room

window, past the first-floor bay (my sister Rowan's room) until you see a tiny window at the top – my attic bedroom.

That's where I've woken up nearly every morning for all of the thirteen years I've been on this planet, and where I'm normally very happy to wake up. Except for one particular morning...

It was weird – for some reason, my whole head was vibrating.

But then, there are plenty of weird things in this world. Like nose hair. I mean, if the point is that it's there for protection, then why doesn't it grow in your mouth too? (Blee...)

And electricity. It doesn't matter how many times the principle's explained to me, I still don't get it. But don't get me wrong, I am pretty *pleased* about it. Dad sometimes likes to light these big, fat, coloured candles we have in the living room, but until they invent a candle-powered TV (that would need a *really* big, fat candle, I guess), I'm OK with electricity, however weird it is.

Of course, plenty of people – including my oldest sister – think our parents are weird for giving their kids odd names (me, I got off lightly out of the four of us), but I think it just goes to show that some people have no imagination. And anyway, when they get to know the story behind each name, they usually think it's pretty cool after all.

Oops, there I go. Getting sidetracked by weird stuff when I was supposed to be talking about the head-vibrating thing. But I do that a lot (get sidetracked, not have a vibrating head) – so get used to it.

Anyhow, it was a Sunday morning when I felt my head vibrate. At first I didn't panic; I just told myself that there must be a giant articulated lorry parked in the street outside, its engine throbbing so hard that it was shaking the house from the foundations right up to my little room under the eaves. That, or maybe it was a low-flying plane, rumbling through the skies above our house, sending tremors from the roof tiles down.

Then I noticed something else – one side of my face and neck were as hot as a very hot thing. A vibrating head *and* a burning-hot face...

OK, so *then* I started to panic. Compared to people like my airhead sister Rowan and my ditzy best mate Sandie, I know I come over like I'm confident and logical. But underneath, I'm basically a world-class worrier...

What had they told us at school about meningitis? Did the telltale signs include victims hearing a persistent droning noise that made their heads vibrate? Was it a common sign to feel one side of your face burning up? I couldn't remember.

Then all of a sudden, the noise and the vibration stopped. In its place, there was silence, broken only by one small noise.

"Snurph."

My eyes flicked open. I was awake, and instantly flooded with relief.

I didn't have the first warning signs of meningitis.

I wasn't about to be carted off to the Whittington hospital down the road.

I turned my head on the pillow and found myself nose to nose with Colin.

"Don't mind me," I muttered, as he moved in his sleep, settling himself more comfortably in the cosy pile of people fur that he'd come across.

As I tried to pull my long, brown hair slowly out from under him, he gave another snuffly cat snore and started off with his loud, droning purr again.

Freeing myself, I flung back the duvet and left Colin to it. I padded over the old, worn carpet and did the morning ritual I've done ever since I was tall enough to reach the ledge on my tiptoes – staring out of my tiny window at the view of the Palace, perched on top of one of London's only proper hills.

"Well, Ally Love," I said to myself, "You could

have been famous; you could have gone down in medical history as the first person to suffer from Vibrating Head Syndrome."

I shot a glance backwards in the direction of Colin, who was now sprawling his whole body and three legs (hey, I'll explain later) across the whole pillow.

Then I thought of something *truly* weird: do cats' heads vibrate when they purr?

I walked back over to Colin, and clamped my fingers round his face.

"Yeee-oow!"

My scientific experiment didn't prove the vibrating theory. What it did do was show that cats really, *really* don't appreciate having their heads squeezed when they're sleeping.

Trust me, I've got the bite-marks to prove it.

Now that I knew I wasn't going to die (well, eventually, yeah – but not right that *second*), I should have been skipping down the stairs to breakfast with a stupid grin of relief on my face.

But I didn't. Mainly because my fear of immediate death had been replaced by an ominous feeling that I'd forgotten something...

Uh-oh.

Chapter 2

LINN'S LOUSY IDEA

"What's up with your hair? You look like you've been dragged through a forest backwards," said my big sister Linn, staring up at me and wrinkling her nose.

"A cat slept on my head."

"Oh," shrugged Linn, carrying on buttering her toast. "Which one?"

"Colin," piped up my little brother, as I sat down at the kitchen table beside him.

"How did you know that?" I asked, rubbing at my nose where it was tickly with stray cat-hairs.

"Ginger fur stuck on your face," Tor muttered, reaching over and pointing his finger right into my cheek.

"Oh."

"And that – that's Colin's teeth-marks."

"Thank you, Pet Detective," I mumbled, looking down the hand that Colin's fangs had dented.

Here's the thing: I close my door every night before I go to bed, but always in the morning some animal's worked magic and wangled its way in (but usually into some cosy corner – getting comfy on my head doesn't happen too often). And I include my little brother Tor in that. It's pretty sweet, actually – whenever Tor has nightmares, which isn't often – it isn't my dad, or Rowan, or Linn he scampers to. It's *my* bed he ends up curling up at the bottom of, like one of the army of hamsters and gerbils he's got stashed in cages all around his own room.

"Rowan up yet?" I asked, helping myself to orange juice from the sticky carton in the middle of the table.

I still hadn't figured out what the thing was that I'd forgotten. Maybe when I was more awake it would come to me...

"You're joking, aren't you? Haven't you noticed it's only half-nine?" mumbled Linn with her mouth full. "The Queen of the Night won't be gracing us with her presence for ages yet."

That was true – Rowan never got up much before noon at the weekends, much to our grandma's disapproval, *and* Linn's. But then Linn gets snippy and grouchy at Rowan pretty easily.

Honestly, my two sisters are about as different as people can get and still be related. Linn is seventeen and sensible, and likes everything neat, tidy, organized and lined up with a set square (believe me, she *would* if we let her). Which is a bit of a shame for Linn, since she has to live in a wonky, ramshackle house like ours. And our whole family's pretty ramshackle and wonky too, when you think about it, and that doesn't please Linn too much either.

You should see her room – it's on the other side of the attic from mine. Where mine's painted sky blue (kind of fitting for an attic, don't you think? The room closest to the real thing?), with posters and pictures and my big old map of the world covering most of the wall space, Linn's is the exact opposite. Everything's so white and streamlined and minimal you'd think she'd ironed it all, from the carpet to her textbooks. Sometimes I catch Linn in there, sitting on the window seat and staring out at her view of central London sprawling away in the distance (approximately eleven and a quarter kilometres, fact fans). At times like that, locked away in her little oasis of calm and non-clutter, I get the feeling that the one thing she'd love to do is get away from sleepy Crouch End – and us.

Now take Rowan's room. You think our living room's bad, with those canary-yellow walls and the navy woodwork? (Mum's choice, by the way, like every other colour scheme in the house except our own bedrooms). Well, Rowan's room is something else. At the moment she's painted it raspberry, and it's like an explosion in a fairy-lights factory. She's got them draped everywhere: round the bay window, along the shelves, the wooden bedhead, and, once, even round Tor.

Rowan had just taken a photo of him all decked out in blinking lights, when Linn barged in and yanked them off him, accusing Rowan of trying to electrocute our little brother. Of course, she was totally right, in a strictly speaking, safety-conscious way, but sometimes I think that Linn doesn't know how to have fun. After all, Tor *did* look pretty cute (and bemused) in the photo, and he didn't seem to mind too much. But then Tor never grumbles about anything. Mainly 'cause he never says much, ever.

If Rowan could get away with wearing fairy lights, I think she'd do it. She's fifteen now, but ever since I can remember, show her anything that twinkles and glistens and she's completely sold on it. It's like with her clothes – ages ago, she bought all these little-old-lady beaded cardies for about zero pence from jumble sales and second-hand shops and wore them all the time. She got loads of weird looks and sniggery comments for it, and then

BLAM! everyone from Miss Selfridge to New Look starts selling them.

And you should see the piles of fashion magazines she's got in her room. One stack of *Elles* comes up to my waist practically, and they've been sitting there so long she's stuck this mad old tasselly table lamp on top.

So, my two older sisters have got different tastes, but that isn't the main reason Linn gets bugged by Rowan. The main reason is that Rowan insists on doing the one thing that no one else does – she calls Linn by her full name: Linnhe.

Boy, does Linn hate that name. I remember her blowing up at my dad once, saying it was cruel of parents to give their kids weird names. I can't remember how Dad reacted – he probably just nodded and agreed with her. It's his usual way of avoiding arguments. But I'm with Rowan on this – not that I'd dream of saying so to Linn. I think Linnhe (think: Linny) is really pretty. Still, Linn hates it so much that she changed it to the more normal sounding Linn. She even went so far as to try and change the spelling to Lynne, but it got too complicated; her name was spelt the old way on everything from her school records to the "Property of Linn Love" notes that she sticks on everything she owns. Including her favourite yoghurts in the fridge. Honest – I'm not joking.

"So, where's Dad?" I asked Linn, sloppily spreading some peanut butter on my toast.

"Out getting a newspaper," said Linn. "And listen, speaking of Dad, I'm a bit worried…"

I paused – was my forgotten thing something to do with Dad? Nah – that didn't feel right. I carried on with my peanut butter.

"Worried? How come?" I asked her, through a mouthful of toast.

"Well, we have a problem…" she sighed.

"Houston, we have a problem…" muttered Tor in a fake American accent.

He watched a programme about rocket launches the night before with Dad, if you want an explanation. But then Tor and his little ways don't need explaining, if you just grasp the single fact that he's a bit of a space cadet in general.

For example, at that moment, I noticed he was drawing a smiley face with his finger in the margarine on his toast, which was completely normal. For *him*, I mean, not necessarily for *every* seven year old. But *our* seven-year-old brother has the habit of moulding *all* his food into some kind of artwork before he eats it. He's very good with scrambled eggs – makes them look like clouds in the sky on his plate. That's why he hates soup; it's really hard to do anything artistic with a bowl of mushroom soup. Try it if you don't believe me.

"What kind of a problem?" I asked my sister dubiously.

The reason I felt a bit dubious is that Linn sees practically *everything* as a problem. Tor merrily announcing that he's found a new walking-wounded, stray animal to clutter up the house with is a major problem. Me leaving my homework till Sunday night is worthy of a drama. Rowan sitting daydreaming instead of taking her turn doing the dishes is virtually an arrestable offence.

Linn gazed at me in despair; I was obviously meant to *know* something, or be *aware* of something. Oops. Since I hadn't a clue what that might be, I just gazed back at her, wondering how she always managed to look so unnaturally together first thing in the morning. It wasn't fair. Her blonde-ish fair hair was dragged neatly back into a ponytail, and unlike me and Tor – who were still in our pyjamas (me: baggy, drawstring-waist trousers and an old T-shirt; Tor: a Wallace & Gromit number) – Linn was already dressed in her regulation black trousers (she has about seventeen thousand pairs, I swear she does) and zip-necked top.

My eyes dropped – as they often do – to the outline of her perfectly formed boobs in that tight top. I was thinking – as I often do – how was it that fate gave her a proper-sized chest, as *well* as everything else, when all *I* got from the Love family gene pool was two mini-mounds that have trouble filling a double-A bra? ("Plenty of time for them to grow!" Grandma always trots out whenever I moan about it. Well, I'll try to be patient – but I won't hold my breath…)

"Don't you realize the date?" Linn said wearily, making me flip my gaze back up to her face smartish. "It's Dad's birthday two weeks tomorrow – and it's his fortieth. What on earth are we going to get him?"

"Uh … a present?" I ventured, knowing I was probably saying the wrong thing.

Tor must have thought so too – he stopped what he was doing and eyed us both warily. Out of the corner of my eye I could see that he was obviously inspired by my encounter with Colin. Beside the smiley face he'd traced in the margarine, he'd been moulding a wobbly, vaguely cat-shaped dollop of gingery marmalade.

"Yes, I *know* we've got to get him a present," said Linn irritably – still, not as irritably as it could have been, knowing her. "But what *kind* of present? I mean, it's got to be special, since it's his fortieth. And it's up to us to make it special; after all, who else will?"

I knew what – or rather who – she was getting at: Mum, of course. But I wasn't in the mood to get into all that.

"Mmm, it *would* be nice to do something special…" I agreed non-committally.

Agreeing with Linn is always the easiest way to go. Like I said, even *Dad* knows that.

"Well," she said, suddenly losing the anxious look, and seeming quite chuffed with herself. "I've had an idea."

"Oh, yeah?"

Me (doing the talking) and Tor (just listening) were both on tenterhooks waiting for this. Whatever was coming wasn't just an idea that we could all kick about and discuss. Whatever Linn had thought of was probably going to happen.

"I thought," she began, a conspiratorial grin breaking out on her face, "that we should … have a surprise party for him!"

Right away, I knew I needed to set her straight, remind her that sweet, shy people like our dad don't really respond to the whole "Oh my goodness – all this for little old *me*?!" centre-of-attention thing. And I needed to remind her that after four years of looking after us on his own (with a little help from Grandma, of course), he hadn't exactly got a lot of time for keeping up friendships.

The surprise was, who exactly was she planning to *invite* to this surprise party?

But of course, I am speaking about my sister Linn – She Who Must Be Obeyed – here.

"Yeah! That sounds like a great idea!" I lied through gritted teeth.

Chapter 3

SENSIBLE ANSWERS ONLY, PLEASE

Considering that my friends' houses are all magnolia-painted neat, with matching towels and plate sets – and chairs, for that matter – it's quite reassuring to know that there's another building in the area that's as beautiful, but as crumbly round the edges as my house.

I ended up thinking just that, sitting on a bench in the park surrounding Alexandra Palace and gazing up at the huge Rose window of the Palace itself. I'd come to the park with the dogs after my conversation with Linn about Dad's birthday present. Walking clears my head, and right now, I knew I needed to come up with an alternative plan to Linn's – and quick.

But so far, of course, all I'd done was daydream.

See, Alexandra Palace is this stunning, big building from a distance, but up close, OK it's *still* amazing, but it's sort of tatty round the edges. One side of the building's semi-restored and shiny, and the other is semi-smoke-damaged and boarded up.

It's really sad when you imagine how awesome it would have looked (all sandstone and glass domes) when it was first built back in 1800-whenever. But then not a lot of people ever had a chance to see it that way – the whole place caught on fire sixteen days after it was finished. What a bummer.

Not that I'm saying a fire or anything that drastic has ever happened to *our* house. It's just that, while it's a really comfy, pretty place to live in, there's loads wrong with it. It's the kind of house where there's always handles falling off the kitchen cupboards and window frames with big, breezy gaps in them and pipes in the wall that sometimes gurgle like they're about to throw up. That's not even *starting* on stuff like the sofa my dad brought home after he "salvaged" it from a skip (it was so full of fleas that the *cats* refused to sit on it), or the ominous cracks in loads of the walls and ceilings that keep getting bigger and bigger ("Subsidence," my grandma occasionally points out darkly). But I wouldn't swap our house – even though it does look like a cross between a craft fair and a second-hand shop – in a million years. (Linn, of course, *would* – in a *micro*-second.)

So, it was late morning on Sunday, and I was sitting staring at the stained glass of the Rose window, views of distant high-rises in central

London behind me, when this frenetic barking started up.

Rolf (our big, hairy dog) barks at anything – the postman, the gate-post, traffic cones, blades of grass, you name it – but the fact that Winslet (our small, hairy dog) was barking too meant only one thing: Billy and Precious were on their way.

I was glad – I wanted to sound out Billy, since he was a boy, about any ideas he had for a good present for *my* dad. OK, so Billy is my age and twenty-seven years *younger* than my dad, but they're both males, so I figured he might come up with *something* useful. I knew I was clutching at straws, but I was desperate to go back home with at least *one* alternative suggestion to Linn's rotten surprise-party idea.

"Hi!" I waved at him, as he stomped over the grass towards me.

"Hi, Ally!" Billy grinned, flopping down beside me on the bench.

Billy's my mate; we've known each other since we were – ooh! – *that* high. I sometimes don't see him too often during the week since he goes to a different school from me (Muswell School for Boys), so whatever we're doing, we always try to meet in the park on Sunday mornings to catch up. He comes over from his side of the Palace

(Muswell Hill), I wander over from mine (Crouch End), and we meet in the middle, on the grass just downhill from the Rose window.

"So how's it going?" Billy asked, keeping one eye on the typical mayhem going on in front of us.

All three dogs were tearing round in a big blurry bundle, playing their favourite game, which involves lots of running in circles, barking and occasional growling (Winslet). Translated into people speak, the game is called "Aw, Go On – Let Me Smell Your Bum!", and the object of it is for Billy's small, white, irritating poodle to attempt to sniff the bottoms of *my* dogs, while Rolf and Winslet do everything short of biting Precious to get him to stop. Personally, I think they're both too polite.

"I'm OK," I shrugged. "What about you?"

"Yeah, great," said Billy unconvincingly. "Except for the fact that I failed two tests at school this week, everyone gave me a hard time 'cause I let in three goals at five-a-side yesterday afternoon, and that really pretty new girl that's just moved in on my street still doesn't know I exist."

At the mention of school, I immediately felt that faint, worrying flutter at the back of my mind again. What *was* it I'd forgotten? I waited for a second, giving my brain a chance to explain itself, but when nothing happened, I turned my attention back to Billy.

"But you said that girl looks about eighteen," I pointed out, knowing I was about to burst his bubble. "She's not exactly going to be tripping over herself to talk to you, is she?"

I'd been starting to notice that Billy was getting a bit predictable lately. We used to have these great conversations about life, PlayStations and everything, but nowadays, he'd always work the conversation round to girls, sooner or later. He was desperate for a girlfriend (that much was obvious), and kept asking me for advice about how you get together with someone and what you do once you *are* together. Like I was some big expert or something. I've only ever been out with one boy – Keith Brownlow – and that only lasted a few dates. (What a disaster my love life is – just don't get me started, OK? I know eight year olds who've had more snogs from boys than me...) Anyway, if you must know about Keith Brownlow, well, *I* decided to chuck *him* when he kissed me right after he'd finished a can of Coke.

(Hot tip, boys: belching in a girl's mouth is *not* too gorgeous.)

"Just kick me now, why don't you," mumbled Billy, pretending to be hurt at my home truths about his chances with the hot-chick neighbour.

"Don't tempt me," I said, aiming a trainer in his direction. "Anyway, there's something I need your help with. It's my dad's fortieth birthday soon. What do you reckon we should get him?"

"A Zimmer frame? Grey hair-dye? Ouch!"

I didn't kick him hard, really I didn't. But boys are such drama queens, aren't they?

"Billy! Stop mucking about and help me out!" I nagged him.

"*I* don't know what you should get him, do I?" Billy mumbled, rubbing his shin. "I mean, he's *your* dad. *You* should know what he wants."

"Well, if I did, I wouldn't need to ask *you*, would I?"

It was my own fault. I should have known it was a waste of time bringing up the subject with him. Billy can quote huge chunks of dialogue out of movies and could tell you the name of every weird alien in every series of *Star Trek*, but he's pathetically hopeless at anything remotely normal and useful.

"What about your sisters?" he asked me. "Doesn't Linn have everything organized? She usually does…"

Billy's pretty intimidated by Linn, and you can't really blame him for that – I think she'd be capable of intimidating the Prime Minister if she was in the right mood (make that *wrong* mood). Whenever Billy comes round to my house for tea he goes really quiet in front of her. But then, he's kind of funny about Rowan and Tor too. He thinks they're weird; Rowan 'cause of the way she dresses and everything, and Tor (Billy calls him "Spook Kid") because he just sits and stares silently over the table at Billy, which is what he tends to do with *any* of the friends we bring home. (Tor even does it to his *own* little buddies, but I guess they mustn't mind, 'cause they still want to hang out with him.)

"You don't want to hear what *Linn*'s thought of. C'mon, Billy – what would be your dream present?"

"Dunno, really," he replied, frowning. "But this morning, I was thinking how cool it would be to own a life-sized cardboard cut-out of Lara Croft."

"Billy, a life-sized cut-out of Lara Croft would be about ten centimetres high. Get it through your head – she's not real. You're in lust with a very small character in a computer game. No wonder you can't get a proper girlfriend!"

I could see that he was struggling with a smart comeback line, but bless him, Billy's not really great at sparkling wit. I mean, he's got a great sense of humour and everything, but he's no match for me. Which is fun. For me.

Not that I can talk, of course, considering the only boyfriend I've got right now is Billy – and that's "boy" and "friend" with a very *big* space between both words...

"Oh, yeah? Yeah?" he fumbled around, hoping vainly that something smart and cutting would come to him. "Well Lara Croft *isn't* just a computer character. What about the *Tomb Raider* movie? She's in that!"

"The thing about the *Tomb Raider* movie," I sighed, "is that it's a *movie*. It's not real life – and just 'cause some actress is playing Lara Croft doesn't make her real either!"

"I know that!" said Billy defensively.

It was a stupid conversation, but then it's pretty typical of the stupid conversations we have. Sometimes Billy drives me crazy when we end up yakking round in circles like this, but most of the time it's kind of fun, actually.

I was just about to tell him that even if Lara Croft suddenly did come to life, he had a better chance of going with one of the Teletubbies than her, when we got disturbed by a sudden kerfuffle.

"Precious!" Billy yelped. "Oi! Precious! C'mere! Oh, God – he's off. Hold on, Al, I'd better go and grab him."

I watched as Billy hurtled down the hill to where the pint-sized poodle was trying to do slightly *more* than sniff the bums of two puzzled Dalmatians.

The guy who owns those Dalmatians isn't exactly the world's biggest smiler at the best of times. A small yappy dog trying to ram its nose up the bottoms of his prize pooches was definitely *not* going to bring a warm, sloppy grin to his face.

And poor Billy – no wonder he let three goals in and couldn't get a girlfriend. Just watching him run, watching the way his long, skinny legs and arms loped about all over the place, you could tell that he was a complete stranger to the art of co-ordination. That's the thing: Billy is *almost* what you could call good-looking, but he's such a clumsy geek that no girl in the Western Hemisphere is ever going to mistake him for Brad Pitt in a hurry.

"Precious! Come here! Precious – heel! Now!" I heard him yell to a totally oblivious dog.

Precious. Can you *believe* that Billy's mum came up with that name for their dog, knowing that her poor son was going to have to use it every time he took the thing for a walk? I'm sure there must be a clause in the Children's Act somewhere that says it's cruel to make thirteen-year-old boys shout "Precious!" loudly in a public place. What was the woman thinking of?

I mean, shouting "Rolf" and "Winslet" gets you the odd look from people in the park – people whose own dogs must be called Dullsville stuff like

"Spot" or "Rover" or something – but it's a thousand times better than "Precious". Who is, in fact, about as precious as a flu virus.

Both my dogs suit their names, I reckon. Rolf – a pedigree mongrel from a long, distinguished line of mongrels – was our first ever pet; Dad got him from Wood Green Animal Shelter as a distraction for Tor when our little brother suddenly clocked that our mum wasn't around any more. Since it was his dog, Tor was allowed to name him. And since his favourite programme in the world happened to be *Animal Hospital* (it still is), presented by the one, the only, the beardy Rolf Harris, Rolf it was.

We ended up with Winslet a couple of years ago when Rowan and Tor found her wandering about in the park, dishevelled, hungry and grumpy (her natural state, we found out later). They did the right thing and took her along to the police station, where Dad inevitably ended up ticking the box on the details form saying we'd take her if she wasn't claimed. She wasn't. So, since Tor already had built up quite a little menagerie at our place by this time, all of whom he'd named, the honours went to him again. He'd just seen *Titanic* and had a huge crush on Kate Winslet, so Winslet she became. (Actually, it was Kate at first, but somehow "Kate" didn't really suit a small, hairy, grumpy dog too much.)

Billy came plodding back up the incline, an indignant poodle writhing in his arms, and breathlessly plonked himself back down next to me.

"You know, if you want to get your dad something special," he panted (Billy, not Precious), "then I think you should get him something original, something he'd *never* think of..."

"Yeah? Like what?"

I was intrigued. It sounded like Billy might just be a lot less useless than I'd thought.

"Huh?" he blinked at me, trying not to lose his grip as Precious wriggled around, trying to escape. "I dunno. That's as far as I got."

"Billy," I said wearily, "your *dog*'s smarter than you."

As if to show off how smart he was, Precious attempted to lunge enthusiastically towards me.

I jerked back, just out of licking range.

There was no *way* Precious was getting within half a metre of my face. Not knowing where that nose had been last...

Chapter 4

SANDIE AND HER AMAZING WRIGGLING HAIR...

All the way home, I racked and racked my brains for some amazing present idea, but I think I'd used up all my energy for the day. Me and Billy had walked the dogs till *they* were tired, *we* were tired, and every other dog-walker in a hundred-metre radius was tired of Precious lungeing his small self at their pets.

My eyes were glued to the pavement, like that might help my concentration or something, when a few doors down from our house, I heard Rowan. She'd got these new mules in a sale, and you could recognize the *flippety-flap*, *flippety-flap* of them three streets away.

"Rowan!" I called after her. My sister's mind works in mysterious ways – if anyone could come up with something unusual and special for Dad, Rowan could. "Where are you going?"

"Just up to the shop," she called back, holding up her hand to shield the sun from her eyes, the multi-coloured Indian bangles she wore jangling down her arm. "We're out of loo roll."

See, that's Rowan for you: who else goes to the corner shop for loo roll in red velvet mules?

"Uh, OK – I'll see you in a bit."

I'd catch her later, I decided, and pick her brain. Tor's too – just 'cause he was little didn't mean he couldn't come up with a smart idea.

Thinking so much about Dad, I jumped guiltily as I walked in the front door and came face-to-face with him.

"Hi, babe! Been walking the mutts, then?"

He's so laid-back and nice, my dad. I know people are meant to love their parents, but I sometimes think they don't seem to *like* them all that much. But with my dad, I think I'd like him even if I was just meeting him for the first time.

My best friend Sandie, she's kind of proof of that; she's round at our house *all* the time, and is always saying how cool my dad is. It's actually a bit of a joke in my house how often Sandie comes round. She does this thing where she seems to leave another bit of clothing or another CD every time she's here; Dad says he thinks she's trying to move in without anyone noticing.

"Hi, Ally!" said Sandie, appearing from the kitchen, a cup of coffee in her hand.

See what I mean?

"Listen, Ally Pally—"

That was my dad. He always calls me that.

"—I'm going along to the workshop for an hour. A whole load of spare parts came in yesterday, and I want to get them sorted out before I open up tomorrow."

"OK," I shrugged and smiled at him. It was perfect, really; if he was safely out of the house, I'd have the chance to talk to Rowan and Tor and even Sandie about ideas for a present without worrying that he'd overhear.

But hold on – the Ally Pally thing. Maybe you'll want to know what that's all about. And if I tell you that, I guess I might as well tell you about all our names while I'm at it. Basically, while my dad had a hand in them, they're all Mum's fault. Which I'm pretty glad about.

So, when it came to naming their Love children (as Mum and Dad liked to call us), it happened like this...

First up, there's Love Child No. 1: Linnhe. Mum and Dad were young, happy, but skint, and had borrowed my grandma's car to go on a camping holiday in Scotland. The plan was to see as many castles and lochs as possible, and the day they checked out Inverlochy Castle on Loch Linnhe was the day my mum sussed out that she was pregnant. When my sister was born, my folks were reminiscing about the trip to Scotland, and it just kind of seemed perfect to call her Linnhe. Linn might not agree, but I think she should count her blessings. The day before, they'd been camping beside Loch Fyne. With a name like Fyne Love, you could imagine the stick she'd get from lads at school. Mind you, it would have come in handy if she'd chosen a career in X-rated videos, I suppose.

Rowan, Love Child No. 2, was due to come along next, and by this time my parents (still skint) and Linn (now two) were living in a grotty and minuscule rented flat in Finsbury Park. The landlord didn't allow them to redecorate, and he also didn't allow children. The children thing, they could get around; every time he was due to visit, they'd frantically hide every toy and kiddy-sized pair of sandals under the bed, and Mum would take the evidence (item 1: Linn; item 2: her own growing tummy) around the block till the coast was clear. The other no-no was a bigger problem. Living in a house with walls that were decorated in depressing "mushroom", with furniture in shades of dull brown, dull-ish brown and *very* dull brown, just about sent my artistic mother round the bend. She told me she bought yards and yards of cheap sari material from the Indian shops up in Turnpike Lane and draped them over everything, but it didn't do much good. She said the only thing that cheered her up was looking through the bars of their basement-flat window at the rowan tree that dripped its red-berried branches over the neighbouring wall and into their bare little backyard. And so, Rowan got her name.

Next, things got a little better for my parents. Dad had worked in bike shops for years (the hardwork, pedal kind of bike, if you were wondering), when he heard about this old guy who was retiring and wanted someone to take over the lease of his small bike workshop in Crouch End. Cue, my dad. It wasn't too long after that that my folks spotted this genteely crumbling Victorian house around the corner from the workshop. Because it needed vats of work doing to it, it was dirt cheap, so they gave up their squashed rented flat for a big, falling-down house, all for the sake of their two small daughters and one big bump (me, Love Child No. 3). On the day they moved in, Mum took one look out of the front attic-bedroom window (my room) and copped a load of Alexandra Palace, and that sealed my fate. Alexandra Love is on my birth certificate, but my dad soon gave me the same nickname as my namesake: Ally Pally.

Three explanations down, one to go.

So, Dad had his business, and we had the house,

but my parents were still what can be technically described as skint. Because of that, the family tradition of camping holidays continued, and one rainy summer, when I was six, we found ourselves stomping up the slopes of Glastonbury Tor in Somerset. It's supposed to be this really mystical place (which, of course, is why my mother wanted to go), but I tell you, it doesn't feel too mystical when you're getting soaked by persistent heavy drizzle and your mum's stopping to throw up halfway to the top. But there you go. That holiday had its good points – well, one, anyway. Mum realised that Love Child No. 4 was on its way. And, in due course, there was a baby, and that baby was Tor (minus the Glastonbury bit, thank goodness).

Sandie loves the stories behind our names; she thinks they're terribly romantic. And you can't blame her. Her parents didn't exactly exert their imaginations when they came up with Sandra, which is what her mum is called too. She was thrilled when I accidentally called her "Sandie" once – after we'd just begun to get friendly last year, when we both first started at Palace Gates comp – and it's all she's let anyone call her ever since.

So, anyway, here we were in our hall – me, Dad, Sandie and two muddy-pawed dogs.

"I was taking a video back to the shop for my mum and dad," Sandie smiled, sticking her thumb back in the direction of the kitchen, where she must have left the tape. "Do you fancy watching it together this afternoon before I drop it off?"

"Yeah, OK," I said, trying to find space on the overcrowded coat-hooks to hang up my jacket. "What is it?"

It was funny, but right at that moment, just looking at Sandie, I got another flutter of that worrying feeling that I'd forgotten something...

"Don't know. It's something with Nicole Kidman in it, so it should be all right."

"Cool," I nodded.

Then I noticed Sandie was doing something weird with her eyes, making them go wide and then darting them to the side.

Normally, I'd say that Sandie's eyes were the nicest thing about her; they're blue and round and pretty, kind of like a character's out of a Disney movie. (Tor thinks her eyes are exactly like his rabbit Cilla's – and I guess he's got a point. She does tend to do that startled, bunny-in-headlights thing a lot.) But today, rolling them around like she was doing, she looked downright deranged.

Dad was still milling about between us, searching for his house keys and the set for the workshop, so

I guess she was trying to let me know something without alerting him. But what it could be, I hadn't a clue.

Looking slightly frustrated at my lack of psychic power in figuring out what she was on about, Sandie dumped her coffee cup down on the hall table and stomped up the stairs.

"Going to the loo," she said needlessly, stepping over a snoozing cat (not Colin) and throwing one of those bizarre boggly-eyed looks at me over her shoulder.

"OK," I shrugged, passing Dad as he pulled his coat on and giving him a peck on the cheek bye-bye.

Then, heading along the hall to the entrance to the kitchen, I suddenly remembered what Rowan had gone out for.

"Hey, Sandie!" I bellowed after her, loud as an alarmingly loud foghorn. "There's no toilet pap—"

It was then that I saw what Sandie was trying to signal with her eyes.

There, sitting at the kitchen table, gently brushing another cat (also not Colin) off the Sunday supplement in front of him, was Alfie.

Alfie.

With my mouth still hanging open where I'd forgotten to finish my sentence, I stood rigid in the kitchen doorway, wondering if it was possible to rewind my life by ten seconds so I wouldn't look and sound like such a dork.

"Hi, Ally..." he said, glancing up at me from the magazine he was – cat allowing – trying to flick through.

It was hardly even a glance – more of a glancette – but the merest eye contact with Alfie tended to have the most traumatic affect on me: I stopped speaking English and started to speak gibberish.

"Huh – uh, hi," I mumbled, stepping forward awkwardly into my own kitchen.

I was walking with these funny bobbing little moves, like an insecure chicken.

"Uh ... where – where's Linn, then?"

"Linn?" he repeated gently, like he was talking to someone who wasn't quite all there. Which I wasn't, in his presence. "I'm just waiting for her. She's on the phone, I think..."

Alfie looked back down at the magazine, which was perfect. It gave me a second to gaze at him, take in the gorgeousness of him, uninterrupted. His short, messily spiky blond hair; those spookily pale, grey eyes; that heart-bursting smile that stretches so wide you can sometimes see the gold tooth he has on one side; that cute leather strappy bracelet thing he wears round his wrist; those skinny but muscular tanned arms... Hey, tell me when you've got an hour. I've only fancied him for ever, so the full list of his many charms tends to run on a bit.

"So," I squeaked, deciding that I should try and squeeze a conversation out of him while I had him all to myself. "What are you two … guys up to to-to-today?"

For some reason I was stammering, which I never normally do. And for some reason, I'd adopted a faint transatlantic twang to my voice, and believe me, I don't make a habit of acting like an extra out of *Dawson's Creek* too often either.

He gazed up at me, and I knew my face must be practically *luminous* pink. My cheeks felt so hot you could fry an egg on them. Except for the fact that it'd keep slipping off them, since I was standing…

Getting sidetracked by the logistics of the egg-frying stuff *might* sound insane, but believe me, having a mind that regularly wanders off on garbage like that really helps sometimes. Like right then – it distracted me from my total and utter fluster and I instantly felt the furnace in my face fade away.

"We're just going into town… Check out Carhartt and that in Covent Garden…"

He spoke in this slow drawl of his, which is *just* delicious. Course I didn't have a clue what he was on about, but I just nodded knowledgeably anyway. It had to be some trendy clothes shop; he was really into labels and stuff.

"Ah. Right. Well ... um ... don't do anything I wouldn't!"

OK, so *now* I knew I'd morphed into some seedy and deeply corny bloke off a building site. I could sense that this was *not* going too fantastically well, and I was considering faking a faint just to put an end to my agony when a blood-curdling scream erupted from somewhere upstairs.

Alfie looked shocked.

"What was that?" I yelped, turning and hurrying out into the hall, hoping the relief I felt at the diversion wasn't written *too* obviously all over my face. I mean, for all I knew, something truly terrible could have happened.

But of course it hadn't.

"Sandie!" I panted, after leaping up the stairs two at a time and staring into every room to find the source of the scream.

Sandie was sitting on the edge of Tor's bed, rigid with fear. If I thought her eyes were mad earlier, it was nothing on the I've-just-seen-an-alien! boggling they were doing now.

"What the hell—" barked Linn, appearing at my side, along with Alfie, who'd followed me up the stairs.

But it wasn't her stare or her gritted teeth that was the freakiest thing. It was the fact that, for some bizarre reason, Sandie had all these *twigs* in her hair.

And, uh-oh...

They were moving.

Chapter 5

ONE SURPRISE, WELL AND TRULY SCUPPERED...

"You shouldn't have done it."

"Why?"

"Because it wasn't nice."

"Why?"

"Because you scared her."

"Why?"

"Why *what*?"

It's hard having a conversation with Tor sometimes. As he's a boy of very little words, it sometimes gets kind of tiring trying to read between his (short) lines.

"Why was she scared of them?" Tor asked, gazing at me across the table, all doe-eyed confusion.

"*Because* when Sandie said she'd like to see them," Rowan explained, as she passed a plate under our little brother's nose, "she didn't think you were going to put the stick insects *on her head*."

Earlier in the afternoon, Linn, Alfie and I were still trying to figure out the best way of removing Tor's latest additions to the household from

Sandie's hair – with Tor anxiously watching and wailing at us not to damage their little stick legs – when Rowan came back from the corner shop. Luckily for the general health of the stick insects, she came up with the smart idea of wafting a lettuce leaf over Sandie's shaking head, enticing them away from the aroma of Head & Shoulders and up on to the safety of much healthier vegetation.

Now, his tea sitting untouched in front of him, Tor blinked and said nothing, but you could tell by the look on his face that he was highly disappointed in Sandie's reaction.

He's always deeply suspicious of anyone who doesn't display at least one hundred per cent adoration for animals*, and when he'd hijacked Sandie on her way to the loo to show off his new pets, the last thing he'd expected was for her to act like she did. (*The one exception to Tor's suspicion list is Grandma. She's not at all fond of the animals, but she's very fond of Tor. And Tor is very, *very* fond of his grandma.)

"Rowan, what exactly *is* this?" demanded Linn, staring at her plate in open disgust.

"Well, remember Dad said we should eat more fish..." said Rowan plaintively, her bracelets jangling as she sat down in her own seat.

She looked hurt, but I don't know why. Linn always has a pop at her efforts every time it's Rowan's turn to cook, so you think she'd be used to it by now. Linn, Rowan and Dad take turns to cook at the weekend. Not Tor, thank God, or we'd probably end up with a tin of cat food, Hula Hoops and hamster mix. (Grandma comes round and cooks tea for us during the week, since us girls are all – ahem – busy with our homework.)

"Yeah, so we should eat more fish. But *this*?"

Linn wasn't being very nice, but then – if I'm honest – neither was our tea. Potato waffles, coleslaw and … kippers. I rest my case.

"Well, it was really busy in the fish shop yesterday and I just got a bit flustered!" Rowan tried to explain herself. "I just … panicked and pointed to the nearest thing when it was my turn!"

If you ask me, the reason she got flustered is 'cause there was quite a cute Saturday boy working in there.

"I'm sure it'll be lovely," Dad interrupted diplomatically. "Thanks, Rowan!"

Rowan gave Dad a grateful smile and reached over for the tomato sauce. Smart move – smothering everything (including coleslaw) in tomato sauce is just about the only way to get through one of Rowan's meals.

"So, Dad..." said Linn, gingerly picking at the fish. "I was thinking, it's your birthday soon. And last year, we all went out for a pizza, didn't we? But this time round, why don't we stay home and cook something special here?"

"Will Rowan make it?" Tor piped up, with a panicky expression on his face.

"No. Definitely not," Linn reassured him, ignoring Rowan's disgruntled tutting.

My heart sank – I knew what Linn was up to. As far as she was concerned, the surprise party was All Systems Go, and making sure Dad didn't want to go out was just Phase One of her masterplan.

"Stay home? Fine by me," shrugged Dad. "You know I don't like a fuss."

See? I felt like yelling at her, *he doesn't like a fuss!*

And correct me if I'm wrong, but you don't get much more of a fuss than a surprise party.

"Speaking of fuss; poor Sandie," Dad laughed. "She must have been so embarrassed today."

He was right there. Poor Sandie. She's a total sweet pea – you'll never find anyone more trusting or kind – but on a one-to-ten shyness scale, Sandie's a nine-and-a-half, no problem, which makes me pretty protective of her actually. She was so traumatized by the stick-insect incident that she just spent the whole Nicole Kidman movie quietly groaning to herself; and even though I kept zapping the pause button and asking if she was OK, all she'd say was that she was fine. But put it this way, she kept covering her face with her hands so often, she couldn't have seen much of the film.

"Yes, she *was* pretty embarrassed," I nodded, wincing inside for her. I mean, *I* wouldn't exactly like to have someone cool like Alfie seeing me in such a total state.

"I can't blame her," my dad continued. "Being stuck in a room with everyone staring at you and *only* you – that's my idea of a nightmare, that is."

My hand froze as I lifted a forkful of fish to my mouth (well, any excuse not to eat it), and threw a glance over the table at Linn.

She'd gone momentarily rigid too.

I flicked my eyes across to Dad, who – unless I'd gone mad (possible) – gave me the tiniest of winks.

Did he know? Had he overheard somehow? Had he suddenly developed psychic powers and sussed out what Linn had in mind for him? Or was what he said just a timely fluke, and the wink was just a twitch?

I didn't know, and I didn't care. All I *did* know

was that the stupid surprise-party idea was well and truly dead.

Long live the next idea.

Whatever that was.

Chapter 6

HEY! LET'S BE FRIENDS! (NOT...)

I was bumbling along the road on my way to school, half expecting to hear the familiar cry of "Alllllllllleeeeeeeeeee! Wait for *meeeeeeeeeeeee*!" from Sandie, but it didn't come. We never plan to meet, it's just that we often do anyway. My sisters go to Palace Gates too, but we all go out of our way not to walk to school together. That would be *so* not cool – for any of us.

Since I was on my own, I guess I should have been doing something constructive with my thoughts – like dreaming up an amazing present for Dad, or maybe even trying to figure out what that I've-forgotten-something feeling I'd had all week-end was about – but instead, inevitably, I thought about Alfie.

More specifically, I was thinking for the millionth time how Linn could honestly be Just Good Friends with someone as totally, omigod beautiful as him. I've never been able to figure it out – what does she see when she looks at him? Doesn't she just want to pounce on him? But, you know, I don't think she does. I've studied her sometimes when she's with him and nope, there's not a trace, not a *hint* of attraction going on there at all.

Same goes for him (I'm glad to report). But that's not to say Linn isn't pretty; she is. (And don't I know it...)

She's more like Mum than the rest of us. She's got Mum's almost blonde-ish wavy hair – not that you can see the waves, since she religiously blow-dries it straight every day – and almond-shaped eyes. (And those perfect boobs, of course.) Me, Rowan and Tor all take after Dad: straight, brown hair and matching Malteser-brown eyes. Of course, the one thing that would make Linn really, *really* pretty is if she smiled more.

Yeah, like *that's* going to happen in a million years.

But with the Alfie and Linn thing, it's not as if I think a girl and a boy can't be friends – I've got Billy, after all. But then, Billy is just, well, *Billy*. And Alfie is just ... *phwoarghhhh*.

Anyhow, I headed into the yard at Palace Gates comp and over to the main entrance, feeling pretty happy after my Alfie daydreams, even though it was Monday morning and I had a whole five days worth of school gaping out in front of me.

And there was still five minutes till the first bell – five minutes to hog a radiator and drool over Alfie in the privacy of my mind.

Or maybe not.

"Ally? Can I have a word, please? My office – now."

It was Mrs Fisher, our Year Head. We got told at the beginning of the school year that we had to look on Mrs Fisher as a friend, as someone we could talk to if we had problems. You know – her door was always open, blah-de-blah.

As *if*.

It took just a couple of gullible pupils to test *that* theory out for the rest of us to know that if ever we had a problem, we'd be better off talking to the janitor, the school nurse, or a random passing stranger about it than Mrs Fisher. I don't know what side of herself she showed off to Mr Bashir the Headmaster to get him to think she had it in her to be this compassionate advisor, but it *sure* wasn't the side we got to see. When it came to irritants like us, she was from the "Don't be silly – pull yourself together!" school of non-sympathy.

Needless to say, my good mood evaporated mighty quick as I obediently and silently followed her along the corridor and up the stairs to her office.

"This," she said, sweeping her door open and wafting her hand impatiently at someone sitting in a chair, "is Kyra Davies. And this—"

She wafted her hand vaguely in my direction.

"—is Ally Love. Ally, Kyra has just joined the school today, and she's going to be in your form class – therefore, I've decided to assign you to look after her for her first week. Show her about. All right?"

All right? I suppose it was. At least I wasn't in some terrible trouble over something I had no memory of, like I'd dreaded when Mrs Fisher had first summoned me. But now the relief that I wasn't about to be hung, drawn and quartered for some unknown misdemeanour was over, I got my first proper look at who I was going to have to babysit.

And I wasn't sure if I liked her.

Kyra Davies was sitting slouched in the chair, an arm sprawled casually along the back of it. She was chewing gum with her mouth open, eyeing me up and down quite blatantly, like I was a sack of potatoes she was trying to guess the weight of.

I tried to brazen it out and stare back at her, but I'm not great at that kind of thing; I don't have the bottle to act that hard (since I'm about as hard as mashed potato). I did stare enough to decide that she was Mediterranean-looking, or mixed-race, even. She was quite pretty – apart from her sticky-out ears that looked glaringly obvious because of the way she'd dragged her dark, curly hair back into a top-knot – but she had this really kind of arrogant manner.

"Well, what are you waiting for, girls?" Mrs Fisher frowned. "The bell just went. You'll be late for your History class, if you don't hurry."

Chop, chop, go, go – that was Mrs Fisher's duty done, as far as she was concerned.

Kyra languidly stood up, hoisting her bag on to her shoulder, and blasted a teeth-baring, obviously insincere smile in the Year Head's direction.

"Thank you *sooo* much, Mrs Fisher," she said in a saccharine-sweet voice just dripping with sarcasm.

"Goodbye, Kyra," muttered Mrs Fisher in response, shutting the door firmly behind us.

"What a frigid old cow!"

I couldn't believe Kyra had the nerve to say that so loud, and right outside Mrs Fisher's door. And I couldn't believe that I suddenly found myself jumping to Mrs Fisher's defence.

"She's all right," I shrugged, walking off in the direction of the History class and just presuming Kyra would follow.

"Not from where *I* was sitting," Kyra snorted, falling into step beside me.

Maybe with someone else I'd have agreed with them straight away, but there was just something about Kyra's cockiness that bugged me, somehow. She'd only been at Palace Gates five seconds and she was mouthing off her opinions. It was a bit much, if you see what I mean.

"So, when did you arrive in Crouch End, then?" I asked, trying to change the subject.

"Last week," she replied, yawning.

I mean, *yawning* – how rude is that?

"Do you like it?"

"Don't know. Looks a bit boring. I told my mum and dad that we should live in south London, not north London, if we were going to move here at all."

"Oh?" I answered through gritted teeth, stomping along the corridor faster.

I know it's crazy, but I really love where I live – I'm really proud of how green and leafy and historic it is, and how many cool shops there are, and how comfy and trendy it is at the same time.

"Yeah – Brixton's much more happening than *this* place."

I couldn't say anything for a second, I was too annoyed. But I tried; I'm not into being rude. Even if Kyra was.

"So whereabouts are you living?"

"Cranley Gardens. The place we're in is a pit."

"Uh-huh."

Cranley Gardens is the sort of place that the local estate agents go all poetic over. It's a "highly desirable turning", apparently, and the way they tell it, every house is "luxurious". But not Kyra's, it seemed. God, just how spoilt was this girl?

"Mmm. So where did you live before?" I asked, relieved to see the door to Miss Thomson's History class in the not-too-distant distance.

"Rye. It's this little place down in Kent."

"I know it. We visited once when I was little."

"Total dump, isn't it?"

"I thought it was nice," I found myself protesting. "All those old, cobbled streets..."

"Yeah? And boring as hell."

Everything was a dump or boring, as far as this girl was concerned. Her boredom was boring me already.

"How come you moved?" I asked, out of politeness rather than actually wanting to know the answer.

"We move a lot. My dad's an assistant bank manager. We get around," she yawned again.

"And your mum?" I asked, eyeing up the approaching doorway.

"She's a professional drinker."

I shot Kyra a shocked look, and her face broke into a lazy grin.

"Only joking…" she sniggered.

What a horrible thing to joke about, I frowned to myself.

But then I guess I'm pretty super-sensitive about stuff to do with mums.

At last, the doorway to the bright, white classroom loomed large.

Everyone was still drifting in, shuffling noisily into their seats. Over by the window, Sandie was already sitting in our usual spot; she shot me a questioning look. From the back of the room, where Chloe and Jen and the others sat, I could practically feel their eyes boring into my head, wondering what the deal was with the new girl.

"Hello, Ally. So this must be Kyra?" smiled Miss Thomson.

"That's me!" trilled Kyra, *really* insincerely.

I groaned inside. Being facetious with Mrs Fisher was one thing, but Miss Thomson was something else. She's too nice and reasonable to muck around with. Actually, she's my favourite teacher at school.

"Right, let's see… Do you want to sit yourself here for the moment, Kyra, and I'll come and chat to you in a second?"

With an almighty sigh Kyra flopped down into

the seat at the desk that had been pointed out to her.

Miss Thomson gave me one of those looks that, like my dad's the night before, *could* have meant something and then again might not. But from where I was standing, her eyebrows definitely shot up and down, as if to say, "*She's* going to be a pain, isn't she?"

But that was me guessing. Or wishful thinking. What Miss Thomson *did* say kind of took me by surprise.

"So, Ally, I was just in the middle of asking Sandie how you're doing with your project."

Our project.

Oh. My. God.

You know that thing I'd forgotten? All of sudden, I hadn't forgotten it any more...

Chapter 7

MORE STRESS? YES, PLEASE!

I'm not mean. Honest I'm not. Well, OK, I've been known to be a *bit* mean to Billy, but that doesn't count. He knows I'm only joking.

Hopefully.

But that Kyra – I was sick to death of her by the end of the day. It was absolutely zero fun, having to drag her around every class, and hear her slagging off the school all the time. (I got a break at lunchtime – I went home to my own place, as usual, after pointing her in the direction of the dinner hall.)

The world according to Kyra went like this: all the teachers she'd met at Palace Gates so far were morons; she was too smart for most of her old teachers and that's why they didn't like her; everybody in her last school was a total nerd; all her old schools were trash, but our school beat them all; everything about Palace Gates was scuzzy, especially the toilets.

Big wow – the toilets! What was she expecting?

Fake-fur-lined seats and toilet-paper monitors handing out individual sheets to everyone entering a cubicle? Get real.

But if I'm honest, Kyra was just an irritation. The *real* problem that was doing my head in was our history project, and the fact that me and Sandie had done precisely nothing about it.

"I can't believe it's come up so fast!" I moaned, as the two of us mooched miserably out of the school gates on this Monday afternoon.

Trying to keep up with homework was one thing; trying to cram a project we'd had six weeks to do into the remaining two weeks was something else.

"I know," nodded Sandie.

"I mean, where's the time gone?"

"I know," Sandie sympathized.

"It's a disaster – we haven't even thought of what we're going to do!" I whimpered.

"I know," Sandie agreed.

We'd been told about this joint Drama and History department project a couple of months back. To celebrate our school's fiftieth birthday, the Drama crew were going to be putting on a play for local primary schools, based around what Crouch End was like fifty years ago. Us lot in the History department had been split up and given different tasks to do: some were helping with research for the play itself, while others – like me and Sandie – were supposed to be coming up with fascinating visuals on a wide variety of subjects to a) decorate the hall outside the auditorium, and b) expand the minds of the visiting small primary kids.

Back when Miss Thomson first told us about it, it had seemed about a hundred kilometres into the future. But now... *uhhhhhhhhh*.

"How could we have just forgotten about it?" I moaned, miserable at my own crapness. It was my leaving-homework-till-Sunday-night outlook to blame, I guess.

"Mmmm."

It slightly jarred that Sandie had stopped saying "I know". What was "Mmmm" supposed to mean?

"Mmmm?" I repeated, staring at my best friend.

"Well..." said Sandie sheepishly.

"Well?" I asked.

"Well ... *I* remembered."

"Remembered what?"

"Um, about the project..."

"You remembered about the *project*?!" I yelped. "All this *time*? Why didn't you *say* something?"

"I was waiting for you... I thought you were thinking up an idea!"

Sandie blinked at me with those blue, saucer-like eyes of hers.

She does this *all* the time – waits to see what I think about something before she says or does anything. ("That girl's got no gumption!" my grandma said once, when Sandie was prannying about at my house as usual, saying, "Oh, I don't know! *You* decide!" when we were working out what movie to go and see at the Muswell Hill Odeon.)

I know what Grandma meant, but it's pretty hard to stay mad at Sandie. She's the kind of friend who's good to have around; she's got a brilliant sense of humour (even if she doesn't have the confidence to be funny herself), and she's so honest that she'll always tell you things straight (but she's also smart enough to know when to tell a little white lie – like saying I look fine when I have the biggest spot in the cosmiverse erupting on my chin).

But you know something? Just this once, I was *really* mad at Sandie. I couldn't help it; it could land us in real trouble. I mean, I know I was a jerk (double jerk) for forgetting about the project, but it was pretty stupid of Sandie not to have said anything about it earlier.

I suddenly felt a bit sick. It was all such a total disaster. Then, just when I thought the moment couldn't get any worse, I heard a sound that made my heart bounce off the pavement.

"Hi, guys," said Kyra, very casually strolling up beside us.

But she didn't fool me – she must have had to run to catch us up, 'cause there was no one behind us a minute ago when I looked back as we were crossing the road.

"Hi," I said half-heartedly. "So ... what did you make of your first day, then?"

"Bo-*rinnnnnnggggggggg*. That teacher, Mr Horse Arse—"

"Horace. Mr *Horace*," I corrected her, quickly.

I was well aware of what all the boys in our class called him. But we'd been taught by him for ages, and since Kyra had sat through one measly class with Mr Horse Ar—, uh, Mr Horace, it did seem kind of cheeky of her to get so casual with his nickname already.

"Yeah, whatever," shrugged Kyra. "Anyway Mr Whatshisname is a complete plonker. He's the worst so far."

I'd had it. If I heard one more whinge about our school and everything in it, I'd have to kill her.

"Um, don't you live over *that* way?" said Sandie tentatively, pointing at the other side of the road we'd just crossed.

I could have kissed my best mate then and there. For once Sandie wasn't just letting *me* do all the talking. And it was a fair point anyway – what *was* Kyra doing coming creeping after us when she lived in the opposite direction?

"I was just … going … to the post office."

No she wasn't. I heard that little hesitation in her voice, and saw her glancing ahead quickly to see where she could pretend to be heading for.

"Oh, right," said Sandie, giving me a quick nudge with her elbow. Looked like she'd sussed out Kyra's porky-pie too.

"Well, bye!" I said cheerily, as we approached the door of the post office.

"Yeah, bye. So I'll see you at the main entrance tomorrow, then, Ally?"

Deep gloom. Being Kyra's school babysitter for the week was just too annoying to contemplate.

"Uh-huh. See you tomorrow," I mumphed, forcing a half-hearted smile.

"God, what's she *like*?!" whispered Sandie, glancing behind to check that we weren't being followed again.

"Like the most pushy, irritating, whining person on the planet?" I suggested, loud enough for anyone in the vicinity – possibly even in the post office – to hear me.

OK, so now I had *three* things to stress over:

1) The fact that the wind was blowing through

the vast, empty wilderness of my imagination every time I tried to come up with an idea for Dad's birthday. At this rate, Linn would be trying to force Very Bad Plan No. 2 on us any second now. And I dreaded to think what *that* could be.

2) The wind was *also* blowing through the vast, empty wilderness of my imagination when I tried to think up some super-amazing idea for the History project too. Not that it had to be super-amazing. An averagely dull idea would have suited me fine by this late stage.

3) And I had this miserable feeling that Kyra was going to be a bit of a cling-on. I worried that she would try and tag along with me and Sandie as the only possible options open to her. After all, from what we'd seen (and heard) of her, people at school weren't exactly going to be queuing around the block to become big buddies with her.

I'd left Sandie a few streets back – both of us vowing to come up with some project ideas overnight (i.e. she'd wait and see what *I* came up with and then agree enthusiastically) – and was quite glad to see my familiar front door looming up in front of me.

Then, walking up the garden path, I heard raised voices coming from inside my house and wondered if I'd done something particularly awful in a past life to deserve such an annoying day.

"What's everyone yelling about?" I asked, stomping into the living room and taking everyone by surprise.

Tor was sitting cross-legged on the floor, petting a cat that wasn't Colin, while Rowan, Linn and Grandma were standing, hovering in a circle around him. From their body language, it looked like my sisters were in the middle of some strop, with Grandma acting as referee.

"Ally, dear, we are *not* yelling," said my gran, contradicting what was so clearly true. "We're just having a debate, that's all."

"OK," I said, chucking my school bag on the sofa and plonking myself down beside it. "So what's everyone debating about?"

"Dad's birthday," Linn replied snippily, settling herself down at the other end of our vast, squishy, old sofa.

It groaned gently as she did so, like a long, low fart, completely ruining her air of superior snottiness.

I threw a glare at Tor that said, "Don't you dare giggle at her – it'll make things worse!" But Tor was smart and knew that already; he'd yanked the black and white cat up into his arms so he could bury his face – and giggles – in it.

"Rowan has had this *stupid* idea," Linn began, ignoring the sofa squelch, "that we should get Dad a session with a feng shui expert for his birthday!"

I glanced around our sunshine-yellow living room – at the old sofa and chairs with their throws, mounds of cushions and magazines and papers spilling off them, then at the fireplace, at the shelves and surfaces, all covered in pictures and ornaments and bric-a-brac and books and plants and candles ... a feng shui expert would walk in here and collapse with clutter-overload.

"I thought that would be right up your street, Linn," I suggested, suddenly remembering I'd forgotten to include assorted pets in the living room inventory. "Getting minimal and everything..."

"Minimal!" squeaked Rowan in alarm. "I thought feng shui people brought you luck by moving the furniture around a bit and sticking a couple of wind chimes up!"

Poor Rowan obviously hadn't swotted up on her suggestion properly. But then, speaking before she put her brain in gear was her speciality.

"I wouldn't mind *any* excuse to get this tip sorted out," sniffed Linn, gazing round the room dismissively, "but it's not exactly something Dad would be into, is it?"

And neither is a surprise party, I thought silently, finding myself irritated with Linn turning up her nose like that. After all, most of the paintings and bits of pottery in here was stuff Mum had made.

"Well, at least I tried to come up with something special," Rowan huffed, the bangles on her wrists jangling with irritation. "At least it's not *boring*, like Linn's idea!"

"Now, girls!" Grandma interrupted, holding a hand palm up in the direction of each of my sisters.

"So what was your idea?" I asked Linn, kicking off my school shoes as I talked.

"Go on! Tell her your idea and see if she falls asleep!" Rowan said stroppily.

"I thought maybe a watch – with a message engraved on the back," shrugged Linn, turning round on the sofa to face me and studiously ignoring Rowan.

"But he's already got a watch – the one Mum gave him," I replied automatically. After all, I couldn't see Dad parting with *that* in a hurry.

"*See?*"

"Enough, Rowan," muttered Grandma. "All this silly bickering over your dad; he would be very upset if he thought you girls were falling out over him."

Nobody said anything then – we all knew she was right.

"Anyway, I thought I might have a suggestion for you," said Grandma, folding her arms across her chest.

"What?" I asked bluntly.

"Well, the most important thing to your dad is all of *you*," she began, now unfolding her arms long enough to point a finger at each of us in turn.

We waited wordlessly, all privately hoping Grandma was about to solve our problem for us.

"So, why don't you give him a family portrait of you four children? That photography shop on Crouch End Broadway always has *lovely* photos in the window of families they've snapped in their studio. They're—"

"Oh, Grandma, *no*!" exclaimed Rowan, looking as horrified as if the government had suddenly announced a ban on the year-round use of fairy lights. "Those posed photos are *awful*! They're *so* naff! All soft-focus and cheesy smiles!"

Grandma frowned at Rowan, then glanced round at the expressions on the rest of our faces.

Even Linn, who was Grandma's right-hand girl, couldn't hide the fact that she thought it was a deeply corny idea.

"Right! If you don't want to listen to my advice, then fine!" said Grandma sternly, turning and heading out the door. "I'd better get started on tea anyway…"

Uh-oh – major huff alert.

Grandma tells *us* lot off for bickering or sulking, but boy, can she do a mean teenage strop when she wants to….

Chapter 8

HACKED OFF...

A word of warning: never, *ever* try to cut your fringe when you're in a bad mood.

I gazed at my reflection in the toilet mirrors while a bunch of girls who were in the year below me charged about screaming and giggling about something or other in the background.

Hopefully, it wasn't my hair, but I couldn't have blamed them if it was. One single, solitary chunk of fringe was cut so high that a big, shiny patch of forehead positively *gleamed* at me in the mirror. My fringe would've looked better if I'd just let Tor's hamsters *gnaw* on it for a while.

You see, Grandma usually trims my hair for me – it's just past my shoulders, with a fringe, so it's not like I'm any challenge to a hairdresser – but last night, she was still huffing too much for me to ask for hair-snipping favours, so I did it myself. In fact, Grandma was huffing so much that she didn't even stay for tea with us like she normally does; as soon as Dad came in she was off, saying there was a programme on telly that she really wanted to catch, which sounded like a flimsy excuse to all of us. Not that any of us let on to Dad that there was a problem – that would have been giving the game away.

So, today, I could add a new dollop of stress to my stress mountain. I had a non-existent History project (no overnight miracles there), no idea about Dad's sodding birthday present, Kyra still bending my ear with her moaning between classes, and now there was Grandma going all grumpy on us.

Oh, and a hairdo from hell.

"No! Don't! No! *Nooooooo!*" shrieked the girls behind me. They were really irritating me – I felt like explaining that it was still possible to laugh without doing it at a level of decibels that burst eardrums. But I was just in a bad mood.

Back to Grandma: she might come over all strict and everything but, underneath, she's a total softie. She tuts and gripes a bit at the state of the house (her flat is like one of those show homes – not a crumb or a speck of dust to be seen. You see where Linn gets it from...), but she's always been there for us. Well, especially since Mum and everything. A couple of years back, she even sold her house up in Barnet and moved to a flat round the corner from us, just to help out more. So even if she was a bit serious and not exactly the kind of person you could kid around with, there's no way I – or any of us – would deliberately want to hurt her feelings. But it looked like we'd managed to...

"Come on! That's the bell! Quick! A prefect might come in an' catch us!"

I moved my eyes away from the vision of hacked hair in front of me in the mirror, and watched the posse of giggly girls tear out of the loos.

I couldn't resist it. I had to have a nosey at what they were all in a tizz about. They'd seemed to be hovering around the cubicle behind me; I stepped across the scuffed vinyl floor and peered in.

Their art teacher wouldn't exactly have been proud of what they'd been doodling on the wall in thick black marker pen. (*I* certainly don't remember any diagrams like that from the sex-education talks Mrs Fisher gave us.) And their English teacher wouldn't have been impressed with the sort of stuff they'd been writing either. I mean, if you're going to scrawl obscenities on the toilet walls, you should at least spell them properly, shouldn't you?

"Nicole is a hoe," I read aloud. "A *'hoe'*?"

Not much of an insult, is it? Comparing a person to something that sits next to the spade in a garden shed, I mean.

But staring at the handiwork of a bunch of girls without a brain cell between them, it did suddenly occur to me that Kyra was right for once: the toilets at Palace Gates *were* pretty scuzzy.

Thinking of Kyra, I breathed a sigh of relief. I'd managed to shake her off at the beginning of the afternoon break, fifteen minutes before, and hadn't seen her since. Could it be that she was as bored as *I* was of us trailing around together? Could it be that at least one of my stress-factors was finished with?

I gave my hair a quick, useless ruffle in the mirror, and hurried out into the corridor.

Where I bumped slap, bang into Miss Thomson, my History teacher.

"Ally!" smiled Miss Thomson. "I've just been talking about you!"

"Oh?" I replied, wondering what was coming next.

"Yes – remember that you told me yesterday in class that you and Sandie were a little behind with your project?"

A little behind? Try four weeks behind...

"Well, I just had a surprise visit at the beginning of breaktime – from someone who could lend you a hand..."

I didn't have to listen as Miss Thomson finished

what she had to say. All I knew was that me and Sandie had just found ourselves with a little helper that we most definitely didn't want.

Kyra sodding Davies.

Chapter 9

SMART IDEAS, WORSE LUCK...

A cat that wasn't Colin started sniffing at the tuna sandwich I'd just made.

"Oi!" I yelped, rushing back from the fridge with a bottle of low-fat salad cream in my hand (it had a "Property of Linn Love" sticker on it, but I was doing my best to ignore that).

The cat that wasn't Colin jumped off the work surface and walked indignantly across the wooden kitchen floor with a clickety-click of its claws. I peered after it, and saw from the funny bend in its tail that it was Frankie. That's the only way I can identify the cats that aren't Colin; by the broken bits on them. Tor, of course, knows every cat by the sound of its purr or the flick of a whisker, but it's harder for the rest of us. It's just that, apart from Colin (being ginger and having only the three legs), our other four cats are all a universal black and white. From a distance, or when they're snoozing in a tight cat-curl, it's hard to tell the difference. Up close, it's easier: Frankie has the wonky tail, Eddie has ears that are so fight-chewed they look like they're lace-edged, Derek is very cross-eyed, and Fluffy makes Frankie look good – he's got no tail at all.

"Your house is amazing! I love all the colours, and all the pictures and stuff!"

I didn't particularly like Kyra, I *definitely* resented having to include her in mine and Sandie's (invisible) History project, and I wasn't exactly *thrilled* at the idea of having to invite her back to my place this Wednesday lunchtime so we could go over our "plans" for the project.

But, hey, I'm shallow enough to appreciate a compliment when it comes my way.

"Thanks," I nodded, handing her a plate with a tuna sandwich on it.

The one Frankie had been sniffing at, of course.

Kyra pulled out the nearest chair, which was directly opposite Sandie, who was already halfway through her sandwich and had been flicking through a mag while Kyra was upstairs in the loo.

"Listen," said Kyra, peeling back the top slice of bread to inspect what I'd given her, "what's going on in the room at the end of the hall upstairs? I heard all these *noises*..."

I hesitated for a second as I blobbed a dollop of Linn's personal low-fat salad cream on my own sandwich, and tried to figure out what she meant. And then I realized – Tor's bedroom is a den of tanks filled with fish, stick insects, lizards and a variety of small things whirring round in wheels.

"Was it squeaking and scrabbling type noises?" I asked.

"Yeah!"

"That's my brother's hamsters and stuff."

"Wow – and you've got those two dogs too?"

Rolf and Winslet had been very excited by the sudden activity in the middle of the day. Normally it was just me and Rowan who were home at lunchtime (me, 'cause I like the peace, and Rowan 'cause – to be honest – she hasn't got any friends at school to hang out with in the dinner hall).

"Yes, and we've got five cats too," I said, yanking out another chair from the long wooden kitchen table and settling myself down.

"Yeah?"

I half-expected Kyra to come out with a sarky comment about smelly animals or something, but she didn't. I was surprised. But not as surprised as what she said next.

"So who's the freak-show sitting in your living room?"

I twitched. How dare she speak about Rowan like that? Although – as much as I didn't want to –

I had to acknowledge (only to myself) that Rowan *had* gone for a very odd look today. She'd twisted her dark hair into all these tight little bobbles on her head, like Björk used to do (which was weird enough as it was), and then tied tiny pieces of ribbon around each bobble. It must have taken her ages to do, and to be honest, the effect wasn't quite worth it.

Still, that *was* a member of my family she was talking about.

"That's her sister!" said Sandie, leaping to mine and Rowan's defence in the face of Kyra's tact-free comment.

"Yeah? Poor you!" snorted Kyra.

I was just about throw a very bitchy comment Kyra's way (if I'd been able to think of one fast enough) when she went all gooey all of a sudden.

"*Oooooh*! *Babe*eeeeeeee! What happened to you?"

From nowhere, Colin hopped up happily into her welcoming arms and set up a rattling purr that would have rocked the foundations of the house ... well, in my dreams anyway.

"You mean his leg?" I said, obviously. "He had an argument with a car, and lost."

"Oh, my God, you must have been so upset!" Kyra exclaimed, stroking an ultra-content Colin.

"Nah, it happened before we got him," I

shrugged. "We inherited him from a friend of a friend of my gran's – they were moving away and couldn't take him."

But then that was the story of all our pets' lives; every one of them was wonky and shop-soiled in one way or another. Like Winslet; apart from her old-lady grumpiness, we also realized when we found two sets of keys, a hairbrush, a hot-water bottle and Dad's favourite jersey hidden under the doggy blanket in her bed that her kleptomaniac tendencies had probably helped lead her to be abandoned in the first place.

And the cats; well – apart from Colin – we inherited Frankie and Derek from nearby neighbours who'd moved in for four months and done a runner in the night, abandoning their four-legged furrballs, while Eddie had just been a stray we'd started feeding. Fluffy is the bad-tempered, feline equivalent of Winslet, who'd had her tail amputated after it was bitten by the Doberman she lived with. In the circumstances, Fluffy and the Doberman couldn't live together any more and, rather unfairly, their owners (people who worked in the grocer's next to Dad's workshop) decided that Fluffy should get herself a new home. Which happened to be ours.

"You're so lucky," murmured Kyra, nuzzling

Colin's head with her nose. "We've moved around so much we've never been able to have any pets…"

I sneaked a look at Sandie, who was sneaking a look back in my direction. If I read her mind right, I knew she was thinking, "What's with *her*?" – same as me.

It was hard to keep up with Kyra's changes of character. In the two and a half days we'd known her at school, she'd been the Snarl Queen. In the five minutes we'd been sitting in the kitchen, she gone from praising my house, to dissing my sister, to practically drooling over my cat and getting embarrassingly slushy over animals in general.

"So, this project," I said, trying to drag Kyra's attention away from Colin before she stroked the fur off his back. "To be honest, we haven't got very far with it."

"Oh?" said Kyra, gazing up at me.

"We haven't done, well, *anything*," Sandie shrugged, nervously scraping her fine, fair hair back behind her ears.

She had little pink spots of guilt on her cheeks too, I noticed.

It's not Miss Thomson we're having a tuna sandwich with! I felt like saying to her. *What are you blushing for?*

"Good!" exclaimed Kyra, puzzlingly.

"Don't mind me..." Rowan's voice drifted into the kitchen. She padded over to the fridge and was about to help herself to some orange juice when her hand hovered over a carton of raspberry yoghurt drink, which she picked out instead. It had a "Property of Linn Love" sticker on it, I noticed.

"Why's that good?" I asked Kyra, turning my attention back to her.

"'Cause I've had this brilliant idea!" she replied. "Well, it's a rip-off of something I did at one of my old schools, but I think it'll work OK."

"Go on..." said Sandie, leaning her elbows on the table and narrowing her big, blue, Disney eyes at Kyra.

"Well, you've got a local historical society here, haven't you? It's just that I bet they'll have maps about where bombs fell in this area during World War Two," explained Kyra, still busily fondling Colin's ears. "At my old school, we did these big posters, showing where the bombs fell, and showing photos from the time, with arrows and stuff pinpointing them on the maps."

"That sounds brilliant!" said Rowan suddenly, a pink yoghurt moustache noticeable on her upper lip. "People are always nosey about stuff like that, aren't they? Trying to see if the street *they* live on was affected!"

"Exactly!" agreed Kyra.

I looked from one to the other. Weren't they both forgetting something?

"Er, hello? Remember us?" I waved at my sister. "Thanks, Rowan, but it's up to me and Sandie to say if it's a good idea or not."

"Well, you haven't *got* an idea, have you? So you haven't got much choice," said Rowan curtly, looking a little hurt.

But then I felt a little hurt myself, with her having a dig at me. As if I didn't feel useless enough when it came to the project.

I watched as Rowan stomped out of the kitchen, back to the strains of some Aussie soap starting up on the telly in the living room.

I sighed to myself. If there's one thing I really hate it's when people are right about something you wish they weren't right about. If you see what I mean.

"So, what do you think?" asked Kyra.

"Mmm," I nodded reluctantly. "Sounds good. Let's do it."

Well, let's face it – it was do Kyra's idea or leave the country before Miss Thomson found out the truth...

Chapter 10

ALL THAT GLITTERS (IS IN ROWAN'S ROOM)

You know that Friday feeling? When it's like you've been set free for a whole, delicious weekend, starting as soon as you get out of the school gates at four?

Well, I didn't have it. Or at least I had it for fifteen whole minutes, till I got home in time to see Rowan storming up the stairs, hiccuping with tears, while Linn was shouting, "Oh, for God's sake, Ro, stop being such a baby!"

"What's wrong now?" I asked Linn, following her back into the living room.

"Ask *her*! I was just trying to have a discussion, and she flounces off. As usual."

Linn flopped down on the sofa and picked up a copy of some magazine. From the way she was holding it up in front of her face and angrily flicking the pages, I could tell I wasn't going to get any more out of her.

I turned and walked out of the room, into the hall – its lilac walls looking more bruised purple as the strange stormy light poured in through the glass panels on the front door – and headed into the kitchen.

"I'm keeping out of it," said Grandma, anticipating what I was going to say.

Beside her at the kitchen table was Tor, sucking unhygienically at the end of his pencil, a jotter with scrawled sums open in front of him.

"But, Grandma, what are they—"

"Ally – Tor and I are too busy doing his homework to worry what silly girls are arguing about. Aren't we, Tor?"

My little brother nodded.

"And silly girls like that would be better off getting *their* homework out of the way on a Friday afternoon instead of bickering, wouldn't they, Tor?"

Tor nodded at Grandma again and looked back down at his sums.

Compared to his sisters, Tor might have been in Grandma's good books for now, but he wasn't all sweetness and light. I could see the slight bulge in the top pocket of his school shirt, and I could see it was moving. Since it was only a small pocket, I guessed that one of his white mice must have been chosen to come down and be his maths muse. If Grandma spotted that she would *not* be amused.

If Linn and Grandma weren't going to tell me anything, then there was only one person who would. And she was upstairs snivelling.

"Rowan?" I said softly, knocking at her door.

There was no reply.

"Ro – it's me, Ally!" I called a little louder, in case she thought it was Linn coming to continue their fight, whatever it was about.

"Mnnnumph!"

I took the trumpeting of her nose to be a yes, and walked in.

It was only twenty past four and shouldn't have been so dark outside, but the purply-orange storm clouds lay low and ominous outside the big bay window. Because it was as if twilight had landed early, Rowan had already switched on her collection of fairy lights and charity-shop lamps. With all her trinkets twinkling in shades of pink and green, red and yellow, the effect was beautiful. Her whole room was beautiful, in an over-the-top, brain-dazzling way. Everything was beautiful – except for the hunched-up girl perched on the bed, her mascara smeared and her nose immersed in a snotty white tissue.

"That's new," I said, pointing to a kind of collage thing on the wall.

It was a sugar-pink fluffy heart mounted on a big

piece of baby-blue art board. All round the edge of the board and the heart, multi-coloured sequins were glued, and in the centre of the fluffy heart itself was a tiny doll, wearing what looked like a little tutu.

"I made it last weekend," sniffed Rowan, blowing her nose again. "Found the doll in a junk shop on Saturday and decided to do something with it."

She seemed a bit happier already – talking about the pictures and stuff she made always cheered her up. Linn maybe got Mum's looks, but Rowan definitely got our mother's love of all things artyfarty. Me, I didn't inherit either Mum's blondeyfair hair or her arty-fartyness. I don't know if I inherited any of her traits at all, really; sometimes my memory of her is a bit hazy. Which is a pretty weird feeling...

"Nice," I commented, though I wasn't sure if I'd have fancied something like that up on my wall.

"Thank you," said Rowan, uncurling her legs from under her and starting to look more composed.

"So, what were you and our lovely big sister arguing about?" I asked, lowering myself down into her green blow-up chair. It was on the semideflated side – my bum was just about touching the floor – but it was still kind of fun to sit in.

"Oh, her!" sighed Rowan, throwing a theatrical

glare at the ceiling. "Linnhe is so bossy it makes my blood fizz!"

Now if I was Linn, I'd have been correcting her at that point, telling her the word she was looking for was "boil", not "fizz". But I didn't bother – that's just the sort of thing that Rowan comes out with and I always find it quite entertaining. My favourite thing is when she's singing along to the radio in the shower or the bath – she warbles along really enthusiastically, but *always* gets the words wrong.

"What's she bossing you about for?" I quizzed her.

"You'll never believe it," said Rowan, her eyes wide and comical with all the black mascara smeared round them. "She's only just gone and decided that this family photo of Grandma's is a good idea after all!"

"What?" I yelped, nearly bobbing out of the inflatable plastic chair in surprise. "How come?"

Rowan flopped back on to her squashy rose-covered duvet.

"That's what I tried to ask – before she bit my head off!"

"What did she say?"

"She said that since me and you hadn't bothered coming up with anything, Grandma's idea was probably the best we were going to get and we should just go for it."

I felt a twinge of guilt at that. Like with the History project, I'd been spectacularly bad in the inspiration department.

"Then I tried to say that I didn't want to do it," Rowan continued, "and Linnhe tells me to shut up unless I had something useful to say!"

I couldn't see Rowan's face at that point, since she was lying on her bed and I was practically down at carpet level, but I could tell she was going all snivelly on me again.

"Don't let her get to you!" I said lamely, as I struggled to get out of the wobbly seat.

There was only one thing for it, I decided: I had to try to come up with a better idea for a birthday present before Linn went and booked an appointment at the photographer's. Linn and Rowan were going to come to blows soon if things went on the way they were, and I didn't suppose Dad would be all that chuffed with a grinning portrait of his family, with his two oldest daughters showing off the black eyes they'd given each other.

Speaking of Dad...

"Hey, Ally Pally! Come to make sure your old dad gets home safely?"

Dad had stuck his head out of the back work-shop at the sound of the bell above the door, and I squelched my way in, trailing wet footprints across the lino.

"Well, you're always reading about old people getting mugged in the street these days..." I grinned at him.

An oily rag came whizzing in my direction.

"What did I say?" I jokingly protested, ducking sideways and letting it fly clean past me.

"Give me a minute – I'll wash my hands and then I'll be ready," he called out, disappearing further into the workshop. "The rain's really hammering down out there now, isn't it?"

"Yep. So, been busy today?" I yelled above the sound of running water in the sink.

"Not really," he yelled back. "Pretty quiet for a Friday. I sold one kid's bike though."

Dad didn't just repair bikes, he sold second-hand ones too – in the teeny-tiny front shop I was now standing in, dripping.

"So, what's brought you round here, Ally Pally?" Dad's voice drifted through.

"Don't know – just felt like a walk," I shrugged to myself.

What a joke. If I'd wanted a walk I'd have grabbed Winslet and Rolf and gone up to the

Palace or to Queen's Woods – not just tootled five minutes around the corner to Dad's shop. And moseying out for a stroll isn't the first thing you generally think of doing when a storm's just broken and the rain's bouncing in sheets off the pavement.

No, I didn't just fancy a walk: unknown to Dad, I was on a spying mission…

"So," said Dad, appearing in his red checked shirt and jeans in the doorway of the workshop, drying his hands with a towel, "you haven't come round to pick my brains about what I want for my birthday?"

Damn. Guess the FBI wouldn't be calling to recruit me soon.

"How did you know?" I asked, slouching in defeat.

"Oh, I overheard Linn talking to Rowan about it last week," he grinned at me. "Tell me, Linn's not still keen on that surprise-party idea, is she?"

"No," I reassured him, remembering that look I thought he'd thrown me across the kitchen table a few days before. "You managed to put her off on Sunday, when we were talking about Sandie and what had happened with the stick insects."

"Good," he smiled, chucking the towel over an old stool and pulling his worn denim jacket off the hook on the door. "I don't want any big fuss. I'm just happy to have all of you guys – I don't want anything fancy."

It was one of those lump-in-the-throat moments. I knew he was thinking of the one person who was missing from the equation, and *he* knew that *I* knew what he was thinking. I blinked hard and tried to say something funny before I started the waterworks like Rowan.

"Don't let on to the others, but keep an eye on things, will you, Ally?" said Dad, sliding his taut, muscular arms into his jacket.

"Sure," I gulped, still feeling that lump in my throat, especially now that Dad had trusted me with his thoughts.

"Maybe you could try not to let things get out of hand," he continued, patting me on the shoulder.

"No problem," I reassured him. "So, no fanfares; no cheerleaders; no ticker-tape parades…"

"Exactly!" laughed Dad, coming and putting his arm around my shoulders and ushering me out the front door.

OK – so now I knew what he *didn't* want. But it still hadn't got me any closer to figuring out what he *did* want…

Chapter 11

CHEEK, AND PLENTY OF IT...

"Ally – look!"

Now, Tor isn't one of those annoying kids that goes loopy in toy shops. You know, the type that just start grabbing anything within a metre radius, whining "Can I have this? Can I have this? Can I have this? Can I have this?" over and over again like a jumping CD.

Nope. I can safely say that I could take Tor into the toy den that is our local Woollies at Christmas, and he wouldn't twitch. But take him to the local pet shop, and that's a different kettle of gerbils altogether...

"Ally – it's pretty isn't it?"

Tor's brown eyes were gazing up hopefully into mine. We were here at the pet shop doing our regular Saturday-morning stint, stocking up on hamster bedding, fish food and whatever little extras Tor managed to wangle out of our budget.

"Uh, yeah, I suppose it's quite pretty," I nodded, peering at the small sponge ball covered in soft, glittery, tinsel spikes. It looked like a strange mating between a hedgehog and a Christmas decoration. "What is it?"

"Cat toy," said Tor earnestly, pointing at the display box full of glitter-spiked balls he'd plucked it from.

"Mmm. Looks more like a Rowan toy," I commented, thinking how much our sister would like something that sheeny-shiny and stupid.

Tor giggled.

It's great having a kid brother sometimes; it doesn't matter *how* lousy your jokes are, they always laugh.

"Better not tell her about these, Tor," I said to him, all mock-serious. "She'll be in here buying the whole lot, and end up glueing them round her headboard or something."

Tor giggled some more. And then he stopped.

"Can I get one, then?" he blinked up at me. "Please?"

He doesn't miss a trick; really he doesn't.

There he was, luring me into a false sense of security, pretending he thought what I was saying was funny and everything, and then *wham* – just when my guard's down, he hits me with the wide-eyed pretty-pleases.

"Well, if we buy this, then we can't go for a hot

chocolate..." I warned him.

That's part of our Saturday-morning ritual too – going for a hot chocolate at Shufda's, a little egg 'n' chips caff a couple of doors up from the pet shop. Unless, of course, we end up spending our "treat" money on stuff like sponge glitter balls.

"That's OK," he shrugged. "The cats'll like it."

So, we headed home early, armed with pet bits and cat toys. With just me and him and no one else around, I felt it was time to pick Love Child No. 4's brain.

"You heard Rowan and Linn fighting yesterday, didn't you?" I asked, as we trudged along the busy pavements, sharing a consolation Kit Kat (well, even if we didn't get our hot chocolate, we still had to keep our sugar levels up...).

"Yep," said Tor, leaning sideways with the weight of his shopping bag.

"It didn't upset you, did it?"

"No."

"Did you figure out that they were arguing about what to get Dad for his birthday?"

"Yep."

"So, what do you think, Tor? Do you think Dad would like a big framed picture of the four of us?"

"Nope."

Like I say, he's a boy of few words. But you always get his drift pretty easily.

"What do you think *would* be a good present for Dad, then?"

Tor looked up at me, his eyes squinting against the sun.

"The zoo..."

"The zoo? Well, I know we want to get Dad something good, Tor, but I don't think even all our pocket money clubbed together is enough to buy the whole of London Zoo..."

"No!" he said, whacking me on the arm with his half of the Kit Kat. "A day out! All of us! And Grandma!"

Ooh, I could just see Grandma there, pulling a disapproving face at the sight of the baboons and their obscenely red bums. Or Linn yawning and looking at her watch. And considering Dad had taken Tor to the zoo one Sunday last month, I didn't think he'd particularly think it was some big-wow birthday treat to go and count the penguins yet again, quite so soon.

"Right, fine. Thanks, Tor – that's, er, another idea to think about!" I lied, as we took the turning into our road.

"Who's that?"

Tor was pointing his chocolate bar into the distance.

"Who's that where?" I asked, peering down the street to see what he could see.

"At our door," said Tor, now nibbling distractedly at his Kit Kat, like one of his hamsters let loose on a carrot.

Fleetingly, I just made out a figure – a dark-haired girl – being let in our front door.

"Wasn't that Von?" I suggested.

Von is one of Rowan's best buddies; one of her two best mates (the other one is a monosyllabic guy called Chazza) whom our gran strongly disapproves of. Mainly because they're quite a bit older than my fifteen-year-old sister (Von and Chazza are both eighteen) and pierced (in Von's case it's her nose, in Chazza's it's his eyebrow), and because Grandma really has a thing against nicknames (Von is short for the hard-to-get-your-head-around Irish name Siobhan, Chazza is playground mumbo-jumbo for Charles). Can you imagine my uptight grandma giving it the old "So, how are you … *Chazza*?" It doesn't come naturally, I'll tell you that. But what choice does poor old Rowan have? All the people in her year give her a pretty hard time, since they think she's so weird and everything, so if Von and Chazza think she's cool, who cares if they're older, pierced, or in possession of crap nicknames?

"No – it wasn't Von," Tor said definitely.

"Was it one of Linn's mates?" I suggested, wracking my brain. "Mary? Or maybe Nadia?"

"No."

I frowned. Who was wandering about in our house right now? If that girl wasn't one of Linn or Rowan's mates, then who was she?

"She had big ears," said Tor simply.

He's a bit spooky sometimes, my brother (no wonder Billy calls him Spook Kid). He has this thing where he hones in on details other people just don't get...

"You couldn't have seen her ears from all this distance away!" I laughed, as we trudged along the pavement.

But as soon as the words were out of my mouth, I remembered someone who did have big ears, when her hair was pulled back tight in a ponytail.

It suddenly occurred to me who the girl in my house really was. And she wasn't a friend of *mine*.

The cheek of Kyra Davies...

Chapter 12

WHOSE HOUSE IS IT ANYWAY?

Rowan was sitting at the table, her knees tucked up inside her white, cotton, Victorian-style nightie. From where me and Tor were standing in the kitchen doorway, it made her look like she had enormous matronly bosoms.

She was still sleepy from her long lie-in – you could tell by the way she was yawning and the way her hair was sticking up at one side. Lucky for her, someone was filling the kettle to make her a cup of coffee.

"Oh, hi! I just got here," said Kyra, ever so casually, as she plugged the kettle in. "I woke Rowan up ringing the doorbell, so I'm making her a coffee to make up for it. Do you want one?"

It's weird seeing someone you don't know or like very much making themselves at home and rummaging about in your kitchen cupboards for mugs. Not just weird; downright INFURIATING!

"Uh, Kyra – wasn't I meant to phone you later, about meeting up?" I said, hoping she'd get my point.

She didn't.

"Oh, it's no problem," she shrugged, clattering cups down on the work surface. "I've already been to the Historical Society – I've got everything we'll need."

Now, you see what I mean about the girl? How presumptuous was that? The plan was supposed to be that I'd call Sandie and Kyra around lunchtime, and work out a time to go to the Historical Society *together*, so we could research and pick out all our reference stuff for the project *together* ... and now look what she'd gone and done. She obviously had some kind of difficulty understanding what "together" is supposed to mean. Like, it doesn't mean "Never mind anyone else; you just go on and do whatever you fancy..."

I was so mad, I couldn't think what to say.

"Yeah, I got up early this morning and was just a bit bored," Kyra blithely continued, turning and placing a cup in front of Rowan.

"Thanks," muttered Rowan sleepily.

"No problem. So I thought I might as well go along and get everything we needed. What do you take in your coffee, Ally?"

I still hadn't said anything, and I was still hovering uselessly in the doorway, carrier bags in hand.

"She takes milk. And one sugar," yawned Rowan, doing my talking for me.

"Well, are you going to sit down?"

I'm an idiot sometimes, I really am. This bossy, pushy girl tells me to sit down in my own house, and what do I do?

I sit down.

"Look, this is what I got," Kyra continued, settling herself into a chair and pulling copies of photos and maps out of a white plastic bag. "All we need to do is get these blown up to poster-size first – does the office at school have a good photocopier, or are we going to have to go to a specialist copying place?"

"I … I don't know," I shrugged stupidly.

"Oh, wow – look! This is Von's street!" said Rowan, suddenly springing to life at the sight of the first photo on the pile.

"Yeah – see this house here? It's completely gone. That's where the bomb fell," Kyra explained.

"Gee, this is going to be really interesting for everyone, seeing if their street was bombed…" mused Rowan, riffling through the other photos. "This must have taken you for ever to sort out!"

"Yes, it did. But the two women down at the Historical Society were brilliant, helping me go through everything."

Do you ever get times where you feel surplus to requirements? That's how I felt right then, watching my sister and this practical stranger sitting with their heads together, cooing over *my* project.

And it was about to get worse.

"Do you like hamsters?" said a small voice.

Because I'd been so stunned at the sight of Kyra Davies swanning round my house like she was my lifelong buddy, I hadn't noticed Tor disappearing from my side. And I hadn't noticed him reappearing, sidling up to Kyra with a handful of fur, teeth and claws.

"Yes I do!" said Kyra, turning and attempting to stroke Mad Max.

"Don't – he bites!" warned Tor.

Damn right Mad Max bites. Tor had inherited him a few weeks earlier from the reception class at his school. Instead of being this sweet, fluffy creature for the little kids to cuddle and love, it turned out that Mad Max was the Rottweiler of the small-mammal world, merrily biting children and teachers at every possible opportunity. If Tor hadn't taken him, Mad Max was destined for a one-way trip to the vet...

I got quite chirpy at that point. Tor was testing Kyra; forcing her to come face to face with his scariest pet, and see how she'd react. Good lad.

"He won't bite me!" said Kyra assuredly, scooping Mad Max right out of Tor's hand and cuddling him to her chest.

Come on, Max, I thought to myself. *Do your stuff!*

"Prrp! Eeeeee!"

"He likes you!" chirped Tor, grinning in delight.

Great.

I couldn't even trust a hamster to be on my side...

Chapter 13

KISSING BILLY (YEAH – LIKE, *RIGHT!*)

The grass was a little bit too damp to lie on, but I didn't care.

Staring straight up, I watched little, ripply clouds wisp their way across the blue, blue sky. Then, accompanied by a far-away roar, a large plane came streaming over the top of Alexandra Palace, its silvery wings glinting with reflected sunlight.

I love skywatching. It chills me right out. Whenever my head gets in a knot, or if I just fancy a daydream, I come and flop down here at the top of the hill and gaze into space. The best part is when the planes swoosh past though – I love imagining who's sitting up there, eating free peanuts, as they gaze down on the amazing aerial view of Ally Pally (the building) and maybe the less impressive and much smaller Ally Pally (me) – if their eyesight's sharp enough. I always wonder where they're going and what their lives are like...

That Sunday morning, I'd happily have swapped places with anyone on the big silvery plane up above me. It wasn't as if anything dramatically *bad* was happening in my life, but I *was* feeling well and truly fed up by how irritating and complicated things can get.

Like the business of Kyra turning up unannounced the day before, and half my family falling for her. I tell you, I'd decided that it was the *last* time I'd take Rowan's side over Linn's, and the *last* time I'd go shopping for spoilt cat toys with Tor...

If only I was on that plane, going somewhere far away... I wished to myself, watching it fly off towards the horizon. *Anywhere that wasn't here would do...*

You know how some people have recurring dreams? Well, I have a recurring fantasy. It goes like this: I'm sitting on a plane that's headed for somewhere tropical and warm and beachy (this week's choice of imaginary destination was Sri Lanka – I'd seen it on a travel show and checked out where in the world it was on the big map on my bedroom wall). Anyhow, I'm on this plane, gazing out of the window at these great, fat clouds below me, when someone asks if I'd mind them sitting in the empty seat next to me. And my heart skips a beat or three, 'cause I recognize that slow, lazy drawl, and I turn round to find Alfie, smiling his gold-toothed smile at me...

Good fantasy, isn't it? Lying up there on the hill, I often try to edge it on a little further than that; you know, start imagining me and him hanging out on the beach together at whatever's my Destination of the Week, rubbing SPF15 on each other's bodies... But somehow, I don't tend to get that far. Mainly because – back in the real world – Winslet will end up padding over and licking my face, just to check I'm not dead or anything. Or Rolf will come and drop a drool-covered plastic disk on my tummy, so that I know that I'm neglecting my Frisbee-chucking duties.

"Yip! Yip! Yip! Yip!"

Winslet had just finished slobbering her dog-food-scented tongue all over my mouth and nose, when I heard her growling at the incoming dog.

"Hi!" said Billy, staring down at me, and blocking out the sun with his back-to-front baseball-capped head. (The baseball cap was back-to-front, not his head. Though with Billy, it's hard to tell sometimes.)

"Out of the way," I replied, motioning him to move over. "I'm trying to beam myself on board that plane, but your big head's between it and me."

Billy lifted his hand to shield his eyes and stared into the sky.

"What – *that* one?" he asked, pointing to the

plane as it headed into the distance, above the skyline of central London.

"Yep," I nodded, pushing myself up on to my elbows.

Further down from us on the grassy slopes, Precious was doing his level best to shove his precious nose exactly where my dogs didn't want it.

"What do you want to be on that plane for?" asked Billy.

"I'm bored of the petty irritations that make up my life," I moaned. "I want that plane to take me away to somewhere exotic…"

"What, Gatwick airport?"

"Huh?" I blinked at him.

"Well, with *that* flight path, and at *that* height, I'd say it's about to land at Gatwick airport," said Billy, crouching down beside me.

Billy doesn't have a romantic bone in his body, he really doesn't. Which is another reason he doesn't have a girlfriend. I mean, I'm not saying he was wrong; it's just that he never knows when a girl doesn't want to hear cold hard facts about flight paths and unglamorous local airports and needs some sympathy and understanding instead.

"Anyway, I don't know what you're on about – you've never even *been* on a plane," he pointed out unkindly. "You don't even know if you'd like it."

"So?" I answered defensively.

But he was right. It's just kind of embarrassing sometimes to admit that your family can't afford to take you on flash holidays. I'm not knocking the camping stuff we've always done (well, I *do* when it rains…), but it can still make you feel like you're missing out compared to other people.

"You all right?" he asked, suddenly noticing my grumpy expression.

"No."

"What is it – your hair?"

I'd tried to brush my fringe into some kind of side parting, but it obviously hadn't covered up my hack job.

"No," I protested, running my fingers through it again, like it would help.

Ha.

"So what's up, then?"

I sighed at the grating memory of Kyra getting cosy in our kitchen with Tor over a packet of milk-chocolate Hobnobs.

"There's this new girl who's started at school this week – and I might end up having to strangle her with my bare hands."

"How come?" frowned Billy, pulling his cap round the right way. "If she's annoying, why don't you just ignore her?"

"Ignore her? Huh!" I snorted. "That's kind of hard, when she's already been helping herself to tea and biscuits at my house!"

I didn't want to ruin another day of my weekend by talking about Kyra, but you know how it is – you have to have a moan. And Billy is quite good to moan to, and knows me better than most. I guess I'm closest to Sandie, because she's a girl and because we go to the same school, but like I said before, Billy's my oldest friend.

We got to know each other when our mums took us to the same playgroup. I liked Billy straight away because he was the only kid who was willing to let me bury him in the sand pit. (He's a very trusting soul.) Oddly enough, my mum and his got to be pretty good friends too. It was odd because his mum's this real neat fiend, who dresses in matching shoes and handbag just to go to Tesco's, whereas Mum was more of a long, baggy skirt and hand-knitted jumper kind of person. And when we were small, Billy's mum would be all uptight, bleaching and disinfecting every surface and every toy in case a stray germ dared to infect her precious little boy, while my mum horrified her by claiming that if everyone licked the kitchen floor each day we'd all be so toughened against germs that we'd never need antibiotics. (We never did though. Lick the kitchen floor, that is.)

Although I played round there a lot when I was small, I don't much like going round to Billy's house now – his mum always gives me these really pitying looks and asks how we're all coping...

Anyhow, that day, Billy ended up sitting on the grass beside me just long enough to hear my whinge about Kyra and to get a wet bum, courtesy of the damp grass.

"And what's she like in class?" he asked, once he'd got the whole story.

"She does that thing where she's totally cheeky to teachers," I explained, "but she does it so subtly, they can't get her for it."

"Like how?"

"Well, you know – they'll ask her a question, and she'll tell them the right answer, but with this really *booooorrred* tone in her voice. Or say 'Yes, *Sir*' or 'Yes, *Miss*' but with this *sneer* in her voice."

"I'd love to meet her."

You could have knocked me down with a sparrow's feather then. After everything I'd said, after explaining how my family seemed to be taken in by her, Billy'd let me down. His girl radar had gone up, and he'd blanked out all the bad bits I'd told him.

"What?!" I yelped.

"Well, I'd like to meet her – just so I could snub her. Show her she's no big deal."

Right then, I could have put my arms around my best mate Billy and given him a great, big kiss.

If the idea wasn't so totally icky.

Chapter 14

GOOD VIBES AND BIG MOUTHS...

"You know, I think it's growing in already," Sandie lied sweetly.

I knew it was just Sandie telling one of her occasional morale-boosting white lies – bless her – so I didn't bother to contradict her, even though my reflection was telling me something radically different.

I rifled around in my bag for the butterfly clips I knew were in there somewhere. My fringe was going to get clamped off my face until it had reached a decent length to be seen in public again.

The reason I decided not to tell my friend that I knew she was spinning me a line was that I'd made a decision; and that was to stop being a moany git.

After I'd seen Billy the day before and sounded off all my woes to him, I'd gone home and idled the rest of my Sunday away, mooching around miserably. There was nothing worth watching on telly in the evening, so I decided to stomp upstairs to my room and dig out my most depressing CD to listen to. But as soon as I walked into my room, before my hand automatically went to flick on the light switch, I saw out in the dark night the glowing vision of Alexandra Palace (don't worry – it wasn't on fire again).

Normally, as soon as darkness falls, you can hardly make the Palace out, but now, all lit up at the top of the hill, it almost looked like it was some fantasy fairytale castle, floating in mid-air. Spotlights shone the length of the Palace's yellow brickwork, the stained glass of the vast Rose window was illuminated like a giant version of something you'd find eating up the electricity bill in Rowan's room, while white streaks of lasers whizzed from the parapets up into the night sky.

OK, so I knew that the Palace must have all lights blazing because they were holding some big corporate do there, but even if this magical apparition was down to the Chartered Surveyors Annual Chartering and Surveying Awards or whatever, the startling prettiness of it still shook me out of the rotten mood I'd been slithering into all week.

Suddenly, I realized that being grumpy was boring me to death.

From tomorrow, I vowed, kneeling on a chair and staring off at the stunning sight of Ally Pally, *I will stop whingeing and whining, and be calm and positive. Hopefully…*

So, here I was, being calm (etc.) first thing on Monday morning, standing outside the main entrance to school, and about to explain my new approach to problems (i.e. Kyra) to my best mate (i.e. Sandie).

"You know something, Sandie?" I said, struggling to get my butterfly clips to stay put.

"What?" Sandie replied, holding up her pocket mirror so I could see what I was doing.

"We shouldn't let this stuff with Kyra wind us up," I mumbled, holding a purple clip between my teeth.

"Yeah?"

"Yes. I've been thinking: we can't get out of doing this project with her, so I think we should just … grin and bear it and make the best of it."

"Oh, OK," nodded Sandie. "And I suppose we've got to feel sorry for her too. Being new and everything…"

See? Sandie always tries to be nice. But sometimes she's *too* nice. Well, she's a lot nicer than *me*, anyway. I was still grumpy with Kyra for doing all that stuff without us on Saturday.

"But Ally…"

Uh-oh – was I wrong? Was Sandie going to have a bit of a moan about Kyra?

"What?"

"Well, I'm confused…"

"What about?"

"Uh, does that mean we are going to be proper friends with her … or not?"

"No, it doesn't mean we have to be *friends* with her," I tried to explain. "It just means that me and you are mature enough to work with her for the next week without any hassle – and then once the project and the play and everything's out of the way, we start trying to shake her off. Gently."

"Oh, OK – I get it," nodded Sandie.

While we'd been talking (and hairstyling), the area around the main entrance had started filling up, full of people like us who were dawdling around, chatting, delaying till the very last moment taking that first Monday morning step into the school buildings.

"Hi, Ally, hi Sandie…"

It was Chloe Brennan, along with Salma and Jen and Kellie. They're like my second-division mates, after Sandie and Billy.

"Not hanging out with your new best friend, then?" Chloe grinned at me.

I like Chloe, but she's a bit mouthy, a bit cheeky

sometimes. Sometimes she winds me up, if you want to know the truth. And twenty-four hours before – when I was feeling all bitter and spiky – that dig of hers would have really bugged me. But now I was calm and serene, and no digs about Kyra Davies were going to get to me.

"No – I just had to show her around for her first week. Thank God."

Oops, that came out a bit bitchy and not too serene.

Must try harder...

"She's a real show-off, that Kyra, isn't she?" said Salma, yawning.

You'd like Salma; she's got this laid-back way about her – as if her natural habitat is lazing on one of those posh, slinky chaise-longues sofas, doing nothing more energetic than chatting to mates down the phone all day. Sometimes the things she says would sound bitchy coming out of anyone else's mouth, but when she says stuff, you know she's only trying to be funny.

"Yeah, she's got a right attitude on her. Did you hear her in French class the other day?" chipped in Kellie.

Kellie's cool, but she's a total gossip queen.

"Oh, yeah!" Jen giggled. "She started arguing with Mr Matthews, didn't she, when he tried to correct her pronunciation!"

Jen's a real giggler – she does it at the most out-of-order moments, like in assembly, or when there's a sad, slushy, romantic moment in a movie.

"It's like she wants to be the centre of attention all the time, isn't it?" Salma commented. "Silly cow…"

Ouch. Maybe Salma wasn't just being funny, for once. Still, at least, it wasn't *me* who was being bitchy. Even if I couldn't help smiling.

"Oh, hey, Ally – did you know that new horror movie's out this week?" said Chloe, suddenly changing the subject.

I knew what was coming next. Chloe is very popular within our little crowd – her dad runs this grocery shop that does a sideline in video rentals, and every time a new movie comes out that we want to see, Chloe can always get her hands on it a couple of days before it's officially meant to go on the shelves. And then that's where *I* come in – all of us take turns having everyone over for a girlie video night once in a while, and it looked like right now, it was my turn to turf the family out of the living room and let my friends invade.

"Cool," I nodded. "Do you want to come over at the weekend to watch it?"

"Nah – it's got to go out on the shelves on Friday, so we'll have to do it before then."

It's stupid, I know, but it's a bit of a buzz for all of us, getting to see something before anyone else, so I had to come up with a better offer.

"OK, Wednesday, then?"

They all murmured and ummed and ahhed, but eventually everyone settled on Wednesday being vid night.

BRRRRRRIIIIIIIIIIIINNNNNNNGGGG!!!

Big mistake – we were standing right under the bell.

"Fantastic!" I grinned inanely at Sandie once the shrill sound had faded. "The start of a whole new week at school! I don't know about you, but there's nowhere *I'd* rather be!"

Sandie grinned back, knowing exactly how I felt. That is, about as pleased as if someone had suggested superglueing my eyelids together...

Me and Sandie had just turned to follow Chloe and the others up the couple of steps to the main entrance, when I felt this weird sensation, like a stare was burning into my head.

I flicked my eyes to one side, and across a crush of people I caught sight of Kyra, hurriedly averting her gaze to the tarmac. Strangely, in that split-second, I noticed her ears – not 'cause they were big (that goes without saying) but because they looked deep pink against her light-brown skin.

("Ah! Ears burning – it's a sure sign someone's talking about you!" Grandma's words rattled round my head. She's very matter-of-fact, my gran, but she still likes to trot out ye olde worlde superstitious sayings from time to time.)

Urgh, I thought, my heart suddenly sinking with guilt. Was Kyra standing anywhere near us while everyone was bitching about her? Had she heard?

Call me a hypocrite, but I hated the idea that she might have caught any of that, and got hurt by it.

Ally Love – you are a hypocrite.

There, I've said it myself.

Chapter 15

SISTERLY LOVE (DON'T LAUGH...)

"No! Don't you dare!"

At Linn's barked command, Rowan stopped dead, her hand hovering over the saucepan on the cooker.

"But it needs it!" whimpered Rowan. "It'll be really boring on its own!"

"Spaghetti bolognese does *not* need curry powder!"

"But—"

Rowan was a braver girl than me (and madder – I mean, curried spaghetti bolognese?). Linn was looking particularly frosty-faced, and arguing with her when she was wearing that expression was just pure insanity.

"Ally – *tell* her, before I ram this spoon down her throat!" Linn beseeched me, waving a tomato-sauce-stained wooden spoon ominously in the air.

"Um," I muttered, hovering in the kitchen doorway.

Both Linn and Rowan were staring at me, waiting for my verdict.

I wished Grandma had been able to make the tea as usual, instead of having to pootle off early to get ready for a someone's wedding-anniversary party this Tuesday night (partying on a Tuesday night? Our gran had a better social life than us...). Then there wouldn't be a battle for cooking supremacy going on between my two sisters, and I wouldn't be stuck in the middle as an unwilling referee.

"I think..." I said slowly, stalling for time. "I think curry is *brilliant*; but I quite like spaghetti bolognese just the normal way."

There – was that tactful enough to satisfy them both?

Nope.

"You *told* Ally to say that, Linnhe!" Rowan burst out.

"*When?*" gasped Linn, laughing at Rowan's plainly ridiculous accusation. "You mean, when I sent her an extra-sensory, telepathic message as she was walking through the hall two seconds ago? On yeah, you are *so* right, Ro!"

"There you go – twisting everything round so you look like you're *so* smart!" Rowan snapped at her, blinking hard like she might be on the verge of tears.

"Yeah? Well, looking smart's not hard, when I'm anywhere near *you*..."

"Shhh!" I hushed them, wide-eyed. From where I was standing, I'd heard the telltale creak of the stairs, even if they didn't.

Linn suddenly turned her attention to stirring the spaghetti, while Rowan grabbed the sponge by the sink and started wiping the work surface.

"Mmm, that smells good," smiled Dad, walking into the kitchen. "Anyone seen my specs? I'm supposed to be helping Tor with his homework, but it might help if I could read what the heck he's supposed to be doing..."

"Oh, they're here, Dad!" said Rowan cheerfully, handing Dad the glasses he'd left lying on top of the breadbin.

"Thanks, Ro. So, you girls all right?"

I knew then that he'd heard the raised voices on his way downstairs from Tor's room.

Me and my sisters, we've got this unspoken rule: never to let Dad catch us arguing. It's not fair to him, you see. He's had such a rough time with what happened with Mum and everything, that he would just get really flipped out if he thought we were ever falling out with each other. So, rows, bickering, disputes ("Debates", as Grandma would say), whatever; they're all kept well away from Dad.

"Yes, we're fine!" I said, probably a little too brightly to be convincing. "Those two were just moaning a bit because I was reminding them I've got my mates coming round tomorrow night!"

"Oh, Ally – don't be silly! You know me and Rowan don't mind!" smiled Linn, playing the part.

She's very good at pretending her and Rowan get on. The only time she lets her true feelings show in front of Dad is when she's confronted by Rowan's terrible attempts at cooking on her nights in charge of the kitchen. But, well, people do have their limits…

"Yeah! I was just reminding Ally that she better remember to tidy up when they've gone – last time her mates came round, Rolf and Winslet were eating spilt popcorn off the floor for weeks! Weren't they, Ally!"

Rowan was positively twittering now. She's a born actress, she really is. Over-acting a speciality.

"Good. Anyway, I better get back up to those multiplication tables!" smiled Dad, as he pushed his specs on.

The three of us girls stood like statues, stupid grins fixed on our faces, till we heard Dad clomp back up the stairs and listened to the creak of him opening and shutting the door to Tor's room.

Then World War Three started again.

"You are so *bossy*, Linnhe! You think you can tell all of us what to do and think!" Rowan hissed.

She was furious with our eldest sister, that was for sure, but considering she had done her hair in these two stubby short plaits, Rowan looked more like she should be going out to milk the cow in an ancient episode of *Little House on the Prairie* than arguing over curry powder in the middle of a kitchen in Crouch End.

"What's this got to do with anything?! What are you having a go at me for?" barked Linn, her green eyes blazing. "And for the ten thousandth time, my name is *Linn*, not *Linnhe*!"

"For one thing, you – you still want us to do this stupid family-portrait thing, even though me and Ally and Tor think it's a totally rubbish idea," Rowan railed at her. "And another thing, you can change it as much as you want – you can say you're name's *Bob* if you want – it doesn't change the fact that Mum gave you the name Linnhe, and that's who you are!"

It went strangely silent again at that point. Linn looked weird at the mention of Mum, like she'd been slapped in the face or something. Rowan looked upset at being forced to bring it up.

I didn't feel too good either, being reminded of the big, yawning gap in our lives. But I remember that Dad once said that your brain has an amazing capacity for protecting you from pain. And right at that moment, my brain obviously decided that it was going to distract me from sad, longing thoughts of Mum by giving me the giggles.

Suddenly, I found myself just struggling not to laugh out loud at the idea of Linn being called Bob…

"If you *must* know," Linn said huffily, pulling herself together and turning her attention back to her stirring, "I don't think we *should* do the family-photo thing now…"

A cat that wasn't Colin swooped round my ankles, alerted by the smell of cooking.

"Why not?" I asked, picking up the battered black and white moggy and identifying it by its crossed eyes as Derek. "I thought you were dead keen on the idea."

Linn pursed her lips.

"That was before I found out how much it costs…" she mumbled finally.

Ah-ha, so *that* explained her frosty features.

Rowan had a triumphant little grin on her face. She was about to say something that would end up with both my sisters yelling at each other again, I could tell.

"How much *would* it cost?" I leapt in, before Rowan could.

"More than we could afford," Linn said firmly.

Rowan was itching to speak.

"OK," I said a little too loudly, anticipating a vindictive outburst from our in-between sister. "So let's think of something else, then…"

"Like what? You haven't come out with any useful suggestions so far!" Linn said to me, pointedly.

Derek was wriggling to be free. He could sense the sisterly tension in the room and, smell of food or not, he was keen to be out of the kitchen and cuddling up somewhere more chilled-out.

"Well, why don't we all go to Camden Market this weekend?" I suggested, letting Derek bounce down on to the floor. "If we can't find something unusual for Dad there, then we'll never find it anywhere."

I don't know if you've ever been to Camden Market, but it's absolutely amazing. It started off years ago as a little patch of stalls in some old buildings by the canal in Camden and it's been expanding ever since, taking over every dilapidated old factory and building in the area. The stalls sell weird, wonderful and bizarre stuff, from clothes to food (OK, so neither of those sound particularly bizarre, but you haven't seen what some of them are like), to clocks carved out of driftwood, knitted pot-plant ornaments and wind chimes made out of old forks. Weird, I know, but good. Trust me.

Linn and Rowan glanced briefly at each other. Without saying anything, it seemed like something had been decided.

"OK," nodded Linn, for both of them. "Let's go to Camden at the weekend."

Phew.

I'd stopped them rowing.

Even if it just meant they'd be saving their worst quarrels for when they tore each other's hair out at the market on Saturday.

Still, Camden Market's so full of buskers and street entertainers that people might watch Linn and Rowan fighting and just presume it was performance art.

I could stick a hat in front of the two of them and see if any tourists chucked money into it...

Chapter (16)

OH, THE HORROR...

"Present for you!" giggled Jen, standing on my doorstep.

"Jen! It's fabulous! You shouldn't have!" I fooled around, taking the tube of Pringles she was holding out towards me. "Come on in – everyone's here already."

Letting her close the front door behind her, I zoomed back into the living room and leapt into the one free armchair.

"Hey, where am I supposed to sit?" Jen protested, looking around at us all.

Chloe had bagsied the beanbag and was lolling on the floor, while Salma and Kellie were both stretched out, at either end of the sofa, like Siamese bookends.

Sandie, meanwhile, was sitting scrunched up to one side of the other armchair from me, looking not entirely comfortable. Rolf's gangly-limbed, furry body took up the rest of the space, his head lounging, *very* comfortably, in Sandie's lap.

Jen stuck her bottom lip out and did a very passable impression of someone who was three years old and about to have a major blub.

A Wotsit came flying through the air and hit her on the face.

"Oi!" she yelped, and took a dive at Kellie – the Wotsit-chucking culprit – tickling her mercilessly till Kellie had wriggled over enough to leave a reasonable gap on the sofa between herself and a cackling Salma.

Jen spotted the space and jubilantly parked her bum there.

At the same time, Rolf – sensing food on the loose – bounded off the chair he was sharing with Sandie and gave chase to the rogue crisp, utilizing her stomach as a handy launchpad.

"Rolf!" I snapped at him, as Sandie grimaced at the sudden impact of a dog diving off her abdomen.

"No, it's all right! I'm OK!" gasped Sandie breathlessly, waving one hand in the air and trying to smile.

She hates "being a bother", as she calls it. If she'd been playing the Drew Barrymore part in the film *Scream*, she'd be lying in a pool of blood at the end of the scene whispering, "No, I'm fine. Honestly! It's just a scratch!"

"Right, chuck me the tape, then, Chloe, and I'll

get the movie on," I said, pushing myself off the chair and kneeling down by the video player. "So, how scary is this one meant to be?"

"Worse than the *Blair Witch Project*, my dad says," Chloe replied. "But wait a minute, Ally – you never answered my question."

"What question?"

My mind was a bit of a muddle; it had been all go since I finished school for the afternoon. First I'd had to go shopping and buy enough crisps, dips and Coke to keep my mates happy for the evening, then I'd had to stop my family from eating or drinking any of it before my friends actually arrived. And despite the fact that my dad is very fair about us all getting a "turn" to have the living room to ourselves like this every once in a while, it had still been a nightmare to shoo them all out before Sandie and Chloe and the others rang the doorbell.

"Before Jen arrived – I was asking about Kyra, remember?" said Chloe. "How it's going with her and the History project?"

Urgh. *That*.

It was all right for Chloe, Jen, Kellie and Salma. Right at the start, they'd been excused from doing anything for the History project, because they'd offered their services in the make-up and wardrobe departments for the play itself. Cushy, if you ask me. Whereas me and Sandie, we had to endure Kyra at close quarters, spending our History lessons stuck exclusively with her and our pile of posters. The Drama group were performing their play starting on Monday, so it was all hands on deck to get everything finished; which is why Miss Thomson had given us class time – and a note to our other teachers to let us have the whole of Friday afternoon off – to get everything finished.

"It's going ... all right," I shrugged non-committally, without catching Sandie's eyes. I knew she'd be thinking I couldn't be telling less of the truth. "But, hey, let's not speak about boring stuff like that. Let's get the movie on!"

"Aw, come on, Ally," said Kellie. "Spill! We already told you how much she was bugging us today in Mr Matthews's class, when she started putting on that stupid over-the-top 'haw-he-haw' French accent."

"Oh my God, yeah!" Jen half-gasped, half-giggled. "Was she taking the mick out of Mr Matthews by doing that, or did she genuinely think he'd be impressed with it or something?"

"Come on, Al," Chloe cajoled me. "You and Sandie have seen more of her than we have. You've even had to put up with her coming round here to work on your project, haven't you? So what's going on with that girl? Is she a big-head, or is she just totally mad, or what?"

"Listen, I can't really be bothered talking about her," I mumbled.

I also didn't want to give up on my own personal resolution not to moan.

"Oooh, are you getting all protective of her?" Kellie sniggered. "Is Kyra your new best friend, then?"

"*Her*? You *must* be joking!" I barked. "I'd rather clean the loos at school with my toothbrush than be friends with Kyra Davies!"

So much for my resolution.

"Who are you bitching about now, Ally?"

Linn stood in the living room door, looking at me in her best snooty and superior older-sister manner.

God, you know, it *really* bugs me when Linn does stuff like that. For one thing, I thought she'd gone out already (Rowan was upstairs in her room listening to music and creating her next junk masterpiece, while Dad and Tor were doing some father and son bonding, watching a repeat of *ET* together on the old portable telly up in Dad's bedroom). For another thing, Linn always seemed to save that snooty and superior older-sister malarkey for when my friends came round. And most annoying of all, it was easy for her to make a glib comment when *she* hadn't had to spend the last few days in enforced close contact with Kyra Davies, getting told "No, Ally, that photocopy's too blurry. Do it again" and "Give those scissors to me, Ally, you're not cutting it straight" and "Don't tint that photo that colour, it looks crap!"

And I'd been good and patient and non-moany, just like I'd promised myself, even though Little Miss Know-It-All was working my nerves so much that she was in danger of finding her *face* getting photocopied.

"I'm not bitching, I'm debating," I tried to say calmly, borrowing that favourite saying of Grandma's.

"Yeah! Like, *right*!" snorted Linn, pulling her jacket on.

I suddenly had a vision of my perfectly featured sister with *her* nose squashed sideways on a photocopier too.

It made me feel marginally better.

"That'll be Alfie…" Linn muttered out loud to herself, as the doorbell shrilled.

My tongue was totally tied and I could feel that my face was about one million degrees hot – partly through my anger at Linn sounding off and showing me up in front of my friends, and partly because

Alfie was in the vicinity…

Then I found myself distracted and infinitely cheered up by the sight of Chloe pulling a face and silently mimicking my sister's nagging. But she soon stopped *that* in a hurry as Linn reappeared in the living-room doorway.

"Another one of your lot," she announced, before breezing off.

Sandie, Jen, Chloe, Kellie, Salma … there wasn't any more of "our lot" to come.

"Hi. I haven't missed the start, have I?"

Six mouths fell open at the sight of Kyra Davies and her bare-faced cheek.

Chapter 17

I HATE HER, I HATE HER NOT...

The young guy with the naff blond-dyed hair job was *not* having a good day. First, he'd fallen out with his girlfriend, *then* he'd gone round to her flat to apologize, only to find that she wasn't up for listening (mainly because she was a tiny bit dead). And now – thanks to the neighbourhood's local friendly axe murderer – Blond Bloke was wearing most of his insides on the outside. And *boy*, that wasn't a good look.

Normally, with horror movies, I'm a total wuss – I watch them from behind cushions, like that'll protect me or something. But this night, I ended up watching the random delights of gore, suspense and more gore with the sort of blank indifference I usually save for the gardening shows my dad regularly tunes in to.

Of course, it wasn't blank indifference I was feeling; it was complete shock. Kyra turning up like that – as if she'd been *asked*, for God's sake – was just so mind-blowingly cheeky that I didn't know what to say to her. Obviously, she must have overheard us all talking about having a girlie video night the other morning outside school, and just ... well ... decided to include herself in the invite.

You know what I said when she asked if she'd missed the start of the movie? OK, before you guess, here's a random selection of things I *should* have said. If I was the kind of girl to have the bottle. Which I'm not.

1) "What gives you the right to turn up here just like this, Kyra? You're *bang* out of order..."

2) "Missed the start? You're going to miss the whole movie, girl. Turn round and leave where you came in..."

3) *"Hellooooo?* Earth calling Kyra! Let me explain: down here in the *real* world we have this cute little custom where we actually *invite* people to come to our houses, not just have them turning up on our doorsteps like *psychos*!"

See, any of those – though not very nice – would, in the circumstances, have been reasonable responses.

But, oh no; Kyra Davies turns up unannounced at my house (for the second time) and, in answer to her question "Have I missed the start?" I faff about and say, "Umm ... no", then watch helplessly as she gazes around the room and settles herself on the floor, leaning her back up against the chair Sandie's sitting on.

"Brought these!" she'd said, opening a white plastic carrier bag and chucking several bags of tortilla chips, kettle crisps and dry roasted peanuts on to the coffee table where the other bowls of nibbles already sat.

Everyone was too stunned to say anything – maybe, since it was my house, they were waiting for me to blast off at her, but I didn't.

Instead, I – oh, the shame – told her to help herself to the two-litre bottle of Coke perched on the table, and immediately pressed play on the remote.

The plot of the movie hadn't even sunk into my frazzled brain, when suddenly a wizened hand burst out of the ground, where the landslide had put an end to the terrible reign of the axe murderer by burying him in choking mud (except it hadn't – you could sniff a sequel coming a mile off).

"What a load of *pants*!" snorted Kyra, as the credits rolled up.

It was a typical Kyra comment, at least from what I knew of her from the last couple of weeks. It didn't make it appropriate though.

"Excuse me?" Chloe bristled, staring across the carpet at Kyra.

Since the video was from Chloe's dad's shop, and it was her little kick to give us the treat of seeing it before any paying customers, she wasn't too thrilled with criticism.

"Come on, it *was*!" protested Kyra, wide-eyed.

In one hand, she held a mound of popcorn; in the other, a full glass of orange juice; and in her lap was a snoozing cat that wasn't Colin.

"And you're some fancy film-critic, are you?" snarled Chloe.

"Don't have to be," shrugged Kyra. "Any moron could see that that was pants. I mean, that bit when the girl feels sorry for the killer and starts singing him a lullaby – no wonder he ripped her head off!"

Actually, you know something? The film *was* pants.

Kyra had the judgement to see that. Sadly, she didn't have the judgement to see that she was getting so far up the noses of everyone in the room that she'd need a native guide to get her back out...

"And that bit when the blond guy saw his girlfriend splattered round the room – couldn't he have at least *tried* to act like he cared a bit more? I mean, has he even *been* to drama school, or did he just walk into that part off the street?" Kyra continued her critique, ramming some popcorn in her mouth after she'd made her point.

"Are you for *real*?" Salma suddenly asked, with this really disgusted look on her face.

OK, so now you're seeing the other side of laid-back Salma. She's quite pretty – she's part Portuguese, or Brazilian or something, I forget – but when she's really hacked off, you'd think from the look on her face that she absolutely despises you. But she doesn't – it's just a momentary thing and it's just the way her face is.

Kyra wasn't to know that. But while anyone else would have spotted Salma's expression and shut up, Kyra didn't seem to notice and went merrily on...

"And the guy's mum!" Kyra carried on, regardless. "Were we really supposed to believe—"

"Erm," interrupted Jen, staring her small, but intense eyes like a shoot-to-kill laser beam at Kyra. "Do you want to shut up for five seconds?"

And for once, Jen *wasn't* giggling.

"What?" said Kyra, furrowing her brow. "Aren't I allowed to have an opinion?"

I felt these prickles at the back of my neck. This was getting really uncomfortable. I was starting to wish I'd never bothered having this video night. I could tell the others were staring at me, expecting me to say something, but I just couldn't think what.

"Well, you *might* have been allowed to have an opinion – *if* I'd invited you here tonight," I suddenly heard myself squeaking.

"Yeah, tell her, Al!" Kellie encouraged me, clapping her hands together.

"What's this got to do with *you*?" Kyra snapped at her. "It's not *your* house, Kellie!"

"No – it's Ally's!" Chloe barged in to the conversation again. "And she didn't ask *you* here tonight, did you Ally?"

I looked across at Chloe, perched forward agitatedly on the beanbag, and nodded, feeling a trickle of sweat tickle its way down my forehead. God, I really *hated* when things got all, y'know, *prickly*.

And it was about to get even *more* prickly...

"What's this got to do with you, Ginger Nut?" snapped Kyra.

Ouch. Double ouch. Chloe didn't mind if you called her a redhead, or auburn or copper or whatever other attractive name you find on the side of hair-tint boxes to describe her natural hair colour.

But start in with the ginger jibes, and you were dead.

"Tell me something," said Chloe, leaning

ominously close to Kyra, her almost transparent white skin even more blanched than usual, "were you born a bitch, or did you have to practise for a really long time?"

Kyra stopped chewing on her popcorn and stared at Chloe.

Something had hit home.

A split-second later, Kyra scrambled to her feet – surprising the cat that wasn't Colin from his slumber and out of her lap. Two seconds later she'd stormed out of the room and through the front door, letting it crash closed behind her.

As the bang of the door was still reverberating, we all gazed at each other in shock.

"Well," said Chloe finally, a small smile of triumph creeping on to her face. "That showed her!"

She was right. Kyra had overstepped the mark by several large, bounding steps, that was for sure.

But you know the weird thing? And this will sound weird – I felt kind of sorry for her...

Chapter 18

DON'T TRY THIS AT HOME

I was late back from lunchbreak, but that was the joy of having Friday afternoon off to finish our History project – I could wander into the empty art classroom we'd been assigned without worrying that I had to explain myself to a teacher.

Mind you, it didn't look like Sandie and Kyra had exactly hurried themselves either. All I had for company was a spooky stone angel statue that some of the Art classes must have been drawing. It looked like it should be smothered in ivy and mouldering away on top of a Victorian grave, not hanging about in a modern school, watching me with its blank eyes and giving me the willies.

Trying to ignore it, I started pushing back tables and chairs to clear a space on the floor: we had six big display posters to finish off, and it seemed like a good idea to get them all laid out together, so we could see what still needed to be done.

If Kyra ever turned up with them, that was. And where was Sandie?

Feeling slightly breathless after dragging and shoving furniture about, I perched myself on the nearest table, and gazed idly round the room. There were paintings and drawings displayed on every available space, as well as some weird and not-especially-wonderful collages made out of what looked like chicken wire and tissue paper. On top of the waist-high cupboards that ran around the perimeter of the room were dozens of half-made papier mâché ... well, *blobs*, and loads of wobbly pottery ... *things*. It kind of reminded me of home. All this room needed was a couple of cats padding about and a large hairy dog skidding across the lino floor and it would've been a dead ringer.

Thinking of home, my heart sank – a vision of our prickly encounter with Kyra on Wednesday night flashed into my head. Since then, I'd given up taking her to and from classes (she pretty much knew where everything was around school by now anyway), and we'd both done an excellent job of avoiding eye contact with each other. Chloe and Kellie and the others were ignoring Kyra too. Even Sandie said she was, but I don't think she was very happy doing it. Sandie's not very good at being mean to people. Even people who deserve it.

And now, I was about to spend a whole after-noon with Kyra. Was she going to mention anything? Or was she just going to pretend it never happened? I hoped so – it's what I planned to do, if I could get away with it. (I know, I know – I'm a coward. You don't have to tell me.)

God, I wished Sandie would hurry up. The idea of facing Kyra and having to make conversation with her on my own didn't exactly make me feel too fantastic.

My heart did a quick couple of star-jumps as I heard footsteps echoing along the corridor towards the classroom door.

Then I heard giggles.

Giggles?

Picture this: my best friend Sandie joking and chatting with Kyra Davies, as she helped her carry in our pile of posters.

Seeing me sitting on the table, Sandie's smile sank like a stone.

Kyra, on the other hand, was as bright and breezy as you like.

"Hi, Ally! All by yourself? Me and Sandie have just been having a *great* laugh about Mrs Fisher, haven't we, Sandie?"

"Mmm!" squeaked Sandie, looking wildly uncomfortable.

I said nothing as the two of them placed the posters on the table beside me and Kyra began unrolling them. But between you and me, I had this funny lump in my throat. I know it was stupid to feel so betrayed, but I did.

"We passed her in the corridor a minute ago and she's got herself the most *terrible* new perm, hasn't she, Sandie?"

Ah, *now* I could see what Kyra's game was: trying to make out to me that her and Sandie were such big mates and make me feel excluded.

That was her revenge for what had happened at my place on Wednesday night.

"I mean, what was it like, Sandie?" Kyra prompted her, acting all chummy.

"Uh ... bad," mumbled Sandie, her cheeks flushed pink.

"God, it was worse than *bad*," Kyra twittered, spreading all the artwork out across the table. "She looks like a sheep, doesn't— Oh, what a pain! I forgot to pick up all the sheets of paper with the captions printed on them! Hold on – I'll have to nip back to Miss Thomson's room for them..."

No sooner had Kyra darted away along the corridor, her top-knot of dark curls bobbing as she ran, when Sandie started blabbering.

"I haven't been hanging out with her, Ally; it's just that I bumped into her coming into school, and that's when she asked me to give her a hand bringing the posters and stuff along here and—"

"It's OK! It doesn't bother me!" I stopped her, even though that wasn't exactly true.

So far Kyra had sucked up to my sister and my brother, even our *animals*, and now it looked like she was doing her best to suck up to my best friend too.

Kyra was like my own personal vampire – sucking my life out from all around me...

"You know, she's all right, really," Sandie blinked her eyes beseechingly at me. "Before we saw Mrs Fisher in the corridor, Kyra was talking about what happened on Wednesday night and saying how embarrassed she was about just storming out like that..."

"Embarrassed about storming *out*?" I said, incredulously. "Shouldn't she be more embarrassed at turning up in the *first* place?"

Sandie shrugged and wrinkled her nose up.

"I know, but I feel sorry for her, Al," she carried on, peeking out of the door to check that Kyra wasn't on her way back already. "She started to tell me that she has a really hard time at home with her mum."

"Like what?" I asked.

I didn't sound too sympathetic, I know I didn't. But I was deliberately being like that; it was all just because Kyra was totally confusing me. One minute she was bossy, aloof and slagging off anything and anyone in her line of vision, the next she was going gooey over my three-legged cat and turning up on my doorstep like my long-lost best buddy. Someone being two-faced, I could just about handle. Somebody having about seventeen faces I couldn't get my head around.

"I don't know *exactly* what's happening with her mum; she never finished telling me, 'cause we caught sight of Mrs Fisher," Sandie explained, making curly-wurly circles with her fingers around her head. "But she *did* say that when Chloe called her a bitch, it really hurt her, 'cause her mum calls her that too! Can you believe that? Her own *mum*?"

My first thought? I was shocked – how could someone's mum say things like that to their face? And then I had a second thought... Maybe Kyra was making it all up, y'know, just for attention or something.

If that was true then it had worked. Sandie had completely bought the story – great big squashy softie that she was.

"You don't honestly think—"

A tip-tap of approaching feet stopped me where I was.

"Right, that's everything!" said Kyra, slapping the stack of paper and a pair of scissors down on the table beside me. "Shall we get started?"

The rest of the afternoon wasn't exactly awash with pleasant conversation, which suited me fine. Kyra spotted a paint-splattered radio on the windowsill, and tuned it into Radio One. Apart from that, there was too much glueing and sticking and finishing off to do; so if we weren't talking about who was doing what, we didn't talk at all.

One thing I couldn't get over was that Kyra didn't once try to bring up the subject of Wednesday night with *me*, even though she'd been more than happy to with Sandie earlier on. It just made it more obvious in my mind that she was deliberately trying to get some attention from Sandie after all. That all this sob story about her mum was just made up. It had to be. Didn't it?

But I tried not to let the whole thing wind me up – we had to get this project finished this afternoon, in time to fix it up in the hall first thing on Monday, ready for the Drama department's first performance on Monday afternoon.

Just get through the next few hours as painlessly as possible, I kept reminding myself, as the hours ticked away, *and that'll be you finished with Kyra Davies...*

* * *

"There!" I said, sticking the *final* caption on the *final* poster.

I stood up straight, and surveyed our handiwork, all laid out on the floor in front of the three of us.

"Looks nice!" said Sandie brightly.

The posters definitely did look "nice". In the centre of each large sheet of artists' card was an A3 enlargement of a section of map, with bomb sites circled in red, and long, thin red lines trailing off to accompanying prints, enlarged from old photos, of what the individual streets looked like pre-war, along with a few Polaroids of what they looked like now.

I had to hand it to Kyra: she'd come up with a really good idea. Even if she was a pain-in-the-neck, conniving weirdo.

"Hmm, I'm not sure…"

"Not sure of what?" I asked, finding myself frowning at Kyra.

"It needs something else … it looks a bit boring like that."

Was she joking? Our project was done, wasn't it? It was twenty to four on Friday afternoon, i.e. twenty minutes to the official start of the week-end, and there was no way I wanted to start faffing about with these posters now.

"What do you mean, *boring*?" I quizzed her, stunned.

"I just think the maps don't stand out enough as a main image," she mused, infuriatingly. "I think maybe they need a border round them or something."

"Mmm … maybe," Sandie half-heartedly agreed, before I got the chance to shoot her a shut-up look.

"Kyra, they're fine the way they are!" I protested, but she'd already walked over to the cabinets closest to us and started riffling through them.

"I know, but they can be *better*," she said brightly, pulling a big roll of masking tape out. "Look – if we paint lengths of this stuff black, it'll dry really quickly, and it'll be easy to cut it to the right length to frame each map. Sandie – see if there's any black paint ready to use in those containers over by the sink, otherwise we'll have to mix some up…"

"Kyra – what's the point of going to all this trouble?" I asked, fuming at the sight of Sandie meekly trotting off sink-wards. "It's not a competition. And anyway the only people who are going to be looking at it are the primary-school kids coming to see the play!"

"So?" shrugged Kyra. "I still want our project to look better than anyone else's. Oh, good, Sandie – you got some!"

"Yeah, there's loads here," said Sandie, walking back towards us with a square plastic container of black poster-paint, left over from someone's artistic efforts that morning.

"See?" Kyra flashed her dark, almond eyes at me. "It's all ready for us – all we have to do is paint the masking tape and tidy away all our rubbish and we'll be done!"

I felt bubbles of irritation rise in my chest. She was just so pushy!

Just be patient for a little while longer, and you don't have to have anything to do with her again... I reminded myself, as my teeth ground together.

"Right! Fine! You know best!" I barked, trying to sound tough, but feeling a choke of angry tears making my voice wobble. "Here, give me the paint, Sandie – I'll do it!"

"Oh, no, you won't – since you seem to think it's such a lousy idea!" snapped Kyra, yanking the plastic container forcefully out of my hands.

Only I hadn't touched it yet.

It wasn't a particularly big container that Sandie was holding out – just about the right size to have held a family-sized chunk of raspberry ripple ice-cream in it (hey, I didn't guess that; the remnants of the label were still visible on its side) – but it sure held enough paint. Enough paint, that is, to send a mini tidal wave swooping up into the air.

It's amazing how far flying paint can fan out, it really is. I'd say try it sometime, but you'd have to be really stupid to give it a go.

Kyra – looking stunned – was left untouched, still clinging to the now empty plastic container. Me, Sandie, even the spooky statue watching over us were, however, covered in what might be described as *ebony* ripple.

Oh, and of course, our project certainly wasn't boring any more. Now, instead of trying to identify their own streets from the posters, all the visiting primary kids could have fun trying to guess what exactly the posters were supposed to *be*, under all those plate-sized splodges of black paint...

Chapter (19)

ONE FOR ALL, AND ALL FOR ... UH-OH

"Ooooooh – isn't that the most beautiful thing you've ever seen?"

I squinted at the object Rowan was holding up. It was a small, fat, gold-painted cherub, stuck inside one of those domed snowstorm ornaments.

Rowan shook it hard, and instead of the usual dandruffy "snow" wafting down over him, a cascade of twinkling gold bits drizzled over his small, fat features.

"It's, er, cute," I commented, wondering what the gloopy liquid was inside those snowstorms. "But it's not exactly the most beautiful thing I've ever seen..."

No, that honour went to stuff like lightning crashing across the sky behind Ally Pally, or our garden in summer, when the wisteria goes crazy and covers the entire back wall in masses of trailing purple blossoms...

God. Who was I kidding? The most beautiful

thing in the world to me was the one, the only (drum roll, please) Alfie.

Sigh.

"What are you looking at?" demanded Linn, appearing at our side.

"Um, this?"

Rowan held up the entombed cherub for Linn to inspect.

"Is that any good for Dad?" Linn asked sternly.

"Er, no," muttered Rowan.

"Well, what are you wasting time looking at it for? If it's not a possible present for Dad, then there's no point, is there?"

Linn should join the army. Sergeant major Love; at your service, *sir!*

The hippie-looking stall-holder stared at Linn, took the ornament out of Rowan's hands, and cradled it protectively to his chest.

"And what's going on?" Linn suddenly barked, scanning all around us.

"What?!" Rowan and I squeaked in unison.

"Where's Tor? Whose turn was it to hold his hand? I *told* you we have to watch out for him. Jeez, this is Camden Market – I *told* you he could get lost in a second in amongst all these crowds!"

Rowan and I exchanged panicked glances. Whose turn had it been to look out for Tor? Obviously *she* couldn't remember any better than *I* could. That's what an hour's worth of shopping amidst this rabbit warren of stalls and crush of people does for you – you end up suffering from the three Ds: Disorientation, Distraction and Death (by older sister, for failing to do your duty).

"I'm not lost!" came a small voice in our midst.

"Oh, thank goodness, Tor," said Linn, her shoulders sinking in relief. "Where did you go?"

"There!" he said indignantly, pointing to a spot all of twenty centimetres away.

Suddenly a surge of gawping shoppers shoved past, sending all four of us almost crashing into the snowstorm stall.

"OK. Enough. Let's get out of this for a while," Linn announced. "Let's go and get some food."

"Noodles!" yelped Tor excitedly.

"Noodles," Linn nodded at him, and off we all trotted (very obediently) behind her.

You know, it's funny with me and Rowan and Linn; OK, so we might niggle and nark at each other, but, boy, when the Love sisters gang up against the world, the world doesn't stand a chance.

There were only a few picnic-bench-type tables beside the takeaway food stalls, and all of them were full. Carefully selecting our victims (Rowan had raised her eyes and nodded towards the group of tourists sitting hugging their all-but-finished coffees) we moved in. Hovering right beside their table with our tinfoil trays of Thai noodles, we three girls started rabbiting away in the most obnoxiously loud, screechy voices we could. The tourists started twitching. They were on the verge of moving, to get away from our irritating banter, but not quick enough for Linn.

Bending down, she whispered something in Tor's ear.

"But I wan' it!" he yelled instantly. "I wan' it! *Whhhhhaaaaaaa*!"

"No! I told you you can't have it! Bad boy!" I scolded Tor in a pantomime voice, winking at my sisters from the corner of my eye.

"Let me have it! I wan' that *toyyyyyyyyyyyyy*! *Whhhhhhhhaaaaaaa*!"

For a boy who didn't like to say much, he could really let it rip.

Loud enough, for sure, to send the tourists scuttling off – leaving the four of us with a roomy place to eat our lunch.

"Good work, Tor!" I grinned, holding my hand, palm-up, just as my sisters were doing.

"High-five!" whispered Tor, grinning as he slapped his small hand against all of ours, one by one.

"Hey, Ally – what's with the black paint in your hair?" asked Linn, twirling noodles round her plastic fork.

"I'm in mourning…" I mumbled, suddenly reminded of the disaster of the day before.

"What for?" Linn asked.

"My History project died."

"What, that thing with the bomb maps and everything?" Rowan exclaimed, raising her eyebrows.

She looked exactly like a movie star when she did that. The only trouble was, it was Minnie Mouse. She'd done her dark hair up in these two twisted knots on either side of her head that looked just like the slip-on ears you can buy in the Disney Store.

"Yes – the thing with the maps. That's the one," I sighed.

"It sounded like it would be really good when your friend … whatshername was talking about it. What happened?" Rowan asked, batting her big, girlie eyelashes at me.

Yep, Minnie Mouse.

"Yes it *was* a good idea. And she's not my friend. And her name's Kyra," I reeled off. "Anyway, it got vandalized yesterday."

"Who by?" gasped Rowan.

"Us," I groaned, slapping my hands over my

face. "We were having an argument, and this container of paint flew over everything."

"Is this what you were supposed to be doing for the Drama department's play?" Linn chipped in, as she worked out what I was talking about.

"I'm coming to see that! With my class!" Tor piped up.

"Are you, honey?" I smiled at him. It hadn't occurred to me that his primary school would of course be part of the audience.

"Well, Tor, you *could* have pointed out your sister's project to all your friends," Linn told him, "but now, you'll just have to point out a big empty space on the wall!"

"Ha, *ha*!" I muttered sarcastically at her, as Tor stood up and tootled off in the direction of the bins with his already empty tinfoil tray.

He's very eco-friendly, my brother.

But Linn was right – there *would* just be a big empty space looming on the wall of the school hall. There wasn't any time to do anything else. And boy, I wasn't looking forward to telling Miss Thomson that, first thing on Monday morning...

"Couldn't you save *any* of it? Was it *all* damaged?" asked Rowan, in-between sucking a noodle up into her mouth.

"It looked totally wrecked when me and Sandie

left yesterday, but then we did have black paint dripping in our eyes at the time..."

"Did your clothes get covered in paint too?" Linn frowned.

That would be her worst nightmare: having her neatly washed and pressed clothes *gunged*.

"Yeah – but they came out all right. Grandma soaked them as soon as I got in."

Neither of my sisters had been witness to my humiliation the afternoon before; Sandie and I had left the classroom as soon as we got over the shock of being splattered. I suppose it was a bit mean to leave Kyra to clean everything up, but all me and Sandie could think about was getting out of school and safely home before the four o'clock bell rang and we had a school full of people pointing and sniggering at us. Back at the house, only Grandma and Tor were privy to the state I was in. And by the time Rowan and Linn arrived home, I was in the shower, and more inclined to keep the whole farce to myself than merrily announce it to the world.

"Couldn't you try to do a rush job tomorrow and put something together?" Linn suggested.

She *would*. But how could you cram all that work into one day, never mind get your hands on all those materials? Not, likely, Linn...

"We'd need a miracle and a few extra pairs of hands to make that work," I replied flatly.

"Well, *I* could help, if you want. I was supposed to be seeing Nadia and Alfie tomorrow afternoon, but I can easily blow them out."

I gawped at Linn for a second; it always takes me slightly by surprise when she's nice. And she *is* nice sometimes – very nice. You just tend to forget it when you're used to her bossing you about every five seconds.

Gazing at my older sister in starry-eyed shock didn't last long – not when Rowan suddenly noticed who was missing.

"Er … where's Tor?" she interrupted.

"He's gone to chuck his rubbish away," I replied, pointing over in the direction of the big plastic dustbin.

Which is exactly where my brother wasn't.

Or anywhere else that we could see.

"Tor!" Linn yelled out in her best sergeant-major boom, alarming everyone at the surrounding tables.

This time, there was *no* small voice saying "I'm not lost!"

Chapter 20

SENDING OUT THE SEARCH PARTY

Imagine every neighbour in your street has their window open, and every single one of them has music blaring out. Walking along the pavement, you hear this weird mix of techno thumping, rock blasting, new age plinky-plonking, classical Spanish guitar-twanging and even Gregorian monks *chanting*, for God's sake.

Add to that the sensation of being in a crowd at a football match, only everyone's wearing T-shirts with band names and slogans on them instead of football shirts.

And that's what it felt like, pushing through the hordes of browsing punters in Camden Market, music pumping from ghetto blasters on every stall, it seemed, while I searched hopelessly for my little brother. I could feel my heart whirring at seventy million beats an hour; I was going into total worry overload. But how could I stop myself? I mean, how can you stop yourself imagining scary stuff, like faceless strangers just silently whisking Tor off to God knows where?

I consciously dug my not-very-long fingernails into the palm of my hands so that the pain gave me something else to think about. It didn't work: all that kept repeating through my head was how on earth me and Linn could ever hope to find Tor – presuming he hadn't (please, oh please) been spirited away – in this crush…

Then above all the din, my ears tuned in to a familiar sound.

Flippety-flap, flippety-flap…

I spun round to see Rowan's panic-stricken face, as she pushed and pattered through the sea of shoppers in her impractical red velvet mules.

"Ro!" I shouted at her, waving to get her attention before she was diverted off, down into a maze of stalls selling second-hand clothes.

"Ally!" she yelped, hurrying over to me with a speeded up *flippety-flap, flippety-flap*. "No sign of him?"

"No," I shook my head, noticing how her Minnie Mouse ears were unravelling as she ran. "But what are you doing? Linn told you to wait back at the tables in case he turned up!"

"I couldn't just hang about and do nothing!" she wailed, strands of hair flopping round her face as her knots unfurled. "I spoke to the guy at the noodle bar – I asked him to look out for Tor and get him to stay there if he came back!"

I shrugged. I guessed it made sense to have all three of us searching, but so far, at least two of us had had zero success, to my knowledge.

With that thought in my head, I looked down at my watch, and saw that twenty minutes had passed since we'd started the hunt. It was time to rush back, as agreed with Linn, to our meeting point by the noodle bar.

"Come on…" I motioned to Rowan. "Linn might be there already – and she might have found Tor…"

As if there was some enormous people-magnet lurking somewhere behind us, a wall of ambling shoppers surged towards us, blocking our way.

I'm not a pushy person, but all of a sudden, sheer fear made me develop elbows of steel, and I found myself ruthlessly barging my way into the oncoming crowds, carving a route towards the muddy courtyard that held the food stands.

A hand suddenly searched out mine, fingers clinging round it desperately. For a split-second, I thought it might be Tor, but the hand was too big to be his. I didn't even have to look round to know that my elder sister was relying on me to get us both through this. And right then, I felt a little bit braver, just knowing that poor Rowan was crumbling around the edges and depending on me.

Still pushing through determinedly, I gave Rowan's fingers a comforting squeeze, and felt her squeeze mine back.

Food stalls, noodle bar, Linn.

No Tor.

"What are we going to do?" whimpered Rowan, edging closer to hysteria. "What if someone's taken him?"

"Stop panicking; no one's taken him," said Linn authoritatively, although the slight wobble in her voice gave her away. "We'll split up and have another look round, then ... *then* we'll think about calling the police..."

At the mention of the police, Rowan lost it completely. Her bottom lip trembled with a life of its own, and fat, hot tears tumbled down her cheeks.

"It's OK, Ro; he'll be all right," I said softly, wrapping my arms round Rowan, being the big sister to my elder sister again.

"Brilliant," sighed Linn, her voice suddenly laden with irony. "What great daughters *we* are..."

"What?" I mumbled, grabbing a serviette that the guy behind the noodle bar was kindly holding out to help mop up Rowan's tears.

"Well," Linn explained, agitatedly, "the plan today was to get Dad a brilliant surprise, and what happens? The surprise turns out to be us managing to lose his only son…"

Chapter 21

LOST: ONE LITTLE BROTHER, HARDLY USED

London's big. London's *very* big. There are about eight million people living in London – and that kind of blows your head off when you know there are only about five million people in the whole of Scotland. (You've got to let me off if I'm out by a thousand or two; I always *was* better at History than Geography.)

And because it's big, one of the moans about London is that it's impersonal. That you could be being mugged by a bloke on stilts with fairy wings and a Bart Simpson mask and people would pass you by without helping, as if it happened every day.

Well, I don't think that's true. Like the guy at the noodle bar? He was on his own behind the counter, and could have carried on serving the queue of hungry customers hovering around his stall instead of helping us.

"Do you need to make a call?" he asked, after I'd taken the serviette from him – the one Rowan was currently soaking with tears and snot.

Now, he was holding out his mobile phone, trusting that a) we weren't going to do a runner with it, and b) we weren't going to call Australia, peak rate.

"Um, no – not right this second," Linn shook her head. "We're going to keep looking for—"

"Wait a minute – Grandma!" I burst out, gratefully yanking the proferred phone out of the noodle guy's hand.

"Grandma?" Linn furrowed her forehead. "What do you want to call her for? You'll just worry her – we might find Tor if we get out there looking again, and she'll never know—"

"No!" yelped Rowan. "Ally's right! Remember that Dad's always taught Tor her phone number, for emergencies?"

"He might have called her..." Linn finished the train of thought, as I hammered Grandma's number into the phone pad.

"Grandma?"

Linn couldn't help it; her Oldest Sister Instinct took over and she snatched the phone from me as soon as she heard me make contact.

"Grandma? It's Linn. No, that was Ally. Listen, have you— Oh, oh God..."

Rowan was clutching my hand again, so tightly that her purple-painted nails dug right into my skin. I squeezed her hand back just as tightly. I could hardly breathe for panicking.

Try as we might, neither of us could make out what Linn's expression meant, as she muttered, "When? Is he...? But how... OK... OK..."

As she pressed the End Call button, the noodle guy and most of his customers were on tenterhooks alongside me and Rowan.

"You'll never guess where Tor is..." she said, looking as if she didn't know whether to laugh or cry.

Tor has his own way of working. It might not be the way that me, or Rowan or Linn would handle things, and he maybe isn't too great at explaining his reasoning (since he's not too fond of the old chit-chat, as you know), but whatever Tor decides to do, it always makes *some* kind of sense. Even if it only makes sense to Tor.

So, what had happened was, our kid brother had wandered over to the bin to chuck his rubbish away, when his well-attuned animal radar pricked up. Straight away, he spotted the pigeon – its wing trailing – huddled between two stalls, as it tried to escape the barrage of passing feet.

Without a backward glance at us, Tor went rushing over, pulling off his sweatshirt as he ran. One poorly pigeon found itself safely wrapped up in a green hooded top, and within minutes Tor was speeding out of the nearby exit with it, and straight into a parked black cab that he'd spotted dropping off passengers.

Looking in the rear-view mirror, the cabbie must have been pretty startled to find a seven year old and a pigeon as his next fare.

In fact, he was concerned enough to try to find out where Tor had come from and who he was supposed to be with. But it was no good; Tor kept repeating the same address over and over again until the cab driver decided that the safest thing to do would be to take him there.

Once at the desired destination, Tor had been very apologetic about not having any money, but the cab driver had to understand, he'd said calmly, that it *was* an emergency.

The cab driver had replied that he'd only let Tor off if he gave him a phone number of someone at home...

Smart thinking. Once Tor had reeled off Grandma's number, he'd scrambled out of the car, with his sickly charge still hugged tight to him. And once Tor had scrambled out, the cab driver was straight on his mobile, phoning Grandma.

"She was just about to leave for Harmsworth when I called," Linn explained, to me, Rowan and anyone else who cared to listen. "But I said *we'd* go and pick him up; we're much closer."

"Harmsworth?" repeated the noodle guy, as he took possession of his phone again.

"It's near the Holloway Road. It's an RSPCA clinic," Linn told him – and the hungry customers who were following the saga of our missing sibling.

"It's where they sometimes film *Animal Hospital* – with Rolf Harris," Rowan chipped in.

The noodle guy looked none the wiser.

"If you knew our little brother," I grinned at him, "it would all make perfect sense…"

HOW TO BE MYSTERIOUS, BY ROWAN LOVE

Rowan added an extra dollop of beans on Tor's plate, right where he indicated.

On his breakfast plate this Sunday morning was a particularly fine piece of food art. A small log cabin (made of toast) sat under a sky full of fluffy clouds (scrambled eggs), with a couple of birds flying high (carved with care from a slice of bacon). Now, Tor was delicately manoeuvring the beans into a radiating sun.

"That's pretty," Linn smiled tolerantly at our little brother. "Now, how about eating some of it?"

She wasn't nagging, though. Her tone was more jokey than bossy. We were all glad to get Tor back in one piece, but Linn especially had smothered him in protective love since we picked him up from the RSPCA centre the day before. And she looked the the most shattered of the three of us after our little heart-stopping adventure; her normally pristine blonde-ish hair was unbrushed and just roughly tucked behind her ears.

I think it was because, being the eldest, she felt very guilty for losing Tor. Course, it wasn't her fault, but *you* try telling Linn something when she's already made up her mind about it. Dad was unbelievably cool about the whole thing and tried to get her to drop the guilt thing too, but I guessed she'd do that in her own time. And in the meantime, Tor was going to have to put up with getting hugged to death by her.

Speaking of Tor, he was fine, if a little quieter than usual. You should have seen his face when the three of us came running into the reception of the Harmsworth hospital; his eyes were like saucers at the sight of these deranged girls descending upon him. Later, he and Dad had a little man-to-boy chat about what had happened, and how while getting the pigeon fixed up was a noble and worthy thing to do, it really would have been better to let at least one of us girls in on the medical drama too.

The pigeon, meanwhile, hadn't broken its wing (much to the relief of Love Child No. 4), but had superficially damaged its feathery bits by doing something unwise like flying into an overhead cable. Its wound had been cleaned, its wing had been bandaged to its fat little body and it was now sitting blinking and looking bemused in the luxurious comfort of our garden shed. (I'd been woken up at six-thirty in the morning – after a sleep filled with nightmares involving Tor going missing in all manner of elaborate ways – by the sound of Tor's bedroom door squeaking open. It turned out he was heading downstairs and out into the garden, off to the shed to check on his pigeon patient for the hundredth time.)

"Hey, about Dad…" Rowan whispered, checking to hear that she could still make out the sound of the shower upstairs.

"Oh, not this business with his present again. I can't think about that. I'm too tired!" Linn whimpered, pushing her hardly touched breakfast away.

She was exhausted. She hadn't had a broken sleep like me – just no sleep at all, after the day's drama.

"But we've got to get him something – and quick," I pointed out. "His birthday's tomorrow!"

What a great day *that* was shaping up to be; a History project with no project, and a birthday with no present. I toyed with emptying my bank account and emigrating, but – sadly – you can't emigrate too far on £33.50.

Linn looked like we'd just asked her to climb up Mount Everest dragging a crateful of tinned beans behind her. Stress and sleep deprivation were playing havoc with her leadership skills.

"Don't worry, Linnhe – I've got an idea for Dad's present!" Rowan hissed excitedly, pulling her antique (i.e. old and holey) kimono dressing gown tighter round her as she sat down.

Linn *must* have been exhausted. She didn't even raise an irritated eyebrow at Rowan for using her whole name. Instead, she just stared wearily at her.

"Uh-huh," she said, flatly. "Hit us with it…"

"Aha! It's a secret! I'm not going to tell you!" Rowan grinned.

"OK, so we're all clubbing together to get Dad a present, but *you're* going to sort it out and keep it secret from us. Is that right?" I asked, trying to spell out to Rowan the ridiculousness of what she'd just said.

"Oh, I don't have the energy to play head games. Just do what you want, Ro, it's fine by me. Right now, I'm going back to bed for an hour," sighed Linn, scraping back her seat and getting to her feet. "And *you*—"

She pointed sternly to Tor, before reaching over and ruffling his hair.

"—stay put! OK?"

Tor nodded, his big brown eyes gazing up at her.

"So, what's your idea? What are you thinking of buying Dad?" I quizzed Rowan, as soon as we heard Linn's tired, slow footsteps trudging up the stairs.

"Who said anything about buying anything?" shrugged Rowan, trying to look mysterious.

Only it was pretty easy to work out what she was up to. If she didn't plan to *buy* him a present, it only meant one thing: she was going to *make* him something.

Uh-oh.

"What are you planning on making, then?" I asked.

Rowan looked a bit miffed that I'd managed to work out her mind-bogglingly complicated conundrum.

"I'm not telling you," she said haughtily. "But I need your help."

I was just about to explain to her that she was facing a no-tell, no-help showdown, when Tor – an eggy cloud stuck on the end of his fork – shushed us, and pointed out into the hall.

Dad was on his way down the stairs, whistling loudly to whatever had been playing on the radio in the bathroom.

"Meet me upstairs; five minutes – your room!" hissed Rowan, getting up and swanning casually out of the room with a piece of toast in her hand.

"What do you reckon, Tor – is she going to make him a bike out of balloons or something?" I whispered. "Or maybe individual zebra-striped, fake-fur covers for his spanners?"

Tor crossed his eyes, cartoon-style.

"Exactly," I nodded at him.

The one good thing about losing Tor (and finding him again – of *course*) was that it had distracted me from the hideous reality of facing Miss Thomson in the morning and explaining *what* we'd messed up and *why* we'd messed up. But then his disappearing act had created another problem in that we'd managed to come home from our shopping trip with a pigeon instead of a fantastic, unique birthday present for Dad. So, as I padded up the stairs to my room a few short minutes after Rowan, I decided that I wouldn't press her to tell me what she was up to, if she didn't want to spill. If she was so keen to solve our hassles and make something, then I should just be grateful, shut up and let her get on with it.

She was sitting cross-legged on my bed, staring up at the big map of the world on the wall above it.

"This," Rowan announced, as soon as she saw it was me, "would look really nice framed."

I shrugged and flopped down on to the bed beside her.

"But if it was framed, I couldn't stick those coloured pins in it," I pointed out to her.

"Mmm, I suppose..." Rowan muttered, her

fingers twirling the little crystal on the end of the silver chain she wore around her neck.

I stared at the pretty piece of rose quartz and felt one of those instant flashback memories fly into my head – suddenly I could picture another set of fingers playing with it, when that necklace used to belong to Mum.

Mum... Most of the time, I only try to think happy thoughts about her. (I know that sounds corny, but it's the only way I can handle it.) But just for a second, I got that ache for her: just 'cause she'd know *exactly* what to do for Dad's birthday. Actually, while Rowan stared at my map, I tried to concentrate really hard, and *will* an answer from her.

But nothing happened. All I could hear was Rowan breathing and my tummy gurgling.

"What do you want me to do?" I asked Rowan, breaking the tummy-gurgling silence. "How can I help?"

"I don't want you to do anything... I just want to have a look in that box you keep. Where is it?"

I knew straight away what she meant. Slipping off the bed, I walked over to my old-fashioned wooden wardrobe and pulled out the wicker box I kept in the bottom of it.

"Guess I can't ask you what you're looking for?"

I said, plonking it on the rug in the middle of the room.

Rowan slithered off the bed and on to the floor, ending up cross-legged again beside the box.

"Don't know myself till I see it," she smiled wryly.

She was coming over all mysterious again, and this time she was succeeding.

Downstairs in the living room is the proper, official record of our family life: a pile of photo albums, with pictures of holidays and birthdays and school plays all neatly stuck inside. But my box is a more random, unofficial record of the lives of the Loves. All the photos floating about in the box are rejects that never made it into the albums: out-of-focus shots of Grandma, taken by Tor, aged three; a selection of snaps of all of us girls, taken in different places and at different ages, but with the same black shadowy thumb effect ruining them all; stupid stuff like the time me, Linn, Rowan and Tor all crammed into the photo booth in Woolworth's and pulled the most horrible faces.

Apart from the artistically lacking photos, there're school reports in there, and corny stuff like Tor's first baby tooth, all wrapped up in cotton wool in a tiny box. And in there somewhere too is a newspaper cutting; a local actress whose name I forget – who used to be in *EastEnders* or something – was promoting fitness in the borough, and ended up perched on a bike outside Dad's shop, with my dad standing beside her, both grinning cheesily at the camera.

As Rowan rummaged, I saw a Polaroid of myself at the bottom. Pulling it out, I stared hard and didn't know whether to laugh or cringe at the sight of me – aged ten – trying on one of Mum's long, flowery, hippie dresses. It had suited her, but it was so big on me that it was like looking at a picture of a rose bush with a head stuck on top.

"Right – this is it!" proclaimed Rowan suddenly, jumping to her feet and heading out of my room.

Rats – I hadn't even caught a *glimpse* of what she'd picked out...

Chapter 23

WHOSE FAULT IS IT ANYWAY?

There was a gentle snoring coming from the pile of laundry I hadn't sorted out yet in the corner of my room.

Well, at least *someone* was getting a good night's sleep, even if it wasn't me.

Yep, for the second night running it looked like my bed was going to be a snooze-free zone: last night, it was down to Tor's exploits; tonight it was down to sheer unadulterated dread of facing Miss Thomson first thing in the morning...

I propped myself up on my elbows to see which four- (or potentially three-) legged friend had invaded my space, but it was too dark to make out anything other than a cat-sized blob on my discarded white T-shirt.

I'd have seen more earlier; when I'd first gone to bed, the nearly full moon had been streaming a bluey light down through the small skylight directly above my bed. But now, it was gloomsville again, which kind of suited the way I was feeling.

Yeah, I know – I should have stuck my bedside light on and read a book or a magazine for a while till I felt sleepy, but I wasn't in the mood to concentrate on anything except what I do best: worrying.

It's a talent, it really is. There are starving refugees carrying all their worldly possessions and their grannies on their backs just to get to UN food camps. There are volcanoes, earthquakes, tidal waves (or tsunamis – see? I might not be sure of the exact population of London, but I *do* remember *some* Geography stuff!) that people have to live through and deal with (or run away from, very, *very* fast…). Anyhow, you get my drift; out there in the big wide world all sorts of big scary things happen to people on a depressingly regular basis, and all I can lose sleep worrying over is a stupid History project. Or a lack of one…

I'd phoned Sandie in the afternoon to have a moan about it, and immediately wished I hadn't. She didn't mean to, but she just made me stress out more.

"Miss Thomson's going to be so mad with us!" Sandie had whimpered pathetically. "She's going to kill us!"

Sandie was overreacting just a *tiny* bit. Miss Thomson wasn't the *Terminator* or anything.

"Well, I guess she isn't going to give us a hug and a kiss and say it doesn't matter!" I'd tried to joke.

"I feel like staying off sick tomorrow!" Sandie whined.

"Oh no, you don't!" I panicked. "You're not skiving off and leaving me to do this all on my own!"

What a hypocrite I am. I'd let the notion of skiving off drift through my head myself, only an hour before. I was only annoyed because Sandie saying it meant *I* couldn't do it.

"You won't be on your own – Kyra will be there!" Sandie had protested feebly.

"Wrong! *You*, me and Kyra will be there!" I'd corrected her.

What with fussing over Tor and helping Rowan select her Mystery Object from my box, I hadn't made my usual Sunday-morning rendezvous with Billy (and dogs) up at the Palace. So, after my less-than-comforting conversation with Sandie, I gave him a ring – just to see if he had any words of wisdom, any insightful thoughts that might put the whole thing in perspective for me.

Fat chance.

"Ssssssssss…"

Billy took a long sharp intake of breath once I'd told him about Friday's fun events.

"What does 'ssssssssss' mean?" I demanded.

"Only one thing for it," he announced.

"Go on, then – what?"

"Pretend you've got chickenpox."

"What?"

"Pretend you've got chickenpox," he repeated, as if it didn't sound stupid enough already. "It's better than an upset stomach; that only buys you a day or two at the most, and you'll *still* have to face the music. But chickenpox is great: you've got a legitimate reason to stay off all week, and the whole project thing will have blown over by the time you go back!"

"OK," I said slowly. "Problem one: how am I meant to convince my family that I've got chickenpox? And problem two: how am I meant to convince my family that I've got chickenpox, since they know I've had chickenpox *already*?"

"People, um, can have chickenpox twice!" he said, unconvincingly. "And, hey, you're a girl; you've got make-up, haven't you?"

"*So?*"

"So, *draw* spots on!"

"Billy," I sighed. "Do me a favour: would you go and bring Precious to the phone?"

"How come?" he muttered, dumbly.

"'Cause Precious might have some useful advice to give me – unlike you!"

And so, here I was, at three o'clock in the morning, trying to talk myself out of worrying by thinking depressing thoughts of starving refugees and earthquake-ravaged cities (not a whole heap of laughs, I can tell you), while my stomach was merrily clenching with tension.

How did I get in this state? I lay there in the dark, asking myself.

Because the project was ruined, I answered myself.

Why was the project ruined?

Because we spilt paint on it.

How did paint get spilt on it?

'Cause me and Kyra were niggling at each other.

Why were you niggling at each other?

Because she's in my face all the time.

Why is she in your face all the time?

Because she's mad.

Why…?

I gave up there. This mess wouldn't have existed if a certain someone had never turned up at our school to start with.

"Are you listening, Kyra Davies?" I said out loud to the darkness and the contentedly snoring cat. "It's all *your* fault…"

Chapter 24

WHO NEEDS *THE X FILES*?

It was one minute past nine.

I peered round the classroom door.

No one was there.

"It's empty," I hissed at Sandie, who was hovering behind me in the corridor, biting her nails to oblivion.

It was the eighth Wonder Of The World: our entire History class – plus Miss Thomson – had vanished into thin air. Like the passengers and crew of the *Marie Celeste*, one minute they'd been chatting normally, the next they'd hit some Bermuda Triangle weirdness and had been spirited away to a parallel universe.

"They'll be in the hall – getting everything set up for the play!" said Sandie.

Well, maybe not *quite* a parallel universe.

"Why didn't you remind me earlier?" I asked her, not really expecting to get a sensible answer.

Sandie shrugged and widened her Disney eyes at me.

See? I was right.

"Come on, then," I said, steering my reluctant feet in the direction of the hall and pretending my hands weren't really shaking. "Let's get this over with..."

Trudging along, I pictured my make-up bag sitting temptingly on the chest of drawers in my room. That dark pinky lipstick I'd got free off the front of a magazine ... that fine make-up brush (off the front of another magazine) ... oh, how easy it would have been to draw on those chickenpox poxy bits...

"Ally! Sandie!" beamed Miss Thomson, suddenly turning out of the hall up ahead and into our path.

I tried to fix something that I *hoped* might resemble a smile on my face, but it probably looked more like I had wind or something.

With every step closer to our teacher and our confession, the knot of dread in my stomach got tighter, and I had this incredible sensation like I was shrinking. At the rate I was going, I'd be ant-sized by the time I'd reached her. Just the right size for her to stomp on me with her heel when I told her what had happened to our project. (And it *would* be me that told Miss Thomson; Sandie would have just opened and shut her mouth like a traumatized goldfish if I'd left it to her.)

"Well done, girls!" boomed Miss Thomson as we drew level.

I was confused – did Miss Thomson *do* irony?

"I really like your posters – they work very well!"

I stared at Miss Thomson, waiting for her to bark "NOT!" and burst into maniacal laughter after what she'd just said.

But she didn't.

"Well, hurry along! Better give Kyra a hand putting them up – she's struggling away on her own at the moment!"

And with a bright smile, Miss Thomson was off, leaving us marooned, in stunned surprise.

There was only one thing that could explain it: it was me and Sandie who were in that parallel universe…

Chapter 25

AND HERE'S ONE I MADE EARLIER...

In the auditorium, there was lots of crashing and banging and shouting going on, as actors and technicians lost their rags due to last-minute-rehearsal nerves.

Out in the reception hall, the walls were awash with posters, photos and rambling captions describing life in our little patch of London half a century or so ago. Some of our History class, finished fixing up their efforts, had wandered off to nosey at the drama unfolding in the auditorium, while others were still faffing about, putting up, taking down and generally rearranging their masterpieces.

Me, I was sitting on a hard wooden bench, staring across the room at the six unstained posters of bomb sites.

"I still can't believe it," I said, shaking my head. "They don't look like they've been touched!"

"Well, the third and fourth ones were the worst; I had to bin them and start from scratch," said Kyra, who was also perched on the bench, in-between me and Sandie. "But the others only had the odd spot on them – I managed to wipe off the black paint almost completely. You can still see it faintly if you go up close, though."

"But when did you do it all? When did you have the time...?" I asked, in wonderment.

"Well, after you two left on Friday, I just carried on, till the janitor came and kicked me out at teatime," she explained, her eyes staring straight ahead at her handiwork. "And I even managed to use the photocopier in the office before they packed up for the day – I re-did all the photos on *that* one and *that* one."

Me and Sandie both stared at the particular posters she was pointing at. "But you couldn't have done all that so quickly!" I protested.

Sandie was saying nothing, I noticed. I think she was still in shock.

"No," Kyra shook her head, her gaze still directed straight in front of her. "I came in yesterday afternoon too. The janitor told me that the Drama lot were coming in to do a dress rehearsal, and he had to open the school up for them anyway, so he didn't mind if I was here as well."

I felt choked. I'd spent my Sunday getting gloomy and sinking into a pit of pessimism, while Kyra was actually doing something constructive.

How dumb did *I* feel?

"You … you did a really good job, Kyra," I mumbled. "Thanks."

"Yeah!" Sandie sighed in amazement from the other end of the bench.

Kyra dropped her eyeline down to the floor, and scuffed at the faded lino with the toe of her shoe.

"Well…" she shrugged shyly. "I felt like I had to do it, really."

"No, you didn't," I contradicted her.

It was true; she didn't *have* to do it. She could have left the posters in the mess they were in and shared the blame with me and Sandie when it came to facing Miss Thomson. And, of course, being the new girl, Miss Thomson might have given her the easier time and saved the bulk of her scolding for me and Sandie.

"But I had to fix things – it was my fault!" said Kyra, finally staring me in the face with her dark almond eyes full of … what? Embarrassment? Remorse? Guilt?

"It was my fault as much as yours!" I found myself arguing.

"And mine!" Sandie chipped in.

See – I told you Sandie was a sweetie. She wasn't the one who was arguing with Kyra, but she still tried to take a share of the blame. I hadn't even thought of that before...

"I'm just ... sorry," muttered Kyra turning away from me.

Suddenly, this close up, I realized what Kyra reminded me of: small face; almond eyes; light-brown skin; a sprinkling of darker brown freckles across her nose; big ears... She was a dead ringer for one of the deer me and Tor go and visit in the deer and donkey enclosure at the back of Alexandra Palace.

"Sorry about what?" I asked, twisting my thoughts back to the project and Kyra's starring role in saving it. "I just said, it wasn't all your fault."

(Yeah, I know – the hypocrite strikes again. That *wasn't* what I'd been saying to myself at three o'clock in the morning...)

"No, not about the project. Well, a *bit* about the project. But I mean, I'm sorry for being ... kind of pushy. For turning up at your house when all your friends were there and everything."

Urgh. What do you say when someone comes out with something as honest as that? "Yes – you *were* too pushy, and you *should* be sorry for turning up unannounced that night"? Maybe, but I couldn't be that hard-nosed. So I did a Sandie and just shrugged.

"I *know* I get too pushy sometimes, and I just can't help it..."

"Why not?" asked Sandie, scoring minus five for tact.

But I was glad she said it anyway. Might as well get straight to the point, instead of circling around it.

"It's just a thing I do, every time I come to a new school," said Kyra, her head hanging. "I arrive, and everyone's already got their little crowd of mates. No one's bothered about trying to get to know the new girl, so I just end up thinking that the only way to get noticed is to be sort of ... pushy. And then I realize I've gone too far, and everyone hates me. And then I'm on my own for a while, till my dad changes jobs and we move and it starts all over again..."

A little cynical voice in the back of my head was whispering, "Don't fall for it – she could still be a nutter..." But what the hell. So I'm a big, stupid softie. So what.

"Must be tough," I said quietly.

"Mmm," Kyra murmured in agreement.

"How come your dad switches jobs so much?" asked Sandie, cutting to the quick again.

Kyra gave a wry little laugh, but still kept up her staring session at the floor.

"He doesn't particularly want to. It's more to do with my mum."

"How come?" I asked.

"Have you got three weeks?" she laughed, without sounding particularly happy. "With my mum, it's a long story…"

Tell me about it, I thought.

Mums and long stories … it looked like Kyra and I had more in common than I'd thought.

Chapter 26

EXTRA FEATHERS ON YOUR PIZZA, SIR?

"Look, Ro – across the road – isn't that your mate Von?"

"Where? Where?" said Rowan, scanning the pavements outside the restaurant window.

As soon as Rowan's attention was distracted, Linn gave me and Tor a wink across the table and promptly dived under it. Me and Tor looked at each other, and ducked down too.

"I can't see her…" we heard Rowan's voice hovering somewhere above us. "Where is she, Linnhe? Linnhe? Oi!"

Rowan joined us under the table, just as Linn was pulling the gift-wrapped present out of the carrier bag at her feet.

"Leave it alone!" Rowan snapped, grabbing the present back out of Linn's grasp.

"Aw, come on – tell us what it is before he comes back from the loo!" Linn whined, as we all straightened up in our seats again.

"No! You'll just have to wait!" Rowan chastised us.

"Can't we just have a feel? See if we can guess?" I suggested, eyeing up the flat-ish, big-ish parcel.

"No!"

"Patience, patience!" grumbled Grandma, with a sigh.

She was sitting at the far end of the two tables that had been squished together for us, while Dad – as the birthday boy – took pride of place at the other end.

We were sitting in our favourite spot in Pizza Bella: right in the window. Not that it had been hard to get – at seven o'clock on a Monday night they don't exactly have queues out the door.

We had been planning to stay at home and order in pizza, but as soon as he'd got in from work, Dad had announced that he'd changed his mind and decided to treat us all instead. We were all pretty pleased, but Tor especially got excited. He's at that in-between age where he seems very thoughtful and grown-up sometimes, and then reverts to being a total kid. And however grown-up he tries to be, we know he still gets a kick when the waitresses in Pizza Bella wander over with a free balloon for him.

"I saw your pictures at the big school today, Ally. Your name was on them," announced Tor suddenly, surprising us all by coming out with two whole sentences at once.

"Did you?" I smiled at him, as he nibbled his way through a straw-thin breadstick. "What about the play? Did you like it?"

He shrugged, which in universal small-boy-speak meant it was OK.

"Hold on; how did Tor manage to see your posters? I thought they were covered in black paint, same as your clothes, after your little accident on Friday," Grandma commented.

"My friend Kyra managed to fix them," I explained.

"Ooh, she's your *friend* now, is she? I thought you said she wasn't?!" Rowan teased me, reaching over to nick a breadstick out of the packet Tor was hogging.

"Well, she must be, to go and do it all herself, if your project was as messed up as you said it was," Linn pointed out.

Over her shoulder, I could see Dad weaving his way back to us through the tables.

"Well, she's not exactly my best mate or anything, but she's all right…" I mumbled, still getting used to how I felt about Kyra now. "Anyway, Dad's coming back – are you going to give him the present now, or wait till the pizzas arrive?"

"Now!" Tor burst out loudly.

"Now what?" asked Dad, sitting down in his place.

"Now," said Rowan, blushing with excitement, "you get your present!"

"Hey! A present!" Dad grinned, taking the package that Rowan was holding out to him. "You shouldn't have – you all gave me cards this morning; that would have been enough!"

"Don't get *too* excited, Dad," Linn laughed. "You haven't seen it yet..."

"Is this from all of you?" he asked, gazing around the table as he tore at the Sellotape.

"It's not from me, Martin; only from the children," said Grandma. "I haven't a clue what it is..."

"Join the club," I mumbled, grinning at Linn.

With a final impatient tug, Dad yanked the paper off, and studied the A3-sized framed picture in his hands.

"Wow!" he gasped, staring with amazement (and slightly twinkly eyes) at the vision in front of him.

The rest of us, of course, couldn't see what it was. All that was visible from our back-view was the blue feathery trim Rowan had edged the frame with.

"Lemme see!" said Tor, lunging impatiently out of his seat and standing by Dad's chair for a bird's-eye view of the present.

"What do you think?!" asked Rowan, looking as

pink and shiny with excitement as the bubblegum-coloured balloon tied to the back of Tor's seat.

"Cool!" said Tor.

"Fantastic!" said Dad. "A family portrait! Perfect!"

Me, Linn and Grandma exchanged looks: unless Rowan had drugged us all and taken us round to the photographer's studio without our knowledge, we hadn't *got* a family portrait done.

"Well, come on, Martin," Grandma chastised him with a smile. "Share it with everyone!"

Beaming, Dad turned the picture round for us all to see.

Apart from the feather-boa-style trim, the main image in the frame was surrounded by a border of Rowan's trademark sequins. And the main image?

It was the strip of weeny photo-booth photos – the ones hauled from my box in the wardrobe – enlarged. There was me, Linn, Rowan and Tor in all our glory, pulling faces and giggling our heads off as we squashed together in the tiny space.

"Hey, Grandma – look!" I pointed out. "It's your idea; the family portrait!"

Grandma shot me an I-told-you-so! look, even if she seemed a bit dubious about Rowan's artistic efforts. I think it's safe to say she'd have preferred a nice soft-focus studio portrait from the place up on Crouch End Broadway.

"It's great!" laughed Dad. "It's just so natural! It's just how I see all of you!"

"Yeah, I got the idea of blowing these pics up on a photocopier from Ally's mate Kyra," Rowan explained. "You know how Chazza's mum's a solicitor? Well, she's got a colour photocopier in her office up in Muswell Hill, so Chazza got the keys off her and me and him went up and did this yesterday afternoon!"

I know it's silly, but I felt all choked up then.

For Rowan to go to all that trouble was amazing. And the picture was brilliant; with all of us laughing and fooling around ... well, you know – it was really nice, really special.

And the fact that Kyra had helped inspire Dad's present was kind of cool too.

You don't need to have a brain the size of a Nobel prize winner or anything to work out that I'd had a big change of heart about her since that morning. All that stuff about moving schools and never being able to make friends – that must have been really lonely for her; especially when you think she's an only child too. And though she didn't go into it too much, her mum sounded like *big* trouble. Apparently, that crack Kyra first made to me about her mum – the one about her being a professional drinker? Well, that's pretty much the way it is. At break this morning, after the decorating of the hall had been finished, Kyra told me and Sandie that her mum is more or less fairly normal, but when she starts to drink, everything changes. She said that her dad ends up being embarrassed by her mum so often – with her phoning or turning up at his work sloshed and shouting – that *that's* why he keeps switching jobs so much.

That's all she said, and neither me nor Sandie felt brave enough to push her for any more details. And bad as that story sounded, I get the feeling that there's more to it than that – Kyra did tell Sandie that thing about her mum calling her a bitch, after all. Well, maybe in time, Kyra will trust us enough to tell us.

And you never know; I might end up liking Kyra Davies almost as much as I *dis*liked her to start with – well, weirder things have happened...

"Happy Birthday, Dad!" Linn burst out, holding up her glass.

"Yeah, Happy Birthday, Dad!" I joined in, raising my glass, along with Rowan, Grandma and Tor.

Crashing our Fantas, Diet Cokes, Cokes and wine together, Dad made a quick speech.

"Thanks, you lot – and cheers to us all!"

A small voice chipped in as the glasses tinkled again.

"And Mum!"

There was the tiniest hush for the tiniest moment: all three of us girls saw Dad exchange looks with Grandma.

"To your daughter," he smiled, raising his wine in the air.

"To Melanie," Grandma smiled back.

"To Mum!" yelped Tor, throwing his Coke so high that both his straws jiggled out of it.

"Mum!" repeated Linn, Rowan and me; Love children one, two and three swapping small, thoughtful smiles.

Our Mum? Don't panic; she's not dead. You didn't think she was, did you? No, she's fine (we think). That beach on the last postcard we got from her – it looked pretty gorgeous.

You want to know her story? Well, it's like Kyra said – have you got three weeks?

But you know something? Colin's sitting right beside me on the desk in my room just now, purring so hard he's hiccuping, and rubbing his vibrating head on my hand. So I think I'd better give up for now and pay him a bit of attention.

Stuff about my mum, about Kyra – and whether she turns out to be cool or a psycho – it'll just have to wait till another time...

* * *

Until then, I'll leave you with my Thought for the Day: always give people the benefit of the doubt. Unless, of course, they're an axe-wielding maniac asking if you happen to be Drew Barrymore.

There's always something going on in

ALLY'S WORLD

Make sure you keep up with the gossip!

2 **DATES, DOUBLE DATES AND BIG, BIG TROUBLE**

OK, so my dad's started ironing his jeans (yes, *really*) – something must be up. I mean, why would he slick back his hair to meet the plumber? It can only mean one thing – Dad is Seeing Someone. Like, a *Woman Someone*. And it can't be our mum, because she's still off travelling the world. There's only one thing for it – serious sisterly espionage. Hey, I know it's sneaky, but we have to uncover the awful (*cringe-worthy*) truth...

Look out for loads more fab Ally's World books!

Find out more about Ally's World at

www.karenmccombie.com

Dates, Double Dates and Big, Big Trouble

"Well, id's obvious, then," said Sandie, matter-of-factly.

"What is?" I frowned.

"Your dad," she continued, "is seeing someone new."

Sandie isn't what you'd normally call intuitive. When it comes to the two of us, she always shuts up and lets me do all the talking or deciding (which drives me crazy sometimes). And she was *well* off-course here; my dad seeing someone new? How ridiculous! It must be those cold germs short-circuiting her brain...

There was no *way* my dad was seeing someone new.

No *way*.

Or...

Or was there?

Also available in this series:

ALLY'S WORLD

DATES,

double dates

and BIG, BIG

TROUBLE

KAREN McCOMBIE

SCHOLASTIC

for aLice MiLLeR (aged 83½)

-the PRiNcess of aLexaNdRa paLace

Scholastic Children's Books,
Commonwealth House, 1–19 New Oxford Street,
London WC1A 1NU, UK
A division of Scholastic Ltd
London ~ New York ~ Toronto ~ Sydney ~ Auckland
Mexico City ~ New Delhi ~ Hong Kong

First published in the UK by Scholastic Ltd, 2001

Copyright © Karen McCombie, 2001
Cover illustration copyright © Spike Gerrell, 2001

ISBN 0 439 99869 7

Typeset by TW Typesetting, Midsomer Norton, Somerset
Printed by Cox & Wyman Ltd, Reading, Berks.

10 9 8

The right of Karen McCombie to be identified as the author
of this work has been asserted by her in accordance with the
Copyright, Designs and Patents Act, 1988.

Contents

PROLOGUE

Dear Mum,

I came across that photo of you and Dad the other day – you know, the one from your first date. The one where you look a bit weird, 'cause you've just thrown up...

Anyhow, it just reminded me how much I loved it when you used to tell me about how you two got together; all the stuff about how he'd come into the jeans shop in Camden High Street where you worked and try on loads of different pairs every week, just to have an excuse to talk to you. (He never bought any, did he?)

And better than that was how *you* used to spend your lunch-hours in the bike shop he worked in across the street, buying a bell one day, a bicycle pump the next, even a puncture-repair kit.

Then, when he finally *did* ask you out, it wasn't till that first date that he found out you didn't even *have* a bike.

It was so sweet the way you told Dad that you didn't mind about him getting the cinemas mixed up that first night out together, and taking you to see a horror movie by accident. *Even though* horror movies and the sight of blood usually made you feel ill. And it was *really* sweet of Dad to still fancy you after you threw up on his lap.

True love.

After all that, I guess I wouldn't have been in the mood to hand someone my camera like you did and get them to take a photo of the two of you (I think if it was me, I'd have wanted to forget the whole thing, after puking all over the place). But I'm glad you *did* decide to do it – or we wouldn't have had a record of the time our parents started seeing each other. I don't know if you had a proper kiss that first night (I hope not, under the circumstances), but it's still one of the most romantic stories I've ever heard – even if there weren't exactly string orchestras playing in the background and rose petals raining from the sky.

Hope it happens to me like that one day (but maybe minus the part about being sick).

Not so long ago, I thought it might ... and that was also right around the time when me and Linn and Rowan started to realize that Dad had found someone to replace you.

I suppose you'd better hear this from the beginning...
Love you lots,
Ally
(your Love Child No. 3)

Chapter 1

THAT FIRST KISS (I WISH...)

OK, so when it comes to the whole romance thing, I admit, I daydream about it a lot. And I mean a *lot*.

I daydream about it when I'm walking the dogs up by Alexandra Palace, looking out over the sprawl of London off in the distance. I daydream about it in bed at night, when I lie in the dark and stare out at the stars through the tiny skylight in the roof of my attic bedroom...

So that sounds very poetic and everything. But then, I *also* daydream about all things romantic at distinctly *un*romantic moments. Like during especially boring classes, or when I'm brushing my teeth, or when it's my turn to do the laundry and I'm sorting through my family's dirty socks, or even when I'm helping my little brother Tor clean rabbit poo out of the hutches in the back garden.

I don't think Juliet thought about Romeo when she was cleaning out rabbit poo. Well, when I think about the film, I certainly don't remember seeing

Claire Danes in a pair of yellow Marigolds day-dreaming about Leo DiCaprio shinning up to her balcony while she was trying to shoo away an irate bunny who's in the mood to bite.

Maybe the fact that I can daydream about romance at really inappropriate times means I'm very imaginative. Or maybe it means I'm a weirdo – I'm not too sure. But anyway, one of my favourite daydreams is That First Kiss. It goes like this...

1) I go to a party and, magically, I look like Joey out of *Dawson's Creek*. (Look, it's *my* daydream, so stuff like that can happen, OK?)

2) The party is amazing, the music's brilliant, and most brilliant of all – I spot *him* across the crowded room. (The *him* part is interchangeable, depending on who I've got a crush on that week. I fall in and out of fancying different boys pretty regularly – but having said that, there's only one boy that I've stayed constantly and truly mad about, and that's my sister Linn's mate, Alfie. Sigh...)

3) During the evening, there's lots of tantalizing staring and looking away going on between us, just to get a bit of a *frisson* going. (Good word, *frisson*, isn't it? Except I said it to my best friend Sandie once, and she thought it was some kind of fish. But I tell you, having a bit of a fish between you *definitely* isn't romantic...)

4) The lights are low and sparkly, my favourite track comes on (that changes week to week, daydream to daydream), and from nowhere *he* sidles up beside me and asks me to dance.

5) Right, this is where it gets good... I've got my arms around his neck, and I can feel myself shiver with goosebumps as he pulls me closer to him, his hands on my back. We say nothing, just look into each other's eyes – reading each other's thoughts and knowing instinctively what's going to happen next. In slow motion, we move towards each other, tilting our heads gently as the moment gets closer. I can feel the warmth of his lips even before they touch mine. And then...

I was sitting on the usual bench on Ally Pally, letting my First Kiss daydream drift through my mind, and was just about to melt mouths with Alfie, when the mood was suddenly ruined.

Well, it's inevitable really, when you find yourself in a headlock.

"Billy! Get off me, you total moron!" I yelled, trying to tug his arm away from around my neck.

Out of the corner of my eyes I could see a middle-aged couple walking along the path looking kind of concerned. They probably thought I was being attacked by some lunatic, and who could blame them? They weren't to know that it was just my mate, acting like a complete prat...

They weren't the only ones looking concerned; my two dogs – Rolf and Winslet – didn't know who to bark at first: Billy, or his yappy little mutt Precious, who was already up to his usual tricks, trying to inspect both their bottoms at close quarters.

"Do you give up?" I heard Billy asking, though I couldn't see him since he was standing behind me and the bench.

He must have been watching that stupid wrestling programme again, I sighed to myself.

"And are you going to give up acting like a six year old?" I managed to growl. "God, no wonder you can never get a girlfriend..."

It was a low blow (Billy's mighty sensitive about his lack of success with the girlies), but still he didn't let go.

It was time to get tough.

I reached back and, after a couple of searching slaps, found his nose and pulled it hard.

"Arghhhhhh!" he whined, letting go of my neck and scrambling over the back of the wooden seat, with me still hanging on to his nose.

The couple walked past at that point, staring disapprovingly at us – a pair of delinquent thirteen year olds spoiling the serenity of their Saturday-morning stroll. They obviously didn't approve of the barking dogs either, eyeing up Precious, Rolf and Winslet like they were the spawn of the devil. (Course, that might be true in Precious's case.)

"Gum on, Ally. Led go," pleaded Billy, nasally. He sounded like he could be in an ad for Night Nurse or something.

But you could tell he was quite enjoying it, since he was now sitting beside me with his hands on his thighs, making no attempt to make me stop.

"You look ridiculous," I told him, as I gave his nose an extra tweak for luck.

"You'll look more ridigulous in a segond when I blow snot all over your hand…"

"You wouldn't dare…" I said, narrowing my eyes at him.

"Wouldn'd I?" he grinned.

He took a big breath, ready for blast-off, when I let go and jumped off the seat.

Rolf and Winslet thought this was a cue for play-time, and bounded over to me, tails flapping about enthusiastically.

"Billy – you are the most disgusting boy I know!" I yelled at him.

He grinned again, put his hand over his nose and made the most grotesque snotty noise.

"And you *laaaaaaaave* it!" he roared, getting up

and running straight towards me, holding his hand out like he was going to rub it in my face.

I was pretty sure he'd just blown a raspberry behind his hand, but I wasn't taking any chances, not where snot was concerned. So I did the only sensible thing – I ran.

I wondered what the couple were thinking now, seeing a screeching girl, hurtling down the hill pursued by three mental dogs and a deranged boy in a baseball cap. They were probably thinking that they were glad we weren't *their* kids…

"Gotcha!"

The red gravel path that led to one of the park entrances was just hurtling into view when Billy grabbed me by the waist and rugby-tackled me to the grass.

"Get off!" I yelped for the second time so far, feeling him land heavily on top of me.

"Aha! You will never get away from the evil Hand of Snot!"

Somehow I managed to twist around underneath him, grab the evil Hand of Snot with both my fists and force it *well* away from my face.

"Billy – grow up!" I panted in his face, trying to sound angry – and trying just as hard not to laugh.

"Ooh! Listen to Ally Love! She's *so* sensible!"

teased Billy, putting on a dopey voice. "Well, we'll have to do something about *that*..."

With his free hand, Billy started mercilessly tickling me, running his irritating fingers from my waist to my armpit to my neck and back down again.

"*GERRROFFFF!*" I squealed breathlessly, between giggles, but he didn't – not that he'd have been able to hear me above the din of three barking dogs anyway, all of whom thought this was an excellent game.

But somehow, I heard another sound above the racket.

They say mothers can tune in to the noise of a crying baby, no matter how faint it is, or even if it's not their own baby. Well, I managed to tune in to a crunch of gravel on the nearby path, and the rubbery screech of bike brakes (when your dad runs a bicycle shop, I guess it's in your blood). Of course what caught my attention most was my name.

"Hi, Ally..."

As I turned to look at the source of the voice, I tried to brush Winslet away with one hand, but she carried on happily licking my face, regardless. I didn't realize it at the time, but I had my other hand right over Billy's face.

"Whas-going-on?" Billy mumbled, trying to shake his face free of my splayed fingers.

But I didn't answer him – I was too busy staring at the vision in front of me, perched on his mountain bike.

"Hello, Alfie..." I smiled stupidly, waggling my dog-licked hand at him in a half-hearted attempt at a wave.

Talk about bad timing.

I had why-don't-you-just-kill-me-now-before-I-die-of-embarrassment timing...

Chapter (2)

LINN IS WAY, WAY, WAY OFF THE MARK

It's funny how you know when you're being stared at.

"What?" I demanded, catching Linn gawping at me for the seventeenth time in the last hour or so.

We were in the living room – me (on the sofa), Linn (next to me on the sofa), Rowan (on one of the armchairs painting her nails silver) and Tor (on the floor, driving his toy cars over a mountain range played by snoozing Rolf) – aimlessly watching a rubbish quiz show after stuffing our faces, this Saturday teatime.

I'd seen Linn eyeing me up earlier over the kitchen table, studying my face like I'd grown another nose or something. And ever since we'd come through and flopped in the living room, she'd kept up the surreptitious scrutiny, even though she was supposed to be flicking through the work section of the local paper in search of a Saturday job. And here she was, at it again...

"What? I'm not doing anything!" said Linn,

opening her green eyes wide and looking shocked at my accusation. "I'm just reading this!"

"Well, if you're trying to read it, then here's a handy hint: keep your eyes on the paper instead of on *me*," I said, sarcastically. "Anyway, who's going to give *you* a Saturday job?"

To tell the truth, I didn't mean to be so mean. And anyone in their right mind would give Linn a Saturday job; she's pretty, well-presented and polite. (Polite to other people, that is. Not to her sisters...) It was just that I'd got myself in a bad mood ever since Alfie had caught me in a compromising position that morning. And it was all Billy's grandad's fault. Well, what I mean is, if his parents hadn't planned to visit Billy's grandad on Sunday, I could have met up with Billy as usual – instead of swapping to Saturday – and Alfie wouldn't have seen me like that: i.e. lying on the grass with Billy sprawled across me like a wet blanket, and a dribble of dog drool dangling off my face, courtesy of Winslet.

"No need to get snippy with me, just because *you're* in a bad mood..." said Linn, in an infuriatingly righteous voice.

My big sister Linn is an expert in being infuriatingly righteous. In fact, I might be wrong, but I think she's doing it as an A-level...

"I'm *not* in a bad mood!" I said, sinking further into my bad mood.

"Mmmm..." muttered Linn dismissively, flicking noisily through the pages of the paper.

"I'm *not*!" I protested.

"Whatever you say..." shrugged Linn.

See what I mean? It makes me so angry when she goes all big-sister-superior on me like that. It makes me want to ... I don't know – ruffle her immaculate hair or go and mess up her colour-coordinated knicker drawer, or something else that would ruffle her perfectly organized feathers.

"Shut up, you two! I can't hear what he's saying!" Rowan snapped at us.

It's not that my in-between sister (in-between me and Linn, age-wise) was particularly wild about corny Saturday-evening game shows; it's just that she's kind of super-sensitive and hates bickering. Even though she and Linn bicker on a practically daily basis.

But, hey – we both shut up. Linn glued her eyes to the newspaper and I stared blankly at the TV screen.

"...*and now, name an animal indigenous to Australia!*" said the cheesy, toothy TV presenter.

"A marsupial!" Tor piped up, not even glancing up from his game.

Rolf snuffled and flicked his tail as a fire engine drove over his furry haunches.

"That's too smart, Tor!" muttered Rowan, fixing the top back on her nail varnish with extended fingers. "All the contestants on this show are picked to be thick, I reckon. They wouldn't be able to *spell* marsupial."

"*Come on, Keith – an Australian animal! You can do it!*" the presenter encouraged, a despairing glint in his eye.

"Duck-billed platypus!" said Tor, as the participant on the screen chewed his lip and struggled to come up with an answer.

"*Still* too smart, Tor," I chipped in, trying to take my mind off Linn and her snide remarks. "All they're looking for is 'kangaroo' or 'koala', and that bloke will win a car. And he can't even get that!"

"*Barrrrpppp!*"

The buzzer meant the bloke on the screen was out of time. Bang went *his* chances of winning some fancy four-wheeled drive.

"*Well, time's up I'm afraid, Keith. Didn't you even have a guess there?*"

"*Um,*" muttered the bumbling bloke on the telly, "*I thought maybe … a sheep.*"

Me, Rowan and Tor burst out laughing –

especially Tor, who saw ignorance about animals as a sign of deep human failing.

But I stopped laughing pretty quickly – as soon as I felt Linn's eyes on me once again…

"What!? What is it?" I demanded to know, swirling my head around quick enough to catch her squinting at my neck.

"Ally, is that a *love* bite?"

"*What?*" I frowned at her.

She'd *got* to be joking. With my track record of pitifully few romantic encounters, there wasn't much chance of me getting *that* lucky.

"There!" she said, extending one finger out to touch me on the side of my neck.

"Get off!" I said, echoing my words to Billy from earlier on in the day.

I leapt up off the sofa and hurried over to the mirror by the living-room door. The mirror was almost a piece of art in itself; Mum made it years ago. She'd bought a plain mirror-tile for a few pence, Dad told us, and then added the whole frame of Fimo flowers and elves that swirled and peeped at you as you stared at your own reflection.

I hauled down the neck of my jumper and tried to see what Linn had seen. Sure enough, there was a dark shadow; but on closer inspection, it was easy to see what I already knew – that it *wasn't* a bruise.

"It's mud! That's all!" I exclaimed, licking my finger and rubbing at the smudge of Ally Pally dirt, still in place after Billy's rugby-tackle earlier in the day.

"Dirt?" said Linn, raising her eyebrows at me. "Well, that's not what Alfie said..."

"What do you mean?!"

"Well, Alfie said that from where *he* was standing this morning, it looked like Billy was snogging you on the grass up on Ally Pally..."

I opened my mouth and shut it again. What could I say to Linn that would put that thought right out of her head, without admitting that the only boy I'd happily let snog me was Alfie?

"What? You and *Billy*!" said Rowan in surprise.

Great – now Linn had *her* believing it!

"It wasn't like that!" I yelped to both of them. "We were just mucking about! We *weren't* snogging!"

"Uh-huh," murmured Linn, disbelievingly.

Arrrgh! She was off again...

"Look," I said, struggling to explain myself. "It's ridiculous. It would be like you snogging Chazza, Ro; or you, Linn – it would be like you snogging Alfie!"

Urgh. The very thought...

"Me and Alfie? As if!" snickered Linn. "Anyway,

stop trying to hide it. If you and Billy have got something going on, then..."

But I'd stopped listening: my radar ears had now tuned into what was going on out in the hall.

It wasn't the fact that my dad was talking on the phone; it was the fact that he sounded like he was *whispering* on the phone.

"What is it?" asked Rowan, spotting straight away that I wasn't paying a blind bit of attention to Linn's wind-up any more.

"Shhhh!" I muttered, with one ear to the living room door.

The door thunked as Linn and Rowan darted over and barged into me, wanting to hear what I could hear. Even Tor slunk up silently, ducking under our arms and placing his ear at pole position at the tiny gap in the door.

"Yes, it was great, just like old times..." we heard our dad say, sheepishly.

Linn stared hard at me, and over my shoulder at Rowan, who was standing behind me, her hot, anxious breath on my neck.

"It's been a long time, that's for sure..."

"What's going on?" Rowan whispered. "What's he on about?"

Shhh! mimed Linn, with a finger

"...yes – definitely. I would love that..." my dad

muttered. And then, with a small, wry laugh, "No, I haven't told them yet…"

Linn fixed her eyes on me, her stare saying exactly what I was thinking. I couldn't see Rowan's expression, but I felt her trembly hand on my shoulder.

"You don't think…?" I whispered.

"Shhh!" said Linn, dropping her gaze downwards to the top of Tor's head.

That was the problem. We'd always protected Tor from stuff, and we couldn't let him know that we were all thinking the same thing.

Was this… Could this be something to do with *Mum*?

Chapter 3

THE TALE OF THE INVISIBLE MUM...

"Ally? It's me – can I come in?" Linn called out softly from the other side of the door.

I'd become very popular all of a sudden. Normally, around eleven o'clock on Saturday night, I'd be the only one in my room (the odd cat included, and *all* our cats are odd), unless Sandie was staying over, which she sometimes did.

But tonight, my room was like a magnet; three (out of five) cats, both dogs and my sister Rowan were taking up space inside my four small walls and under my slanted roof. The cats – Frankie, Colin and Fluffy – were already here when me and Rolf padded upstairs after a non-eventful night in front of the telly with Dad and Tor (my social calendar wasn't exactly packed this particular Saturday night). And Winslet had followed Rowan in when she'd come tapping at my door (Winslet – smart but grumpy dog that she is – obviously sniffing out that this was the place to be).

At this rate, I was expecting to open the door

and see Mad Max the hamster leading a procession of iguanas, white mice and stick insects up the stairs from Tor's room at any second.

"Yeah – come on in!" I replied, keeping my voice low.

I didn't really want to alert my dozing dad that there was a bit of a family pow-wow happening upstairs in the attic.

Linn had only opened the door a crack when a cat that wasn't Colin slithered his black and white body through the gap. He scampered past me and Rowan, who were sprawled on the floor, and leapt – light as a furry feather – up on to my bed. At closer range, I checked out the fight-chewed ears and sussed out it was Eddie. All we needed was for cross-eyed Derek to come scratching at the door and we'd have a full house in the feline department.

"Oh..." said Linn, looking a little put out to see that Rowan had beaten her to it.

"Hey, Linn – how did it go tonight?" I asked our eldest sister. "You're back early, considering you were going to a party."

"I left early – I wasn't in the mood," she shrugged, shutting the door behind her and joining us on the floor. "I kept thinking about Dad..."

I couldn't blame her; I'd spent the whole evening pretending to watch whatever was flickering on the

TV screen, when all that was really running through my head was Dad and that weird phone call.

(Still, imagine being at a party with Alfie and choosing to leave! But then Linn doesn't see Alfie the way *I* do. That girl's *got* to need specs – it's the *only* explanation. Specs, or a brain transplant. One of the two...)

"Me too," said Rowan, running her hands through her dark curls and sending her Indian bangles jangling. "I was round at Chazza's tonight, and he was showing me and Von what he could play on his new guitar—"

Linn rolled her eyes at the thought of how boring *that* sounded, but thankfully, Rowan was too distracted by Frankie padding on to her lap to notice.

"—but I couldn't stop thinking about Dad," Rowan continued. "And what he was saying on the phone and ... everything."

Everything ... meaning Mum. Or at least our suspicions that his conversation had been to do with her.

Or even *with* her.

"So, Ally – did he say anything about it tonight?" asked Linn, leaning back on her elbows on my threadbare carpet, then sitting up again smartish when she felt how uncomfortable that was going to be. "Anything at all?"

"No," I shook my head. "He just made jokes about what was on the telly, then went up and read Tor a bedtime story. The usual."

Me and my sisters hadn't had the time or the opportunity to talk before Linn and Rowan had gone out. For one thing, Tor was there (and we didn't want to set his little mind whirling), and for another thing, Dad came blustering in to the room as soon as he'd finished the call, cheerily demanding to know what rubbish questions he'd missed on the quiz show.

(You should have seen how fast the four of us moved when we heard the phone go *ping*! as he put the receiver down. One second we were behind the living-room door – the next we were all back in our places on the sofa etc., trying *very* hard not to sound out of breath.)

"But once Tor went to bed," Linn continued to quiz me, "didn't he even give you a little hint then?"

"No, he didn't say anything. No hints, nothing."

I'd just been through all this with Rowan, and I knew what Linn's next question was going to be, mainly 'cause Rowan had asked it thirty seconds before Linn came knocking.

"Couldn't you have pumped him for a bit of information?" asked Linn, right on cue.

"No. I thought about it, but I couldn't work out what to say that didn't let on that we'd been listening in on his conversation," I tried to explain.

But it was no good – my two sisters were looking at me with total disappointment. I'd been their only hope to solve the riddle this evening and I'd failed miserably.

"So, do you think he *could* have been talking to Mum?" asked Rowan, finally saying out loud what we'd all wondered.

I'd thought of nothing else for the entire evening, but to be honest, I couldn't see how it could be true. I couldn't believe that Dad would keep anything to do with Mum a secret from us (except for Tor – we *all* kept things secret from Tor, for his own sake). Especially not after four whole years...

So maybe it's a good time to tell you what happened with Mum. It's more complicated than you might think, mainly because there're are *two* versions: the short one and the long one (otherwise known as the white-lie version and the truth). I might as well tell you both, since the first one doesn't take up much room...

Tale of the Disappearing Mum (the short version): this is the one Tor believes. Mum loved all of us so much that she felt terrible about all the children in the world that have no one to care for them. That's why she decided to go away for a while – leaving us in Dad's safe care – and work for a charity that sends her to faraway places. There are lots of countries out there and lots of children to look after, and that's why she's been away so long. But she'll be home one day…

Tale of the Disappearing Mum (the truth): basically, Mum was only seventeen (and Dad was twenty-two) when the two of them started going out. Mum had just finished school and was working in the jeans shop in Camden, but was planning on hiring a craft stall in the market to sell all her paintings and pottery, then using the money she'd make from that to take off round the world for a year, before going on to art school. That was the plan. Then – oops! – she found out she was pregnant with Linnhe (think: Linny. Not that anyone calls her that. Except Rowan, that is).

Anyway, once they'd got over the shock, Mum and Dad were blissfully happy; and, by the time Mum was eighteen, she found herself in her own little flat, married to Dad and with a small bundle of baby to look after.

Fast-forward through ten very happy years (and they *were* happy – I remember lots of it, even though some of it's kind of hazy now), to the time when Mum had Tor. All of us knew that Mum had changed a little bit; she still laughed and had fun with us, but we'd sometimes catch her looking sad, even though she'd say she was all right ("Post-natal depression that just didn't get better," Grandma explained to us much, much later). Then, when Tor was three, Mum and Dad had this long chat with us girls one night (Linn was thirteen, Rowan was eleven and I was nine), and announced that Mum had decided to go travelling for three months, to see some of the places she'd meant to visit on that long ago year-round trip she'd had to cancel. It didn't sound too long to us; we were big girls and could cope, helping Dad around the house. It would be an adventure for us too.

Next thing, she'd been gone six months – always sending cheery letters and postcards home to us – and we three girls began to get suspicious. We *definitely* got suspicious when Dad started to get gloomy and Grandma sold her house and moved to a flat just along the road "so she could look after us better". I don't know when it was exactly that we all began to think she *wasn't* coming back, but eventually that's the way we all saw it, and the way we've expected it to be ever since…

(But you can see why we stick to the first version for Tor. You don't want a little kid to think he's the one to blame for his mother disappearing off into the sunset, for ever. It would be pretty tough to handle, figuring your Mum got ill 'cause she brought you into the world. The nice, fluffy, charity-work story is a lot better for him, if you see what I mean.)

So here we were now – the three eldest of the Love children – wondering if we'd got it wrong; if Mum really was closer at hand than we'd thought.

"Well, all that 'it's just like old times' and 'no I haven't told them yet' stuff Dad was saying on the phone," mused Linn. "It definitely *sounds* like he was talking to her."

"And he did go out on Wednesday night," Rowan chipped in, her face all taut and tense. "Remember? He said he was going for a drink with the guy from the plumber's next door to the shop."

"Oh, yeah…" I muttered, remembering Dad hastily scrambling out of the door, looking slightly overdressed just to go and sink a couple of pints in a local pub.

And we were bound to notice when Dad went out; he did it so rarely. After Mum left, I think he felt he had to over-compensate for the fact that we were one parent down, and he always tried to be around for us.

"And he'd done his hair that funny way – all

greased back. Like it was in some of those old photos of him and Mum when they were young. We were teasing him about it," Linn reminded us.

"Wow, do you think the pub story was just a cover?" asked Rowan, wide-eyed.

Frankie was trying to wriggle out from her heavy-handed stroking, I noticed.

"Maybe," shrugged Linn. "Maybe he got all dressed up to go and meet *Mum* somewhere…"

"But, hold on," I said, scrambling to my feet and going over to the big map of the world on my wall. "We got a letter from Mum last week, and she was *here*…"

I pointed to a blue pin stuck on a small island in the Pacific Ocean. Every time we get a letter from her, I check where it's from and mark it on my map.

"So?" said Rowan. "What difference does that make?"

I can be a prize-winning worrier, but Rowan *really* gets herself in a stressed-out mess. You know, forgets to engage her brain, she's so busy panicking. And right now it wasn't just the look on her face that was giving her away; it was the fact that she had Frankie in a vice-like grip in her arms. Poor Frankie – he'd only been looking for a warm lap to sit in and he'd found himself being used as a feline worry-bead.

"*Think* about it, Ro," I urged her. "Mum wrote that she was planning to stay where she was for a couple of weeks, so—"

"—so she *couldn't* be back yet," Linn finished off my train of thought.

"Probably not," I replied, not sure whether to be reassured or hideously disappointed by that realization.

"So, if it wasn't *Mum* that Dad was talking to on the phone," Rowan said slowly, "where does that leave us?"

"Back at square one," I sighed, flopping down so hard on the bed that Eddie – much to his surprise – found himself bouncing off the duvet and up into the air.

Chapter 4

SANDIE'S SMART THINKING

Q: What's white and red, and drips all over?
A: My mate Sandie.

Well, that would be the answer, this one particular Sunday afternoon.

Sandie's face had gone waxy white, but her rotten cold had left her with a scabby red nose and upper lip as a fashionable contrast. Add to that two nostrils that were running like taps, and you get the picture. (And it wasn't pretty...)

"How are you feeling?" I asked.

Stupid, really, since it was so obvious how she was feeling. And that was *lousy*.

I noticed that the carpet beside her bed was strewn with soggy, scrunched-up paper hankies, even though there was a wicker wastepaper basket strategically placed within chucking distance. But not placed strategically enough, by the looks of it.

"I feel absoludely derrible..." sniffed Sandie, punctuating her medical update with a parping blow into a man-sized tissue.

Her big Disney eyes were particularly pathetic – all dewy-wet and sad. Or maybe she looked more like one of the bunnies out of *Watership Down*. Maybe the one with myxomatosis...

"You don't *seem* very well," I agreed, which was an understatement.

I was perched on the end of her bed, well out of the catchment range of tissue-chucking.

"Id's really sweed of you to come – bud you shouldn'd have," she scolded me with a grateful smile. "You mide cadge this cold!"

"Great! I get a legitimate excuse to stay off school!" I joked.

I didn't mean it. It wasn't like I loved school to pieces or anything, but I'd much rather have been going to classes than looking as bad as Sandie did right there and then.

I moved further back on the bed, and hoped I was well out of the germ radius.

Maybe it would have been a better idea to just phone rather than visit.

"So, I guess *you* won't be coming back to school tomorrow..." I said, astutely. Not.

Sandie shook her head. She was like this disembodied head (a white, red and dripping head) above a sea of cutesy teddies. Cutesy teddy duvet cover, cutesy teddy pillowcase, matching cutesy teddy pyjamas. All bought by her mother, I hasten to add. No fellow thirteen-year-old friend of *mine* would willingly sleep amongst cutesy teddies if he or she had freedom of choice...

"Mum says I'll have to sday in bed a couple of days ad leased," she mumbled forlornly, through her bunged-up nose.

I couldn't blame her for sounding down. Sandie's mother was one of those suffocating, over-protective mums at the best of times. But if Sandie was ill, she'd be even worse – fluttering about, plumping up pillows and shovelling her daughter full of medicine every five seconds.

The thing is, much as they love her, Sandie's parents are the reason she comes round to my place so much. They're both about a hundred and ten (OK, so I exaggerate, but her folks *are* old), and treat Sandie (their only kid) like she's a cross between a china Dresden doll and a precious, delicate butterfly. Thank goodness they approve of me, or Sandie would have no fun at all. Mind you, they've never seen my house. They would probably never let her through the door ever again if they saw how ramshackle our place is (despite my Grandma's best efforts to civilize it). And if they knew how many animals there were, they'd be apoplectic about Sandie catching cat-flea allergies, or distemper from the dogs or something.

"Ally, can you do me a favour?" Sandie sniffed, pointing over to the candy-pink painted table by her bedroom door.

Honestly, you should see her room. Everything in it is pink; and not that mad, raspberry pink that Rowan's done her room in (which sears your eyeballs to the back of your brain, but is still somehow cool). No, everything in Sandie's room is in shades of candy or bubblegum pink. With frills. It's like being in Life-Sized Barbie's room, for God's sake.

And Sandie hates it.

I know, I know, it was her choice in the first place ... but that was when she was *eight*. She's been desperate to redecorate it for the last three or four years, but her parents won't let her. They think her room is "just adorable". If you ask me (and even if you *don't* ask me, I'm going to tell you), I think it's 'cause they want to keep their little girl *little*, if you see what I mean. Growing up, having periods, snogging boys; I think they've blocked all that out and are just pretending it's *never* going to happen.

(And, just for the record, Sandie *is* growing up – she's got bigger boobs than me, but then *every*one does; she *has* started her periods – aged twelve at my house and Linn sorted her out; and she *has* kissed boys – even though it was just during games of Spin the Bottle and that kind of stupid party stuff.)

"What is it? What are you after?" I asked, scanning the top of the table, and hoping Sandie didn't seriously want the white teddy sitting on it with the silk heart that had "We wuv you!" embroidered on it. (A Christmas present from her parents. *No*, not when she was at primary school; *this* year…)

"Can you pass me thad new box of dissues off the dable?" she asked.

I had to laugh.

"You sound just like Billy did yesterday," I smiled at my own joke.

"Whad – does he have a cold doo?" frowned Sandie, all concerned.

"No," I shrugged. "I was just torturing him by twisting his nose off."

"Why?" Sandie quizzed me, looking confused.

"He's a boy, he's annoying … what more is there to say?" I shrugged.

It's funny; Billy's my oldest mate and Sandie's my best mate, but they just don't really hit it off together. They like each other and everything, but they just don't seem to gel. We do all go out as a threesome sometimes – mostly to the movies, where they don't have to speak to each other too much – but usually I see them separately. Billy's told me he thinks Sandie's too quiet, and he doesn't know what to say to her. But to be fair to Sandie, he *does* tend to act more stupid and show-offy in front of her. Nerves, I suppose. And Sandie says she thinks he doesn't like her, which to me translates as Sandie feeling a bit insecure about me having another close friend, other than her.

It gets on my wick a bit, actually, but I like both of them so much that I don't let it bother me most of the time.

"So whad did you do lassed nide?" asked Sandie, using her nail to spear the new box of hankies I'd just given her.

It took me a second to translate what she'd said from virus-speak to English.

"Last night? Nothing..." I replied.

"Billy nod up for doing anything?" she asked, checking I wasn't getting too friendly with him behind her sickly back.

"No – he was seeing some guys from his school," I told her. "And I phoned Chloe and the others, but no one was up for doing anything."

Sandie looked quite pleased. I think she'd have felt like she was missing out if I'd ended up spending a brilliant Saturday night out with Billy, or Chloe or Salma or any of our other friends from school. And who could blame her – I'd probably be the same if it was the other way around.

"So whad did you do?" she asked.

"I just stayed in with Dad and Tor and watched telly," I explained. "But something weird *did* happen…"

Sandie's enormous eyes seemed to light up. But maybe that was just fever.

"Whad?" she demanded through her blocked nose. "Whad happened?"

You could tell how bored she was after two days of being incarcerated at home. The remotest *hint* of something gossip-worthy had got her going.

"My dad – me and the others overheard him having this phone call. He was saying all this stuff like 'I can't wait till next time' and everything…"

"Whad – like he's been on a *date*?" she practically squealed.

Sandie loves anything remotely romantic, she really does.

"Well, me and Linn and Rowan *almost* thought he might have been out with … with our mum."

Sandie's jaw dropped.

Like Billy, she knows the whole story to do with my mum and her disappearing trick. To everyone else at school, I just say my mum lives abroad. No one gives me a hard time about it – I guess one good thing about so many people my age coming from broken and re-modelled families means that having a mum living abroad doesn't raise anyone's eyebrows or interest too much.

"Do you really think id's your mum?" she gasped.

"Actually, no – I don't think it can be," I admitted. "It doesn't add up – she's still supposed to be out on the Cook Islands for a while. We had a letter; she *couldn't* be back…"

"Well, id's obvious, then," said Sandie, matter-of-factly.

"What is?" I frowned.

"Your dad," she continued, "is seeing someone new."

Sandie isn't what you'd normally call intuitive. When it comes to the two of us, she always shuts up and lets me do all the talking or deciding (which drives me crazy sometimes). And she was *well* off-course here; my dad seeing someone new? How ridiculous! It must be those cold germs short-circuiting her brain…

There was no *way* my dad was seeing someone new.

No *way*.

Or…

Or was there?

Chapter 5

RING, RING – WHO'S THERE?

I squinted at my plate, and tried to figure out what it was we were supposed to be eating.

It was Rowan's turn to make the Sunday tea again. How did her turn come around again so quickly? What had we done in a previous life to deserve it?

"This is—"

Dad stopped to cough.

"—lovely, Rowan. Er, what is it?"

Bless him, he always tries to pretend Rowan's efforts are edible. (I know I serve up fish fingers, spaghetti and beans with boring regularity when it's *my* turn to make meals, but at least people don't get *food* poisoning from it...)

Linn swirled her fork round in the pink sludge with a look of pure horror on her face. And she hadn't even tasted it yet.

"Is it pudding?" asked Tor.

"No," said Rowan, sitting down at her place round the kitchen table and looking slightly flustered. "Who ever heard of getting just *pudding* for tea?"

"Well, if it's not pudding, why's it pink?" Tor asked her straight out.

"It's *pink*," sighed Rowan, as if she was a world-class chef who was being questioned by a lowly punter, "because it's got *beetroot* in it."

"Beetroot's red," I pointed out.

And not unfairly, I don't think.

"I put it in the liquidizer, with natural yoghurt," Rowan explained. "To make a sauce…"

I gulped.

I had to ask the next question, if no one else would.

"To make a sauce for *what* exactly?" I asked, gingerly poking about in the lumpy pink goo with my fork.

"Roasted vegetables," she replied.

"Roasted vegetables?" said Dad, raising his eyebrows enthusiastically. "*They're* good for you!"

"And fruit," Rowan added.

"*Fruit?*" squealed Linn, spitting out her first, tentative mouthful. "What kind of *fruit?!*"

"Peaches," said Rowan defiantly. "I found a tin in the cupboard. I thought it would make it a sort of … sweet-and-sour thing."

You know, sometimes I think Rowan stares at the fairy lights in her room too long…

Suddenly the phone shrilled out louder than

Linn's protests, and Dad went rushing out to the hall before any of us could get up off our seats to get it.

"Look – he's shut the door!" Linn hissed over the table, the terrible tea soon forgotten in the face of more secrecy on Dad's part.

"Yeah – he must be expecting this call, and doesn't want us to hear!" Rowan pointed out.

"Why not? Why doesn't he want us to hear?" Tor piped up, reminding us all that we should keep our mouths well and truly shut in his presence.

"Because it's just boring business stuff," I assured our little brother, wrinkling up my nose. "Hey – doesn't that sound like one of the cats yowling outside?"

It was smart thinking on my part – in a split-second, Tor had leapt out of his seat and tugged open the back door, heading out into the garden in search of any four-legged friend (or three-legged, in Colin's case) in need of his help.

"Listen," I whispered to my two sisters, while we had a moment to ourselves. "Sandie said something today…"

Linn rolled her eyes. At a time like this, she wasn't exactly scintillated by the notion of listening to whatever my best friend had to say – *that* was plain to see.

"What? What did Sandie say?" asked Rowan.

Bless Rowan – she's a weirdo, but at least she's a weirdo who's prepared to listen.

"Sandie said that maybe..."

I lost my nerve for a second.

"...Um, that Dad maybe has a new girlfriend," I finished off. "Maybe."

Linn and Rowan's jaws dropped till they nearly hit the hideous pink creation on their plates. But they said nothing, so they were obviously considering the idea.

"I think..."

I stared at Linn, waiting to see what she made of it all. Normally, I was quite happy for my know-all big sister to keep her opinions where the sun don't shine, but tonight, for once, I actually wanted to hear what Linn thought.

"I think," she began again, "that Sandie could be right."

Rowan looked like she might cry. She hangs out with her cool, older friends and everything, but she's all marshmallow inside, really.

"So, what do we do?" I asked Linn, hoping she had a smart answer.

"We watch and listen," said Linn, staring from me to Rowan and back again.

"Spying, you mean?" Rowan gulped.

"If that's what it takes, yes."

Linn would make a great Bond girl, she really would…

Chapter 6

I'LL TELL YOU MINE, IF YOU TELL ME YOURS

There's this kind of broad, tree-lined avenue that leads into Alexandra Palace (one of about seventy thousand ways to get into the whole park area).

It's not really open to cars, except when there's some big, fancy exhibition going on at weekends. But during the week, it's shut off as a road by these big ornate gates, with just the odd cyclist using it as a scenic short-cut, away from the traffic, or people with pooches on their way to the grassy expanses of the park.

Course, there are times of the day when the avenue – and all the old wooden benches that line it – gets busier. Like after four o'clock on week-days; that's when it becomes the unofficial snogging (and smoking) venue for loads of people from our school.

I was there this one Monday, idly wondering if the greeny-coloured, damp mould that covered the bench I was sitting on was going to stain my trousers. I was also letting my finger run along the groove of a badly carved heart, with the initials "E.K. luvs S.W." inside. I wondered if they belonged to anyone I knew. I couldn't help feeling momentarily jealous; I hate vandalism of any sort (and hacking love-hearts on park benches with a pen-knife is vandalism, I suppose) but I couldn't help wondering if there'd ever be a time when someone scratched "X.X. luvs A.L." on a lump of wood for *me*.

Though, I think I'd prefer someone more literate. Like someone who could spell "love" properly, for a start...

Now before you get the wrong idea, no, I wasn't there snogging anyone. And no, I wasn't there smoking either (please, credit me with a *brain*). I was there because the avenue is also quite a good place to hang out and gossip (usually about the people who are snogging), if you're not in the mood to hurry home.

Today, since Sandie was still lying in her snotty sickbed, I found myself sitting on a bench chatting with Kyra. Or more like *not* chatting with Kyra.

I stopped picking at the carved initials and stared at her as she checked the messages on her mobile phone. The one she was listening to seemed to be going on for ever, and whatever was being said wasn't exactly lighting up her life.

"Sorry about that," she apologized, finally clicking off her phone and slipping it back into her bag. "I was hoping for something a bit more exciting than my mum ranting on about the fifty million things I've got to pick up from the shops on the way home…"

I shrugged like I hadn't noticed how long she'd been. I wasn't really sure what to say either; the ins and outs of Kyra's relationship with her mum were still a mystery to me (all I knew was that it was bad, and that her mum had some kind of drinking problem). And since I didn't know Kyra well enough yet to go noseying into her life, I'd decided to keep stum till she told me herself. *If* she ever wanted to.

"So, I see Teresa Smith's got zero taste in men!" said Kyra, brightening up.

I looked where *she* was looking and saw Teresa Smith – only the prettiest girl in the year above us – losing her street cred with amazing speed. There, in front of anyone who cared to watch, she was holding hands and staring slushily into the eyes of some non-entity in a Muswell School for Boys uniform. It wasn't the fact that he wasn't anything special that was ruining her reputation; it was the fact that with the hand she *wasn't* holding, he was slowly and unself-consciously scratching his bum.

And not just a genteel one-finger scratch. Oh, no – this was a full-handed gouge worthy of any of the baboons down at London Zoo.

"Hope she's not going to hold *that* hand now…" I muttered to Kyra.

"It's one of those times you wish you had a video camera, isn't it?" giggled Kyra. "We could send it into that TV show; make ourselves a bit of money!"

I knew she was only joking (wasn't she?), but it didn't seem like Kyra particularly needed any extra money. Apart from living in one of the poshest turnings in Crouch End, Kyra had a few trimmings that definitely spelt "dosh", and plenty of it. Like, her phone – it wasn't any old standard mobile. It was one of those snoot, tiny ones I'd seen advertised for more money than my dad pulled in at his shop in a slow week.

Not that my dad would buy stuff like mobile phones even if he *had* the money. Technology kind of passes him by. We clubbed together and bought an answering machine for the shop one Christmas, but Dad just ended up taking it back to Argos and swapping it for a new tool box because he couldn't figure out how to work the thing. And as far as computers go, he can't get his head around websites and the Internet at all, even though Tor's tried to explain it to him loads of times.

Plenty of my friends have got their own phones and computers. It doesn't really bother me that I don't, and it doesn't bother me that the most gadgety thing in our house is a video we've had for five years (that was second-hand in the first place), mainly because I know how tough it is for Dad to keep everything together for us on his one, unspectacular wage. It doesn't bother Tor or Rowan either, but I know it *really* bothers Linn. That's why she's been frantically looking for a Saturday job – so she can start keeping herself in the style to which she'd *like* to become accustomed.

"Hey, what's up?" Kyra suddenly burst into my thoughts. "You're not drooling over Scratchy Boy, are you?"

I realized I'd had my eyes fixed a little too firmly on the bum of Teresa Smith's repulsive boyfriend for the last few seconds while I daydreamed. No wonder Kyra had got the wrong idea.

"No! No way!" I grimaced. "Disgusting geeks aren't exactly my type!"

Scruffy, I don't mind. A boy with the manners of a pig, I don't *think* so.

"So what *is* your type?" asked Kyra, narrowing her eyes at me.

We were still at that getting-to-know-you-better stage, me and Kyra. And Sandie, of course. Ever since we'd had the bust-up and make-up over the History project we'd done together, we three had all started to hang out a bit more. My other friends – Chloe, Jen, Salma and Kellie – thought me and Sandie were insane. They still reckoned that Kyra was a number-one show-off and a pain-in-the-doodah (and I understand why, since I used to see her in exactly the same way). But I'd come round to thinking that it was just a bad case of new-school nerves that made her try too hard and come over so bolshy and full-on.

"*I* don't know about what *type* of boy I go for!" I said, trying to laugh off her question.

Which was a downright lie, actually. Like most people, I can fancy all sorts of different boys for all sorts of different reasons, but I wouldn't need to do much thinking to come up with my *perfect* boy.

"Come on!" said Kyra, nudging me in the ribs with her elbow. "You tell me your type, and I'll tell you mine!"

The only person (apart from me, natch) that knew about my mega-crush on Alfie was Sandie, and I wanted it to stay that way. But what harm could this do? I could describe Alfie, without ever saying exactly who he was…

"Well," I mused, "I guess I like boys with short, messily spiky blond hair…"

"And?"

Kyra raised her eyebrows at me, egging me on.

"And light-grey eyes," I sighed. "You know – the sort that make you go a bit wobbly when you look into them, they're so spooky and pale."

"Go on!"

I didn't need much encouragement. Speaking about Alfie, even anonymously like this, was pretty much a pleasure.

"And I like guys who have great smiles. And maybe a little gold tooth somewhere at the side. That's cute. And I don't like jewellery on boys much, but you know those leather strappy bracelet things you get in Camden Market and places?"

Kyra nodded.

"Yeah, I like them," I continued, "on boys with skinny, muscular arms."

"So," said Kyra, staring at me intently now. "Who is this guy?"

"What guy?" I replied nervously. "You just told me to tell you what type I liked!"

"Come on, Ally!" she grinned. "That's not a type – that's a police photofit! You've obviously got one person in mind…"

I'm *so* transparent, I really am. I think I'm being clever and subtle and everything, but all the time I'm easier to read than a Year One ABC book.

"There's no one!" I blustered on, hoping against hope that she'd believe me. Kyra laughed out loud.

"You liar!" she giggled. "This guy sounds all right by your description, so what's the problem with him? Why can't you say who he is? What's the catch – is he only eleven or something?"

"He's four years *older* than me, actually!" I contradicted her bad-taste joke, and at the same time walked right into her trap.

"Aha! So we're getting somewhere!" shrieked Kyra, clapping her hands together as if prodding at my love life was the best game in the world. "Does he go to our school?"

"No. He goes to a sixth-form college over in Highgate..." I mumbled.

"Well? So tell!" she shrugged. "What's the point in keeping it from me?"

I couldn't think of *one* point, right at that moment, and although I thought I'd probably regret it, I ended up telling her who it was.

"His name's Alfie. He's best mates with my sister Linn," I explained, sheepishly.

"Does Linn know you fancy him?"

"God, no!" I squeaked.

The very idea made my blood run icy. Linn would *not* approve of one of her sisters fancying her best buddy – that would be far too juvenile for her. She'd never bring him around to the house ever again.

"Does he fancy you?"

"God, *no*!"

If only.

If only I could speak to him without turning into a gibbering, babbling fool, that would be a start.

"Why not? What's so weird about that?"

I was stumped. What a strange concept – Kyra honestly couldn't see why Alfie might not be interested in me. I'd spent the last few years stacking up all the reasons why someone like him could never be interested in someone like me, and now Kyra was putting a completely different spin on things.

Maybe it wasn't such a terrible idea talking to her about it after all...

"Oh – that's my phone! It could be him!"

Kyra jerked at the twittering tune jangling from her mobile, and dived into her bag to retrieve it.

I was feeling instantly deflated now that our Alfie conversation had been interrupted.

"Him who?" I asked distractedly, as I watched her practically turn her bag upside down to find her mobile.

"My new boyfriend!" Kyra grinned and whispered quickly, before she answered her phone.

Her new boyfriend?

Since when?

She hadn't even got round to telling me what *type* she went for yet, and now she had a *boyfriend*?!

Chapter 7

CUPID STRIKES AGAIN (NOWHERE NEAR ME...)

You know what was doing my head in? The fact that Kyra Davies had lived in Crouch End for about five minutes, and she'd got herself a boyfriend, just like that.

Me? I've lived here all my life, and all I've managed to chalk up is four (lousy) dates with Keith Brownlow when I was twelve and had no taste.

All the way home from the park, I couldn't help festering over how jealous I was. Not jealous of *Kyra* exactly (it wasn't like I wanted to get a voodoo doll of her and stick pins in it); just jealous of the whole idea of having a boyfriend. And that made me really mad with myself – it was so pathetic that I wanted one anyway. What was the point? My two friends who *had* had boyfriends (Salma and Jen) spent half the time they were supposed to be happily dating just moaning on about the boys, and how they never phoned when they said they would, drooled over other girls when they were out with them, and how generally useless they were. Their experience of boyfriends (as well as my *own* fleeting experience) should have put me off the whole idea.

But it didn't.

"Hello!" I shouted to no one in particular, as I barged grumpily through the front door.

I let my schoolbag drop with a clatter on to the floor and shoved my jacket on to the coat rack.

"Hello," I heard a small voice say, as I stomped past the staircase towards the kitchen, where Radio Two was blasting out some corny old song.

(Me and my sisters always retune to Radio One at breakfast, and Grandma switches it back to Radio Two when she gets in after picking up Tor from school.)

"What are you doing?" I asked, stopping to squint at my little brother.

Tor had his legs wrapped round a pole in the bannister, and was dangling backwards, his finger-tips nearly touching the wooden hall floor.

"Being upside down," he stated, slightly breathlessly.

"Your face is bright red," I pointed out, turning my head around to get a better view of his beetroot-tinted features.

"Is it?" he replied, seeming quite pleased about it.

"Shout if you need a hand down," I told him, as I strolled off into the kitchen, where the smell of something good managed to lift my spirits.

Ah, the joy of Monday to Friday, when Grandma makes our tea. When everyone's guaranteed not to moan, or end up with violent indigestion.

"He's still upside down, is he?" muttered Grandma, leaning down and prodding at something in the oven.

"Yep," I said, flopping on to one of the wooden chairs around our big old table. "What's he up to?"

"They did something about bats in school today," she replied.

Well, that explained that. Tor loved animals so much that it wasn't a great surprise that he was trying to turn into one.

"What are you making, Grandma?" I asked, sniffing the air like I was one of the dogs. (Talk about *Tor* turning into an animal…)

"An aubergine and mascarpone bake."

"Huh?"

"Well, a vegetable and cheese bake, in plain English," Grandma explained, closing the oven door and straightening up. "Saw it on *Ready, Steady, Cook* the other day."

"Smells great," I nodded.

Grandma's always trying out new recipes off the

TV on us. And I'd just like to take this opportunity to personally thank all the programme controllers for putting so many cookery shows on – if it wasn't for them, our weekday teas would be a lot less interesting.

"Well, you'll just have to tell me what this one's like – I can't stay and eat with you tonight," said Grandma, peering into the small mirror beside the back door and primping up her already immaculate blondey-grey hair.

"Why – what are you doing?" I asked, while marvelling at how neat Grandma was.

Not just in the way she looked and dressed, but the way the kitchen was so spotless and ordered, even though she'd been busy throwing food together for us five seconds before. I'm the total opposite – I even manage to make a mess at breakfast. There's always sticky bits on the table where I've poured (and dribbled) orange juice, and I always have to do a toast-crumbs-in-my-hair check in the hall mirror before I leave for school.

"I'm going out…" Grandma hesitated, looking uncharacteristically flustered for a second. "I'm going on what you girls would probably call a *date*."

Well, knock me down with a vegetable and cheese bake. One minute I'm in the park with Kyra, getting told she has a boyfriend (and being deserted two seconds after she gets off the phone, 'cause she's got to meet him, and promising she'll tell me more later). Next thing I'm home, and my Grandma is telling me more or less the same thing.

"Who is he?" I demanded, feeling even more rejected and loveless now that even my sixty-year-old grandmother had pulled.

"His name's Stanley, and I met him at my friends' wedding-anniversary party a couple of weeks ago," said Grandma, matter-of-factly.

"Is he nice?" I asked, a little more warmly.

It was silly to be so grumpy with her. It wasn't her fault that *I* wasn't going out with anyone, and it wasn't as if I was going to be too jealous of her new bloke.

"Very nice. He's a retired engineer."

Yep, I definitely didn't have the hots for Stanley the retired engineer.

"So, where are you two going?" I asked, wondering if I should push it and make a joke about her being sure to get home to her flat by eleven o'clock or she'd be grounded, but Grandma looked a little too self-conscious about the whole thing to take a joke.

"Just one of the restaurants near Crouch End Broadway. I forget which one he said," muttered Grandma, wafting her hand vaguely around in the air. "Anyhow, Rowan's outside taking in the washing. Why don't you give her a hand?"

I was dismissed. Grandma had had enough of gossiping about her love life with me, that was for sure. It's funny; her and Linn are so alike. If they're done talking to you, it's like the shutters come down and that's that.

Pulling open the squeaky back door, I saw Rowan wrestling for control of a pink, flowery pair of pants with Winslet.

"Let go! Leave! I said, *leave*!" she squeaked.

But Winslet didn't *want* to leave. She'd carefully selected the pants from the mound of newly dried clothes in the laundry basket lying on the grass, and was planning on adding them to the ever-changing collection of stolen items hidden under her doggy blanket. (She may be a short, hairy, grumpy dog now, but she *has* to have been a magpie in another life – it's the only explanation.)

"Need a hand?" I asked, bending down and grabbing Winslet by the scruff of her neck.

(It's a good trick that Tor taught me: get hold of a dog or cat by the scruff and they automatically open their jaws and drop whatever's in them – toys, mice, stolen pants...)

"Thanks. Yeuchhh! *These* are going straight back in the washing machine..." said Rowan, wrinkling up her nose and holding the knickers at arm's length.

"Those are Linn's, aren't they?" I asked, peering at the floral pants.

"Oh, yeah, so they are!" said Rowan, brightening up. "Oh, well – I'm sure they'll be fine. I mean, what's a little dog saliva between friends..."

She dropped the knickers back in the pile of clean clothes and turned back to the washing line, a small, smug smile playing at her lips. Well, it's not often she manages to get one over on our bossy big sister.

"So," I began, holding out my cupped hands for Rowan to drop the pegs into. "What about Grandma having a date tonight, then?"

"Well, it's not really a big deal, is it?" Rowan shrugged. "Not compared to this stuff with Dad..."

Urgh – I'd managed to forget about that. Call me a coward (you're a coward, Ally Love), but I suddenly understood why ostriches bury their heads in the sand when trouble lurks. I'd put any thoughts about the business with Dad away in a small, dusty corner at the back of my mind, and now here was Rowan, reminding me about it all over again.

"I suppose so," I mumbled, as I half-heartedly shooed Winslet away from the laundry basket.

"Anyway, you know what Linn said about us

keeping our eyes open?" Rowan whispered, peering over my shoulder at the open back door.

"You mean, about spying on him?" I said, more frankly.

"Yeah," Rowan nodded, making the halo of tiny, metallic butterfly clips holding her dark hair off her face glint in the late-afternoon sun. "Well, I found something!"

"Like what?" I asked, bending down and grabbing Winslet by the neck.

Automatically, the thief-dog dropped one of Tor's Pokémon socks and stared ruefully up at me.

"Like, I spotted the notepad beside the phone this morning," Rowan garbled, her eyes wide and shiny with her secret. "And on it, it said 'Wednesday', with these doodles of stars all round it!"

"OK, so he must have done that when he was on the phone last night – that call where he closed the door on us…"

"Exactly!" Rowan agreed with me. "So he must be going out with *her* again on Wednesday!"

Suddenly, I realized that I didn't care about Kyra having a new boyfriend. And Grandma seeing someone was just sweet. But what I did care about very, very much was the whole idea of Dad getting romantic with someone.

Someone who *wasn't* our mum…

Chapter 8

KYRA GOES TWINKLY

"Hi, Ally," said Kyra, hurrying along the school corridor towards me. "Listen, sorry I disappeared yesterday, but I *had* to meet Ricardo."

"Ricardo? Is he Italian, then?"

I hadn't even found out his name the day before, Kyra had been so desperate to sprint off and meet Wonderboy.

"Well, his family are, way back, I suppose," Kyra shrugged, leaning up against the radiator I was parked on. "Ricardo Esposito... Sounds really nice, doesn't it?"

Kyra was looking totally twinkly-eyed. The way she'd said it I had the feeling she'd already played that game of running your name together with his. "Kyra Esposito..." nah – I wouldn't run down to the registrar's to book the wedding straight away if *I* was her.

It was the start of breaktime on Tuesday morning, and I was idly mooching around, waiting to meet up with any of my friends who happened to amble by. (Not Sandie, though – she was still at home sinking under the weight of soggy tissues and being smothered by mother love.)

"So, come on – tell me about him," I grinned. "What's he like? When did you meet him?"

I'd decided I might as well be enthusiastic about this. If I didn't have a love life of my own, I might as well get a kick out of somebody else's.

"Well—" said Kyra, her light-brown skin flushing unexpectedly.

She comes across so loud and over-confident normally that it's always a surprise when you see little chinks of shyness like that (never mind the big chunks of insecurity I know are hidden away there too).

"—I went shopping in Wood Green with my dad on Saturday, and we ended up in one of those car-phone places. Anyway, it looked like Dad was going to be in there for *ever*, so I said I'd wait for him in Burger King."

"And?"

I was intrigued. Girl Finds Love in Burger King. It didn't sound too promising...

"And Burger King was mobbed. So I spot this *really* cute lad sitting on his own at a table, and I asked if I could sit there for a while," Kyra gushed, her bushy, high ponytail bobbing as she talked. "*He* tells me he's keeping the table for his mates, but then he says of course I can sit down, if I want to!"

Amazing. If *I* saw a really cute lad sitting at an empty table, the last thing I'd do is ask to sit down. I'd never have the nerve. I'd just cower in a corner and stare longingly at him from a distance. But then maybe that's why Kyra had got herself a boyfriend and I hadn't.

"And then he asks my name, and I ask his, and we get talking… We must have been talking for about half an hour; then I look up, and see my dad coming in. So I say, 'Here's my dad – I better go', but he says, 'Quick – write down your phone number!' and shoves a serviette across the table at me. And I scribble down my number with this old eyeliner pencil I found at the bottom of my bag!"

"And he phoned you yesterday?" I asked.

"Yesterday? Huh! That was the *third* time he'd phoned me," Kyra beamed happily. "He already called on Saturday night, *and* Sunday afternoon!"

It was official: I was impressed. Compared to my one, pathetic attempt at going out with someone, this was like a Hollywood blockbuster.

"What's he like, then?" I quizzed her.

"Like I said, he's cute. He's got dark-brown hair, big brown eyes, a big cheeky smile. Looks a bit like he could be in a boy band. And he's dead chatty and funny."

So, definitely *not* like Keith Brownlow.

"When you saw him yesterday, what did you do?" I asked, raising my eyebrows at her, and getting a little cheeky myself.

"We just hung out. He jumped on a bus from his school—"

"Which school?"

Kyra frowned and glanced around like she was trying to figure out which way was north. She still hadn't been in this part of the world long enough to get the geography sorted out in her head.

"Um, can't remember the name. It's somewhere over that way, I think."

"Wood Green?" I guessed from the direction she was pointing, through a set of school walls. "I wonder which one it is..."

"Whatever," Kyra shrugged, not interested in boring details like schools. "So we just hung out for a while and talked."

"And ... anything else?" I ventured.

She knew and *I* knew that we were talking snogging. It just seemed a bit tacky to come right out and say, "Did you snog, then?" even though it was the one thing I wanted to know.

"Maybe," grinned Kyra, shooting a sideways look

at me. "But anyway, best of all, we're going out properly tomorrow night!"

"Where to?"

"Skating up at Alexandra Palace."

It's good up there. Good for boy-spotting that is, not for skating. Well, very good for skating if you *can* skate – which I can't. Tor has to hold my hand and literally *drag* me round the ice whenever we go there.

"That'll be fun," I mused.

Lots of hand-holding and giggling – skating has great touchy-feely potential. Good choice, Kyra.

"But you know what's stupid?" Kyra shrugged.

"What?"

"I don't know what to wear! I mean, on Saturday, he just saw me in my old combats and a T-shirt, and yesterday I was in school uniform. Tomorrow I'd really like to look different. Y'know – really nice!"

I knew the feeling. Whenever there's a party or something, it always takes me about a week to work out what to put on. All my mates are the same, and we have this thing where we try on outfits in front of each other just to road-test them. It's a real laugh, and we always end up swapping and borrowing stuff from each other. Maybe that's what Kyra needed – a bit of the dress-rehearsal treatment...

"Well, why don't I come back to yours after school today and help you choose something?" I offered.

OK, so I had an ulterior motive: I also wanted to check out her posh house in her posh street. And maybe get a glimpse of this mother she didn't get on with.

"Uh, nah – it's OK," she said, looking suddenly ruffled. "I'll probably just shove on a jumper and my padded vest top. We're going skating, after all, so I guess it'll just have to be warm stuff..."

Did I hit a raw nerve? I wondered to myself. *Doesn't she want to have anyone back to the house?*

"Um, anyway, I better go to the loo before the bell rings," she suddenly muttered.

Ooh, it did look like she wanted to change the subject.

"OK," I shrugged. "Shall I wait for you?"

"No, it's all right," she shook her head. "You go on without me!"

I got the hint.

Just as I turned to head towards my Maths class-room, as the end-of-break bell trilled, this horrible image popped into my head: Keith Brownlow. All this love stuff had brought it back to me – i.e. our rubbish attempt at dating – when I'd done a really good job of forgetting it for a long, long time.

You see, it started in that way that it often does in real life, and never, *ever* in movies. Keith Brownlow was this kind of cute-looking boy in a crowd of lads in the year above me. Then one day, out of the blue, one of his mates comes over and says, "My mate Keith fancies you. Do you want to go out with him?"

Now, I did a stupid thing: I was *so* flattered that someone cute-looking (and in the year above!) was interested in little old me, that I persuaded myself in two seconds flat that I was madly in love with him.

And so me and Keith Brownlow went out four times (twice, we just hung around the park; once, we went to Pizza Hut; and once, I watched him play football and hung out with him afterwards).

And it was all a horrible disaster. Partly, it was my fault, because I was spending all my time trying to persuade myself that I fancied him, when I didn't really. The rest was his fault – I mean, he may have looked cute, but he hardly ever *talked*. Every time I saw him, I ended up babbling like crazy, and all he'd do was grunt in reply. And I should never have let him kiss me. To be honest, I didn't even know he was going to *do* it. One minute he was hovering outside my gate, slugging on his Coke, after walking me home (in silence) from the football match. Next thing I know, he's lunged at me, suctioned his lips on to mine, and done that unforgettable burp, right in my mouth. Talk about a memorable first kiss.

I think he knew he'd blown it then. I scurried inside the house after he walked me home and hoped against hope that he'd never phone me or come near me again, and luckily he didn't. We'd both done this thing ever since, where we never looked at each other at school. Maybe it was juvenile, but it was a lot easier to pretend we'd never met than to remind ourselves what a huge, embarrassing mistake it was.

I shook the memory out of my head and tried to concentrate on where I was going. Right now, there were about a million people coming down the stairs that I was trying to go up, to get to my Maths class.

"Don't push!" I yelled, as this surge of Year Seven boys came towards me.

But of *course* they took no notice of me, and of *course* they kept on pushing. Next thing, I'm on the floor, with everything in my bag spilt everywhere.

I was just thanking my lucky stars that I'd decided to wear trousers and not a skirt that day (landing on your bum in full view of loads of people is bad enough – having your skirt over your head at the same time would be just *shameful*), when something made me look up.

Stepping over my scattered books right at this second was the one, the only, Keith Brownlow. He was doing our trick, I noticed, as I scrambled, red-faced, to my feet. He was staring down at the tiled floor and pretending he couldn't see me.

Phew.

And then I spotted what he was actually staring at.

The little blue box I kept in my bag had burst open, and my tampons were fanning out across the shiny red floor tiles...

Nice one, Ally! I told myself, wondering if I should just ram my empty bag over my head and make like an ostrich.

Chapter 9

SPEAKING IN DISGUISE

I was sitting at one end of the sofa, with my school books spread all around me, when Linn came bustling into the living room.

(Grandma had left ten minutes before, which is why I had my homework with me in the living room instead of upstairs at my desk. She's got this pet theory that you can't study properly in the same room as a TV; and to be honest, she's right. Instead of doing anything remotely swotty, I was gazing blankly at some holiday programme, while simultaneously reliving my humiliation in front of Keith Brownlow the previous day and stroking Colin the cat, who was gently snoring on top of my opened textbook.)

"I just saw Dad come out of the bathroom..." Linn hissed, scooting over and shifting some of my books so she could sit down.

At Linn's pronouncement, Rowan roused herself from flicking through her magazine. And Tor stopped playing his game of Spin the Bottle on the floor (which consisted of him hugging Rolf or Winslet, depending on where the empty plastic Coke bottle ended up pointing).

"...and he's done his hair all fancy!"

It was Wednesday night – the night we girls were primed to watch out for signs of Dad going out again. And you didn't get much more of a sign than Dad doing his hair.

"He's greased it back?" I asked, feeling my heart rate pick up.

For a long, long time we'd only ever seen it as short-ish, curly-ish and style-free. But years ago – and we had the photographic evidence in the albums in cupboard – he always wore it smoothed back, all slick and shiny like the teddy boys did in the fifties. That's what had first made our mum and dad fancy each other; they were both really into fashion – only fashion that was several *decades* out of date. Dad had this kind of rockabilly style, with his greased hair and checked shirts, worn with turned-up jeans and Doc Marten boots. Mum's style was straight out of the seventies, with her long wavy hair, velvet jackets and hippie dresses. They must have made a weird couple. But cool too, I think.

So Dad's retro hairdo *had* to mean something. He'd done it like that the previous week when he'd disappeared off for the pint or two with his "plumber mate" – but strangely enough, he hadn't said anything about going out tonight. Only the scribble on the phone pad had given that away.

"He's coming down the stairs!" whispered Rowan, hearing the thudding of footsteps a microsecond before the rest of us.

We must have looked like dress-shop dummies when Dad came into the room. Rowan, Tor, Linn and I were silently and stiffly glued to the TV, as if the story about scenic coach-trips for the over-sixties was just about the most fascinating thing we'd ever seen.

"Um, listen, I forgot to say…" said Dad, hovering in the doorway, awkwardly. "I'm just going out for a couple of hours. Just … popping out for a pint."

"With the plumber?" I asked, hoping I looked innocent.

"Um … yes, with the plumber. Jake, yeah…"

He didn't sound too convincing. And he didn't *look* too convincing either. He was wearing his best white shirt, and both it and his jeans were ironed, if I wasn't very much mistaken. What bloke would iron jeans (that were never normally anywhere within an eight-kilometre radius of an iron), just to go to the pub with a mate?

"Sorry, guys," he apologized. "I should have checked with you first. None of you are going out are you? Is someone OK to look after Tor?"

"Of course!"

"Yes!"

"Sure!"

The colliding voices of his three daughters must have caught Dad by surprise. I don't think he'd ever heard us sound so definite when it came to babysitting duties.

"Well, all right. Thanks, you lot," he said sheepishly, as he disappeared into the hall. "I won't be late!"

Linn darted over to the window as soon as we heard the front door shut.

"OK, he's gone," she said, ventriloquist-style through clenched teeth, as she smiled and waved Dad off.

She spun round, ready to talk over events with us, when something made her stop.

"What's happening?" asked Tor, narrowing his eyes at all three of us.

Tor – we'd forgotten about him in all the intrigue. He'd silently listened to us gossiping about the business of Dad's hair, and he'd played along with keeping quiet and watching the telly when Dad had walked in the room. But really, he hadn't a clue what we were all up to – and we wanted it to stay that way. After all, the night before, he got kind of worked up when Dad and us had been joking around about Grandma's hot date (we knew he was worked up because he didn't make his food into any shapes before he ate it, like he normally does). We finally got it out of him that he was scared Grandma wouldn't love him as much if she had a boyfriend. And if he was scared of *that*, then we sure didn't want him freaking out about Dad seeing someone else...

"We're just taking the mickey out of Dad, that's all," I tried to reassure him. "Just 'cause he's putting all that slimy gel in his hair!"

"It's wax, actually," he corrected me, earnestly.

You've got to watch it with kids sometimes; they're smarter than you think.

"Hey, do you suppose I should run after Dad?" asked Linn, trying to sound normal but staring meaningfully at me and Rowan. "You know – to check he's got his *keys*?"

It suddenly clicked – we were about to have a conversation in code. Me and my sisters sometimes do this when we want to keep stuff well over Tor's head. (And Grandma's, now and again. There *are* times when you don't want your gran to know *everything* that you're up to.) According to the code so far, Linn was letting me and Rowan know that she planned to follow Dad and see where he was going … and who he was *really* meeting.

I glanced over at Rowan to make sure she'd sussed the code thing – sometimes she's too busy being an airhead to notice what's going on. But Rowan shot me a quick look back and I knew we were all on the same wavelength.

"That's a good idea!" I nodded at my eldest sister. "We might be in bed by the time Dad comes back, so he'll need his keys to get in!"

(Translation: "Go for it, Linn!")

"But he *took* his keys!" Tor piped up, before Linn could head for the door.

"Er, no he didn't!" said Rowan.

"He *did*! He was jingling them in his hand!"

Never underestimate the observational skills of a seven year old.

"Was he?" I smiled at Tor, "Well, that was clever of you to notice."

Annoying, more like.

Me, Rowan and Linn were silent for a second, stumped, now that our first attempts at proper spying had been stalled.

"Oh, I think I'll go to the shop!" Rowan burst out, scrambling out of the armchair. "I really fancy … some … Wine Gums!"

(Translation: "Now that Linn's plan is down the dumper, I've tried to come up with an alternative excuse to get out of the house and follow Dad.")

"*Grrandma* says Wine Gums stick in your teeth and rot them," Tor squinted at Rowan dubiously.

"Well ... maybe I just fancy having rotten teeth, OK?" Rowan shrugged, searching the floor for her shoes.

(Translation: "Leave me alone, Tor – I know it's lame but it was the first stupid thing that came into my head!")

"You'd better hurry, Ro – the shop might close!" said Linn sternly.

(Translation: "Hurry up if you're going, or you'll never catch up with Dad!")

"But the shop stays open past my bedtime!" Tor chipped in.

I gritted my teeth together and knew my sisters would be doing the same. It was like living with a junior member of MI6.

"I think the shop is closing early tonight. I'm sure I saw a sign in the window saying that..." I tried to pacify him.

(Translation: "Tor, we love you but shut up and let us lie to you!")

"I can't find my other shoe!" whined Rowan,

knowing that time was ticking away. "Winslet – have you taken it?"

(Translation: "I'll never catch up with Dad at this rate, because that stupid dog's hidden my shoe under a bed somewhere!")

"Ro, listen: forget the Wine Gums," Linn sighed, shoving her hands on her hips. "You can get them another day."

(Translation: "Give up. Dad'll be *well* gone. We'll try another time when Inspector Tor isn't listening in.")

Tor glanced around and seemed to notice that all of us were deflated for some reason or other, and he didn't like it.

Since I was the only one still sitting, he fixed on me.

"Winslet would like a cuddle," said Tor, struggling to pick up and carry the reluctant, hairy sausage of a dog over to the sofa, and scrambling up next to me with her.

(Translation: "Tor would like a cuddle.")

And who was I to refuse those big brown eyes. (Tor's, I mean, not Winslet's...)

Chapter 10

LOVE AND CHIPS

I know I moan about Linn, but she was really cool when Billy phoned and begged me to come out and see a movie with him before his brain exploded with boredom.

OK, so it was obvious that it didn't need all of us to stay home and look after Tor while Dad was out with ... well, *whoever*, but in the circumstances, I felt like I should be there, showing solidarity with my sisters.

But as soon as I came back in the living room and said how I'd told Billy I couldn't come out, she'd told me not to be so silly and to get back on the phone and tell him I'd meet him up at Muswell Hill Odeon in half an hour.

And so here I was, sitting in the darkness next to Billy, nudging him to pass me the giant bucket of popcorn he was hogging.

The only problem was, the new sci-fi movie we were meant to be seeing (Billy's choice) was sold out. So we'd been forced to give up until another day, or opt for this romantic comedy thing that was starting around the same time. And since neither of us was in the mood to go home (me, because I'd just worry about what my dad was up to; Billy because, well, he was plain *bored*) we stuck it out.

"Ally, how come that girl keeps on crying?" Billy whispered loudly, pointing up at the screen as I wrestled the bucket of popcorn from his other hand.

"Because she loves that blond guy," I whispered back, "but she thinks she doesn't stand a chance with him."

Boys aren't too sharp at picking up emotional stuff, are they?

"Oh, OK..." Billy nodded, but sounded unconvinced. "But how come the bloke with the blond hair keeps being horrible to her?"

"Because he loves *her*, but he's trying to hide it."

Even in the semi-dark, I could see Billy frowning.

This film wasn't doing much for his understanding of the intricate ways of romance. And who could blame him for struggling with it? After all, the two characters we were watching would spend an hour and a half going through a whole pile of complicated misunderstandings, but just before the credits rolled – shazam! – they'd come to their senses, realize how in love they were and live happily ever after. And surprise, surprise, life's not like that. (If it was, after all these years of fumbling, blushing conversations and awkward silences, me and Alfie would be well on our way to announcing our engagement or something by now.)

"I don't get it – who's this other guy *here*?" asked Billy, forgetting to whisper now, which must have been just fantastic for the people sitting around us.

"He's her boss. He's in love with her too."

While I was trying to explain the film's ludicrous romantic entanglements to Billy, for a fleeting second, I thought not of Dad and his mystery date, but of the other hot date that was going on – Kyra and Ricardo, slip-sliding their way around Ally Pally ice rink.

I immediately shoved the thought to the back of my mind. The best *I* could do with my Wednesday night was explain storylines to my dense mate. And speaking of that, it suddenly struck me that I'd just learnt an important life lesson, which is: only attempt to watch romantic movies with a) girl mates, or b) boyfriends. Girl mates are always up for a good chick flick, and boyfriends will at least *pretend* to like them, for the sake of their girlfriends. But romantic movies and single boys don't mix – it brings out the worst, most cynical streak in them.

Basically, watching a romantic film with a boy who *isn't* your boyfriend is just *asking* for trouble.

"*Burrrrrrrrrrrrrrrrrrrrp!* Oooh, sorry!" sniggered Billy.

As the tutting started behind us, I slunk so low I practically slipped off my seat...

OK, another life lesson is *not* to tell Billy anything vaguely important and expect a useful answer.

"But you don't know for *definite*!" said Billy, through a mouthful of tomato-sauce- and (blee!) mayonnaise-drenched chips.

We were strolling along Muswell Hill Broadway, heading towards my bus stop. I had been a bit dubious about telling Billy what was going on with Dad, but for some strange reason (I think the film was so bad in the end that it turned my brain to mush) I told him everything that was rattling around in my muddled head.

The reason that I *hadn't* planned on telling him was the fact that he's not too brilliant with "sensitive" stuff. (Put it this way: he isn't Sandie, who's so sensitive that she can cry at *car ads* on the telly, if they're slushy enough.) Here's an example: there was this one time, years ago, when I got a bit upset at how long Mum had been gone, and all Billy did was go very quiet, then tell me I could borrow his Gameboy for an unlimited period if I wanted. I mean, OK, so it was really sweet, bless him, but a girl buddy would give you a hug, wouldn't they?

(Actually ... you know something? There I am moaning on, but I've suddenly just remembered that I was quite chuffed at the time. I'd never had a go at a Gameboy before and within one minute of playing on it, I'd got totally addicted and managed to forget about Mum for a bit. Maybe Billy isn't so useless after all. And maybe I'm just a bit of an ungrateful moo...)

But anyway, as we queued at the fish and chip shop opposite the Odeon, common sense was telling me that I should stick to talking about how much he'd hated the movie (loads); how much his school was bugging him (loads); if he still had a crush on the eighteen-year-old girl who'd moved in next door to him (most definitely); the usual stuff. But instead, I blurted. Well, Billy and I have known each other since we were little kids, so it's hard *not* to tell him what's going on. Even if he generally doesn't have anything remotely helpful to say about it.

"What do you mean, I 'don't know for definite'?" I asked, wondering how he had room in his skinny body for the mound of chips he was stuffing his face with. He'd already hoovered up *triple* his fair share of popcorn in the cinema.

"Well, you don't know for *certain* that your dad is out on a date with a woman," Billy shrugged.

"What are you saying – that he's out on a date with a *man*?"

I know I was deliberately misunderstanding him, but I was a bit irked at Billy's unwillingness just to go with what I was telling him.

"No! I don't mean that. It's just that I think maybe you've got it wrong!"

"Look, Billy," I said, regretting that I'd ever opened my mouth, "I think I know my own father pretty well, and I know when something weird is going on!"

"Yeah, but I still think you're overreacting!" he mumbled, as he rammed more chips in his mouth. "I mean, my mum and dad go out all the time, and *I* don't know what they're up to. They're just out – like tonight – *doing* stuff."

"Billy – you can't compare me and my dad to you and your parents!"

"Why not?" he blinked at me, looking slightly hurt.

I couldn't feel sorry for him, though. Not while he had this disgusting dribble of tomato sauce oozing down his chin.

"It's totally different!" I tried to explain. "Dad is really close to all of us – we all know what's going on in our family!"

Well, that wasn't quite true. None of us knew what Dad was up to this particular evening; *that* was the problem.

"So, what are you saying – that I'm not close to my mum and dad?" asked Billy, coming to a halt beside my bus stop.

"Well, you're not, are you?"

It wasn't like Billy and his folks didn't get on – it was just that they all drifted about in their biggish house, all doing their own thing. Whenever I went round there, Billy's mum was always popping out to her coffee mornings and the garden centre and her evening classes. And his dad was always the same – saying a cheery hello to me and then burying his head in the paper for the rest of the time.

"We *are* close!" Billy protested.

"Billy – you don't even know what your dad does for a *living*!"

"I – I do! He works for … an insurance company!"

"Doing *what* exactly, Billy?" I tested him, my hands on my hips.

Boys are rubbish at knowing important details. They really are.

"Uh…"

Billy was saved by the fact that my bus drew up just then, opening its doors with a swish of hydraulics.

"See you up the park on Sunday, if I don't talk to you before!" he yelled, as the doors swooshed closed behind me.

I felt a bit mean going on like that at Billy, and tried to make it up by hurtling up to the top deck and waving at him like mad before the bus whizzed round the roundabout and dipped down the steep hill towards Crouch End.

As Billy waved his greasy fingers back at me, the bus driver did the usual kamikaze trick of hurtling down the forty-five-degree incline at an alarming rate, hurtling me bum-first down on to the seat. Normally, I hate this part of the journey (I tend to play out a whole morbid scenario in my mind: the screech of brakes, the bus tilting over, the local-paper headline, "Bus Careers Out Of Control On Perilous Hill – All Passengers Horribly Squashed"), but tonight I quite enjoyed the sensation. With the top of the bus to myself and the carpet of lights of London spread out down below, it was kind of like being on a Disneyland ride.

I was almost disappointed when the bus finally squealed to a halt by the junction at the bottom of the hill. But just as I stuck my feet up on the back of the seat in front and relaxed, something caught my eye.

The couple huddling in the bus shelter on the other side of the road were doing some seriously steamy snogging. It was better than anything in the film I'd just watched, that was for sure. I squinted for a better look; the way they were going, it was like a cross between mouth-to-mouth resuscitation and a WWF wrestling competition.

It was at that second that a passing car illuminated the couple in the glare of its headlights. Although I couldn't see her face, I recognized the girl's high, bushy ponytail instantly.

Oh. My. God. What was Kyra Davies *like*?!

Chapter 11

DAD SLIPS UP

"He's whistling!" whispered Rowan, as if Dad whistling first thing in the morning was the wildest thing to happen in our house all year.

Rowan was attacking some bread on the worktop, waving the long breadknife at me ominously as she made her point.

"So?" I whispered back, as I grabbed myself a glass out of the cupboard.

Speaking of wild things, Rowan's hair would've scored a definite nine out of ten on any wild scale this morning. She had it done up in two short plaits (nothing wrong with that), but the bottom of her plaits were tied with whole streamers of different coloured ribbons that trailed down over her white school shirt. If she stood still for too long, she was in danger of having small kids use her as a maypole.

"*So*, if he's whistling like that, maybe it means he's happy. You know, maybe he had a good time last night!"

I heard what Rowan was saying, but I glanced

over my shoulder to check that Tor hadn't. Luckily, we had the radio up loud and Tor was pretty much absorbed in carving his toast into something specific.

"Ro, whistling doesn't mean anything. We need more to go on than that..."

Rowan looked a little huffy with me. She grabbed the mound of bread she'd just cut (all squint), turned and plonked it down on the table.

"Hi, guys!" Dad's voice suddenly boomed above the radio.

"Hi, Dad!" said Rowan, Tor and I, simultaneously.

"Ah," exclaimed Dad, settling into his usual chair at the table, and rubbing his stomach. "Pass me some of that bread, Ally Pally – I'm starving!"

At that point, Linn breezed into the kitchen, looking as immaculate and ironed as she always does.

By contrast, an uncomfortable damp sensation made me look down at the cuff of my own white school shirt, which was currently soaking up a pool of orange juice right by my plate. I yanked my arm up and sucked at the cloth, and wished – for a split-second – that I was just slightly *less* of a clumsy geek and slightly *more* like Linn. (And you don't hear me say that too often...)

"What's this about being starving?" smiled Linn, bending over to peck a kiss on Dad's forehead before she sat down. "What have you been up to that's made you so hungry, Dad? Bit of a night last night, was it?"

Good one, Linn! I thought proudly, as my big sister launched today's offensive before she'd even had any cornflakes.

"No, no," Dad shook his head, concentrating intently on buttering his wonky slice of bread. "Quiet night, really. Few drinks, and a bit of chat. That's all."

"What pub did you go to, Dad?" asked Rowan, getting in on the act.

"Um, it was just that one off the Broadway," he muttered, vaguely.

I watched Rowan open her mouth and then close it again. She was obviously just about to question him about which of the many pubs off the Broadway that he meant exactly, when she realized she might incriminate herself. (I guessed Rowan didn't *really* want Dad knowing what me and Linn already knew – that she'd been in most of those pubs at one time or another, thanks to hanging out with her two best mates, who were both eighteen.)

My turn.

"So how's Jake?" I asked, studying Dad to see if he'd give himself away.

"Jake?"

A hint of a puzzled frown crossed Dad's face.

Aha! Got him... I thought, desperate to glance over at my sisters and check that they'd spotted that too.

"Oh, Jake! Yes, fine," Dad attempted a recovery. "Yes, Jake's ... OK."

Yeah, *right*. And just how long have you had this imaginary friend, Mr Love?

"And what did you two talk about, then?" I continued, practically giddy now that I was sure we'd caught Dad out in his lie.

"Um, just ... sport. That kind of thing," he said casually.

To add weight to his casual act, Dad picked up the marmalade jar and pretended to be fascinated by the wording on the label. Who was he kidding? And what was with the "sport" conversation? Dad watched cycling stuff like the Tour de France on telly, but beyond that he knew as much about sport as he did about the nutritional value of marmalade.

"Don't we have any *normal* stuff?" Tor suddenly interrupted, while trying to ram a piece of bread that lurched from being ten centimetres thick at one side to a sliver at the other into the toaster.

"Sliced? No we've run out. We've only got that," said Rowan slightly tersely, feeling her culinary skills were being criticized once again, even if it was only bread in question.

"But I can't finish what I'm making with this!" Tor whined, flopping the bread in the air.

"What *are* you making, Tor?" I asked, squinting at the carved piece of toast already on his plate.

Tor trotted back to his place at the table and put the toast up to his face.

"Cool!" mumbled Rowan, nodding at the sight of the Chris Evans style (toast) specs our brother was balancing on the bridge of his nose.

"I needed more toast for the arms!" Tor explained, looking at us all through the holes he'd so expertly cut out, while pointing at the space between his home-made glasses and his ears.

The technical specifications of his work of art were certainly making our normally monosyllabic little brother very chatty this morning. I was just about to quiz him on how he'd planned to *fix* the arms to the rest of the edible specs when a screech from Dad's chair alerted me to the fact that he was on the move.

"Where are you going?" asked Linn, seeing our prey slip away.

"Um, I just remembered there's an early delivery

due at the shop this morning," said Dad, heading out of the kitchen armed with his bread and marmalade. "Better get round there now..."

"Damn!" muttered Linn, under her breath.

"I *heard* that..." muttered Tor, disapprovingly.

So, we got nothing out of Dad. But luckily, *someone* was willing to talk – and tell all. Even if it was on a totally different subject.

"...and then he was skating *straight* towards me, and I was screaming and everything, but he *deliberately* crashes straight into me, grabbing me and cuddling me." Kyra giggled at the memory. "And we were laughing like mad, and then he says, 'I'm freezing – do you fancy warming me up?' And *I* said, 'Sure – you want me to buy you a coffee from the machine?' Geddit?"

I got it. So much for Kyra giving a cool back-hander to his saucy line; it sure looked like they were doing a good job of warming each other up when *I* saw them the night before – and that was what I was *really* interested in hearing about. I still hadn't quite got over the shock of seeing Kyra and Ricardo re-enacting a scene out of some steamy movie, specially since the setting was a bus shelter on the W7 bus route.

To be honest, I wasn't exactly blown away by

the sound of Ricardo's unsubtle charms, but I was having quite a good time listening to Kyra's tales, or at least as much as she could squeeze into the short journey along the corridor between English and Maths classes.

"And he definitely wants to see me again!" gushed Kyra, her upturned nose crinkling as she grinned, so that her sprinkling of freckles disappeared. "He's asked me to go to his mate's party in Muswell Hill with him on Saturday!"

"Yeah?" I said dolefully, a sinking feeling suddenly washing over me, so that I totally forgot to tease her about the bus-stop snog-fest.

"What's wrong?" asked Kyra, scanning my face.

"Nah, it's nothing," I tried to laugh, thankful that the door of the Maths class was looming up and I'd be spared any further explanation of my Party Complex.

So I didn't want to tell Kyra about it there and then ('cause I didn't want to sound like the pathetic, sorry-for-myself geek I know I can be), but basically, *this* is my Party Complex: hearing about a party that you *know* you're going to get an invite to is exciting. Hearing about a party that you're *not* going to get an invite to is just sheer torture.

I mean, parties can be rubbish, can't they? But

there's always that potential; the potential to have a brilliant laugh with your mates, to meet new people, to meet new boys... (Uh-oh, I'm off on the boy thing again.)

But that's the problem with hearing about parties and knowing you're not invited – all that potential is going on and you're stuck at home playing Junior Scrabble with your little brother while your kleptomaniac dog keeps running off with random vowels.

OK, I'm speaking about myself here, but you get my drift.

"Anyway, I'll keep you posted!" Kyra grinned at me conspiratorially, before she darted off to her own class.

"Yeah, keep me posted on what fantastic things are happening next in your charmed life, Kyra," I mumbled grumpily.

Chapter 12

STUNNED? ONLY A *HUGE* BIT...

"Yeeeeoooooowww!"

Grandma, who was busy pulverizing some potatoes into submission with a masher, shot me this look that said, "I told you so!"

And she was right. When you've got an old coffee jar (painted bright blue with paper stars stuck on it – one of Rowan's early artistic efforts) that's stuffed with kitchen utensils, it's really dumb to try to turn the fishcakes you're frying just with your fingers.

I was just about to run my stinging hand under the cold-water tap, when I heard the phone ring in the hall.

"I'll get it!" I yelled, hurrying through to grab the receiver.

I presumed it would be Sandie; she was going to phone me back once she'd had a think about what video I should bring round with me on Saturday night. I'd called her as soon as I'd got in from school to see how she was getting on with her pet virus. Her horrible cold had turned into some even more horrible gastric thing, and she'd been confined to her little pink bedroom for the entire week by both her doctor and her mother. She was now going completely round the bend after days' and days' worth of mollycoddling (her mother was asking for regular updates on the state of her "bowel movements" for goodness' sake), and was desperate for me to come and inject some normality in to her life. ("Do you want me to bring anything?" I'd asked her. "Just a video. Oh, and maybe you could get me something from the hardware shop too." "What?" I asked, wondering if the virus had affected her brain. "One of those big industrial padlocks," she sighed. "So I can lock my stupid mother out of my room...")

"Hello?" I said down the phone, suddenly aware that I could smell something fishy at close quarters...

"Can I speak to Ally, please?" said a voice that wasn't Sandie's, but that *was* vaguely familiar.

"Yeah, it's me," I replied, sniffing at the hand that was holding the phone and sussing out that it was the one I'd been flipping the fishcakes with. Poo.

I cradled the receiver awkwardly, between my head and neck, and – using my non-burnt, non-smelly hand – lifted a corner of my shirt and wiped away the grease from the plastic handle.

"Oh, hi! I thought it was maybe one of your sisters," I heard the girl's voice say, as I transferred the phone to my other ear with my clean hand.

"Kyra?" I said, clicking who it was.

"Yeah, it's me! What are you up to?"

"Not much…" I shrugged, holding my greasy, fishy-fingered hand well away from me.

What could I tell her? That after I heard that she was going to a party on Saturday night with her new boyfriend, I spent the whole of Maths feeling particularly hacked off? And then I'd walked home from school (feeling particularly hacked off); tried to do my homework but couldn't concentrate (because I was too hacked off); phoned Sandie on her sickbed to see if I could come round and see her on Saturday night (so I wouldn't be the only one hacked off at not going to a party); and finally that I'd nearly deep-fried my hand because I was too hacked off to pay attention when my grandmother told me to use a spatula instead of risking third-degree burns?

"Hey, listen, Ally," said Kyra. "I've got a bit of a proposition for you…"

I was intrigued…

"Like what?"

"Do you remember what I told you at school

today? About Ricardo's mate having a party on Saturday?"

Did I remember? The fact was only *seared* into my brain...

"Yes, the party. I remember something about that..." I mumbled, trying to sound like I couldn't care less.

"Well, do you fancy coming?"

A wave of happiness steamrollered over me. I wanted to scream "YES, PLEASE!!", but I decided very quickly that that would not rate too highly on a cool scale.

"Uh, yes – sure, I'd like to come!" I squeaked, instead.

(While a small voice in my head was also shouting, "And what about Sandie?" and I was doing a wonderful job of ignoring it...)

"Great!" said Kyra. "Only there *is* a catch..."

Isn't there always?

"What is it?" I frowned, becoming aware of a rasping sensation on my fingers.

I glanced up and saw Colin the cat, perched on a stair at shoulder-level to me, stretching his neck through the bannisters and enthusiastically licking my fishcake-scented fingers.

"It's like this," Kyra began. "I was just talking to Ricardo on the phone, and he was saying that he wants to bring this mate of his along to the party too, so I said, 'Well, can I bring *my* mate as well?' "

Me. *I* was her mate. And if I wasn't very much mistaken, I was just about to have my very first blind date.

"—and Ricardo says, 'Hey, it'll be like *Blind Date*!' "

Kyra didn't look much like Cilla Black, but I can't say I cared. And I know blind dates can sometimes be a disaster, but on the boy front, it was the best offer I'd had all year. And in a week where I'd not only made a fool of myself in front of Alfie, but also in front of the only boy I'd ever been out with too, I kind of thought I deserved a change of luck.

"No problem. It could be a laugh," I giggled, trying to keep the wobble of hysteria in my voice under control.

Wait till I tell Chloe and the others at school tomorrow! I thought frantically. *Wait till I tell Sandie! Er, on second thoughts...*

I was debating whether to phone Billy and boast about it, or leave it till I saw him on Sunday to blurt my news out, when Kyra wrapped up the call pretty suddenly.

"Oh, gawd ... my mum's just come in. I've got to go. Speak to you at school tomorrow!"

And with a clatter from her end she was gone.

Slowly, I put the receiver down and walked back into the kitchen in a daze, only narrowly avoiding falling over Colin, who was weaving (make that *hopping*) his way around my legs, in the vain hope that I was carrying any spare fish in one of my pockets.

"All right, Ally?" asked Grandma, giving me one of her X-ray looks.

She must have thought I was ill, the way I was wandering about like a zombie. Probably thought I'd contracted Sandie's Horrible Thing.

"Grandma – I've got a date on Saturday!" I blurted out.

"Have you, dear? Well that makes two of us!" she smiled brightly, clattering plates on the table.

"Stanley again?" I asked, remembering her dinner date earlier in the week.

"Of course it's Stanley. What do you think I am, some wanton woman going out with two men in the same week?" she said, brusquely. "And who are you going out with?"

I didn't take offence at the brusque business – it's just the way Grandma talks. Mum isn't like that, though; she's more ditzy, like Rowan (well, from what I remember). It's funny how it kind of skipped a generation, with Linn ending up like a mini-clone of Grandma.

"That's the thing," I said, responding to Grandma's question. "I don't know his name. Well, not yet."

"Blind date, is it?" Grandma frowned. "You're not meeting him on your own, are you?"

"No, I'm going out in a foursome with my friend Kyra. This lad's a mate of her boyfriend's."

I felt myself blushing as I explained it to her. I was probably going to spend the next two days blushing about it. I'd be luminous *red* by the time I finally got introduced to this boy. He'd probably think I had some strange tropical disease and insist on a note from my doctor before he'd go anywhere near me.

"Hello, girls! What are you two gossiping about?" said Dad, coming into the kitchen and scooping Colin up into his arms and away from my legs.

"Nothing much," shrugged Grandma.

She's great that way. She knows when there's things that we might not want to tell Dad about. I mean, I *would* tell Dad before I went out on Saturday, but only once I'd stopped being a gibbering, girlie wreck about it.

"Well, it didn't sound like that to me!" Dad

grinned, standing in the middle of the kitchen in his bare feet, oldest faded jeans, scruffiest black T-shirt and with the purriest cat in his arms.

And with his hair normal and curling, he didn't look anything like he had done the night before, when he'd seemed so smartened up (for *him*, I mean; my dad's not exactly the kind of guy you'd ever see in a suit...).

"Just girls' talk, Martin," said my Grandma, in that tone of hers that means "that's it – you're not getting any more explanation than that!".

"Oh, that's right!" he teased us. "Just you two keep your little secrets from me!"

"Ah, now, speaking of keeping things from you – I nearly forgot," said Grandma, glancing up at him from fixing the table. "Someone rang earlier, when you and Tor were out feeding the rabbits in the garden. I was going to come and get you, but she told me not to bother."

She?

At the mention of that one word – that one *pronoun*, if we're going to get pernickety – I came out of my date-induced walking coma.

"Er, who – who was that, then?" asked Dad, looking suspiciously sheepish.

"Sorry, can't remember her name. I should have written it down," said Grandma, clattering the forks and knives into place. "All I remember is the message."

"And that was…?" asked Dad, his voice sounding ever so slightly strangled.

"If you're still up for Sunday, then give her a call. Does that make sense?"

Grandma looked up at Dad with her steely grey eyes.

"Uh … yep. Yes – that makes sense. Oooh, smells like tea's nearly ready. I better give everyone a shout!"

Dad – and Colin – were out of the kitchen door at the speed of light.

I looked at Grandma.

She looked back at me.

I saw her fractionally raise one eyebrow and, in that unspoken second, *I* knew that *she* knew that *I* knew that *she* knew *something* was going on.

If you see what I mean…

Chapter 13

SMALL, BUT SMART

We were just heading out of the doorway of the pet shop when Tor tugged at my sleeve.

"The parrot!" he whispered to me, his eyes wide and earnest.

I glanced back at the shop's resident grey parrot, whose cage stood above the cash desk.

"What *about* the parrot?" I asked, ducking to one side to let another customer in.

"He said my name!" gasped Tor.

Tor does this thing, where – after we've chosen what we need to keep our menagerie going – *I* do the dull stuff like queuing up to pay, while *he* talks Tor-talk to the mice and hamsters in their cages. He also tries to bond with the resident parrot by giving it long, meaningful stares.

I thought about it for a second as I hustled Tor out of everyone's way and pointed him in the general direction of the café a couple of doors along. Call me cynical, but to me, the sound the bird made was your basic "squawwwk!" type parrot noise. But I guess it *could* sound a bit like "Torrrrr!".

If you stuck your fingers in your ears and hummed a bit, that is.

Still, who was I to burst Tor's bubble?

"Wow! He said your name? That's cool!" I nodded down at Tor, putting my hand firmly on his back and steering him into Shufda's.

As we waited for our two hot chocolates – a regular treat after our Saturday-morning pet-shop expedition – Tor took out the new goldfish scoop-net we'd just bought from the plastic bag and proceeded to capture the salt cellar with it.

"Watch you don't knock it over, Tor," I whispered.

Tor's a good kid – you can take him most places and never be embarrassed by him, unlike a lot of other children. Even when he was really little he was kind of laid-back. Other two year olds would be having screaming hissy fits on the bus because they weren't being allowed to eat the bus ticket or something, and Tor would just stare at them with his big, brown eyes, like he was trying to figure out what their problem was.

"I'm being careful!" he assured me, as the waiter came over with two steaming mugs.

"OK. So how've things been at school this week?

Are you friends with Freddie again?"

I liked these chats we had on our own. I mean, I always did most of the chatting (no surprise), but it was still pretty nice, just the two of us.

"Uh-huh," nodded Tor, licking chocolatey froth off his spoon.

"What was it you two were fighting about, anyway?"

"Stuff," Tor shrugged.

Tor maybe didn't say much – especially at school – but he was still a popular guy. There was always a procession of small chums from his class trampling around our house being introduced to all the pets. Maybe different things make you popular when you're older, but when you're seven, having the equivalent of Rolf's *Animal Hospital* at home works pretty well.

"What kind of stuff?" I pushed him.

Today in particular I was quite up for losing myself in Tor's world. It distracted me from what was looming in front of me ... i.e. my blind date. I was planning on keeping myself really busy until it was time to get ready, just so I wouldn't go round the twist thinking about it.

"Stuff," shrugged Tor again, taking a slurp of his drink. "I did a picture of a snail and Freddie said it looked like a big poo."

I know ('cause I remember) that when you're Tor's age, things like that matter – a *lot*. But still, if that was all he had to worry about, then I was pleased. He had plenty of time to grow up and worry about life, the universe, exams and everything.

"You and Linn and Rowan..." said Tor suddenly, fixing me with a serious stare.

I was tempted to lean over and wipe away the frothy chocolate moustache on his upper lip, but I thought he might get grumpy about me babying him.

"What? What about us?" I asked, sneaking a look at my watch. (Nine hours to go before I had to meet up with Kyra...)

"You all think Dad's got a girlfriend."

I choked so much on a mouthful of hot chocolate that it nearly sprayed out of my nose (mmm!). Frantically, I tried to think of something to say – some reassuring denial – but my mind let me down. Several pathetic explanations popped into my brain, and were so pathetic that they popped right out again.

Tor kept staring at me as his nose disappeared back into his mug.

He may be a weird kid, but he's so smart. Smarter than his three sisters put together, that was for sure. We thought we were so clever, hiding everything from him, and he saw through it all.

"He's going out with her on Sunday," said Tor matter-of-factly, wiping his mouth with the back of his hand.

It was just as well I hadn't taken another slurp of hot chocolate, or it really would have been spraying out of my nose in surprise at *that* little pronouncement. It seemed that Tor not only knew what *we* knew, he knew *more*...

"He's going out on Sunday? How do you know?" I quizzed him, giving up any pretence at denying anything. Why bother?

"I asked Dad if we could go to the City Farm on Sunday," Tor explained. "He said he couldn't, he had to do a *thing*. And he went bright red."

Look at that – my brother was even smarter than our *dad*, seeing through his excuse straight away. (Still, saying he was doing a "thing" was a pretty *pitiful* excuse on Dad's part and not *that* hard to see through, I guess.)

"Are you going to follow him this time?" Tor asked straight out.

I was slap-bang stunned. Again.

"Did you know that's what Linn and Rowan were trying to do on Wednesday night?" I asked him, remembering how his questioning had put a stop to my sisters' attempts at spying.

"Uh-huh," nodded Tor, playing around with the

fish-scoop again.

"Why didn't you tell us you knew what was going on?"

"You were leaving me out," said Tor simply.

I guess he had a point.

"Listen, we'll talk to Rowan and Linn when we get home," I told him. "And we won't leave you out again, OK?"

Tor nodded happily. I guess we thought we were protecting him, but all the time we were making him feel lonely and pushed out with our sisterly secrets.

Still, it looked like Love Child No. 4 was just about to join the family firm of private investigators.

Dad didn't stand a chance.

Chapter 14

THIS WAY FOR A SPEEDY EXIT...

Time was dragging. It had been a busy (and draining) day, but this last couple of hours before I was due to go and meet Kyra were stretching out like the world's biggest elastic band...

My day had gone like this: after my brother's little bombshell in the café, the two of us had traipsed home, rounded up Rowan (Linn was out), and filled her in on Inspector Tor's powers of deduction. What Tor had said about Sunday tied in with the suspect message Gran had given Dad the other evening, but until we could get hold of Linn, there was no point working out what to do about it.

After that, I went round to see Sandie. I was in serious grovelling mode; she'd said on the phone that she didn't mind if I blew her out for the party (and the date), but I knew she was gutted really. She'd asked me all these questions: "What's this boy like?" (I didn't know); "Where's the party?" (I didn't know); and "What are you going to wear?" (Yep, I didn't know – since none of my other friends were going, the dress-rehearsal ritual hadn't happened). And all the time, Sandie kept looking at me with her big Disney eyes all soulful and sad.

I finally escaped (from the guilt) when her mother came up to take her temperature and check she hadn't developed the *plague* or something. On the way home, it suddenly struck me that Sandie was probably worried that me and Kyra had got too buddy-buddy while she was stuck at home with her gastric-flu thing. It wasn't really like that, but I could see why she thought it might be.

But as they say, that was then and this is now. And right about now, I was standing under the shower, feeling very, very sick.

(Mind you, it's not hard to feel ill in our bathroom. Mum painted the walls deep ruby red, 'cause she wanted to put lots of plants in here, and thought the greenery would look great against it. Only it practically gives you a *migraine* if you stay in the room more than ten minutes.)

His name was Bobby, this guy I was feeling sick about. Kyra had told me that much, and that was *all* she'd told me, apart from the fact that him and Ricardo went to the same school. I guess that was as much I could expect from Kyra, considering she'd only been going out with Ricardo for a week, and probably didn't know that much about him either (apart from an intimate knowledge of his snogging technique).

So, with two hours to go, I was standing in the shower, letting the torrent of water batter over my head, and – get this – trying to think of things I could talk about with Ricardo's mate.

How pathetic was that? But you know, that was (actually, it still *is*) something I worry about a lot. A *lot*. I mean, what are you meant to speak to each other about on dates? Once you've run through all the stuff about *likes* and *dislikes*, and who your mates are and everything, I worry that you just dry up. At least, it was like that when I went out with Keith Brownlow (urgh, don't remind me...), and even though we're about a million light years away from *ever* dating, it's like that with Alfie too – my mind just goes blanker than blank when I get the chance to talk to him.

Now Billy, that's different – 'cause he's just a mate, same as Sandie, or Chloe or the others (well, with a couple of genetic differences...). I can talk to Billy for *hours* about *anything* (mostly rubbish, if you want to know, but it's always pretty entertaining rubbish).

So what happens to your brain when you fancy someone, or you're out on a date? Why does it seem like having a normal conversation is about as alien as nipping to Saturn for your summer holidays?

My eyes suddenly started stinging with shampoo, so I rammed my face under the flow of the water, and tried to distract myself from the pain by coming up with things I could talk about.

And this was all I managed...

1) Ask him what subjects he's doing at school. (Nah – it would make me sound like a total swot...)

2) Ask him what football team he's into. (What's the point? I don't know anything about football, so it would be a really *short* conversation. Him: "And what football team do you support?" Me: "Uh, none." Him: "Oh." See? Not exactly scintillating...)

3) Tell him the stories behind my brother and sisters' names. (Nope – he'll think we're all weirdos. Which isn't far off the case when it comes to Rowan...)

4) Ask him what he wants to do when he leaves school. (Sounds too heavy. He'll expect me to ask how many children he wants and if he's got a pension plan next...)

5) Tell him that I share a house with two dogs, five cats, three hamsters, too many white mice to count, a one-eyed iguana, four rabbits, a couple of

tanks of fish, a pile of stick insects, a recuperating pigeon and whatever else Tor's brought home lately. (*Definitely* not – I want him to think I'm this cool, desirable girl, not Dr Dolittle...)

It was no use.

I gave up, turned the shower off and stepped out of the bath, dripping. The water pipes to the shower shuddered to a halt, like there was a tiny man behind the wall, hammering like crazy. (Maybe there is – who knows? Or a poltergeist of an irate Victorian plumber?)

Wiping away the steam on the old, chipped, wood-framed mirror above the sink (a junk-shop treasure my mum once came home with), I checked out my reflection – and saw a big pink prawn staring back at me. I'd obviously stayed in the shower just a *little* bit too long. In fact, I was *so* pink, I clashed horribly with the red walls. I had to get out of there – get up to my room, open the windows wide, and cool down. How could I go and meet the mysterious Bobby if I looked like I'd fallen asleep under a sun-lamp?

Rifling through the towels in the cupboard, the only one I could find that was big enough to cover my bits was one of those emergency towels – an ancient, threadbare, ratty one that you keep in case the others are all in the wash, and hope you never need to drag out. But it would have to do; today was laundry day and all the half-decent towels were outside twirling on the washing line along with the clothes.

"Mmm – very sexy. *Not*!" I murmured at my dripping, pink, ratty reflection.

The old bolt on the bathroom door was as sticky as ever, and I had to give it a good tug to get it open.

Does nothing in this stupid house work properly? I moaned to myself, realizing immediately that I was starting to sound worryingly like Linn. If she had her choice, Linn's dream house would be some ultra-modern, ultra-sleek, ultra-minimalist effort like you see in those interiors magazines – not a pipe-rattling, door-sticking, madly-painted wreck like our place.

In my general stress-induced state of grumpiness, I hadn't noticed the creak on the stairs coming up from the hallway. Suddenly, I saw Alfie's scruffy blond hair coming into view, just when I was about as far away as I could be from the escape route of the stairs to the attic (which were at the other end of the landing).

Emergency! If there was one thing I was sure of, it was that I did *not* look like a moist-skinned, semi-nude goddess. I looked like I'd been *stewed*, for God's sake, and I could feel an ominous draft whistling round my bum, from what must have been a large hole in this disgrace of a towel.

Up till now, I'd had precisely zero chance of ever going out with Alfie. If he saw me like this, my chances would dip down to minus a *million*.

Thankfully, Alfie's face was turned and looking back down at Linn, who I could hear chatting behind him. This gave me a split-second's grace to vanish, before I embarrassed myself more than I'd ever been embarrassed in my life (and there were plenty of times *that* had happened, I can assure you...).

The closest door to me led into Dad's room and, quick as a pink flash, I slipped in there, shutting the door silently behind me. Sighing, I leant my whole weight against the door. (What for? In case Alfie had caught a glimpse of me and tried to barge his way in after me, unable to control his passion at the sight me in my peek-a-boo towel? I don't *think* so.)

As my heart rate began to slow down (from frantic to only marginally *less* frantic), my eyes drifted across the room. It was flooded with a cosy orange glow, partly from the early evening sunlight streaming in through the window, and partly because the walls themselves were orange (a kind of ginger-cat colour – Colin was completely camouflaged whenever he came in here for a snooze).

Outside on the landing, I could make out the mumble of conversation and the squeaky tread of stairs, as Linn and Alfie headed up to her room. I could relax... Or at least give myself a chance to cool down, and nick a pair of jogging bottoms and a T-shirt from Dad's wardrobe so that I could get back up to my room with a little more decorum.

I walked over to the wardrobe and pulled the door open. It was packed – but not all with Dad's stuff. There were loads of Mum's dresses and everything in there. All beautiful, patterned fine cottons and Indian silks, a couple of velvet jackets, and some cheesecloth tops. I knew without looking that all her favourite chunky old jumpers would be where they always were, folded up in the big bottom drawer of the chest by the bed. Dad's kept all her stuff just as she left it – perfume bottles, make-up (not that she ever wore much) and an old hairbrush all sit on the dressing table, in case she just happened to stroll through the door and want to pick up where she left off...

There are reminders of Mum all over the house – not just in the way she decorated it, but her paintings and pottery and everything are on every wall and on practically every spare surface. But this room in particular is like a mini-shrine to her, and it's nice to come in here now and again, just on those weird occasions when I feel like I'm starting to forget little things about her, and smell her perfume or pull out her favourite clothes.

And of course, there's her self-portrait right above the bed. Not that you might recognize it as a self-portrait, since it's just all a mass of swirly oranges and yellows. In case you were wondering, it represents her aura. (An aura is some spooky electric current that we all have around us, according to ... well, people who read auras. Normal people can't see them, but aura readers can; and one of them told Mum that hers symbolized "awakening". I think I go through so many feelings and moods in a day that *my* aura would be brown – like when you get all those brilliant Plasticine colours that turn to sludge when you mix them.) Anyhow, my mum came back home after getting her aura reading done at a Mind, Body and Spirit Festival at Alexandra Palace, and immediately started working on this painting. She left home on her travels about two weeks after that, so I reckon that aura reader's got a lot to answer for, if you ask me...

But back to that afternoon, when all I had on

was that awful scabby towel. Suddenly, I found myself sitting on the edge of Mum and Dad's big old squeaky wooden bed, staring at her painting and remembering the Sunday mornings when we all used to pile in – even Linn. Nowadays, Tor still dive-bombs Dad occasionally (along with Winslet and Rolf), and it's funny to see, but it's not the same as those long-ago times when all us girls and Mum were part of the fun.

I shook myself, aware that I was starting to get too sad about everything. Quickly – before the tears had a chance to get hold of me – I got to my feet and began hunting through the wardrobe, yanking an old denim shirt off a hanger and hauling it on. Some more searching, and I'd found a pair of Dad's jogging bottoms that were far too big for me but at least made me look more human and less like pond-life.

I went over to the dressing table to check out my general redness levels, when I spotted something lying open by the side of the bed.

It was a photo album – one of the ones that normally lived in the cupboard in the living room. What had Dad taken it up here for?

I flopped down on the floor and pulled it round to face me. It was open at a page of photos of Mum: Mum holding her long skirt up and paddling in the sea; Mum laughing at some unknown joke; Mum in the long, wispy lavender dress she got married in; Mum grinning by a muddy stream, wearing wellies, dungarees and stroking her round, pregnant tummy.

What had made Dad dig these out?

I glanced up again at the large framed painting hanging over the bedhead.

"Oh, Mum," I mumbled, wishing I was looking at her face for real, instead of a bunch of stupid orange and yellow swirls. "What do you think's going on? Do you think Dad's feeling guilty about something...?"

Chapter 15

BLIND DATES AND FRAYED NERVES

It was the first time I'd ever seen Kyra without her hair scraped back into her bunched-up ponytail. With her curls waxed, her mid-brown hair looked darker and glossier, pinned back from her face with coloured butterfly clips.

It suited her. You know how she's got those sort of sticky-out ears? Well you couldn't even tell they were sticky-out at all with her hair like that. Not one bit.

"I know I've said it already, but you look really nice," I told her, in a squeakier-than-normal voice.

It was a tough job keeping my frayed nerves under control. I couldn't do much about my voice, but at least I could stick my hands (which were suffering from a bad case of tremble), deep down in my trouser pockets.

"Thanks! You look pretty OK too!" she smirked, raising her eyebrows at me.

We'd just got off the bus and were heading for Ricardo's house, with Kyra holding a scruffy bit of paper with directions on it. We were now on the north side of Alexandra Palace, not a million miles away from Billy's house (I hoped we wouldn't bump into him – he'd have killed himself laughing if he'd seen how dressed up I was). Now that we were here, I realized that if I'd known how close Ricardo's house was, I'd have suggested that we just walk over the park.

But then I took a look at the black, satiny wedge sandals that Kyra had on her feet, and knew that grass, earth and those shoes would definitely *not* go...

I was just wearing a pair of trainers (but my best pair, of course). I can't wear anything with heels – they make me walk like a duck. And unlike Kyra, who was wearing a little chiffon, flowered skirt, my legs were well covered up, in my cut-off khaki trousers. Kyra had dared to bare with her top (a little black halterneck thing), but again I played safe, sticking to my favourite T-shirt: the khaki one with the red star on the chest.

It wasn't so much my clothes that would have made Billy laugh – it was my make-up. Or more like *Kyra's* make-up. When we'd met at the bus stop, she'd frowned at me, then rummaged in her bag and pulled out a little pot. Next thing, she's holding up a mirror and showing me the twinkles of glitter she's daubed on my cheeks and eyelids.

"That looks so cool on you!" Kyra had announced, and I didn't have the guts to contradict her.

A couple of lads in a car honked their horn at us as we trotted along the road, still searching for Ricardo's street. I didn't know whether it was the sight of Kyra's long brown legs that had driven the boys to hammering on their horn, or if the glitter on my face was blinding them and they were trying to let me know I was a traffic hazard.

"Is it far now?" I asked, trying to sneak a peek at the squiggles on the piece of paper Kyra was holding.

"No – this is the road here!" she announced, swinging a left into a street full of small terraced houses.

"Thanks again for inviting me," I muttered, even though at that point I felt so nervous I was pretty tempted to turn and run – very fast – all the way home.

"No problem," said Kyra, brightly. "I kind of felt sorry for you after what you were saying earlier in the week…"

Great. She hadn't fixed me up on this double date because I was smart, or funny, or interesting or pretty – she'd invited me because she felt *sorry* for me. How useless did that make me feel?

"After I was saying what exactly?" I quizzed her.

I tell you one thing: getting defensive is a good way to stop feeling nervous.

"Oh, it was when you were talking about fancying that friend of your sister's. The one you said you don't stand a chance with," said Kyra, bluntly. "So, I just thought it might cheer you up to snog Ricardo's mate."

An avalanche of nerves descended upon me again.

Oh my God. Did this guy *assume* I was going to snog him? If Kyra was sure it was going to happen, then her boyfriend must be sure too, and – naturally – his mate as well. I mean, I had no objection to the idea of kissing someone if I really liked them, but the thought that everyone expected it to be a done deal was only completely petrifying...

I didn't have any more time to think about it (or invent a sudden illness that had struck me out of the blue so I could get away *fast*) – Kyra was sashaying up to a navy-blue front door and ringing a bell.

I gulped, and just knew I'd gone pink again.

"Hi!" said a dark-haired lad, pulling the door open.

He glanced my way for a nano-second, then grinned slowly as he eyed Kyra up and down. Joey out of *Friends* had nothing on this guy.

"Hi, Ricardo!" Kyra smiled coquettishly, twirling and swaying on the doorstep. "This is Ally…"

"Yeah? I couldn't remember what you said she was called," said Ricardo, with minimum tact and charm.

Mmm, it might be a bit of a struggle to like this guy, I decided.

"Anyway, this is my mate," he continued, pointing his thumb back over his shoulder in the general direction of the hallway, where a tall, shadowy figure ambled towards the doorway.

"Hi, Bobby!" said Kyra, wafting her fingers in a wave towards Ricardo's buddy.

I took one look at Bobby and froze.

He took one look at me, and seemed like he was going to laugh or hurl – one of the two.

"His name's not Bobby," Ricardo snorted. "It's Billy!"

"Bobby … Billy," Kyra shrugged off her mistake with a cheeky air of casualness. "What's the difference?"

It's the difference, I felt like telling her, between having a proper blind date, and being set up with your own best *mate*…

Chapter 16

THAT'S *SOME* PARTY TRICK...

I glanced around the room. Yep, it was just like I suspected when we first walked in: everyone at this party seemed a *lot* older than us – fifteen or sixteen at least. I hoped I didn't look as young as I suddenly felt.

Just as I was nervously checking everyone out, I became aware of a pair of eyes staring at me, from only a few centimetres away.

"What *is* that stuff on your cheeks?" asked Billy, wrinkling his nose up as he inspected my face.

"Pure gold dust. What did you think?" I replied, sarcastically.

Some party this was shaping up to be. The whole of the flat we were in was crowded with people (i.e. boys) I'd never met, and I'd never get a *chance* to get to know any of them – not with Billy in tow. Even if a cool sixteen year old was interested in going out with someone who was only thirteen. (Like, fat chance...)

It's at times like these you suddenly appreciate

the differences between female and male friends. If I was with Sandie or Salma or someone, people would assume I was single. But standing with this lanky berk of a boy – especially when he was pawing at my face the way he was – anyone was bound to suppose we were an item.

"Gerroff!" I moaned, pushing his finger away from my eyeball.

"I just wanted to see what that stuff was!" he whined. "Is it like little bits of metal, or what?"

"It's a gel, with glitter in it," I sighed, knowing I'd better give him an answer or he'd just keep annoying me. "Kyra's got a little pot of it. Why don't you go and ask her if you can try some?"

I stared over at Kyra and Ricardo, who were busy getting to know each other better on the sofa (i.e. recreating their snogathon at the bus stop when I saw them the other night).

"Nah, I won't bother," grinned Billy. "Just looking at you, I can see that it's crap."

"Thanks!" I said, rolling my eyes.

I still hadn't quite got over the shock of finding out that Billy was my date for the night. Billy, of course, thought it was the funniest thing in the world. It turned out that Ricardo had only told him he was set up on a blind date about half an hour before me and Kyra arrived (like I said before, boys are useless when it comes to important details).

"He told me your name was Emma, or Wendy or something," Billy had told me, as we'd headed off to the party after our bizarre "introduction" on the doorstep – *and* once Kyra and Ricardo had stopped wetting themselves laughing.

"But didn't you even recognize Kyra's name when he was talking about her?" I'd asked him.

Kyra was pretty unusual (the name *and* the girl), and he'd heard me moan about her enough when she'd first started at school and got right up my nose.

"I didn't know what she was called. I just knew Richie had a new girlfriend, that's all," he'd shrugged. (See what I mean about being useless?)

And there was the other twist of the night. Ricardo wasn't an unknown quantity to me at all – Billy had mentioned him loads of times in the passing, but as Richie, not Ricardo. He wasn't a close friend of Billy's or anything, it was just that they played on the same football team. The one nugget I'd remembered hearing about "Richie" was that he was a real success with the girls. Billy was slightly in awe of his success rate in actual fact: Richie seemed to be going out with a different girl practically every week.

Which didn't exactly bode well for Kyra...

"Come on – let's dance!" said Billy, trying to drag me into the centre of the room as a hip-hop track burst on to the sound system.

"No, I'm not in the mood," I shrugged.

"Aw, Ally!" he pleaded, tugging at the bottom of my T-shirt and doing this goofy little dance in front of me, rolling his shoulders and jumping around on the spot.

"No!" I giggled, shaking free of him.

He's such an idiot, you can't help laughing at him sometimes. And the thing is, he just *looks* funny as well – like he grew too quickly and bits of him haven't caught up yet. It's like his whole body's skinny-boyish, but he's got this big, man-sized nose and these huge hands and feet.

God, I'm not selling him too well, am I? I mean, despite all that, he *is* kind of cute-looking. To be honest (and I'd never tell him this), I don't really get why he hasn't got a girlfriend yet...

"*Course* you want to dance!" Billy grinned at me, grabbing me round the waist and lifting me into the centre of the room, and into the throng of dancers.

"Billy – put me down!" I squealed, battering on his shoulders with my fists. See what I mean about goofy?

As he let me slither to the ground, I noticed

something behind him. Over by the far wall, a couple of guys were watching us. They looked like they might be about sixteen, and one of them – dressed in baggy skate gear and with spiky short dark hair – was grinning this cute grin. At *me*.

I checked again, just to make sure he wasn't looking at some gorgeous model-type girl lurking behind me. He wasn't – there was that grin again.

I decided to stop protesting and dance. I'm a pretty good dancer. I know that sounds big-headed, but there are plenty of things I'm *not* good at (and I'll be the first to say so), so when there *is* something I can do quite well, I don't think it's too awful to admit to it.

Anyhow, I figured that I might just impress Skate Boy, if he was still watching me. I'm rotten at flirting (see? *There's* a thing I can't do!), so dancing well was my best shot at getting his attention. Maybe.

Three tracks later, and I'd worked up enough courage to sneak a peek in the direction of the wall.

No Skate Boy, or his mate.

Well, that was a waste of time, I grumbled to myself.

But I can't say I wasn't surprised. And anyway, I felt kind of nervous about the whole idea, if you want to know the truth. It's like, if I didn't know what to speak to Keith Brownlow about, I sure didn't know what I'd find to speak to a really cool sixteen-year-old boy about, if he'd decided to come over and talk. Which he hadn't.

"Billy – I'm going to the loo," I yelled in his ear, above the music.

"OK!" Billy yelled back, still dancing.

I'd kind of needed to go to the loo for ages, but because I'd been on my mission to impress, I'd put it off. I wished I hadn't, though – there were already three people queuing outside the bathroom door.

To take my mind off my expanding bladder, I started to daydream about the Skate Boy. What if I caught him looking at me again? What if he asked me to dance? What if we got talking? What if he asked for my phone number? What if tonight I ended up with a date after all? But I was rushing way, way, *way* ahead of myself.

I took a long, slow, deep breath… Once I'd been to the loo, I decided, I'd trawl through the flat, and see if I could locate him in the crush of people. I might not have the courage to go right up and talk to him (like, duh!), but at least if I hung out in the same room as him it would up my chances of getting to know him. And I'd just have to worry about what to say to him when (if!) it happened…

"Ally! Oh, brilliant – you're next!"

Kyra appeared at my side, irritating everyone who'd started to queue behind me. While I'd been daydreaming, I hadn't even been aware of the fact that the three people in front of me had been and nearly gone.

"I'm absolutely desperate, Ally – can I nip in before you?" Kyra pleaded. "I'll be quick!"

"Well..." I said, dubiously, knowing I was about to get steamrollered.

"Aw, thanks!" Kyra smiled, crossing her arms across her chest and doing tiny hopping move- ments from side to side.

At that moment, the bathroom door opened, and practically before the poor girl had come out, Kyra was barging past, dragging me in tow.

It seemed we were to have our first girls- gossiping-in-the-loos moment.

"So how are things going with your hot date?" giggled Kyra mischievously, as she plonked herself down on the loo.

"Don't!" I moaned. "And it's all *your* fault. If you'd remembered which school Ricardo went to, and got Billy's name right in the first place, I *might* have sussed it out..."

"Whatever," yawned Kyra, in that irritating way she's got.

But that's what Kyra's like – really good fun and also kind of infuriating. But as I was getting to know her, I was slowly learning *not* to get too wound up by the infuriating side of her character.

"So?" I asked, sensing that she was probably more interested in talking about her own situation than mine. "Are you having a good time?"

In the harsh bathroom light I couldn't help noticing the vivid red rash below her bottom lip and on her chin. A telltale sign of her snogging marathon...

"Well, yeah. It's OK..." Kyra replied, scrunching up her face slightly.

"*That* doesn't sound too enthusiastic!" I frowned.

I'd expected her to be raving on about how fantastic Richie/Ricardo was. What was going on? Had something happened? Maybe Richie/Ricardo was up to his old tricks; maybe Kyra had spotted him eyeing up next week's potential girlfriend.

"Well, I've decided I'll probably chuck him," said Kyra matter-of-factly, as she stood up, smoothed her skirt back down and turned on the sink tap to wash her hands.

I knew it was my turn to go, but I was too surprised to do anything about it.

"You want to *chuck* him?" I gasped. "How come?"

"I'm kind of bored with him. He's really into football and stuff that's just dull, dull, dull..."

Kyra was gazing into the mirror above the sink, inspecting her reflection and running her finger under her eyes where her mascara had started to run.

"Are you going to chuck him *tonight*?" I asked.

I felt almost sorry for Richie/Ricardo, even if he hadn't done or said anything to make me like him. It looked like the heartbreaker was in for a bit of a shock.

"Nah. He's a good kisser. I won't chuck him till tomorrow."

Maybe I'm really dumb, but I always thought you needed to *like* someone if you were going to kiss them. But then, Kyra was pretty good at baffling me.

"I thought you needed to go?" said Kyra unemotionally, glancing over towards the loo.

"Yeah, yeah," I muttered, distractedly unbuttoning my trousers and taking my turn.

If I *was about to chuck a boy*, I thought to myself, *I think I'd be a wobbly pile of jelly*.

Kyra was being so cool it took my breath away. I wondered what had happened at her other schools. Had she been out with lots of boys? Was she always this hard-nosed about them?

"And what about you, Ally? Seen anyone you like here?" asked Kyra, fluffing her curls up with her fingers and readjusting some of her butterfly clips.

"Um, well, I saw this cute boy when I was dancing earlier..." I said, slightly shyly.

"Yeah? What's he like?" she asked, her eyes lit up at the prospect of gossip.

Before I could tell her, there was a hammering at the door.

"Hurry up! Get out of there! NOW!" came a muffled male voice, along with other mumbles from a variety of voices.

I glanced at Kyra, both of us a bit shaken at being yelled at like that, even if there was a large chunk of wood between us and the shouty lad.

Quickly, I got myself together, flushed the loo and opened the door – only to be pushed aside by two lurching boys falling into the room.

"Jeez! Too late!" growled a guy I recognized as Skate Boy's mate, just as Skate Boy hurled projectile vomit all over the bathroom floor.

And Kyra's satin wedge sandals...

Chapter 17

IT'S ALL DOWNHILL FROM HERE...

It wasn't particularly late (we'd left the party early, because it had turned out to be so rubbish), but on the road that circled round the walls of Alexandra Palace, there wasn't a car to be seen.

"Look – see that flashing red light away in the distance?" I pointed out to Kyra. "That's Canary Wharf, down in the Docklands. And that light over there? That's the Telecom Tower, in the West End."

"Wow!" said Kyra, pulling her little black cardie tighter around her body in the chilly evening air. "I'll have to bring my dad up here – he'll love it!"

"You get a better view in the day, though," Billy chipped in. "You can make out the Dome then too."

"Why didn't you point out this stuff when we came up here to the skating the other night?" Kyra chastised Richie/Ricardo.

Richie/Ricardo just shrugged.

I felt like pointing out to her that they were probably too busy snogging when they weren't actually skating at the rink. And when you've got your eyes closed and someone else's face in your way, it's hard to appreciate a view.

"And since we're sightseeing," said Billy. "You see that bench down there?"

"No," replied Kyra, peering down into the unlit, grassy expanse of the park below.

"No, neither can I," Billy, the big joker, agreed with her. "But anyway, there *is* a bench down there, and that's where me and Ally meet up every Sunday, with our dogs. Isn't it, Al?"

"Yep," I nodded, as I turned off the pavement and started walking down the steps into the darkness.

"Where are you going?" asked Kyra, sounding a little concerned.

"We're going down the hill," I told her.

The boys had offered to walk us to the other side of Ally Pally, where – back in the glare of the street lights – me and Kyra could make our separate ways home.

"What – straight down the hill?!" frowned Kyra dubiously. "But I thought we'd just follow the road around!"

"But going down the hill's much quicker," I explained.

(I was trying to convince myself as well as Kyra

at that point – I knew my dad would flip out if he knew we were cutting across the park at night; he thinks that's way too dodgy. OK, so I wouldn't do it on my own, or – like that night – if it was just me and Kyra, but since the boys were going to keep us company, and it wasn't exactly *late* late, I figured it would be fine, just this once. And I planned on sticking the money Dad had given me for a taxi back into his jeans pocket, since it's not like he's got gallons of money to chuck about.)

"And going down the hill's more fun!" grinned Billy. "Come on – run!"

And with that he grabbed my hand and pulled me after him, running headlong into the darkness, where only the tallest branches of the trees stretching up into the starry sky showed any shape.

Half-laughing, half-shrieking, I tumbled after him.

"*I'm* not running down there – it's dark! I could step in dog poo and not realize it! Why can't we just— No, Ricardo! Ricardo! *Waaaaaaahhhhhhh!*"

From the thudding of running footsteps and shrieking giggles coming from Kyra, it didn't sound like Richie/Ricardo had given her a choice. They were right behind me and Billy as we crashed through the rustling, tall grass, halfway down the hill.

Mind you, I didn't know why Kyra was so bothered about the risk of getting dog poo on her precious shoes – not when they'd already been barfed on that night. Even though we'd done a good job of cleaning them up at the kitchen sink, they were still pretty much ruined...

Actually, I think it's safe to say that after the barfing incident, me and Kyra both had a change of heart about our boys. Once we'd cleaned off her shoes and made our way back to the living room (Kyra leaving a trail of wet footprints where she walked), it suddenly became blindingly obvious that practically every lad at the party – not just Skate Boy and his mate – was horribly, obnoxiously drunk. By comparison, Richie/Ricardo and Billy were reassuringly sober, and it was a relief to be back in their company.

"Where have you been?" Billy had asked me when I finally found him, now slouched on the sofa beside Richie/Ricardo. "I thought you were off trying some of that lethal cocktail stuff. I thought I was going to have to roll you home!"

The cocktail stuff that Billy had heard about was the reason so many of the lads (and loads of the girls) at the party were trashed. Billy had heard that someone had found a big bowl and was pouring *everything* alcoholic into it – whatever bottles people had brought had been chucked in there, as well as stuff that had been raided from the house.

I felt kind of sorry for the boy whose party it was – his parents were going to kill him when they saw how trashed their house was and how much of their own booze supply had been raided. But Billy told me not to waste my time: the guy whose party it was the one who was making the "cocktails"…

"Yeah, suckers – we're beating you!" Ricardo called out, streaking past us with a yelping Kyra, the two of them just hazy blurs in the darkness.

"You want a race? You've *got* a race!" Billy yelled after them. "C'mon, Al!"

I gasped breathlessly as we hurtled headlong down the hill, Billy still holding my hand tight. It was funny; I'd been building up the party in my head since I'd heard I was going, and yet this – acting like a ten year old, with my best mate – was much more fun than anything else had been the whole night. (Although, in a *weird* way, I'd quite enjoyed Skate Boy's little party trick – it was just the novelty of a boy making a fool of himself in front of *me*, instead of the other way round…)

Finally, the hill slipped away into the flat, grassy expanse at the bottom, and the occasional window light from the flats that backed on to Ally Pally lit our faces with a watery light.

"We won!" Billy panted, holding my hand aloft in the air.

Richie/Ricardo and Kyra didn't say anything – they just grinned and tried to get their breath back. But I noticed the way they were standing with their arms round each other. It looked like Kyra might have changed her mind about chucking him quite yet…

"Hey," said Richie/Ricardo, once he could speak. "You said you lived over in Palace Heights Road, didn't you?"

He was talking to me (and I suspected he still didn't remember my name).

"Yes," I nodded.

"Well," he panted, "that entrance over there is closest to you. But the entrance over there is closer to Kyra's. So we're going *that* way…"

Even in the faintly lit gloom, I could see the way that Kyra was gazing mushily into his eyes. Looked like the two of them were telling us in no uncertain terms that they were off for a romantic stroll – and we were not invited.

As we waved the two of them off, I turned to Billy.

"You don't have to come any further," I told him. "You'll just have to go all the way back up over the hill."

"Nah, it's all right," he shrugged, starting to walk down towards the alleyway. "I'm thirsty after all that running. I'll walk you down to that twenty-four-hour shop on the main road and get a Coke or something, and then maybe get the bus home."

OK, so I was doing a total turnaround. Suddenly, I remembered one of the advantages of male friends compared to female friends – they can act like your protector the way a girl can't.

We had just come out of the alleyway into a sleepy little street, when Billy came out with something that nearly squeezed what little air I had left right out of my lungs.

"Hey, I meant to say," he shrugged, his hands shoved in his jeans pockets. "What was my mum phoning your dad about the other night?"

"Huh?" I blinked at him.

Sure, my dad knew Billy's mum, but only vaguely. My own mum had been quite pally with her – they'd met when Billy and I were in playgroup together. But Dad didn't know her or Billy's dad particularly well at all. I mean, if they bumped into each other round Crouch End, then they'd stop and say hello and stuff, but calling each other up?

"What, didn't he say she'd phoned?" asked Billy.

I shook my head, silently.

"Well, maybe I got it wrong. It was just that I heard her call whoever it was 'Martin', and I just thought of your dad. It was probably some other guy she knows. She knows loads of people. She's got a better social life than *me*."

I tried to tell my befuddled head that that was the answer. She was talking to someone else, not my dad. No way.

"You know, it must have been someone else, 'cause she was arranging to meet them on Sunday. Tomorrow, I mean," Billy shrugged.

There were shivers zipping up and down my back. I didn't know what to think, what to say, what to do.

"Billy," I suddenly found myself choking out, "thanks for walking me over the hill, but I've got to run, I'm really late..."

I didn't even give Billy a chance to say bye as I pounded the pavement at top speed. I didn't even think about the fact that he must be wondering what I was on about (late? How could I be late when we'd ducked out of the party early?). All that was in my head was the memory of Gran passing that message on to Dad on Thursday.

"If you're still up for Sunday, then give her a call," I muttered, repeating the message as I ran, my heart pounding.

Call "her".

Billy's mum.

I just couldn't believe it...

Chapter (18)

IT CAN ONLY GET WORSE...

I stared at the map on the wall, faintly lit by the light from the street lamp outside my window, since I'd left my curtains open.

I felt restless and hot under the covers, and kicked my duvet off me.

An indignant "Prrrp!" from the bottom of the bed made me realize that a small, furry entity had been adding to the temperature of my overheating bed.

"Sorry," I whispered, to a cat that wasn't Colin, as I sat upright and hauled the duvet off it.

Before I could identify which cat it was, it thumped off the bed in a grump, heading off to another part of the room where its sleep wouldn't be so rudely disturbed.

Now that I was sitting, I let my hand stretch up the wall and touch the jutting-out coloured pins that mark all the places Mum has sent letters home from. Sometimes the pattern of the pins confuses me; they seem so random, like she's doubling back on herself a lot of the time. One time, she'll be in

Thailand, then a couple of months later we'll get a letter from America, then it'll be back to Indonesia again. "How can she afford it?" I asked Linn once, when I was old enough to work out that travel wasn't free. "All the long-term backpackers know how to live on next to no money," she'd told me, like she knew the answer to everything (which she usually does). "They all tell each other where the cheapest places are to stay, or where they can go and work for a while. And look what Mum's said when she's written – she's painting T-shirts and selling them, or waitressing sometimes too. That's how she pays for travelling."

What was most annoying was that she was on the move so much, she never had an address long enough for us to write back to her. That was hard, only having this one-way contact with her. There'd been plenty of times when I really, really felt that I needed to talk to her. Like now...

But what could I possibly write? "Dear Mum – remember your friend Sharon? Billy's mum? Well, it looks like she's having an affair with Dad..."

I shuddered at the thought and felt suddenly cold. Gathering up the duvet, I bundled myself up against the headboard, and – with only my nose sticking out – I stared off out of my window at the faraway outline of Alexandra Palace.

I mean, Billy's mum, of all people! She's *so* not like my mum. She's this neat-freak with a house full of stuff that's so new it's practically still got the price tags on. She runs some clothes section in a department store in Wood Green. The kind of clothes she sells, they're all sort of *womanly* and *middle-aged*, if you see what I mean. You know – jackets with gold buttons and knee-length skirts, worn with smart, high-heeled shoes. I know she's got to dress like that at work, but she dresses like that at home too. I think if I ever went round to Billy's and saw her in a pair of jeans and without her hair blow-dried, I'd faint.

I know I might sound like I'm judging by appearances (guilty!), but there's another thing about Billy's mum – she orders people about in that patronizing management way in the store, and does *that* at home too. "Billy," she'll say, lifting his feet off the coffee table, "we have standards!"

I don't know how Billy's dad stands it. (Not that I know Billy's dad too well even after all these years; he's one of those people who looks at children and teenagers like they're an unknown species, as if he's never been one himself and has no idea how to communicate with them.) Billy says his dad just agrees with everything his mum says and keeps his head down in his newspaper or whatever.

Well, he might not have to do that much longer … not if his wife's running off with my dad! I thought gloomily, feeling a sorry-for-myself pool of tears forming in my eyes.

A thump on the bed heralded the return of a cat that wasn't Colin. Tor always says that animals can sense your emotions (I don't know if that goes for stick insects too), and that they'll come to you when you need comfort. I reached my hand out from my duvet cocoon, and stroked the purry furrball – and when I felt the short stump of tail, I knew it was Fluffy.

"Hey, puss – what's going to happen, eh?" I whispered.

Fluffy rubbed her face against my nose in response.

"What if she tries to move in here?" I muttered. "She'll want to paint everything – she'll want to throw all our furniture in a skip. She'll want to get rid of loads of our animals, just so she doesn't get pet hairs on her precious business suits!"

I jolted as soon as I'd said it.

Precious.

She'd want to take her horrible, yappy, manicured poodle to live with us, while Rolf and Winslet would be relegated to a hut in the garden, or worse.

Then another thought struck me.

Billy – Billy would be my half-brother!

I flopped back in the bed and flung the duvet over my face.

It was all too weird and it was making my head go positively twisty...

Chapter 19

ACTION STATIONS!

If it was twisty before, my head was totally muzzy when I woke up.

There was too much noise and barking and voices and sounds blaring from the TV and the radio for this early in the morning. I forced one eye open and looked at my alarm clock – and got a shock when I saw it was half-eleven already.

I felt a dead weight on my legs and peered down the bed, to see that Fluffy had transformed into Colin at some point. He snuffled in his sleep, as I pulled my feet out from under him and swung them off the bed.

Dad and everyone must have thought I wanted a long lie-in this morning, since I was partying last night, I decided, as I pulled an old cardie over my PJs and headed for the door.

Dad had been snoring in an armchair in the living room when I got in the night before – the house was still and quiet apart from the tappity-tap of Rolf and Winslet sleepily padding over the wooden floors to investigate who'd just got in. But it wasn't the party that had tired me out and let the morning slip by – it was the fact that my brain was working overtime and hadn't shut down till who knows what time in the early hours of the morning.

"Morning, Ally – or should I say afternoon?"

I blinked down the stairs and saw Grandma gazing up at me from the hall. She was helping Tor into his jacket. Tor, meanwhile, was swapping a packet of Wotsits from one hand to the other, while trying to keep them out of Winslet's reach. So *that* was what all the barking was about.

"Hi, Grandma," I replied, rubbing my eyes and stepping down the stairs. "What are you doing here?"

"Me and Tor are going to the City Farm, aren't we?" she said, turning back to my little brother.

" 'Cause Dad can't take him…" I muttered, remembering what Tor had told me over our hot chocolate the day before.

"That's right – he's busy today," said Grandma, giving me what looked like a hint of a meaningful stare.

"Busy," said Tor, giving me a *big* meaningful stare.

I suddenly felt wide awake. I had to talk to my sisters – Linn in particular – to find what our plan of action was.

"Is Dad still here?" I asked Grandma, at the same

time nicking a Wotsit out of Tor's upheld bag, now that I was standing beside him.

"Yes. He's in the shower, I think. Right then, Tor – are we ready?"

"Uh-huh," nodded Tor, heading for the door.

"Have fun. Bye!" I called out, as I padded off towards the kitchen.

"Ally…!"

I turned and saw Tor at the opened front door, holding his thumb up to me.

That was "good luck" in code, if I wasn't very much mistaken. I nodded and put my thumb up in return.

"At last!" said Linn, looking up from the Sunday supplement she had open on the kitchen table in front of her. "Even Rowan's beaten you to it this morning."

That was amazing. Rowan was always the last to emerge from her bed at weekends. But there she was, sitting in her tartan, flannelette pyjamas, looking only three-quarters still asleep.

"Sit down, Al," Linn practically ordered me. "We haven't a lot of time. Dad's going out in half an hour. Says he's going to help 'Jake' fix his bike this afternoon!"

Linn's voice dripped with disbelief at Dad's lame excuse.

Before I did sit down, I stepped back to the kitchen door and pushed it closed. Then I walked over to the radio and turned it up louder – there was no way I wanted Dad earwigging on *this* conversation.

"Has Rowan told you what Tor heard?" I asked Linn, who was fully dressed in a black top, black jeans and trainers. Me and Rowan must have looked like bag ladies beside her...

"Yeah, she told me last night. I just wish you hadn't slept in when we needed to talk about this!" said Linn, a little snappily.

The longer I hadn't come down, the more up-tight she'd been getting, by the looks of it.

"Listen," I began, ignoring her snippy tone. "You're not going to believe what Billy said to me last night!"

"What?" asked Rowan, pushing her unruly hair back off her face.

"He said..." I paused, checking in my head that I hadn't dreamt the whole horrible thing, "that his mum had been on the phone to Dad – arranging to meet up with him today!"

Linn and Rowan stared at me with similar open-mouthed expressions. For once, they actually looked alike.

"Your mate *Billy*? His *mum* and our *dad*?" Linn repeated, incredulously.

Both of them knew who she was. At least, they knew her to say hello to, if nothing much more than that.

"Billy's mum?" squeaked Rowan, her brown eyes the size of saucers. "But isn't she married? To Billy's dad, I mean?"

"Well, *yes*," I said, rolling my eyes at her.

"What's Billy saying about it? Was he freaking out?" asked Linn, almost managing to slip back into her organized and in-control self after the shock.

Still, her skin looked paler than pale against her almost-blonde hair.

"No! He didn't get the significance – and I didn't really want to spell it out for him," I told her.

"What did he say exactly?" asked Rowan.

"Just what I said. Literally, just that he overheard her talking to 'Martin', saying she'd meet him on Sunday."

"Ally – quick, before Dad gets downstairs," said Linn urgently. "Phone Billy; ask him if he heard where they were supposed to be going!"

"If he heard it, he won't remember!" I protested. "He's a boy! Boys don't remember details!"

"Ally, you've got to try!" Linn flashed her eyes icily at me. "It's going to be really hard trying to follow Dad if we don't know where he's going, but if Billy *has* overheard something, it'll make it much easier!"

I sighed – there was no saying no to Linn.

"I'll try," I promised, pushing my chair back and heading for the hall. "But don't get your hopes up. It *is* Billy we're talking about after all…"

"Just do it," said Linn firmly.

Peering up the stairs, I could hear Dad still singing in the bathroom, while the taps in the sink rushed and the pipes gurgled and rattled.

Quickly, I dialled Billy's number.

"Hello?" came his familiar voice, after a couple of rings.

"Billy? It's me," I told him.

"Oh, hi, Al! I was just heading off for the park. Aren't you coming?"

"Uh, I hadn't thought about it," I replied, slightly flummoxed.

My brain was too fried to deal with ordinary, run-of-the-mill habits. But he'd pricked my conscience – I gazed around me in the hall, and saw two expectant doggy faces gazing back up. Rolf even had his Frisbee in his mouth.

"What are you phoning for, then?" asked Billy. "Are you OK? Did you get home all right last night? You ran off pretty fast. I thought—"

"Billy," I interrupted him, lowering my voice to a whisper, even though the singing and pipe-rattling showed that Dad wasn't about to walk out of the bathroom on me. "I need to ask you a question."

"Fire away," he said, sounding intrigued. "But why are you whispering?"

"It doesn't matter – just listen," I snapped at him, Linn-style. "Is your mum still there?"

"Uh … no. She's just gone out. About five minutes ago."

And Dad was leaving soon too. Urgh, the whole mess *had* to be true…

"Billy, this is going to sound weird, OK, but when you heard your mum on the phone the other day – you know, when she was speaking to my dad or whichever Martin she was talking to – did you hear her say *where* she was meeting him on Sunday? Today, I mean?"

"Uh … I don't remember."

Wow, what a surprise.

"Are you sure?" I pushed him.

"Hold on!" he said, brightly. "Dad's just through in the living room. He might know. Wait and I'll ask—"

"No!" I yelped down the phone.

It was complicated enough trying to work out what was going on with Dad and Billy's mum – we didn't need to alert Billy's dad to the fact that his wife might be cheating on him. Well, not *quite* yet…

"Why not? What's up?"

Any other day, I might have been able to come up with a sharp excuse (i.e. white lie) to cover my tracks, but since my brain was as scrambled as the eggs going cold and rubbery on Tor's plate through in the kitchen, I failed miserably.

"Billy, can you come round here? Now?"

"Why?"

"Just come, will you?"

"Um, OK. I'll be there in about half an hour. I'll take Precious with me…"

"No!" I yelped again.

My wide-awake nightmares came flooding back; I didn't want Precious coming here, trying to get his horrid little paws under the table.

"Why not?" asked Billy, sounding confused.

"Just come, will you? And quick – come on your bike?"

"Why?"

The singing suddenly stopped, and the pipes were gurgling to a halt. Dad was going to pull that door open at any second.

"See you in ten minutes!" I hissed down the phone, before slamming it back on the receiver.

Rolf nuzzled his damp nose under my hand and whined.

"I feel like that myself today," I muttered, ruffling the spiky fur on his head.

I SPY WITH MY LITTLE EYE...

I don't know if Dad thought it was weird or anything, the fact that the four of us were all hovering about down at the end of the garden, but there wasn't much else we could do. The trouble was, he was wandering up and down the house too much, getting ready to go out, and the garden was just about the only place we could talk without risking him overhearing.

"*My* mum and *your* dad!" Billy exclaimed for the fortieth time since I'd told him what we suspected.

He'd taken it better than I thought he would, but to tell you the truth, I don't think it had sunk in. He had this stunned-yet-dumb expression on his face, like he'd just heard that Lara Croft had come to life and moved into the house across the road from him.

Me, I was feeling marginally calmer after my middle-of-the-night flip-out, but only marginally. I mean, I still felt really down about it all, but not so *frantic*. I know it's the sort of thing Grandma comes out with, but that stuff about "things always look better in the morning" is true, kind of. I maybe still felt totally weird about my dad being up to something with Billy's mum, but at least I'd got over that *ridiculous* idea of Billy being my half-brother. I mean, *as if*!

(Oh, please, please, *please*, God, don't let it come true!)

"Billy, are you *sure* you didn't hear where your mum was supposed to be going today?" Linn tried him again.

She was perched on the old swing, while the rest of us (and both the dogs) were hunkered down on the grass. Even at a time like this, it was pretty funny to see that Linn was still making sure her clothes stayed clean and free of grass blades.

"Nope, that's all I heard her say on the phone." He shook his head.

"Damn!" hissed Linn. "I suppose I'm just going to have to follow him when he leaves, and hope I don't lose him..."

"I'm sorry," shrugged Billy, petting Winslet, who'd moseyed up beside him and flopped her head in his lap.

"Hold on, Linnhe – how come you're saying '*I'm* going to follow him'?" Rowan demanded, peering at our sister through the pink, hexagonal sunglasses she'd shoved on to come outside. "Why should *you* go? Why don't we *all* go?"

Rowan had a point. But I had a better one.

"If anyone goes, it should be me and Billy – since *his* mum's involved in all this…"

"Rowan," said Linn flatly, completely ignoring the fact that I'd spoken. "For a start, you couldn't spy on anyone – they'd spot you a mile off."

Rowan opened her mouth to protest, then shut it again, with a slight wobble of her lip.

Linn was right, of course, and even Rowan could see that. Our in-between sister didn't know the meaning of dressing down, and no matter how well she hid, it would be practically impossible for Dad not to see a *glint* of something to do with Rowan, out of the corner of his eye.

"And *you* two," Linn continued, turning to me and Billy. "Well, OK, I see your point, but I'm coming as well."

Aha! She *had* heard me after all. And now She Who Must Be Obeyed had spoken, so it looked like the three of us had better get our spy-heads on…

"Winslet! Leave Billy alone!" I said, suddenly noticing that our small, hairy monster was showing her terrier side and trying to bury her way into Billy's jacket pocket.

"It's OK," Billy grinned, trying to gently remove her frantically snuffling nose from the inside of his jacket. But it didn't do any good. "I must have a couple of doggy biscuits left over in there from walking Precious."

There was nothing for it but forcible removal. I grabbed Winslet round the tummy and lifted her off her feet and out of Billy's pocket.

"Ewwwww! What's she eating?" cringed Rowan.

I turned her round to face me and heard the crunch of doggy treats. The trouble was, Winslet hadn't been very selective about what exactly was in Billy's pocket and also seemed to be chewing on an old snotty hankie and a piece of green notepaper.

Time for Tor's trick: I plopped her down on the grass and grabbed her by the scruff of the neck. And *voila*, her jaws flipped open and out tumbled the remains of her snack.

Winslet let out a long, low growl of irritation.

"Sorry, Billy," I apologized, picking up the piece of scrawled-on green paper by the least-chewed side. "Is this important?"

"Nah, I can't even remember what it is," he replied, flipping it round from one side to the other. "Oh, yes I can – it was just the name of this new Dreamcast game Richie phoned me up to tell me about. That's all. It's noth ... oh."

"Oh?" I repeated, watching as Billy squinted at the writing on the other side of the note.

"'The Chesterton Hotel, W1. Sun. 1 p.m.,'" Billy read out in a monotoned mumble. "Hey, this is my mum's handwriting!"

"Bingo!" I cried out, feeling my heart leap at our unexpected breakthrough.

"Really?" said Linn, out of the blue, her eyes ridiculously wide. "Hey, sounds like a good party!"

Me, Billy and Rowan stared at her. Had the sun gone to her head?

Then it clicked – we were talking in code. Dad must be in the area.

I turned around, shielding my eyes with my hand.

"Hi Dad!" I chirped, hoping I sounded cheerful (and innocent).

"Hi guys!" said Dad, wandering over in his normal weekend jeans, T-shirt and old denim jacket.

If he hadn't have slicked his hair back with gel or whatever, he wouldn't have looked at all suspicious.

"So what are you lot up to?" he asked, gazing around at all four of us.

"Oh, just hanging out. Talking about the party Ally and Billy were at last night," said Linn, very convincingly. (Give the girl an Oscar!)

"Good, was it?" he smiled down at me and Billy in particular.

"Hu-unghh…" Billy croaked, obviously too fazed by the situation to communicate in English.

"Yes!" I answered brightly, to make up for him.

"Great stuff!" nodded Dad. "Well, I better be going. Um, see you later, guys…"

"Have fun fixing Jake's bike!" Linn couldn't resist calling after him, as he strolled back to the kitchen door.

"Linn!" I hissed, once Dad was safely inside. "That sounded really sarcastic!"

"No, it didn't – you're just paranoid," said Linn, pushing herself off the swing. "Right, as soon as Dad's gone, I'm going to have to make a quick call to Alfie and blow him out – I was supposed to meet him this afternoon. Rowan, like I said, you can't come. But make yourself useful and look up the address of that hotel in the Yellow Pages. OK?"

"Uh-huh," nodded Rowan, looking none too excited by her role in the action.

"Come on, Billy," I said, standing up and hauling my brain-numbed friend to his feet. "Operation Parent-catcher starts here."

Billy blinked at me for a second, then turned the collar of his jacket up and the brim of his baseball cap down.

"Ready for action!" he saluted me.

"Billy," I sighed, "you look more like a failed member of a boy band than a spy."

I yanked the brim of his hat down till it covered his whole face...

Chapter 21

THE FOUR MUSKETEERS...

"How much longer do you think we'll have to wait?" Billy whinged.

"For as long as it takes till they both come out," Linn said, her voice tinged with irritation.

Billy was drumming one knee up and down so fast under the table that our nearly empty cups and saucers were rattling gently on the formica table. I knew that was going to drive Linn insane (it was bugging me too, but Linn's levels of irritation are *infinitely* more finely tuned than mine...).

I stuck my hand across and grabbed Billy's knee – then pushed down hard.

"What?" asked Billy, his eyebrows knitted in confusion.

"Quit it," I told him, eyeballing him hard and trying to communicate to him through my stare that he was testing Linn's patience.

Billy scrunched up his face into an expression that said "Huh?"

Subtlety goes right over boys' heads, doesn't it?

"You're drumming your leg. It's annoying. Stop it," I spelt out for him more graphically.

Billy flopped his elbows on the table and rested his chin on his hands in real hangdog mode, but I didn't have the energy to talk him round. My nerves were ... well, all the things nerves *are* rolled into one. You name it and they were doing it: straining, fraying and jangling. And the pathetic thing was, it wasn't just the tense waiting game that was causing it, it was all because we had an extra spy in tow...

When Linn had phoned Alfie and told him she couldn't hang out with him that afternoon and why, he'd only gone and decided to invite himself along. It was a bit of a cheek really – as if he was joining us on some excellent adventure, instead of trying to find out something that could have pretty far-reaching implications on both our families and futures.

Well, that's what I'd have thought of any *other* person muscling in our spying mission, but we *were* talking Alfie, here. And I know I've got the invisible version of Rowan's rose-tinted sun-specs on when it comes to him, but what can a girl do? When your heart goes ping! your heart goes ping...

"What time is it anyway?" I asked, glancing round the café for any sign of a clock.

My heart skipped a beat or three as I spotted Alfie's messy blond hair over by the counter, where he'd gone to buy us more refills.

"Coming up for three o'clock," Linn muttered, staring down at the watch on her wrist.

We'd been sitting in the café, which (lucky or what?) was right across from the entrance to the Chesterton Hotel. By the time we'd got into town (the Tube seems to run in slow motion on Sundays), it was just after one o'clock. We weren't too bothered about missing seeing either Dad or Billy's mum heading into the hotel: as long as we knew they were there, we were happy to wait. (OK – bad choice of words: we were *willing* to wait...)

There was one little problem, though – a small niggle that kept pulsating through my mind. I wanted to say it out loud, but I was a bit scared. Scared of Linn *growling* at me over it.

Still, time was ticking away. For one thing, I had to say it out loud now, before Alfie came back to the table and I turned back into the burbling birdbrain I always was in front of him. (Luckily, both the bus and the Tube we'd taken into town were crowded, and Billy and I had had to sit at a safe distance away from Alfie and Linn. Safe, because I was far enough away not to open my mouth and say something stupid in Alfie's hearing, but not so far away that I couldn't ogle him from time to time...)

The second reason I had to make my point was that Dad and Billy's mum could come out of the hotel at *any* moment. Therefore...

"Um, Linn...?"

"What?" said Linn, staring intently over at the entrance to the hotel.

"Linn – if, I mean *when* Dad and Billy's mum come out," I began, sheepishly, "what are we ... well, what are we going to do?"

"Video them and send it in to *You've Been Framed*?" Billy jumped in, before Linn could say anything.

(I blamed mild hysteria for his bad joke. But then *all* Billy's jokes are pretty bad...)

Linn was frowning. I wasn't sure whether it was Billy being frivolous that had irked her, or me daring to question her authority (i.e. ask awkward questions). But I had a feeling I was about to find out.

But before Linn opened her mouth, someone else spoke.

"I just think you guys should play it cool..." Alfie's voice drifted down, as he hovered by my side with the tray of drinks.

I couldn't look up at him – I was frozen to the spot. I'd never, ever been this close to him before. My heart did a backflip as he leant right across me – the heat of his breath brushing my face – passing a coffee over to Linn.

"How do we play it cool?" asked Billy. "Do we say 'Hi, there! So you two are having an affair? Hey – no problem!'"

Linn flashed her eyes at Billy for daring to take the mickey out of whatever Alfie had said.

"No – I just mean, don't go out there yelling or something," Alfie drawled in his lazy, laid-back voice.

I went cross-eyed staring at his lightly tanned arm as it passed dangerously close to my nose. As he dumped a can of Lilt in front of Billy, I turned into Winslet and sniffed the air manically, trying to breathe a bit of Alfie in.

"Like, if I was you, I'd just walk along the opposite side of the pavement, saying nothing, till they saw me. Then let *them* do the talking..." Alfie continued, putting a steamy cup down in front of me. "Hot chocolate, wasn't it, Ally?"

I had to respond. I would look like a total twerp if I didn't – I'd already sat for two hours at this table letting everyone else do the talking so I didn't have to make a fool of myself.

"Cue!" I squawked.

(Translation: "Thank you!")

I turned and focussed my eyes on his face, only centimetres from my own. Those bony, high cheekbones, that long, thin nose, those pale, pale grey eyes ("same colour as a collie dog's!" Tor had so kindly pointed out once), those lips...

Er, rewind to the pale grey eyes. Where exactly were they staring right at this minute?

Only at my hand, the one that was still clutching Billy's knee next to me.

And – once again – I'd managed to make the one boy I'd *always* fancied think I was going out with the one boy I'd *never* fancy...

Chapter 22

WATCHING AND WAITING. AND WAITING SOME MORE...

"What time is it now?" I asked Linn.

"Nearly four," she mumbled, without dragging her gaze away from the entrance to the Chesterton.

She'd got into the habit of checking her watch every few minutes like a reflex action, and was probably counting every second in time with her heartbeat.

"*Yeahhhh!*" came a loud roar from the back of the café.

Linn narrowed her eyes and shot a dark look at the two boys playing on the fruit machine.

It had seemed really considerate of Alfie to suggest a turn on the machine to Billy, when Billy had begun to look a bit maudlin earlier and started mumbling stuff about his "poor dad". But half an hour later, and it looked like they were enjoying their game just that little bit *too* much; like they'd somehow managed to forget the whole purpose of our "jaunt" today...

"Boys..." tutted Linn, folding her arms across her chest. "They've got the attention span of a *newt*."

"Yep," I agreed with her.

Although, to be honest, I was kind of glad they'd moved away. I hadn't been able to look at, never mind *talk* in front of Alfie since he'd clocked me clutching Billy's knee.

"You don't think Dad and Billy's mum have left already, do you?" I asked my all-knowing sister, while systematically tearing apart the plastic cup I'd just drunk my Coke out of. (The café owners must have been toying with giving us *shares* in the place, the amount of time and money we'd spent in there.)

"Left? How could they have left?" said Linn, sounding a little short with me. "We've been sitting here watching that entrance for nearly three solid hours. Well, at least *you* and *me* have..."

"I know," I tried to agree with her. "But maybe they snuck out the back entrance or something. You know, just in case they were spotted!"

"For one thing," sighed Linn, "they aren't *expecting* to be followed, so there's no *point* in them sneaking out the back. For another, they wouldn't *go* sneaking out the back because they're not *film stars*, for God's sake. It's only *famous* people who sneak out through the kitchens – or hadn't you noticed?"

Forgive me for having such a lowly brain compared to yours, Miss Smart Alec! I felt like saying.

Except I didn't.

"Hey, I was thinking," I said instead, while eyeing up the phone box on the other side of the road, just along from the entrance to the Chesterton. "Rowan'll be at home going crazy – we should let her know what's going on."

Or *not* going on. Watching a Sunday afternoon's worth of traffic zip by was about as interesting as it had got.

"Yeah, good idea," nodded Linn.

The tension was starting to show on her, I noticed. It wasn't just her excessive snappiness (a couple of degrees up on her *normal* snappiness), it was also the fact that a couple of tendrils of hair had escaped from her scraped-back ponytail, and she *hadn't bothered fixing them*.

I rest my case.

"I've got some change. I'll go and call her from over there," I pointed to the phone box opposite.

"OK," said Linn, sounding weary.

It was all getting to her, it really was. Linn does such a good job of hiding all her emotions away (apart from the grumpy ones) that I think the very *effort* of doing that tires her out more than the rest of us.

I glanced back into the café as I made my way out of the door, and saw Billy staring intently at the display on the fruit machine while he hammered away on the buttons. At the same time, Alfie was cheering him on, grinning his wide grin and showing off that twinkling, gold back tooth.

I felt my knees buckle...

But my knees had to behave themselves once I got out in the fresh air (or traffic-polluted air, since we were in the West End of London). I had to make it across the road and into the phone box quickly, just in case Dad appeared at the front door of the hotel at that moment. I didn't really fancy getting stuck in the middle of the road and confronting him with "What exactly do you think you're doing, Dad?" while a stream of black cabs thundered in front of me, drowning me out.

Once I was safely (and breathlessly) in the phone box, I dialled our home number, then turned to stare back at the now-nearby hotel entrance while I waited for Rowan to pick up.

"Hello?" I heard her say.

"Ro?" I panted. "It's me. Listen—"

"No, hold on, Ally – I'm so glad you phoned! I've got some news..." she interrupted me.

As she began to tell me her news, I stopped staring off into the distance. Instead, I just saw my own reflection in the glass panels on the phone-box door. And all over my face was written "Oh. My. God."

The pips sounded – my twenty pence had run out. But it didn't matter; I'd heard all I needed to hear.

I replaced the handset and pushed the door open. But instead of crossing the road straight away, I made my way along the pavement to the entrance of the hotel. Right before I walked up the few marble steps that would take me into the foyer, I glanced across at the café, and saw Linn sitting where I'd left her, in the window seat, frowning over at me and mouthing "What are you doing?"

"Hold on!" I mouthed back, holding up my hand to her.

I didn't need to go all the way in to see what I needed to see. From out here on the top step, I could peer through the glass double doors at the noticeboard standing just inside. The noticeboard that had all the details of what was going on the hotel's various function suites.

"So it's true!" I heard myself say out (very) loud, as my eyes fixed on what Rowan had told me to look for...

DAD'S DARK SECRET (AHEM)

"Wow. I mean, *wow*!"

It was all Sandie had been able to say since we'd filled her in on the whole sordid story. (Not, thankfully, that there was anything too sordid about it in the end...)

Sandie was sitting on the swing next to Kyra's, wrapped up (by her mother) in a padded black coat that looked a bit like a duvet. She must have been sweltering – it was a warmish Sunday evening and the rest of us weren't even wearing jackets.

"So you and Billy spent three hours sitting in some café this afternoon for *nothing*?" said Kyra, a hint of a teasing smile on her face.

I was mildly tempted to run over and shove her off the swing that she was twirling on, but I couldn't be bothered untangling my crossed legs and getting up off the ground. Also, it seemed a bit mean, since I was feeling practically giddy with relief right now.

"Well, it wasn't exactly for *nothing*, was it?" said

Billy, perched on the saddle of his mountain bike and leaning on the handlebars. "I mean, we had to try and find out what was going on, or *if* anything was going on!"

"But like you say, there *wasn't* anything going on – well, not what *you* two thought, anyway!" Kyra laughed, leaning her head languidly against one of the swing chains.

During the last couple of weeks of the Dad Drama, I hadn't breathed a word about it to Kyra. In fact, I hadn't told any of my friends except Sandie (because she's good at being super-sympathetic) and Billy (because I *had* to), and that's the way I thought it would stay. But as soon as we'd arrived at the park this evening, Billy had blabbed it all to Kyra – by accident.

What had happened was that me and Billy had arranged to meet up with Sandie in Priory Park at seven o'clock. (Billy had stayed at mine for his tea – well, after dragging him into a drama that was, after all, *not* a drama, asking him to stay for tea was the least I could do. And Rowan wasn't cooking, so it was safe.)

I was desperate to tell Sandie what we'd found out that afternoon, and Sandie was desperate to get out of the house and away from her pink cell, so the kids' playground – mercifully free of small, shrill children at that time in the evening – was where we'd decided on to meet up and catch up.

What we *hadn't* expected when we got there was to find Kyra dangling on a swing, waiting to meet Richie/Ricardo (who obviously wasn't quite dumped yet). And what *I* personally hadn't expected was for Billy to suddenly launch into a blow-by-blow account of everything that had happened that day, which was supposed to be for Sandie's ears only. I guess with the business of the party and everything, he'd just figured (wrongly) that me and Kyra were a couple of stages further along the friendship trail than we actually were. But you could tell he was regretting it now; he wasn't as used to Kyra's cheekily sarky ways as me and Sandie.

"Where's your boyfriend? Isn't he late?" I said to Kyra, changing the subject. "Maybe you got it wrong – maybe he meant for you to meet him at the kids' playground up at Ally Pally instead. That would be closer to his house..."

"Nice try, but you're not getting rid of me that easily!" grinned Kyra, seeing through my feeble attempt to distract her. "I'm enjoying hearing all this stuff far too much!"

Actually, I didn't particularly mind her teasing.

After the stresses of the last little while, it was kind of nice to have a laugh about it.

"Awww!" sighed Sandie, out of the blue, a soppy little smile on her face.

"Awww, what?" I frowned at her, wondering what planet she was currently residing on.

"I was just thinking about Tor – it's so sweet that he sorted out this whole mystery!"

You know how I said she can turn on the waterworks really easily? Well, right then, it looked like she was in danger of going all gushy over my little brother. Her eyes were looking suspiciously dewy. (But then she *had* been ill with gastric flu all week. Maybe she was just suffering from a case of conjunctivitus.)

"Fnar!" snorted Kyra. "That's the funniest thing about all this, Ally! While you and your sisters all managed to convince yourselves that your dad was up to no good, a blimmin' *seven* year old is busy sussing out what's *really* going on!"

"Thanks, Kyra. Rub it in, why don't you!" I grinned back at her.

But she was right. It did seem ridiculous when you looked at it that way. After all, while me, Billy, Linn and Alfie had spent our Sunday afternoon acting like the cast of *Scooby Doo* (er, minus Scooby Doo) on the trail of skullduggery, Tor had got to the bottom of the mystery in one easy step: by asking the right person a straightforward question.

"Dad's acting weird," Tor had begun, as he and Grandma sat on the bus on the way to the City Farm. "Do you know why?"

And, as I should have expected, she did. Not much gets past our gran, whether it's something to do with us kids, or her grown-up son-in-law.

"So did your grandma know all along?" asked Sandie, so entranced with the whole story that Kyra's sarcasm was shooting over the top of her head.

"No," I replied, stretching my legs out in front of me. They were going to sleep the way I was sitting. "Like I said, she'd had her suspicions that something was going on, but it was only after she took that message for him – the one from Billy's mum – that she asked him what was up."

And here's what *was* up.

Billy's mum had no intention of getting her perfectly manicured claws into my dad (phew). Instead, it turned out she was trying to do the Girl Guide thing and do a good deed: she'd bumped into my dad on the Broadway one day a couple of weeks back, and started giving him a hard time about never getting out and having no social life (ever since Mum had gone, natch). Dad had wittered on about being happy to stay at home with us lot (bless him), but Billy's mum kept on at him. Finally, she persuaded (i.e. bullied) him to come along to the regular Wednesday evening class she and Billy's dad did.

What could Dad do? He's so easy-going, he'd never be able to say no to someone as determined and persistent as Billy's mum. And so, he found himself – wait for it...

Line dancing.

I know. Shocking, isn't it?

"No wonder your dad didn't want to tell you what he was doing!" sniggered Kyra. "I mean, *line* dancing, for God's sake! How corny is that?"

Exactly. That is *exactly* why he hadn't told us what he was up to. He said as much when we spoke to him about it this afternoon, when he'd arrived back home and seen from all our expressions that We Knew.

(Me, Linn and the boys had beaten him back to the house. After Rowan told me over the phone what was going on – Grandma and Tor had filled *her* in after they got back from their day out – I'd double-checked by reading the board in the hotel lobby. As soon as I saw "Ambassador Ballroom: Line dancing workshop, 1–5 p.m.", I'd run across the road, spilt my news, and we'd all beaten a hasty retreat back to Crouch End.)

"So you know, then?" Dad had said sheepishly, confronted by us all in the kitchen.

(By the way, we just let him believe we'd heard about his heel-toe-tapping adventures from Grandma. Admitting that we'd been trailing him halfway across London was just too sad and pathetic, and was one of those times that a white lie comes in very useful.)

"But, Dad, *line* dancing?!" I'd squeaked, incredulously.

"I know, I *know*. I don't even like country and western music!" Dad had laughed, his cheeks pink. "That's why I didn't tell you all. It was too embarrassing. And I kind of thought I'd go just the once to pacify Sharon – oh, no offence to your mum, Billy!"

"No problem!" Billy had said brightly, glad that his mother didn't have an illicit lover after all – only a stupid hobby.

"But then…" Dad shrugged and paused.

"Then what?" Linn had pushed him impatiently.

"I realized – and don't hate me for this – I *quite* enjoyed it."

None of us had a go at him for such a shameful confession. (Although it was on the tip of my tongue to beg him *never* to buy a cowboy hat, if he truly loved us.)

"So, my parents do line dancing?" Billy smirked. "My dad too?"

Scary, isn't it? That a boy can live in the same house as his folks and not have a clue what they do with their lives. Scary, but typical, if you ask me.

"Well, yes – didn't you know?" Dad had replied.

Billy shook his head.

"But your father couldn't come to this workshop at the hotel today," Dad had continued, "because of his bad back."

Billy looked confused.

"From hurting it at work?" Dad prompted him.

Billy had looked just as confused.

Not a clue about important details. Not one, tiny clue...

And Billy didn't have much of a clue about learning to shut up, either, as I realized now, sitting in the kids' playground this Sunday evening.

"Still, Ally, if your mum ever comes home, at least she won't find out that your dad's shacked up with someone new!" he said, tactlessly.

Sandie took a sharp intake of breath, knowing that wasn't an entirely sensitive thing to say. But that's Billy for you.

I saw Kyra pause on her swing and narrow her

eyes at me, knowing that there was more of a story to my family than I'd ever let on. But she didn't push me this once, mainly because she's got more of a story too.

And I did find out her story, eventually ... only I won't tell you now. I can't concentrate any more on my writing, 'cause Dad's playing some dreadful country and western track really loud downstairs and Rolf and Winslet are howling along like out-of-tune walruses.

Before I go downstairs and tell Dad that I'm going to report him to the social services for extreme mental cruelty to his children (there's no other way to describe that music), what I *will* say is that Billy was kind of right: I am glad that if Mum happened to wander through the door, all smiles and suntan and outstretched arms, the only romance she'd be hearing about is Grandma and Stanley's (going very well, apparently).

And I'd also like to say that while I love Billy like a brother, I'm so, *so* glad that he isn't going to be one to me.

That would have been *very* weird indeed...

So, until next time, I'll leave you with my top tips for avoiding embarrassing situations:

1) ALWAYS keep spare tampons safely stored in

a zipped-up purse – they have a life of their own and tend to escape from bags when you least expect them to;

2) AVOID any home-made "cocktails" at parties, unless you enjoy being violently sick; and

3) Never EVER tell anyone that your dad does line dancing…

There's always something going on in

ALLY'S WORLD

Make sure you keep up with the gossip!

(3) BUTTERFLiES, BULLiES and Bad, Bad HabiTS

Rowan's been acting strange (well, OK, *more* strange than usual). One minute she's crying over who-knows-what, and the next she's tripping into the house with all this new stuff (which *has* to come from the shopping fairy, since I *know* she's got zero money). Then there's the graffiti at school: "Rowan Love is a muppet" (and I don't think it's meant in a friendly, Kermit-is-cool kind of way). Just *what* is going on with my sister?

Look out for loads more fab Ally's World books!
Find out more about Ally's World at

www.karenmccombie.com

Butterflies, Bullies and Bad, Bad Habits

Just then, my eyes settled on something scribbled on the back of the cubicle door. It was right at the end of this really boring, long piece of graffiti that's been going for a couple of months; graffiti that had started out with someone writing "*Ellie F is a total muppet*", then someone underneath added "*I know who you are, and YOU are the muppet!*", then in completely different handwriting, there was "*No, you are the muppet, you big MUPPET!*", and it went on and on and *on* like that.

But now there was a new addition to the slagging.

Who's getting it this time? I wondered, bending forward to make out the red-penned scrawl.

Then I wished I hadn't bothered.

"*The biggest Muppit at Pallace Gates*", wrote someone who couldn't write, "*is Rowen Love*".

Unless a new girl with a ridiculously similar name – give or take the odd vowel – had started at our school, then it looked like my sister had just been voted this week's muppet.

Uh-oh...

Also available in this series:

The Past, the Present and the Loud, Loud Girl
Dates, Double Dates and Big, Big Trouble
Butterflies, Bullies and Bad, Bad Habits
Friends, Freak-Outs and Very Secret Secrets
Boys, Brothers and Jelly-Belly Dancing
Sisters, Super-Creeps and Slushy,
Gushy Love Songs
Parties, Predicaments and Undercover Pets
Tattoos, Telltales and Terrible, Terrible Twins
Angels, Arguments and a Furry Merry Christmas
Mates, Mysteries and Pretty Weird Weirdness
Daisy, Dad and the Huge, Small Surprise
Rainbows, Rowan and True, True Romance?

ALLY'S WORLD

BUTTERfLiES, BULLiES and Bad, Bad HabiTS

KaReN McCoMbie

SCHOLASTIC

for Rebecca Petrie

(P.S. Hey Rebecca, hope you realize this means I'm
expecting a dedication in return in one of your books!)

Scholastic Children's Books,
Commonwealth House, 1–19 New Oxford Street,
London WC1A 1NU, UK
A division of Scholastic Ltd
London ~ New York ~ Toronto ~ Sydney ~ Auckland
Mexico City ~ New Delhi ~ Hong Kong

First published in the UK by Scholastic Ltd, 2001

ISBN 0 439 99870 0

Typeset by TW Typesetting, Midsomer Norton, Somerset
Printed by Cox & Wyman Ltd, Reading, Berks.

10 9 8 7 6

Contents

PROLOGUE

Dear Mum,

How are you doing? We're all fine ... now. It's been a funny old time for us all, but mostly, of course, for Rowan. Do you want the good news, or the bad news? Well, I guess I'd better choose, since you aren't able to answer. And since I can't send you this letter anyway.

I don't mean to make you feel guilty about that – I know you move about too much to have an address that we can write to. By the way, we got that letter from you today; the one from Frankfurt. Only Grandma got a bit funny when Linn showed it to her – she said that she didn't understand why you were going on about how "steely and grey" the sea was there, 'cause her boyfriend Stan's been over there lots of times for work and it's apparently nowhere near the sea. (Like I wrote before, Grandma's been seeing a lot of this Stan bloke, although she hasn't taken him round to meet us yet. And she'd kill me if she heard me describe him as her "boyfriend", although that's what he *is*.)

Anyway, Linn just shrugged and said it was probably just you being poetic, trying to make a boring, industrial town sound romantic for our sakes, but Grandma just tsk-tsk'd some more.

Oh, I'm forgetting about the good news/bad news stuff, aren't I? Well, the bad news is that Rowan got into a lot of trouble recently. I mean, a *lot*. Some of it was her fault and some of it was absolutely *not* her fault. Even the stuff that was her fault wasn't, if you see what I mean. Um ... well, you *will* see what I mean if you read all this stuff I've written down.

And the good news? I guess it's that we got it all sorted out. Not completely, but *kind* of sorted. In a funny sort of way.

I'm not telling this too well, am I? But if you love Rowan – and I know you do, wherever you are – you really need to read this.

Clear as a big bowl of porridge, I know.*

Love you lots,

Ally

(your Love Child No. 3)

---

* Blee! Porridge – Grandma's always on to us to eat that stuff. I'd rather eat *hamster* bedding. Actually, do you think porridge is just juiced

hamster bedding? I'd better not talk to Tor about this or he'll have a bunch of hay and stuff in the liquidizer before I can stop him...

Chapter 1

JUST DON'T MENTION THE PUPPIES...

"They're all DEAD!" yelled Tor, gushing tears like burst water pipe.

"Who's dead?" I asked, dumping my schoolbag down on the floor and running around the kitchen table to comfort my little brother.

I'd kind of dawdled on my way home from school. I'd stopped and chatted with my best friend Sandie at the corner of her street, and then she asked me to come up to her place and hang out for a bit. It seemed cool, it didn't seem like I'd miss much back home.

It seemed I was wrong.

"Who's all dead, Tor?" I repeated, crouching down and wrapping an arm around him.

On the other side of Tor, Rolf the dog was staring at him with big puzzled eyes, whining quietly in sympathy.

But Tor was inconsolable – beyond human speech. It was taking all his energy just to try to *breathe* between these great big, lung-busting sobs.

☆ 4 ☆

At that point Grandma bustled into the kitchen, with a box of man-size tissues (for Tor's non-man-size nose) and plonked them down on the table in front of him.

"There you go Tor, dear," she said in her usual kind-but-efficient way, ruffling his hair as she breezed past him. "Now, what about if I look out some carrots, and you can go and give the rabbits an extra treat?"

She's smart, our Grandma, she really is. She knows that the best way to humour Tor isn't to offer him sweets or crisps or staying up late – the quickest route to his heart is to spoil some of the (zillions of) fluffy, scaly or flippery inhabitants who happen to share our house. And it's pretty nice of her to do that, considering that she isn't actually too fond of animals (only don't tell Tor that).

Anyhow, I was relieved: if whatever was wrong could be solved by feeding carrotty titbits to the rabbits, then nothing that serious could have happened. I mean, I couldn't have lived with myself if a freak typhoon had hit the house and swallowed up my whole family while I was round at Sandie's watching telly and raiding her biscuit tin.

"Who's dead?" I whispered to Grandma, while I patted Tor on the back to try to get rid of the hiccups he'd got through too much crying.

As she started roughly chopping up carrots beside the sink, Grandma tilted her head, motioning me over to her.

"Penny the Labrador-cross – she lost all nine of her puppies," Grandma whispered.

"Ah, *Pet Rescue*," I nodded, getting the point.

It's one of Tor's favourite TV shows. But then, *every* TV show about animals is his favourite. He's got the times, channels and evenings when they're on all programmed into his head, and woe betide any of us if we want to watch anything on another channel while the *Ickle Cute Sick Wombat Show*, or whatever, is on. And if we've forgotten that one of those *was* on the viewing schedule, Tor has this funny little way of reminding us... Right before the theme tune starts, he disappears upstairs and runs back down with his Save the Seals T-shirt on (required uniform for the viewing of *every* animal show, and an item of clothing that's very hard to wash – there are a LOT of animal shows on every week, so the window of opportunity to smuggle the smelly thing out of his room and get it washed and dried is very small...).

"All the puppies got sick!" Tor hiccuped, as the sobs started to subside and he got enough breath back to talk.

"What made them sick?" I asked, going back to keep Tor company at the table.

"Just dog flu, I think," Grandma muttered matter-of-factly, obviously keen to get the subject closed as quickly as possible to prevent more Tor and Rolf howling duets.

"Parvo virus!" Tor corrected her, before blowing his nose loudly into a paper tissue that was big enough to engulf his whole face.

Behind him, I could see Grandma rolling her eyes. It must be weird to be put right by someone who's about sixty years younger than you.

"Ta-DAHHH!!"

I spun my head around towards the source of the cheerful whooping. It seemed pretty inappropriate when Penny – bless 'er – had just lost all nine puppies.

Rowan stood in the doorway of the kitchen, holding a T-shirt up to her chest, striking a model pose, with a great big grin slapped across her face. Though that went quick enough when she clocked the state our little brother was in.

"Uh-oh. Something died on *Pet Rescue*, didn't it?" she asked rhetorically, letting her arms, and the T-shirt, drop.

"Yes, but let's not talk about it any more, shall we?" said Grandma breezily. "Why don't you show us what you've got there, Rowan, dear? Is it a new top?"

The smile pinged back into place on Rowan's face.

"Yes – I went to Wood Green after school with Von and bought it. It's lovely, isn't it?"

Grandma pursed her lips slightly as she eyed up my sister's latest purchase. It wasn't that she disapproved of the top – a lilac T-shirt with an iridescent butterfly on the chest – it was more that she doesn't think too much of Von. I think she'd prefer it if Rowan hung out with a mate who was the same age (i.e. fifteen), and not the legally pub-friendly eighteen. And preferably a mate who didn't have a pierced nose and a tattoo (actually, Grandma doesn't know Von's got a tattoo – that would just be something *else* to disapprove of). All round, I think Grandma worries that Von will lead Rowan astray, but accompanying my sister shopping in Wood Green High Street doesn't seem all *that* wild and raucous to me.

"Gorgeous, isn't it?" Rowan beamed, rubbing her hand lovingly over the butterfly. "I've got a party a week on Saturday – I think I'll wear it to that."

Yeah, *right* – if she didn't buy herself about twelve other tops in the meantime. Rowan loves shopping – although, it has to be said, she isn't the type of girl that's going to help make many designers into millionaires in the near future. Her big kick is to get bargains, and she loves cruising the charity shops around Crouch End and picking up strange second-hand bits and pieces she can adapt and transform into something weird and hopefully wonderful (her trademark).

"And how much did that cost you?" asked Grandma, as she placed a plastic bowl of carrot chunks in front of a recovering Tor (he was down to only gentle snuffles now).

"Not much!" trilled Rowan, twirling around in her red velvet Chinese slippers.

(Our school uniform isn't too strict: a black blazer, a black or grey skirt or trousers, a white shirt, a stripy black, grey and white tie. But when it comes to shoes and coats and stuff, you can wear what you want and, believe me, my sister exploits that to its full potential. Last winter, she wore this ratty old fake leopard-skin coat that she'd got from the Cancer Research shop over her uniform. She thought it was very arty and cool. But it actually looked more like she'd been pounced on by a geriatric leopard which had then just *died* on her.)

"How much is not much?" I asked, wondering where she got the not-much-money from.

I knew for a fact that she was skint; she'd been

moaning that she'd blown all of her allowance by Wednesday, and Dad doesn't dish out our money till Saturday.

"Well, I had to borrow a tenner off Von," she shrugged. "So I'll have to butter up Dad and see if I can get an advance on next week's money."

"And then what are you going to do for cash *next* week?" I asked pointedly.

"Borrow off the *next* week's money?" she suggested blithely.

Rowan might be Queen Bargain-Hunter, but she still has zero common sense when it comes to actual pounds and pence. *Tor*'s got a better concept of money than her. Actually, *Rolf*'s probably got a better concept of money than her.

"What's wrong with *him*?" frowned Linn, taking us all by surprise as she strode into the kitchen.

We'd been so engrossed in Rowan's amazingly poor grasp of economics that no-one had heard our eldest sister come in.

"Guess!" I replied, glancing over at Tor with his red-rimmed eyes.

"Oh, *that*," said Linn, knowingly, and settled herself down on to the chair opposite mine. "You've got to stop watching that, Tor. There's always something dying on it, and it just upsets you. So, what died today?"

"Puppies," mumbled Tor, cuddling Rolf so tightly around the neck that he looked in danger of becoming another dead-dog statistic.

"Nine of them," I mouthed to Linn, holding the right number of fingers up in the air.

"Oh," she grimaced, acknowledging the higher than average mortality rate, and Tor's resulting grief.

"So, Grandma, is Dad around?" asked Rowan, blanking Linn and glancing up at the kitchen clock.

"Not yet," Grandma answered, while ushering Tor (and Rolf) out of the back door with the bowl of carrots. "He's working a bit later tonight – he's rushing to get a bike ready for someone's daughter's birthday tomorrow."

"Ooh, extra work!" Rowan smiled. "That means extra money – maybe Dad will just give me the ten pounds as a one-off, and not take it off my allowance!"

"Well, that wouldn't exactly be fair!" snapped Linn.

"Why isn't it fair?" Rowan asked her petulantly – sticking out her bottom lip ever so slightly.

(The way it works with Linn and Rowan is like this: Rowan comes up with a stupid, half thought-out, hare-brained scheme – and Linn shoots it down in flames. The End.)

"Think about it!" Linn sighed wearily. "If *you* get

extra money off Dad, then he'd have to give me and Ally and Tor extra money too, wouldn't he?"

"Not necessarily…" mumbled Rowan, knowing she was beaten, but refusing to give in.

A big old slanging match was about to kick off in about two seconds flat, unless I came up with something to divert it.

"You're late home from school, Linn. Where've you been?" I asked, not bothering to fill her in with pointless little details like the fact that me and Rowan had only been in minutes before her ourselves.

"Me?" said Linn, arching her pale eyebrows and looking pretty pleased with herself. "*I* have been for an interview. And *I* have got myself a Saturday job!"

Linn had been going on about getting a Saturday job for ages. We all knew how much she really wanted a mobile phone, but as it didn't look like either Dad or Santa was going to get round to fixing her up with one of those in a hurry, she'd sussed that she was going to have to find a way to pay for it on her own. And now it looked like she had.

"Where did you get a job?" I asked, knowing instantly that it wasn't going to be stacking shelves in the supermarket. Linn wouldn't consider any job where she might risk working up a sweat. She was too all-round prissy and neat for that.

"You know those clothes shops on Crouch Hill?" she asked.

"Oh, yes, they're all very nice!" Grandma marvelled, already impressed.

Please, I thought, *please let her say she's working as a cleaner in the pub opposite them!*

"I'm starting on Saturday at the one in the middle – Seasons," she said, smugly. "It's got more proper designer labels than the other shops…"

Oh, well, *not* the pub, then. Life isn't fair, sometimes, is it?

"Do they do staff discounts?" Grandma asked, her steely eyes lighting up, if I wasn't very much mistaken.

"Yes – I'll get fifteen per cent off. So that means I'll have lots of great new clothes, and plenty of money to spend on myself!" Linn boasted, smoothing down the front of her immaculately smooth white shirt with an air of self-satisfaction.

It's hard to be happy for someone when they're acting that pleased with themselves. It's not as if Linn doesn't have her moments of being likeable, it's just that she hides them pretty well. Instead, she just prefers to be smug and superior and gorgeous and perfect – a constant reminder to me and Rowan that we're ever so slightly inferior, lacking in gorgeousness and most definitely *im*perfect.

I glanced over at my fellow imperfect sister to see how she was taking Linn's news. Rowan's long, thick, dark hair was scraped back from her face with this mad metal hairband covered in little jewels: making her big brown eyes more obvious in her pale face. And right now those big brown eyes looked sad, and jealous and pathetic.

"So, Linn!" I said, turning to face Love Child *numero uno*. "You don't think Rowan should ask Dad for that money?"

"No," Linn frowned at me, wondering why we'd returned to the topic.

"Well, if *you're* going to be so rich now, why don't *you* lend Ro the money?!"

I already knew what the answer was going to be, but I couldn't resist being cheeky and asking it anyway.

"You must be joking! I'd nev—"

"Right!" said Grandma loudly, stepping in as referee. "Here, Rowan – this is from me ... but I want it back – a pound a week. OK?"

"Oh, thank you, Grandma!" gushed Rowan, running round the table to take the note Grandma was holding out and to give her a hug.

"I've had enough hassles today, what with dead

puppies," Grandma sighed, patting Rowan on the back, "and I don't want any more hassles over money. Do you three hear me?"

"Yes, Grandma," I nodded, hearing my words echoed by Rowan and Linn.

But as soon as her back was turned, Linn shot me a withering glance across the table. I nearly shot her one back, but I was trying too hard not to laugh at the sight of Rowan standing behind Linn's chair and pulling a face behind her back.

That's the trouble when me and my sisters start niggling at each other – we're a bit too big to get palmed off with carrots and bunny-feeding...

Chapter 2

FOR RICHER, FOR POORER...

When you're trying to watch a video, it's very hard to concentrate when there's a constant *thunk, thunk, thunketty-thunk* going on in the background.

"Dad, what are you doing? Why don't you come and watch this with us?" I asked, over the back of the sofa.

"No, it's OK, I've got these bills to go through," Dad muttered from the wonky writing desk in the corner of the room, not even looking up from the cheque book he was scribbling in.

I turned back to the screen, but the *thunketty-thunk* was really spoiling the mood. Out of the corner of my eye, I could see Linn's foot tapping in irritation. Half a second later, she'd slid Tor off her lap, grabbed a magazine off the floor, and walked round to Dad and the desk.

"There!" came her muffled voice, as she bent down out of sight and shoved a wodge of paper under the one short leg of the desk.

Brilliant – no more *thunketty-thunk* when Dad was writing.

"Thanks, Linn," smiled Dad. "Must get that fixed sometime…"

Ha. That's his catchphrase about everything in our rattling, crumbly, falling-down house.

"Come on, Dad, like Ally says, why don't you stop for a while?" Linn urged him, straightening up and standing beside him. "Come and watch the video with us!"

That's what the rest of us were doing – watching *A Bug's Life*, for Tor's sake. Before she'd escaped back to the sanity and calm of her own flat after tea, Grandma had come up with the smart idea of renting the video and letting Tor stay up a little later to watch it. As soon as she'd suggested it, I was on my bike and headed for the video shop. Without a burst of cheerful Disney-ness before bedtime, Tor was bound to have bad dreams. And when he has bad dreams, it's usually *my* bed he crawls into in the middle of the night. And since there's usually a succession of cats and dogs making themselves comfortable on my duvet during the night, the further addition of a small boy generally means I have to sleep with half my body hanging out of my own bed.

"Yeah, come on, Dad!" said Rowan, switching the video to pause. "You can even have this chair!"

Dad rubbed his stubbly chin at her offer, and then shook his head.

"No, it's OK. You three look too comfy to move," he replied, nodding over at Rowan and her lap full of snoring cats.

It was true; Eddie and Fluffy were dozing away happily, entangled in a blur of black and white fur so it was hard to see where one cat started and another cat ended.

"Anyhow – I've really got to get these bills out of the way tonight," Dad muttered more seriously, as he turned back to the paperwork. "Some of them are red ones..."

"Red's bad," said Tor, getting on his knees and staring at Dad over the back of the sofa, same as me.

"Yep," Dad nodded, "red is bad. Specially this one for the electricity. It's days old, but I only found it tonight..."

"How come?" I frowned.

"I saw the corner of it sticking out from under Winslet's blanket when I went to pat her earlier," Dad grinned.

Tor and I turned to the dog we were sharing sofa space with and frowned at her. Winslet snuffled guiltily, whipping her ears flat back and dropping her hairy head on to her hairy paws.

"What are you stealing bills for, Winslet? *Stupid* dog!" I told her off, waggling my finger in front of her nose.

She stared up at me with sorrowful eyes, knowing she'd done something wrong, even though all she heard was "Blah blah blah blah blah blah, Winslet? *Blah* blah!"

In a past life, Winslet must have been a pick-pocket. Usually she steals things that make vague sense: food (pretty straightforward), squeaky or fluffy pet toys (so Rolf and the cats can't have any fun) and random bits of clothing from us (preferably unwashed, but she isn't fussy – as long as it's chewable). But stealing letters was a new one. What was the point? Unless she was trying to teach herself to read...

"Are there *lots* of bills, Dad?" asked Linn, bending over the desk and trying to make sense of what was spread out on it.

"Yes, unfortunately. They've all kind of sprung on me at the same time, for some reason," said Dad, pushing the rolled-up sleeves of his checked shirt further up his arms. "And there's a whole load that's just landed on me for the shop too."

"But you'll manage to pay them all, won't you?" asked Rowan, with a slightly alarmed squeak to her voice.

"Urm, I'm sure I will," he said, unconvincingly. "Only I haven't quite figured out *how*, exactly…"

There was silence for a second, as we four Love children suddenly realized that while Dad might be smiling, he wasn't joking.

"Are we poor, Dad?" asked Tor, bluntly.

"Well, we're not rich," Dad laughed wryly. "And right now, we're *particularly* not rich. Put it that way!"

"Are we in trouble, Dad?" I asked, hoping he was going to tell me not to be so stupid.

Only he didn't.

"It's, um, more like — what do those banker-types say? — a cash-flow situation. Still, let's go crazy," he said, getting to his feet and clapping his hands together. "We've still got that big tub of ice cream in the freezer — why don't I get us all some and we'll cheer ourselves up?"

What a weird Thursday night this was turning out to be. First it was the drama with the puppies (RIP), then me and my sisters got all spiky with each other over Linn's supposedly good news, and now Dad was *not* quite managing to hide from us the fact that we were in a state of financial ruin.

"That's it," Linn murmured quietly, as soon as Dad had left the room. "I'm not going to take my allowance from Dad any more – I'll just manage on my wages from the shop…"

My head was a whirl (what's new?); what could I do to help?

"I'll get a Saturday job too!" I blurted out, determined that I'd start looking straight away.

"Mice!" said Tor.

"What?" I asked, my normal ability for interpreting Tor-speak failing me this once.

"I could ask my mice to have babies," he explained simply. "And I could sell them. But only to my *special* friends."

I could just see Tor now, rolling up to his friend's houses with his clipboard and pen, vetting their homes as suitable or not for his precious pets. He'd never be able to part with them – we'd just end up with gallons *more* mice scuttling about with the rest of the menagerie in his bedroom.

"Er, we'll talk about that later, Tor," said Linn hurriedly, obviously thinking along the same lines as me.

Then I realized that the only one of us that hadn't made a suggestion (useless or not) was Rowan.

"Ro?" I said, swivelling back round into a sitting position to look at her.

"We're … *poor*!" she gasped theatrically, clasping her hands to her chest.

There's one thing you can always count on with

Rowan – if there's the slightest reason to flap, she'll flap. If there's a tizz to get in, she's your girl.

"Ro – it's OK," I tried to reassure her. "This isn't the Victorian times; we're not going to get sent to the poorhouse!"

I was trying to be funny (and failing). I saw the first hint of wateriness in Rowan's eyes and knew I'd have to act fast.

Lunging over, I grabbed the remote from the arm of her chair and pressed play.

"Just watch the movie and don't think about it," I ordered her.

Rowan blinked rapidly at the screen and did as she was told.

Honestly, sometimes she's so flaky you'd think Rowan was the youngest of us all, not the second oldest.

Only you know something? I was feeling pretty flaky and frightened too...

Chapter 3

ROWAN GOES WEIRD(ER)

"...and that's your assignment, boys and girls. Sorry to have kept you!"

Don't you hate it when teachers make you wait? (Especially last period on a Friday afternoon.) And don't you hate it if they call you "boys and girls" when you've been out of primary school for about a hundred years?

Just before I thudded my book shut and stuffed it in my bag, I glanced at the notes I'd just scribbled down and realized they were illegible. But I wasn't going to hang around and ask our English teacher, Mr Samuels, to go through it all again, not when the bell went five minutes ago and I knew Rowan would be waiting for me outside.

"*That* was boring," muttered Kyra, as we scrambled out of the door along with everyone else.

"Tell me about it!" I moaned, trying to do up the buckle of my bag as we walked.

"Do you fancy hanging out for a while?" Kyra asked, wrinkling her little upturned nose at me questioningly. "Maybe go over to the park or something?"

"What's the matter – not seeing Richie?" I asked her, wondering if I was her second choice.

"Ricardo? No, I'm bored with him," she shrugged.

She'd been going out with Richie/Ricardo for about three weeks by then, and it was pretty funny to see how often she changed her mind about him. Either she was madly in love with him, or madly fed up with him and on the point of giving him the chuck.

It looked like he was on the downward spiral right then, and one of these days, I hoped it would stay that way – I thought he was a bit of an obnoxious creep, to be honest. It's like with the whole Richie/Ricardo name thing: just to impress her and sound more romantic or something, he told Kyra his name was Ricardo when she met him (even though I don't think anyone except maybe his granny's ever called him that). It wasn't till my mate Billy pointed it out, that I realized "Ricardo" was actually his buddy from school, otherwise known as Richie Esposito to his mates.

I mean, it would be like me telling some guy I fancied that he had to call me Alexandra, even though my full name is so unfamiliar to me that I wouldn't look round if someone yelled it out in the street.

"So what about it? The park?" Kyra repeated, as the front door of the school loomed closer.

"Nah," I shook my head, "I can't. Got to meet my sister and go and get some shopping up at the Broadway."

"Your sister? Which one?" asked Kyra, shoving some chewing gum in her mouth. "The pretty one or the weird one?"

Me and my weird sister arrived up at the Broadway, after walking up the road together in virtual silence.

It wasn't just the fact that we never do this kind of thing usually (me, Linn and Rowan *never* walk to or from school together – I guess because we see enough of each other at home, and because we tend to meet up with our own friends on the way. Well, me and Linn do anyway – Rowan doesn't actually have any proper mates at school). No, today, for some reason, Rowan was being *extra* weird, going all huffy and wobbly on me for keeping her waiting outside school, like I could *help* Mr Samuels being a pain and keeping my whole class back.

"Where've you been? I've been waiting on my own for ages!" she'd narked at me.

Which was a lie on *two* counts: for one thing, it hadn't been ages, and for another thing, she wasn't on her own – there were still a couple of girls from her year kicking around the entrance when we got out. Anyway, what was she so scared of? Dying of boredom?

So I'd gone in a huff at her huffiness. (And yes, I know how dumb that sounds now.) But as we got closer to the shops, I had to resume communications.

"Where do we need to go? What's on the list?" I asked her.

"Um … it's all just vegetables," she replied, scanning Grandma's scrawly handwriting. "So, just the fruit and veg shop over there, I guess. Or do you think we should go round a few of them? Work out who's got the cheapest Brussels sprouts or something?"

I was just about to tell her she was being pathetic, when I sussed out that maybe *that* was what was up with her.

"But Ro, we don't have to *panic* about money – you heard what Dad said this morning at breakfast," I told her, as the green man beeped and we crossed over at the traffic lights towards the Clocktower.

I think Dad realized he'd freaked us all out the

night before. Even though we'd all pretended we were cool, and watched *A Bug's Life* and ate our ice cream and pretended everything was fine, he saw through it, I'm sure. That's why this morning, he'd taken the opportunity to tell us things weren't as black (or as red) as they might have seemed the night before.

"We just all need to be a bit careful when it comes to spending at the moment, that's all," he smiled round the table at us all. "So no buying any diamond tiaras this month, OK, girls?"

I was just about to cross at the next set of traffic lights when I realized I'd left Rowan behind.

So much for Dad's funny lecture and my reassurances – she was standing with her nose practically superglued to a gift-shop window dripping in trinkets.

"What are you looking at?" I asked her, half-expecting her to say "Everything...". It was Rowan's favourite shop in Crouch End, stacked floor to ceiling in jewellery, candelabras, painted glass doodahs and tasselly, silky lampshades.

"That CD rack," she muttered, pointing to a rectangular wicker and wire affair.

"What do you need a CD rack for? You've got one already," I pointed out, thinking of the plain white Perspex one she'd bought in a sale and customized by glueing on sunflowers cut out of a sheet of wrapping paper.

"Not for me," she sighed, leaving a fuzzy circle of steam on the window. "For Carla. For her birthday next week."

"Who's Carla?" I asked, trying to keep up with the mystifying twists and turns of Rowan's mind.

"Von's mate from college. The one whose party I'm going to next Saturday."

"Oh, *right*..." I mumbled, remembering her saying something about that when she was showing me and Grandma her new top the day before.

"I've been to her flat, down in Finsbury Park. It's really cool. And I thought that CD rack would be a good present to buy her. But I guess I'll have to go without taking her anything, since we're so skint at the moment..."

"She probably won't expect you to bring anything, since you're not like her best mate or anything," I pointed out, trying to console her.

It didn't seem to do the trick. Rowan still kept on staring through the window at the CD rack, like it was the Holy Grail.

"Or you could just *nick* it – *that* would be cheaper," I joked, in big, bad taste. "The only trouble is, if you stick something *that* shape up the front of your blazer, everyone's going to think you've got these huge, square boobs..."

OK, something was wrong. I knew it was a minus-one-out-of-ten kind of joke, but I did expect Rowan to giggle a bit, even if she followed it straight up by telling me how deeply rotten it was.

But Rowan stayed straight-faced, staring, staring, staring through that window...

Chapter 4

LINN GETS LUCKY (ONLY IT'S *BAD* LUCK)

We shouldn't have. We *really* shouldn't have. But we couldn't help ourselves...

"Look, there she is – wave!"

Tor did as he was told and waved frantically at Linn with his one free hand. The other was clutching a bag of pet-shop goodies (well, necessities – like us, the Love house menagerie were going to have to manage on short rations for a bit).

"Why is she looking at us funny?" he asked, squashing his nose flat up against the plate-glass window of Seasons clothes shop and breathing his steamy breath out like a halo on it.

"I think she's just shy, that's all. With it being her first day and everything," I murmured, grinning and sticking both thumbs up at our big sister.

Course she wasn't shy – just furious. Furious that we'd merrily ignored her order NOT to come and bother her on her first Saturday working at the shop. But she'd told us that at teatime the night before, and hey, it *could* just have slipped our minds. Well, it could have. Even though it hadn't.

("Shall we go home now?" I'd asked Tor, when we came out of the pet shop. "OK," he'd replied. "Or, shall we go round and see how Linn's getting on?" I'd ever-so-casually suggested. "OK," Tor had shrugged. See? It was that easy.)

There were no customers in Seasons at that precise moment – just rails and rails of expensive-looking clothes and two sales assistants. One was a middle-aged, very groomed woman, who was grumpily trying to force a roll of paper into the till. The other was Linn, who seemed like she was trying to look useful, straightening clothes that were already straight. At least, that was what her hands were doing. Her face was doing something completely different; twisted up into this weird, shocked frown thing. No wonder Tor thought she was looking funny.

"What's she saying?" he asked, breathing another steamy circle on to the glass.

With her neatly plucked blondish eyebrows practically bouncing up to meet her hairline, Linn was most definitely mouthing something silently at us.

"I don't know," I lied, waving all the harder at Linn, now I knew I was most definitely annoying her.

"I think she's saying something rude!" said Tor. "I think she's saying 'F—"

"OK!" I interrupted him, before he translated Linn's words too loudly for a busy, bustling street.

I was just about to give up my most splendid game of embarrassing Linn and start hauling Tor homewards when I saw something I couldn't resist.

"Look, Tor – that other lady's gone into the back of the shop. Quick, let's run in and find out how Linn's getting on..."

Before he could say anything, I bundled my brother through the doorway of Seasons, into a world where Sting crooned through the sound system and the smell of pot pourri or fancy oils or something filled the air. It was all very laid-back and posh. In fact, the only thing spoiling the atmosphere was a small black cloud (invisible, of course, except to me) hovering in the middle of the shop, right above my tight-lipped sister.

"Go away! You'll get me sacked!" she growled, mean and low, while frantically casting her eyes back towards the counter, where I'd seen the middle-aged woman glide through a doorway seconds earlier.

"Don't be silly! How could you get sacked, just because your brother and sister have come in to say hello?"

It was a guess on my part that she couldn't get sacked just for that. But I figured that she *might* get sacked for working in such a snooty shop under false pretences. I mean, no matter how neat and trendy and together she appeared to be, having me and Tor turn up on her employer's doorstep looking like we were on our way to an eco-warrior, tree-saving, tunnel-digging road sabotage might just blow her style cred.

Poor Linn. She'd made a super-human effort to outdo herself that morning – it was as if she'd run the iron over everything from her super-smart Gap khakis right up to her hair (scraped and gelled back into a ponytail that was *so* tight it practically gave her a facelift). Then there was me, with my hair hanging shapeless and longish and in need of a wash-ish, wearing a grey T-shirt that had strange brown splodges on it from when I helped Tor creosote the rabbit hutches the weekend before, and a pair of combats and trainers that were both so battered they looked like they'd been in a war zone (well, when you're only aiming to trudge to the pet shop with your little brother on a Saturday morning, there doesn't seem much point getting glammed up).

However, my bag-lady look was still better than what Tor was wearing. I didn't realize his T-shirt was on inside out and back-to-front till he took his sweatshirt off (hey, size labels worn under your chin *could* be the next big craze). His jeans might have looked all right from a distance, but the problem was that they were quite new, i.e. too big, and he'd forgotten to put a belt on, to hold them up. So the world at large was being treated to a lovely view of a sizeable chunk of Tor's Tigger pants.

"GO AWAY!" Linn hissed urgently.

OK. Now that her face was so close up to mine, I could see that she was really, truly mad at me. I was in serious danger of going just that weeny bit too far…

"Fine! No problem! We're going!" I said, all innocence, grabbing Tor by the hand and turning to head for the door. "*All* we wanted to do was wish you luck, but if *you* don't want—"

"Aaaarrrghhh!"

Can a scream ever be whispered? I'd never have thought so, but right then, Linn was definitely screaming quietly.

"What's wrong?" I asked, whipping round to see what was flipping her out.

"Uh-oh…" mumbled Tor, spotting what was wrong before I did.

Thanks to a hole somewhere in the plastic bag

Tor was carrying, there was a grainy trail of hamster food leading from the door to Linn's feet and back again, as we'd tried to make our exit.

"I'm sorry, Linn!" whined Tor, blinking hard at the mess on the pale grey carpet.

"Oh my God! How am I going to clean that up?" Linn stressed, her hands clutched over her nose and mouth.

"Hoover?" I suggested unhelpfully.

Linn narrowed her eyes at my flippant remark. I could practically feel the little arrows of hate that were shooting out of them.

Quickly, me and Tor scrambled for the door, casting another flurry of grain on to the carpet.

I did feel bad for her, honest I did. But as Tor and I trotted off down the Broadway towards home, I couldn't help smiling.

Rowan was going to *love* hearing about this...

Chapter 5

FOUR HOTDOGS AND A PACKET OF WINE GUMS PLEASE...

"Is this screen one or screen two?" I frowned at Chloe.

"Huh?" Chloe frowned back, walking into the room with a big bowl of popcorn in her arms, and staring at me, Sandie, Jen, Kellie and Salma, all sitting squashed in a row together.

"This *is* Finchley Warner Village, isn't it?" I continued, pointing at the huge blank screen in front of us.

"Yeah, when does the movie start?" asked Sandie, in a wobbly voice (she's no good at wind-ups, really she isn't).

"Uh, have we missed the ads?" said Jen, blinking hard at Chloe.

"Yeah, and what about the previews? Have we missed them?" said Kellie, all wide-eyed and innocent.

"Do we have time to get some hotdogs?" I continued, trying to keep a straight face.

"Wine Gums for me!" Salma grinned.

That started Jen off with the giggles (not a hard thing to do – Jen gets the giggles as often as the rest of us *breathe*). Not that she was laughing out loud, but I could feel her shoulders shaking right next to me. And it was infectious; there were snorts of suppressed sniggering coming from further along the big, wine-coloured leather sofa. Sandie and Kellie, I reckoned – Salma's really good at keeping it together during wind-ups.

Chloe narrowed her eyes at each of us in turn, her pale face scrunched in concentration as she tried to work out what we were on about. Then she looked at the big black monolith on the the other side of the room and finally twigged.

OK, so we were just goofing around and teasing her, but her new telly really was *vast*. I mean, *super*-vast.

"Ha, ha – I'm laughing so hard inside that it hurts," she muttered, with lots of eye-rolling at our pathetic gag about her back room turning into the latest multiplex.

For extra effect, she tossed her wavy red hair back and plonked the bowl of popcorn down on the table with a clatter. Chloe likes dramatic gestures.

Now that our feeble joke had been played out,

Salma and Kellie wriggled off the sofa, grabbing a couple of overstuffed cushions each and settling themselves on the floor. And since we had more room, Jen, me and Sandie kind of expanded sideways, getting into suitable slobbing-out mode to watch whatever new video Chloe had grabbed from her dad's shop downstairs.

"Widescreen..." murmured Jen longingly, staring straight at her reflection on the black screen. "I wish *my* parents would buy one of these. Our TV is so small it gives me a migraine when I try to watch it for more than an hour at a time."

Tell us about it. Out of all of our houses, the least popular place to go to on one of our girls' video nights is round Jen's. Chloe's flat is the best because even though it doesn't look much from outside (it's right on the main road, right above her dad's shop and you have to get to it through a grungy back alley), it's really big and impressive once you're inside. *And* it has this separate TV room as well as a living room, so she doesn't have to plead with her mum and dad and brothers to get out when us lot are coming round.

My house is next favourite (even though our telly is so unreliable that sometimes it moves from being in colour to showing programmes in varying shades of *green*). All the girls love our comfy, sunshine-yellow living room with its squashy second-hand sofa and armchairs and its clutter and cats and stuff (even though Chloe sometimes likes to moan about how the pet hairs make her allergic – but Chloe likes a good moan, full stop).

Sandie's place is OK, but her mum can be a bit much – she pops through about a million times whenever we're there and glued to a video. She offers us loads of cakes and nibbles and that kind of thing (which is great), but we all know (especially Sandie) that it's not just a case of her being thoughtful and nice; it's also because she wants to have a nosy and check that we're watching a nice safe fluffy movie and not some X-rated slasher flick (we save those for when we're round at one of the other houses). Poor Sandie – she gets absolutely mortified; you should see the shade of pink she turns when Mrs Walker hovers about in the doorway saying, "Any of you girls want another nummy hotty chocolate?" Urgh...

Salma's place is OK, but we can hardly ever go there, 'cause of all these manic tiny toddlers running about the place. Salma's mum got re-married a while back and has three-year-old twin girls. But Salma's nineteen-year-old sister has a little girl too, and she's always round at Salma's place as well. I mean, I like little kids and everything (well, I like Tor), but this lot are so LOUD. When you go round to see Salma, you need earplugs 'cause of all these small, shouty hurricanes thundering about the house. And I can never tell them apart ("Rosa's the one who has the sulky screaming fits," Salma once tried to explain when I was at her place and getting all the toddlers' names muddled up. "Julia's the one who has hysterics if you try to pick her up, and Laurel is the one who just shouts all the time."). Rosa, Julia and Laurel – pretty names for miniature monsters. I still can't figure out which is which, but maybe that's 'cause they're always a blur of racing arms and legs. And I can't figure out how Salma manages to look so calm and serene all the time, considering she lives in a house that's about as relaxing as the middle of the M25 at rush hour.

A night at Kellie's is always a real laugh. She lives with her mum in a tiny flat, but the way her mum cooks, it's like she's feeding a really hungry rugby team. We turn up there on a GVN (Girls' Video Night), and guaranteed, get hit by an amazing smell of food as soon as we go in. Her mum makes mounds of all this Caribbean stuff and by the time we've watched a movie, our stomachs all look like we've swallowed a beach ball.

But back to Jen ... her parents are nice and

friendly and everything – and they're quite cool 'cause they know a lot about music and bands and stuff – but they are the kind who disapprove of too much television; like it'll melt your brain or something. So they bought the world's titchiest telly just to make sure watching it is as little fun as possible. Torture, actually – it's true what Jen says about the migraine thing; I always come out of her house with a blinding headache after squeezing my eyes so hard to try and focus in on whatever was flickering over the screen. Her parents might think they're doing the right-on thing, but while they're stopping Jen and her sister from getting brain-melt from watching *Who Wants to be a Millionaire?* and *Emmerdale*, they should realize that they're permanently damaging their kids' vision into the bargain. Actually, maybe *that*'s why Jen has such tiny, button eyes ... maybe she was born with eyes as big as a bush baby's and then years of straining to look at a doll's-house-sized telly made them the way they are.

And if you ask me, Jen's mum and dad – bless 'em – must be really dense to think that Jen and her big sister Rachel don't just go and get their TV fix somewhere else. I mean, haven't they figured out that *that*'s why Jen spends so many evenings a week at Kellie's place in the next street? Maybe

Mr and Mrs Hudson have this notion that Jen and Kellie are expanding their best-buddy teenage minds by studying origami or reading poetry to each other or something, but sorry – they're just curled up on the sofa in front of *Brookside* with Kellie's lovely, cuddly mum and a family-sized pack of Hob-nobs.

But anyway ... back to Saturday night at Finchley Warner Village. I mean, Chloe's posh TV room.

"So what are we watching tonight, Chloe?" asked Sandie, her big blue eyes blinking questioningly at our friend. (Sandie's got a normal, watchable telly, so, see? My eye-strain=TV-size theory might *just* be right.)

"Well, I'm so angry with my dad," growled Chloe, as she crouched down in front of her flash new telly. "The new bunch of movies that were due in today? They're not going to be in till Monday now!"

I thought that was just a bit unfair. It's not like it was her dad's fault or anything, but then we were dealing with Chloe Brennan here, and I wasn't about to contradict her. She's a bit bolshy, is Chloe – one of those people who even when she's wrong, she's right, if you see what I mean. And after knowing her for a couple of years, I've come to realize that the easiest thing is just to shrug and let her believe whatever she wants to believe.

Of course, I don't always listen to my own advice. It was like the week before, I had another go at trying to explain why me and Sandie hang out with Kyra now. Even as the words were coming out of my mouth, I knew I was wasting my time...

"Kyra was saying—" I'd started, forgetting for a second how much my other friends were still wary of her.

"Kyra Davies?" Chloe had spat out. "I still don't get why you bother with her. She's a total psycho."

Now, to be fair, that's what I thought of Kyra when she arrived at school recently. But also to be fair, I soon realized that all the loudmouth stuff she pulled in class was all part of her trying to cover up her awkwardness at being the New Girl. But try convincing *Chloe* of that, when she'd already made up her mind.

"Actually, it's like I've told you before: Kyra's OK when you get to know her," I'd shrugged, as Sandie stood back and let me do the talking. "*Isn't* she, Sandie?"

Sandie's nod was practically invisible to the naked eye. She obviously thought it was kind of pointless to push this with Chloe. Which I should have known too, if I had a brain.

"Kyra Davies is a psycho and she's got you two

wrapped round her little finger," Chloe had announced, her arms crossed defiantly against her chest.

Behind her, Salma, Jen and Kellie just stood in silent agreement.

"But she—" I'd started to protest, feeling how unfair it was that none of my so-called mates were willing to give Kyra a second chance.

"She's a psycho," Chloe interrupted.

"She's not; she just—"

"She's a psycho."

"But Chloe—"

"She's a psycho."

I gave up then. The crazy thing is, Chloe and Kyra are kind of similar in a lot of ways (loud, bolshy, opinionated) which is why they don't particularly like each other. But it does bug me that Kellie and the others all just end up agreeing with Chloe for an easy life.

And it bugs me that I do it too. I mean, no matter how much I like her, there's no way I'd invite Kyra along to one of the GVNs (and that doesn't include the time she turned up at one uninvited, back when I still thought she was a psycho too). And that's all down to Chloe.

God, I'm pathetic, aren't I? For not standing up for what I believe in. Mind you, you haven't had

Chloe stare at you with her dark eyes and her white cheeks all flushed and tetchy. It's like trying to argue with a she-lion. Or my sister Linn. In fact, I'd rather take my chances arguing with a lion with a grudge than argue with Chloe or Linn...

"So if there's no new movies, Chlo, what are we going to watch?" yawned Salma, stretching out across the floor and grabbing a handful of popcorn.

"I got the DVD of *The Sixth Sense* out," said Chloe, slipping a shiny CD-type thing into one of the layers of matt black decks stacked under the new telly.

"You've got a DVD player now *too*?!" gasped Jen.

"*Yes*," sighed Chloe, as though it was as ordinary to get a DVD as it was to pick up a toaster. "I know we watched this ages ago when it came out on video, but the DVD has all this extra stuff, like showing you what all the clues were."

"Wow..." I heard myself muttering.

"Why 'wow'?" asked Jen, flopping her head around on the sofa to stare at me. "You guessed all the clues the first time around!"

"I didn't mean wow about the extras on the DVD," I grinned at her. "I mean wow about being able to afford all this stuff. My dad can't even afford to pay the bills this month!"

I don't mind mentioning money (or lack of it) in

front of the girls. Although Chloe's family are pretty well off (obviously), and Jen and Sandie's parents seem OK that way, Salma and Kellie's families sometimes have it pretty tough. And although Chloe could act all show-offy about stuff in her own house, she never made the rest of us feel like our own houses were crummy by comparison. Well, not deliberately.

"Is everything OK?" asked Kellie, leaning up on her elbow and gazing at me with concern.

"Yeah, kind of," I shrugged.

(I could feel Sandie's eyes boring into me from the other end of the sofa; I hadn't sounded that casual when I'd been whingeing on about it on our way round here.)

"Isn't your dad's bike shop doing very well?" Chloe frowned.

"It's OK, I guess," I answered her, shrugging again. "I think we've all just got to be careful with money for a while. Like my sister Linn – she's got herself a Saturday job now. She just started today – in that clothes shop Seasons, just off the Broadway."

"Oooh, I'd love a job somewhere like that..." sighed Salma.

(Or anywhere else. As soon as Salma turns fourteen, she's planning on writing to every shop and business in a five-kilometre radius of Crouch End. It's not just the money she's after – it's just that it'll get her away from her flat full of sprogs for a whole, entire day.)

"Me too," I nodded. "In fact, I'd love a Saturday job right now!"

"Yeah? Well, I know where there's one going, if you're *that* desperate!" said Chloe, leaning back on her arms in front of the giganta-telly.

"Where?" I asked her, feeling my heart immediately race into a gallop.

"Just along the road, in that corny little card shop," Chloe replied, chucking her thumb to the right. "There was an ad in the window for a Saturday girl when I passed there this afternoon."

Instantly, I knew the one she meant. Crouch End is full of very trendy card and gift shops, but there are a couple of more old-fashioned card shops – the sort my Grandma likes to go into; the sort where she isn't going to tsk-tsk at the extortionate price of a card with a dried daisy glued to the front of it. ("Daylight robbery! You could make a meal for a family of five for the price of this!" she'd grumble, if me and Rowan ever dragged her into one of the fancier gift shops.)

"That would be brilliant!" I beamed, my mind already visualizing my dad's grateful expression when I announced I'd be helping supplement the family's income. Or at least, the fact that he wouldn't have to give me pocket money any more.

"Umm..."

I could hear Sandie's little squeak from the other end of the sofa and I knew she was about to say something that would burst my bubble. I'd know that negative-sounding "umm..." anywhere. That was the "umm..." that she did when I came back from the loos at the last end-of-term disco and told her excitedly that Ross Stewart had been eyeing me up and down (after her "umm..." she broke it to me that I had a metre of toilet paper attached to the heel of my shoe). And that was the "umm..." she did the time I told her I had a really good feeling about the magazine competition I'd just entered (after *that* "umm..." she pointed out the entry coupon with my address on it that was still lying on my bedside table, instead of being in the envelope I'd just posted off).

Basically, "umm..." meant "bummer".

"What's up?" Kellie asked Sandie, asking my question for me.

"Well, they wouldn't give Ally the job, would they?" Sandie muttered in a teeny-tiny voice. "I mean, she's not fourteen yet, is she?"

OK, so at the back of my mind I knew this. But

it didn't make me any the less disappointed now that Sandie had pointed it out.

"Awww," muttered Jen, spotting how downbeat I suddenly looked (and felt) and putting her arm around me. "That's not fair, is it?"

"Well, there's an easy way around that!" Chloe announced.

"Huh? How?" I asked, hoping that Chloe would have an amazing plan.

"Lie!" Chloe grinned. "Go round there on Monday after school and just *say* you're fourteen!"

Somehow I'd hoped Chloe's amazing plan would be just a *little* bit more amazing than that.

The thing is, I know some people can lie really easily, but whenever *I* try to, bits of me start randomly twitching – which means people can work out pretty quickly that I'm fibbing for Britain, or else they assume I'm telling the truth but have a strange medical condition.

Either way, it's not good news.

Nope, lying just isn't for me.

"OK – I'll do it!" I heard myself saying. "Since it's for my dad…"

Hey, I thought. *Wouldn't Dad be proud if he could hear me? Not only am I planning on lying, but I also manage to keep my resolve for about two seconds flat, and then blame it all on him.*

What a lovely, trustworthy daughter.
Not.

Chapter 6

CHAMPIONSHIP FRETTING

Feeling terrible through lack of sleep is OK if you've done something amazing the night before.

Something amazing like going to a great party (not that I've been to many of those), or having all your girlfriends round for a sleepover and talking rubbish with them till dawn (done that plenty of times), or being abducted by friendly aliens who beam you out of your bed, take you on a speed-of-light tour of the entire galaxy and deposit you back in your bedroom in time for breakfast (it's never happened, but then you never know, do you?).

But sitting at the kitchen table this Sunday morning – with a plateful of cold and spongy scrambled eggs sitting uneaten in front of me – I felt truly terrible through lack of sleep, and it wasn't for an amazing reason at all. It was because I'd lain awake for hours, merrily fretting about money, lack of money, Saturday jobs and lying.

"Look, Ally, it's only a case of adding a few months to your age, and it *is* in a good cause!"

Chloe had said to me, before me and the other girls had left her house after our GDVDN (Girls' DVD Night) the previous night. "Just don't make such a big deal of it!"

Don't make a big deal of it, don't make a big deal of it... I'd repeated silently in my head, as I lay poker-straight under the duvet.

But, of course, that's exactly what I did do, for hour after sleepless hour. Make a big deal about it, that is.

Outside my window, there were white lasers darting across the cloudy sky, thanks to some fancy event going on at Alexandra Palace. Normally, I'd have been perched on a chair, my nose practically pressed flat against the glass, staring at Ally Pally – all lit up like a fairytale castle on the hill – happily imagining what glitzy event was going on inside. But instead, I was running through a million problems in my head.

Like...

What if I went into the card shop on Monday after school, and the Card Shop Woman demanded proof of my age?

What if I went into the card shop on Monday after school, and the Card Shop Woman just somehow psychically *knew* that I was only thirteen?

What if I went into the card shop and couldn't

even *ask* about the job, because I was twitching so much due to the stress of lying about my age?

What if the Card Shop Woman gave me the job, but on my first day, some kind of Age-Checking Wardens from the council came in and demanded to know how old I really was?

Were there such things as Age-Checking Wardens? How could I find out if there were or not?

What if I was working there and people from my class came in and the Card Shop Woman worked out that they were only thirteen – so I must be too?

What if I went into the card shop on Monday after school and the job had already gone?

How could I help Dad out with money then?

How poor were we really?

How was Dad going to manage?

Where was Mum when we needed her…?

Oops, and I'd managed to work myself into a state about Mum, on top of everything else, which was really stupid.

That's the thing: me and my family pretty much try to think happy thoughts about Mum and where she is and what she's doing (Tor especially, but then he only knows the rose-tinted "Mum's-working-with-starving-sick-children-round-the-world" version of what happened anyway).

Somehow, during the last four years that she's been planet-hopping (just the one planet – earth – I mean; it's not like she's intergalactic or anything), Dad's been really good at getting us to think that way. "It's like this, girls," he once said to me, Rowan and Linn, "if she'd stayed here, she'd have been unhappy, even though she loves us all. If she's happier travelling the world, then we should be pleased for her – not sad. And she'll come back when she's ready…"

But there were times – like now – that I couldn't be happy that my hippy mum was off somewhere staring at stupid Roman ruins or tickling endangered sea turtles in Turkey or whatever the hell she was doing. All that mattered at times like this was that she wasn't around. And no matter how many cheery letters and postcards she sent home, it didn't help.

And now, here I was, after a night of championship fretting, lost in this lack-of-sleep pool of misery. I was still staring down at the remains of my yukky eggs when I heard Dad suddenly rustle his Sunday paper and say something.

"What?"

That was it; that was all he said. For a second, I thought he must be talking to me. Quickly, I plastered a fake half-smile across my face – there was no way I wanted to add to Dad's troubles with my worries – when I realized he was talking to Tor.

"What?" Dad repeated, staring at my little brother across the big table. "What's up, Tor?"

Tor hadn't said anything, but then he didn't have to. He has this way of just staring at you till you realize almost telepathically that he's got something to tell you.

"Can Freddie come round and play this afternoon?" said Tor.

Focusing in on Tor, I noticed that he had a teeny tiny bit of bacon in one hand, pulled off the rasher on his plate. As he spoke, he dropped his hand under the table. When it arrived back up beside his unfinished breakfast, there was no bit of bacon.

"Freddie?" frowned Dad. "But I thought you weren't friends with him any more?"

"Am now," said Tor, his marble-like brown eyes gazing straight and steady at our dad.

Maybe Tor thought he could hypnotize Dad into not noticing the fact that he was feeding bits of breakfast to a small something under the table. Dad wasn't too hot on feeding any of the animals titbits like that. It wasn't as if he was worried about hygiene or anything like that; it was just that Dad was scared of Grandma. Grandma *really* disapproved of Rolf and Winslet and the cats hovering around and begging at teatime, and since she came round and made our tea and ate with us every weeknight, we had to try to make sure it didn't happen.

"Well, of course Freddie can come round and play," said Dad, saying nothing about the rapidly disappearing bacon (maybe Tor *had* managed to hypnotize him).

"But if you've asked him round to play in the garden, better do a check with the pooper-scooper first," said Linn, emerging from behind a Sunday fashion supplement at the far end of the table.

In my drowsy daze, I'd forgotten she was even there. But I wasn't so drowsy that I didn't notice Tor's hand disappearing under the table again. I half-fancied bending down to see who was wolfing down the brown-sauce-covered bacon, but I didn't want to draw Dad's attention to it and get Tor into any hassle.

"Oh God, yes, Linn – you're right. Last time Emily was round, she got poo on her shoe and I didn't hear the *end* of it from her mother..." said Dad, pulling a face.

"Rolf didn't mean it!" said Tor, passionately. "He never does it on the grass! He just had a funny tummy that day!"

Yeah, I thought, *probably had a funny tummy*

from eating too much bacon covered in brown sauce or whatever else Tor was smuggling to him that day...

But it wasn't Rolf getting the benefit of animal-unfriendly snacks this particular morning. While Tor was being (unusually) talkative and jumping to our dopey dog's defence, he was suddenly slacking from his duties as bacon-smuggler. As he pleaded Rolf's innocence, a small ginger paw appeared from under the table, scrabbling in the air for more treats.

It looked like Colin was doing an amazing balancing act (well, amazing for a cat with only three out of four legs). And it looked like Dad, who hated telling any of us off, was about to finally notice what Tor was up to.

Only it wasn't Tor that got the telling off. Surprise, surprise ... it was Rowan.

"Aaaaaarrr*uuuummpphhhh!*" she yawned, padding barefoot into the kitchen and yanking out the chair next to Tor. "Give us the toast, Ally!"

Rowan doesn't like getting up early at weekends. But when she does get up, at least she normally looks vaguely human. This morning, though, she looked like she'd been in the tumble dryer all night and come out all rumpled and puffy and creased. I decided I probably looked perky as a breakfast-show presenter next to her.

"Rowan, what time did you get in last night?" Dad suddenly asked her outright – none of the cheeky remarks like "Morning, Ro! Or should I say *evening*!" that he normally comes out with.

He said it in this weird, uptight tone of voice, too, and Dad *never* speaks like that to any of us. He's always really cool about what time we come in – he knows we'd never take the mickey and stay out later than we're supposed to (well, at least that was what I thought *then* – I was soon to see how wrong *that* was). And as for that weird tone in his voice; it kind of knocked me off balance a bit. Well, enough that my arm wobbled frozen in mid-air, still holding on to the plate of toast.

I noticed that two little spots of pink had appeared on Rowan's face. She obviously hadn't expected that stuff either.

"I wasn't late!" she mumbled, looking hurt.

"Ro – you were supposed to be home by eleven."

My arm was starting to hurt. I remembered it was still hovering, and tried to stick it down on the table as quietly as I could. I shot a look at Linn, who shot a look back. It seemed as if she was as stumped as me at what was going on.

"I ... I *was* back by eleven, Dad!" protested Rowan. "You ... you were asleep in front of the TV!"

Rowan's eyes were really dark underneath. I wondered if she was ill, then I realized that it was just eye make-up that had slithered south.

"Yep, I did fall asleep in front of the TV," said Dad, his skinny face taut and tense, "but I woke up when I heard you come in. And it was nearly half-past two, Ro..."

Me and Linn's eyes darted towards each other in shock. Rowan had broken the rules. Not just Dad's rules, I mean – *our* rules. Our rules that us girls never, *ever* give our sweet and funny and kind dad any grief, since he's had enough with Mum going off like she did.

Only our sweet and funny and kind dad didn't seem too sweet and funny and kind right now. He was doing textbook Stern Dad stuff: Chapter 11-and-a-quarter – "Getting Really Mad When Kids Stay Out Too Late".

"It's not fair!" Rowan yelped, screeching her chair out from under her and getting to her feet. "You're always telling me what to do! I can't take it any more!"

I felt like I was still dreaming. Where did Rowan get that from? When had Dad ever come across like a bossy parent? (Apart from right this minute, of course...)

"Ro!" exclaimed Dad, frowning at her with

concern. "Calm down! I was only worried about you! I mean, anything could have happened—"

"Get off my back!" wailed Rowan, her eyes getting all filmy and teary. "It's not fair – Von and Chazza can do whatever they want! No-one hassles *them*!"

"Rowan!" Dad protested. "Why are you talking like this? Like I said, I was just worried about—"

"Leave me alone!" Rowan choked out. "I'm just – I'm just sick of everyone interfering in my life! I wish everyone would just LEAVE ME ALONE!"

And with that, she flounced off. Well, as much as you can flounce in a pair of tartan flannelette pyjamas.

"You OK?" I asked Tor.

Tor nodded back, his face glum. He now had Colin on his lap and was cuddling him hard. Colin, meanwhile, was chewing on a whole rasher of bacon and looking blissfully happy.

"Well," muttered Dad, his face pinched and white, as if he'd been slapped in the face. "Better go and see what all *that* was about..."

As Dad got up slowly – sighing a bit, and not really looking at any of the rest of us – Linn burst into efficient action, just like Grandma would have done if she'd been here.

"Come on, Tor!" she smiled brightly. "Let's take

all this toast to Priory Park and feed the ducks!"

"But—" murmured Tor, staring at our big sister like she'd gone mad.

"No buts! Come on!" she smiled, grabbing an old plastic bag from the utility room, and chucking the plateful of toast straight into it. "Get your jacket, Tor!"

It was nice of Linn to try to bustle Tor out of the house and take his mind off what had just happened. The only thing was – as Tor and I both knew – there weren't any ducks at Priory Park. In fact, the only bit of water in the whole place was a little kids' paddling pool, and I didn't suppose the little kids' mums would take too kindly to Linn and Tor chucking hard bits of toast at their children.

The other reason Tor had said "but..." was obvious to me as soon as I saw Linn bundling Tor's arms into his anorak sleeves and ordering him to step into the red wellies she'd plonked in front of him.

But I didn't say anything – not when I saw Tor's grinning face.

It looked like he thought it was going to be fun to go out and feed invisible ducks still dressed in his Spiderman jim-jams.

* * *

Precious… Never in the history of dogdom has there ever been a dog with a name that suits it less.

Sitting on the park bench, I couldn't even *hear* what Billy was wittering on about, his stupid dog was making such a racket.

"…so *Steven* goes to me, 'You're a total—"

Yap! Yappetty-yap! Yap!

"An' so *I* says to Steven, 'Well, you can just p—"

Yippetty-yap! Yap! Yap!

"An' then Hassan starts up and *he* says—"

Yap! Yap! Yippetty-yippetty yap! Yap! Yap! Yap! Yap!

I stared at Precious, willing the stupid poodle to shut up, but it didn't work. The yappy bundle of white fluff was meanwhile staring at Rolf and Winslet who were hunkered down on the grass, their scruffy heads resting between their front legs, looking like they wished with all their doggy hearts that it was physically possible to put their paws over their ears and drown out the noise.

"An' so *I* says, 'Hold on, Hassan, you don't know what's going on here!' "

Yippetty-yappetty yap! Yippetty-yippetty yap! Yap! Yap! Yap! Yap!

"Billy!" I yelp. "Never mind Hassan! *I* don't know what's going on – I can't hear you for Precious!"

Yippetty-yap! Yippetty-yippetty ... hmmphhh!

Reaching over, Billy had scooped up the hideous Precious with one hand and put his other hand over his mouth, clamping its over-worked jaws shut. Suddenly, it was as if peace and tranquillity had descended over the whole of the parkland around Alexandra Palace.

"Sorry," Billy grinned, holding Precious on his lap. "You know what he's like. He just gets excited when he sees your two..."

Poor Rolf and Winslet; I sometimes think that for them, playing with Precious must be as much fun as having a colony of fleas partying in your fur. Only louder.

But now that the world had gone quiet, "my two" were giving themselves a shake and a stretch (although not very far in the case of Winslet... Fate might have given her the long, hairy body of quite a substantial dog, but then it played a trick on her and gave her fun-size-Mars-bar legs).

"So anyway, what were you saying? About Steven and Hassan?"

"Well," said Billy, carrying on as if he didn't have an indignant poodle on his lap, growling quietly in protest at its mouth being clamped. "Like I was saying, there we were on Muswell Hill Broadway, arguing about all this stuff, when..."

I knew I was nodding at him, but really, my mind was drifting away. I didn't want it to – in fact I really wanted to listen to Billy's tales of what him and his mates got up to the night before (and that didn't happen very often; not when all that they usually did was hang around somewhere talking about Nintendo and then go back to some guy's house and *play* Nintendo). Still, I wanted to give my brain a rest from everything that was running through it, and my mate Billy's boring Saturday night seemed like the perfect antidote.

But then off my head went again, getting in a tangle over the idea of asking about this job tomorrow (and lying); about Dad getting uptight with Ro (must be down to worrying about money, I'd decided, when I escaped the house with the dogs after Tor and Linn had left); about Rowan going crazy and shouty (who knew what was up with *her*?).

I gritted my teeth and tried again to forget all that stuff, and tune into whatever Billy was wittering on about.

"...and it was then that I saw Rowan," I suddenly heard Billy say.

"What about her?" I frowned at him.

"Well..." said Billy, looking sheepish.

It wasn't going to be good news, I could tell.

"...she looked pretty out of it, Ally."

"You mean drunk?" I asked, feeling my heart do a triple-jump lurch.

The thing is, I knew Rowan sneaked into pubs sometimes along with Von and Chazza (*I* knew it and *Linn* knew it – not Dad, of course), but I didn't think she necessarily *drank* when she was in one. Well, not *alcohol*, I mean.

"I suppose she was drunk," Billy shrugged. "Or maybe she was stoned or something."

Oh God ... it was getting worse.

"It was just that she was with this crowd, and those mates of hers – the ones that are all pierced –" Billy continued, not knowing what else to do since I'd gone quiet, "and she was staggering around a bit; like I say, kind of out of it."

He was swaying around on the bench, trying to do an impression of Rowan, I supposed. Any other time, I'd have started giggling, he looked so silly – especially when he was doing it while holding a bad-tempered dog on his lap that looked as if it was about to explode like a fur-covered time-bomb.

But this wasn't any other time, and I didn't laugh.

Rowan was maybe sometimes a little weird, but right now, something *super*-weird was going on with her...

Chapter 7

BIG WIGS AND PLASTIC HEARTS...

If you didn't know Kyra Davies, and you just saw a photo of her standing still – I mean, *totally* still, with no expression on her face and none of the posing, attitudey stuff she pulls – you'd probably think she was really cute and sweet.

Ha.

That's the trouble with first impressions. You see this girl that looks like Bambi (long skinny legs, fawn-coloured skin, little snub nose with sprinkles of freckles, almond eyes) and you decide she's *got* to be sweet and cute. Then she opens her big gob.

"Working in a card shop? Are you *joking*? That's sounds really naff!"

I was glad Sandie was sitting in-between us on the bench. I might have had to accidentally stamp on Kyra's foot. Hard.

I was beginning to wish I'd never told her about it. But it *was* Monday morning, and what are you meant to do during break but catch up on what's been going on over the weekend with your so-called mates?

"And you'd never get me to do a Saturday job, full stop," Kyra yawned, looking around the playground with a bored expression on her "cute" face. "It's bad enough being *here* all week; the last thing I'd want to do is spend part of my precious weekend in some *boring* shop serving *boring* people..."

Don't know where she got this "precious" weekend stuff from. She'd only just finished telling me and Sandie that she'd been bored to bits the last couple of days and that the high point had been phoning Ricardo to finish with him. (But then she got *so* bored by Sunday night, she ended up phoning him to say she'd changed her mind, even though she'd decided she doesn't like him very much. How desperate does that sound?)

"And if you're so skint, Ally, why don't you just ask your dad to give you more pocket money?" Kyra suggested blithely. "Your dad seems really nice – I'm sure he wouldn't say no..."

Doh! Spoken like someone who's never had to worry about money in their life.

"I'd love a Saturday job," Sandie sighed, before I had a chance to reply to Kyra's dopey comment. "But my parents would never let me..."

"How come?" asked Kyra.

"They just wouldn't," Sandie replied, dropping her head down and scuffing at the tarmac with the toe of her black shoe.

"Are they quite strict or something?" Kyra frowned, scrunching around in her seat to face Sandie, now that the conversation had taken a more interesting turn for her.

"They're not exactly *strict*..." Sandie shrugged, tucking her fine, straight hair behind her ears.

"They just treat Sandie like she's three, not thirteen," I explained.

Poor Sandie ... it's hard being the only child when you have parents like Mr and Mrs Walker who just want to staple you up in nice, safe bubble-wrap and smother you in love. I swear they'd never let her out of the house and into the big, bad, germ-filled world if it wasn't against the law. And they'd certainly never dream of letting their Perfect Little Princess spend her Saturdays stacking shelves in Tesco.

Kyra slumped slightly, looking disappointed. I think she'd hoped for something more dramatic than that.

"Oh, look," she said, suddenly perking up again. "There's your weird sister, Ally. What's she doing?"

I swivelled round and spotted Rowan straight away. In a bobbing sea of people dressed in black, grey and white school uniform, Rowan stood out like a luminous life-raft. Her blazer and long skirt might have been black, but her accessories certainly weren't. On her feet she was wearing her current favourites: her red velvet mules. With those, she had on clashing pink tights (ouch). Her schoolbag was something she'd made herself – a big, mental, fluffy orange number with a yellow felt buttercup-type thing hand-stitched on it. Shoved high on her nose was a pair of heart-shaped purple sunglasses that I hadn't seen before.

But it wasn't the explosion-in-a-Fruit-Pastille-factory colour scheme that made me stare at her (that was pretty standard Rowan stuff, after all) – it was what she was doing: just slapping the heel of her hand against her forehead over and over again.

"Is she all right?" asked Sandie, tilting her head to one side and peering at my sister.

"Back in a minute…" I muttered, getting up off the bench and making my way over to her.

Rowan saw me and stopped with the head-smacking before I got within talking range.

"Ro? You OK?" I asked, feeling a bit funny.

Funny, 'cause we hadn't spoken about what had happened with her and Dad at breakfast the day before. When I'd got back from walking the dogs, Dad had explained to us that Rowan hadn't been feeling well, and was sorry for upsetting everyone. He told us she felt very silly and that it would be a good idea if we pretended nothing had happened and acted like normal. Which was pretty hard for me, considering what Billy had just told me up at the park.

And I guess that's why I felt funny too; for the moment I was keeping that bit of information secret till I could figure out exactly what to do with it...

"Yeah, I'm fine," Rowan nodded, making all the tiny, coloured plastic butterfly clips in her hair glint in the sun.

"What was with the..."

I did the *thunk-thunk* thing with my palm against my forehead.

"Oh ... it was just ... nothing," Rowan replied hurriedly. "I ... um ... found out we've got a test next period and I haven't swotted for it."

She blinked at me through the purple lenses of her sunglasses.

Are they new? I found myself wondering.

Suddenly, I found myself a bit annoyed with Rowan. Not so much for being a drongo and forgetting about a test (well, I managed to forget a whole *project* not so long ago); it was just the fact that our family was supposed to be on a mission to save money just now, yet here was Rowan, with another new trinket for her collection of tat.

"When did you get those?" I asked, pointing my finger so close to her that she went cross-eyed.

"What – *these?*" she asked, fidgeting with one arm of her sunglasses and trying to sound all casual. "I've had them – oooh! – for ages!"

That wasn't true. And I knew that for two reasons: first, any time Rowan gets something new she parades it around me and Linn and Dad and everyone, like it's the most fantastic thing that's ever been invented; and second, those pink spots on her cheeks were getting pinker.

Yep, Rowan was definitely a liar, liar, though I didn't fancy checking to see if her pants were on fire.

"Um … got to go! See if I can cram any revision for this test thingy…"

And with that, Rowan slipped inside the building, in a blur of technicolour.

"Well? How was the Weird One?" asked Kyra, as I moseyed on over to the bench again.

"OK – just freaked out about a test she's got," I shrugged.

I didn't really want to go into it any more with

Kyra, somehow. For her, whatever was going on with Rowan was just a bit of fun gossip, and I didn't want to do that to Rowan, even though I was kind of miffed with her right at that moment.

Just then, I felt Sandie link her arm around mine, and I knew that *she* knew there was more to it than what I'd just told Kyra. I looked at her questioning face and gave her arm a little squeeze (best-buddy sign-language for "I'll tell you later") and she mouthed me back a silent "OK".

Of course, Kyra didn't notice any of this – subtlety isn't really her thing. But then, just as I'd written her off as being too annoying to bother with this morning, she suddenly came out with something that made sense...

"Listen, Ally, I was thinking," she began, as she held out her hands and studied her nails. "If you're *really* up for this scuzzy Saturday job, why wait till after school to do something about it? It could be gone by then. Why don't you phone now? Before the end of break?"

Sometimes it takes someone else to state the obvious. So, in the space of five minutes, I'd borrowed a phone book from the school office, shoved twenty pence in the public phone in the hall, and found myself connected to someone who sounded very batty indeed.

"Aloha!" crooned a woman's voice.

"Um ... I'm not sure if I've got the right number," I mumbled, not expecting anyone Hawaiian to answer the phone.

"And who did you want, dear?"

"Um, I was trying to get through to Something Special..."

"Ooh, and you are through to Something Special, dear ... something very special indeed!" tittered the voice.

I could instantly put a face to the voice now. Whenever I'd passed the Something Special card shop, I'd half-noticed the Grandma-aged woman who ran the place. She had the most amazing head of fancy blonde curls I'd ever seen. It looked like a (only slightly) scaled-down version of something Marie Antoinette might have worn. ("Wig..." Grandma had muttered sniffily, patting her own elegant grey crop one Saturday, when we'd been strolling past and I'd commented on the vision of blondeness.)

"Well," I gulped, and tried to continue, "I was wondering ... the Saturday job. I was wondering..."

I wasn't doing this very well. Either my money was going to run out or the end-of-break bell was going to blast off above my head before I got any further. But I have this funny thing about phones

☆ 73 ☆

sometimes. It's just that I find it really hard to communicate with someone I've never spoken to before, if I can't look them in the eyes. It's like I'm talking into this big void down the phone and I don't know what the other person is thinking at all, since I can't see their face to figure it out. Does that make sense?

I bit my lip and tried again, this time imagining Wig Woman and her towering pile of blonde curls at the other end of the line.

"I wondered if the Saturday gob was still jo-ing."

Nice! I winced, cringing at the mess I'd made of that. Even if the "gob" was still "jo-ing", she wasn't going to give it to someone who couldn't even speak.

"The Saturday job?" the Wig Woman trilled. "Yes, I still have a vacancy for that. Do you want to come in and see me about it?"

A wave of relief whooshed over me. Suddenly it seemed so easy. After stressing out the whole weekend since Chloe had first told me about it, here I was, being offered an interview. Just like that. Even after I got completely tongue-tied and nearly goofed up.

"Yeah ... I mean, yes. Please. But I'm at school right now..."

"Fine! So why don't you just pop along this

afternoon, when you finish?" Wig Woman suggested. "Just come in and ask for Mrs Merrill. And what's your name, dear?"

"Ally," I smiled stupidly, as if she could see me. "Ally Love."

"Ooh, how pretty!" cooed Wig Woman. "Look forward to seeing you later then, dear!"

And that was it. Perfect timing too, 'cause just as I put down the receiver (with my hand wobbling like it was made of rubber or something), the bell blasted off.

"I've got an interview!" I whispered to myself, setting off for my next class with a grin slapped right across my face. "I might get a job!"

As I started running up the stairs, with a million other people storming up behind me, something made me glance down through the stairwell. A certain sparkle that yanked my eyes like a magnet: Rowan was standing just outside the loo doors, holding something in her hands ... her new sunglasses, which looked – strangely – like they were now in two separate bits.

Serves her right, I thought, as the crush of people behind me shoved me further up the stairs. *If she blew money we can't afford on a stupid pair of sunglasses, she deserves it if they've been broken.*

But even if Rowan *did* deserve it, it still made

me feel kind of gutted to see how totally sad she looked, holding a stupid, purple, plastic heart in each hand...

Chapter 8

ROWAN AND HER SPEED-OF-LIGHT MULES...

"I'll get the job…"

I yanked a leaf off the small branch I was holding in my hand.

"I'll get the job … *not*."

Yank – another leaf gone.

"I'll get the job…"

Yank.

"I'll get the job … *not*."

Yank.

It was five past four on Monday afternoon, and I was heading along the pavement towards Crouch End Broadway, mumbling to myself and leaving a trail of hedge bits in my wake. I'd been walking along, doing my usual tummy-flipping panic thing (about the interview and about the fact that I was about to lie to get the job), when I'd idly let my fingers trail along someone's garden hedge. I'd only meant to pull off one leaf, but tension must have made me stronger than usual and I ended up tugging out this whole sodding branch. I couldn't exactly stuff it back in, so I'd started with my alternative to the daisy petals and the "He loves me, he loves me not" routine, just to have something to concentrate on till I got to the card shop.

"I'll get the job..." I continued to mumble.

But before I could dissect the next chunk of shrubbery, I heard a horrible sound.

It's funny how you can recognize the sound of bullying, isn't it? It's the tone of the voices, even if you can't hear the exact words. It's like if a mate is shouting to you to wait for them, it sounds friendly, doesn't it? But when the yelling is about something nasty, it's like you can make out the poisonous atmosphere a kilometre away.

I glanced across the road, but it was hard to make out who was doing the bullying and who was on the receiving end; the traffic was madly busy and the whole of the opposite pavement – like the one I was walking along – was heaving with people in school uniforms, all streaming off towards home.

Suddenly, I forgot all about the bullying bellows, because right then, in the middle of everyone, I spotted a flash of bright pink, and could just make out Rowan, rushing past everyone; squeezing and excusing herself as she bolted ahead, her red velvet mules flippety-flapping at top speed.

Why's she hurrying so much? And where she going? It's not the most obvious way to go home... I thought to myself, peering through the constant zoom of cars and buses and lorries and wondering if I could possibly get across the road at any time in the next month.

Glancing left, right, and left and right again, I saw a gap in the traffic and took it. But while I'd been concentrating on getting over the road, Rowan had conveniently vanished from view.

I stopped standing still like an idiot (being jostled and stood on wasn't the best fun in the world) and decided I should just get on with it – I had an interview to go to after all....

"...and over there are the condolences cards, although I do hate to sell those – it always means that a tragedy's happened to some poor family, doesn't it, dear?"

The Wig Woman – Mrs Merrill – rubbed her hands in contemplation and shook her head sadly. Normally, when someone shook their head that way, you'd expect to see some movement, but there was no mobile-hair action going on with Mrs Merrill's rock-hard locks. Those curls stayed stubbornly curled, without a bounce in sight. Yep, Grandma was right – it had to be a wig.

Mrs Merrill had done nothing but yatter at me since the second I'd walked through the door and stammered my name, which was quite a relief, since all *I* had to do was nod and look interested.

The only dodgy moment had come when she'd pointed out a bowl full of birthstone keyrings for sale beside the cash register and asked me which one I was. I gulped and had to admit I didn't know. Mum probably told me what my birthstone was when I was little; when I wasn't paying attention because I (foolishly) supposed she'd always be around and that I could ask her things I'd forgotten whenever the fancy took me. Mrs Merrill seemed to frown a bit when I said I didn't know, and it did make me worry that that was one big black mark against me. Although her shop was full of pretty corny, sensible ranges of cards, she herself seemed to come from Planet Looney Tunes (the big, mad hair, the fact that she was singing "Oh I do Like to be Beside the SEASIDE!" at the top of her voice when I walked in), and I was sure knowledge of birthstone keyrings would figure high on her list of priorities.

"...and now the till. Have you ever worked one, dear?"

I dragged my eyes away Mrs Merrill's hairline (I was sure I could just see some normal grey hair poking out from under it) and tried to concentrate on what she was saying as she moved behind the counter. Behind her, the cars and buses hummed past outside the big plate-glass window.

"Um, no ... I haven't. Used a till, I mean," I shook my head.

Like a normal person, my long brown hair fell around my shoulders when I moved.

"Never mind! Won't take long for a sharp young mind to pick it up!" she said cheerfully.

Phew – it looked like being a novice in charge of a till full of money was less of a problem for Mrs Merrill than a shocking lack of knowledge about birthstone keyrings.

"All the buttons are very simple, and it's very easy to correct if you make a mistake. In fact, all you have to do..."

I stopped listening at that point. Not because I was bored, or I'm horribly rude or anything – it was just that I was curious to see Rowan on the other side of the road, with her mate Von. Von, dressed in black canvas army trousers and a long-sleeved black T-shirt, looked years older than Rowan in her (weird-around-the-edges) school uniform. I mean, I know Von is three years older than my fifteen-year-old sister, but somehow the age gap seemed even bigger – and maybe that was because Rowan looked like she was just a miserable little kid, the way she was mooching alongside Von, with her head hanging down.

"...so, what's your phone number, dear?" I heard, tuning back in to what Mrs Merrill was saying just at the right time.

Mustering a smile, I took the pen she was holding out to me and scribbled our number down on the pad where she'd already written my name.

Rowan would like this pen, I found myself thinking, as I doodled the green ink across the white paper, the huge baby-blue feathers glued to the top of it nearly tickling the end of my nose.

Finishing, I straightened up, handed the pen back to Mrs Merrill, and tried to sneak a peek out of the window again – but Rowan (and Von) were nowhere to be seen.

"Lovely! Well, I've a couple of other people to interview, Ally, dear," Mrs Merrill beamed, "but I'll give you a rinkle-tinkle as soon as I've made up my mind!"

It wasn't till I was halfway home – musing over what was going on with Rowan and wondering when exactly Mrs Merrill would give me a "rinkle-tinkle" – that I realized she'd never even bothered to ask me how old I was...

Chapter 9

HOME ALONE(ISH)

I really like all my friends, and they all really like me (hopefully). But there is one thing I prefer to do without them.

It's nothing drastic; nothing exciting. It's just that Chloe, Jen, Salma and Kellie always stay for school dinners (and maybe that's why the four of them are such a tight little clique), while I like to bumble on home and have lunch there. Sandie goes home too, but that's just 'cause her mum demands it – she can't bear not to see her "snookie-cookums" all the way from breakfast through to home-time, so doing anything but sharing a bowl of home-made soup with Mummy dearest is not an option. Kyra goes home too, but I don't think *her* mum calls her stuff like "snookie-cookums", not from the little she's told us about her mum and her drinking problems. Poor Kyra ... every time she bugs me I should always remember that she's got *that* hassle going on in her life.

Anyhow, the reason I like to go home at

lunchtime is that, after the noise and hassle and crush of school, the house seems calm and cosy and lovely by comparison. And, much as I love Dad and everyone, it is kind of nice to go back to this quiet house, where there's only the sound of Radio One, me flicking through a magazine, and the odd purr and pant from the various cats and dogs.

Apart from the sound of the telly in the living room of course – that's where you'll find Rowan at lunchtimes; flicking channels with the remote control while eating her beetroot and cottage cheese sandwich, or whatever weird concoction she's slung together.

We (normally) get on great, me and Ro, and we can (normally) talk to each other for ages about stuff, but lunchtimes are funny. We both really like our own space, so while she does her TV thing, I leave her alone, and while I'm mooching in the kitchen with a magazine, she leaves *me* alone. Generally the only thing we say to each other at lunchtimes is "Hiya!" when we come in, and "See ya!" when whichever one of us heads back to school first. And that's just the way it seems to work.

But today was different. Today – Tuesday – I was twitching away at the table, *totally* not concentrating on the *Get the look of Joey from Dawson's*

Creek! feature in front of me and staring through the kitchen door out into the lilac-coloured hall, wondering what was going on with my big (but not biggest) sister.

I couldn't put it off any longer. I couldn't put off ignoring what Billy had said, and ignoring how she'd flipped out at Dad on Sunday morning, and ignoring that I saw her looking all miserable with Von the day before...

So, I chucked the rest of my sandwich in the bin (i.e. Rolf, who was waiting patiently beside the bin with his mouth open and a hopeful expression on his doggy face), and walked through to the living room.

"All right?" I said, casually as I could, flopping down on to the sofa.

"*Yeah*," muttered Rowan, giving me a "Why are you through here?" glance from the armchair, where she and Winslet were sharing a peanut-butter-smeared Ryvita.

But I knew she wasn't all right. She had the news on, for goodness' sake. Rowan *never* has the news on. If there isn't some soap or chat-show type thing to watch, she'd rather stick on an old video of *Friends* or Tor's ancient *Bob the Builder* video than watch the news. It isn't that she doesn't give a hoot about the world and current affairs and stuff

– it's just that it tends to upset her too much. You know how you see some stuff about a famine or a war and you see the kids and you feel sad? Well, Rowan doesn't just feel sad – she feels gutted, and then she uses up half the tissue reserves of the *world* sobbing over what's just happened.

So the fact that she was sitting glued to the news was *not* a good sign.

"What are you watching?" I asked stupidly, not sure how to start asking her what I wanted to ask her.

"The news," she replied, staring straight ahead at the screen, while Winslet took the last hunk of Ryvita out of her hand and swallowed it whole. Rowan didn't seem to notice. Or maybe she didn't care.

She didn't look herself today, I suddenly noticed. Her dark hair was scraped back into a ponytail with a dark scrunchie. Her tights were black. Her shoes, lying on the carpet beside the armchair where she'd kicked them off, were an old pair of black cotton Chinese pumps. In fact, the only glint about my normally ultra-glinty sister was one spangly yellow grip pinning her hair off her face in a side parting. And that was it.

"The news..." I repeated, even more stupidly.

I didn't know how to start with everything I had

to say. So I didn't. I copped out.

"So ... are you ... OK just now?" I asked her vaguely, hoping she'd make my life easy and just start pouring out whatever was bothering her.

Like, *yeah*.

"Course I'm OK. Don't I look OK?" she answered me, sounding a little snippy.

And before I could work up the courage to say anything else, she hit the volume button and started to look really interested in the news piece about the petro-chemical industry in Angola or wherever.

I knew I shouldn't have, but I gave up at that point. Maybe I should have tried harder, but until I'd worked out a smart way of getting her to talk, I thought I was probably just going to irritate her rather than help her.

"Well ... I'm heading back to school," I mumbled, pushing myself upright off the squashy sofa. "So ... see ya!"

"Yeah ... later!" she called, as I walked out into the hall.

"What's up with her?" I whispered to Rolf, who was now settling down for a doze on top of the wellies and shoes by the door after having his lunchtime snack – my leftover sandwich.

"Harrr-umfff," he replied, as I lifted my blazer off its hook and pulled it on.

Maybe it was just a doggy burp, but I felt like Rolf was agreeing with me.

"Exactly," I nodded down at him.

I reached up again to grab my bag, and stopped dead – frowning at a couple of white stringy blobs on the back of Ro's jacket. What were they?

I frowned some more and focused harder, then realized it was bits of chewing gum. I know I got some on my jeans a couple of times when morons had stuck gum on the seats on the bus, but how had Rowan managed to get some on her *back*?

Still, the mood Rowan was in, I wasn't about to ask her.

Chapter 10

GURGLES AND GROANS

Sandie was sitting bent over the desk in my room, her fair hair flopping forward and her tongue sticking out of the corner off her mouth as she concentrated.

The tape had finished, and even though Sandie was closer to my stereo than I was, she was too caught up in what she was doing to notice.

I was lying on my stomach on the bed, my head propped up in my hands, staring vaguely at Sandie and wondering if I could be bothered to get up and turn the tape over.

For a few seconds, the only sound in the room was my stomach gently gurgling. Grandma had made an excellent tea – home-made pizza and strawberry cheesecake (boy, was Sandie pleased she'd hung around this particular Wednesday night!) – but my stomach didn't seem too happy about it. It was making more noise than the groany old water pipes that rattled the length of our house whenever you even *looked* at a tap, never mind turn one on.

"Greeee-oooow-*nooooof*!!"

That was it. That was enough with the stupid stomach noises.

"Sandie – go and flip the tape!" I begged her, since I had zilch energy to move from my comfy position.

"In a minute…" mumbled Sandie.

"But Sandie, it's too quiet in here. We need music!"

"There!" Sandie announced, suddenly sitting up straight and grinning at me. "What do you think?"

She was holding out her hands towards me, wiggling her fingers wide, to show off the new nail varnish she'd just put on (a freebie that she peeled off the front of the magazine she'd brought round with her).

"Yuk!" I said, automatically scrunching up my nose. "It looks like your fingers have got the plague!"

I didn't mean to be horrible – it's just that I couldn't figure out how anyone could sit in a lab or wherever they made nail varnish, and decide that the most groovy colour they could come up with was a kind of sickly grey-blue (not forgetting the special sheeny-shiny effect it had, like the sheeny-shiny lustre of an oil spill…).

"Yeah, it *is* pretty yukky," Sandie agreed with

me, replacing her smile with a little scowl. "Got any nail-varnish remover?"

"Linn'll have some – I'll get it off her before you go home," I mumbled, sinking my head down into my hands so that my knuckles squished my cheeks further up my face.

"You look like a cross between a frog and a chipmunk when you do that," said Sandie.

"Thank you," I mumbled, without rearranging my face in any way.

"Do you want me to try out one of the quizzes on you?" asked Sandie, pointing to the magazine in front of her.

"Go on, then," I muttered, without much enthusiasm.

Reaching over to the stereo, Sandie expertly flipped the tape around with one hand, while flicking her hand through the pages of the magazine with the other.

"Here's one!" she announced, letting her finger drop on one page, while the music started up behind her. "OK... so this one's called '*Are You A Happy Bunny?*'"

"Shouldn't you be trying this out on Cilla instead of me?" I said grumpily, thinking of the fat, fluffy, carrot-cruncher who'd be snoozing out in her rabbit hutch as we spoke.

"Ha, ha," said Sandie brightly. "Right, so the first question is… *'There's something making you feel a bit blue just now. Is it … a) Worrying about your sister, b) Stressing out about the fact that the woman in the card shop hasn't phoned you back yet, or c) Both of these'*."

Now it was my turn for the fake laugh.

"Ha, ha," I said, dropping my elbows and flopping my head down on the bed, so that my face was buried in my cloud-patterned duvet.

"But it's true, isn't it? You're getting all stressed out about the job thing, *and* about Rowan, aren't you?" I heard Sandie ask.

"Yuff," I mumbled, my words (well, *word*) getting muffled in amongst the cotton clouds.

She was right. I was letting it all get me down, and apart from telling Sandie about it, I was being truly rubbish and doing nothing to sort any of it out. And, bless her, though Sandie's a great listener and brilliant at being sympathetic, she's not that great at giving me any advice.

"I mean, with the lady at the card shop – why don't you just go in after school tomorrow, and ask her if you've got the job or not?" Sandie suggested.

Because I couldn't bear the humiliation of her telling me to my face that I haven't got it, I thought to myself. *I'd be so embarrassed that I'd have to cross the road every time I'm passing by the shop...*

Sandie was silent for a bit, giving me the chance to say something back, but I didn't. I just made a non-committal noise.

"Humf," I grunted.

"And, with Rowan, why don't you just tell your dad about Billy seeing her drunk on Saturday, and that you're worried about how weird she's being?"

Because Billy is lovely but he can be a real berk sometimes, and what if he got it wrong? And what if I've put two and two together and come up with something completely stupid? I mean, if she was getting into booze or something, would those really be the symptoms? Flying off the handle on Sunday morning maybe, but dressing nearly normally (like today) and looking all peed off when I saw her with Von (like yesterday) doesn't mean there's anything serious going on with her...

Look at that – my mind is very good at worrying (I think I'd get an A+ if they did exams in Worrying). It's just that my mouth is sometimes not very good at saying it all.

"Humf," I repeated.

Then the phone jangled into life, which in turn jangled me out of my soggy mood.

"Why is no-one answering that?" I asked, lifting my head up.

Dad was at his evening class (well, it's actually his line-dancing class, but that's almost too embarrassing to mention), but last time I looked, Rowan and Linn were both downstairs in the living room with Tor.

The phone kept trilling away.

"My stupid sisters!" I grumbled, pushing myself off the bed and stomping my way to the door and down the attic steps.

But just as I reached the first-floor landing, the ringing stopped, and so did I.

"Hello, this is Tor. Who are you?" I heard my little brother say.

I hovered about in case it was Billy. Sometimes, me and Billy only see each other once a week, when we meet up with the dogs on Sunday morning. But we speak to each other loads – usually 'cause Billy gets bored easily and likes to phone me up and tell me how bored he is.

"You sound funny," I heard Tor giggle.

What was Billy doing? *Yodelling* down the phone?

"I'm seven. How old are you?"

Well, it wasn't Billy. Tor knew that he was thirteen, same age as me.

"Huh? She's in her bedroom."

I glanced around the upstairs hall and saw no

light shining under Rowan's door, and Linn's door had been wide open into a darkened room when I sped down here, so I quickly worked out (duh!) that the call *had* to be for me. I started down the last flight of stairs, looking over the bannister at Tor's dark head bobbing below.

"Uh-huh. OK. I'll shout for her. *Allllllyyyy!*"

"I'm coming! I'm coming!" I said out loud, and mouthed "Who is it?" at him.

Tor shrugged and held out the phone towards me, but just as I got within two footsteps of him, I saw his eyes light up and he thudded the receiver back to his ear again.

"Are you the old lady with the w—"

In one smooth move I yanked the phone away from him and closed my other hand over his mouth.

"Hello?" I said tentatively.

"Is that Miss Love?" came a sing-song voice that could only belong to Mrs Merrill.

"Yes," I answered breathlessly, hoping against hope that she a) was going to tell me good news, and b) hadn't worked out what my darling little brother had been about to say.

"That was the Wig Woman, wasn't it?" Tor asked me, when I finally hung up the phone and let go of his mouth.

"Don't call her that!" I reprimanded him.

"Why not?" he blinked at me. "You did at teatime."

Oops.

He was right. I'd been moaning to Sandie – when only her, me and Tor were left at the table having our second helpings of what was left of the cheese-cake – and I'd called Mrs Merrill Wig Woman.

"Well, we can't call her that any more," I smiled at him. "It's rude, and anyway, her name is Mrs Merrill."

After all, I couldn't be horrible about her now. Not when the lovely, gorgeous, mad-as-a-very-mad-fruitbat Mrs Merrill had just offered me a one-day try-out at her shop on Saturday...

Chapter 11

TOM HANKS? NO THANKS.

"You can't put *him* on your list! He's old! *And* he doesn't qualify!" Chloe barked at Jen.

It was only meant to be a laugh, a stupid game of list-making that filled an otherwise dull Wednesday-afternoon breaktime. But for once, Jen didn't giggle. She looked really offended that Chloe wouldn't let her have Tom Hanks (her favourite ever actor) on her Top-Five Totty list. But to be fair to Chloe, she *had* specified that the list had to be made up of boys we actually knew, or knew-ish. *And* they had to be boys. Forgive me for being pernickety, but as Tom Hanks doesn't live in Crouch End, London, N8 and he's several decades older than any boy we know, he didn't qualify on either count.

"Well, I can only think of four people round here that I fancy – so why can't I put Tom Hanks on to make it up to five?" Jen protested.

"Because he's disgusting," Chloe said flatly, putting a blunt end to Jen's argument.

"Yewww…" shuddered Kellie. "I don't know how you can fancy him anyway, Jen – why can't you go for someone who's less than a hundred years old?"

"He was good in *Forrest Gump*, though," said Sandie, slithering away from my side and trying to show some solidarity to Jen, who was looking seriously wobbly now that someone had dared to have a dig at her ultimate Hollywood human.

"Yeah, but plenty of actors are good in films – it doesn't mean you have to get a crush on them," Salma blinked slowly at Jen and Sandie. "Specially when they're as minging as Tom Hanks…"

While my friends were debating just how "minging" Tom Hanks was or wasn't, I found myself staring at my own Top-Five Totty list, which the girls had all been teasing me about right before Chloe started on Jen.

So, I'd written down Alfie's name five times. So what?

Quickly, I scrunched the list up and aimed it right at the bin. The last thing I needed was to have it flutter out of my pocket at home, only to be discovered by Linn. I've done a stunning job so far of hiding the fact that I have a crush the size of France on her best friend, but – and I might be wrong here – a list headed "Ally's Top-Five Totty" followed by "Alfie!" x 5, and with loveheart doodles all around it might *just* give the game away.

But my perfectly projected ping! missed its mark. Or at least, the flight path of my scrunched note was interrupted – instead of landing in the bin, it boinged off the side of a passing teacher's head and rolled right under a radiator.

"Sorry!" I cringed, as Mrs Wilson from the English department gave me the evil eye.

She threw me the sort of do-that-again-and-it's-detention dirty look that teachers specialize in, and carried on walking. For about half a second.

Omigod, she'd stopped. Omigod, she was turning round. Omigod, it looked like she'd decided not to let me off with just the regulation dirty-look thing after all.

"You're Ally Love, aren't you?" she said, holding her plastic folder and pen clenched tight to her chest.

"Yuh-hung..."

It's hard to get words to do the right thing when you're about to be charged with assaulting a teacher with a lethal paper-ball and all your friends are watching open-mouthed.

"So, how's your sister?"

I hadn't been prepared for that. If Mrs Wilson

had said, "Get to the Headmaster's office NOW!" or "That's it – you've got detention till you're 35!" or something, then I wouldn't have been so shocked. Mortified, maybe, but not shocked.

"Which one?" I asked, trying frantically to remember whether it was Linn or Rowan who had the (dis)pleasure of being taught by Mrs Wilson.

"Rowan," she replied.

The wind whistled through my empty, clueless head. What was the silly old bat asking about Rowan for?

"She wasn't in class this afternoon?" said Mrs Wilson, giving me a huge hint.

"Ahhhh..." I mumbled in a long, drawn-out breath, to give myself time to think.

Mrs Wilson stared hard at my gently reddening face, waiting for a response. To one side of me, I could practically *hear* the silence as my mates held their breath.

"Rowan ... is ... I mean, *has*..."

The corner of my mouth started to vibrate as the lie began to form.

"...diarrhoea!" I finally exclaimed.

"Mmm," muttered Mrs Wilson, narrowing her eyes and believing me not one bit.

Which was fair enough since it was a big, fat lie.

"Tell her to get better soon, then."

"I will," I nodded at Mrs Wilson.

I'll tell her, all right, I thought to myself. *I'll tell her right after I've killed her for making me cover for her like this...*

Chapter (12)

NUH-UH...

OK, so when Mrs Wilson corralled me in the corridor, my first reaction was to suspect Rowan was skiving.

But then, as soon as I'd parked my bum on the uncomfortable stool in the science class, my highly attuned Worrying Gland kicked in.

And my pattern of worrying went like this...

Stage 1. *Why would Rowan skive off? She's never done it before, as far as I know.*

Stage 2. *She's dead!*

Stage 3. *Stop it – she's not dead. She was making herself a tuna and pea sandwich when I went home at lunchtime (blee). And she left for school a couple of minutes before me, so if she'd been run over by a rampaging milk float or something, I'd have come across her lying in the gutter, covered in semi-skimmed.*

Stage 4: *Aaargh! But she could have been abducted – it can happen so fast; one minute you're there and the next you're gone...*

Stage 5: *I've got to ask Miss Kyriacou if I can leave class, so I can go and tell someone that my sister's been abducted!*

Stage 6: *But what if I tell people Rowan's been abducted, and she really is just skiving? I'll get her into terrible trouble...*

Stage 7: *But what if I keep my mouth shut, and she really has been abducted?*

Stage 8: *Don't panic – she hasn't been abducted. She's just skiving. I hope.*

Stage 9: *Return to Stage 1, and repeat for two lessons and the entire walk home after school...*

By the time I got to my front door, I had an ulcer. Well, not a proper one, but a serious burny, churny knot. And it was burning, churning and knotting because I had convinced myself that I'd open the front door and find my whole family weeping and wailing over my poor squashed-in-the-road/abducted sister.

But instead, there was the sound of giggling, shooing and cooing...

In order of appearance – as I followed the sounds and bumbled through to the kitchen – there was Tor (doing the giggling), Grandma (with a tea towel in her hand, doing the shooing) and Britney the pigeon (doing the cooing. And the pooing, actually – right on the kitchen floor).

"Tor, dear, stop laughing and help me get this bird out of the house, please!" ordered Grandma, staring sternly from the small, smirking boy to the puzzled-looking pigeon flapping around on the table.

Britney is a fairly recent addition to our house-cum-zoo. Tor found her, battered, bruised and dragging her poorly pigeon wing about, when we were at Camden Market a couple of months back. He took her home to recuperate, and after regaining her strength and unruffling her feathers in our garden shed, Tor held a very dramatic release ceremony, which was compulsory for all of us in the family to attend, as well as a few of his buddies from school.

But the release wasn't as dramatic as we'd expected: after Tor had come out of the shed and launched Britney skyward (with lots of accompanying "Ooh!"s from us lot), she'd promptly fluttered into the nearest tree, and has stayed there ever since. Except, of course, when she's down on the bird table, eating the nuts and old bread that Tor sticks out for her every day. Or when she's got impatient for her waiter to bring her her tea and has flapped her way through the open back door to see what the hold-up is in the kitchen...

As I watched Tor try to tempt Britney out of the

door by wafting a Jaffa Cake under her beak, it suddenly occurred to me to ask for any sightings of my elusive sister.

"Hey, have you two seen—"

"Hello! I'm home!" I heard a voice interrupt me from the hallway.

There was a bang as the front door slammed shut, and a familiar *flippety-flap* as Rowan tripped up the stairs.

She wasn't getting away that easily…

Turning away from the bird-baiting drama in the kitchen, I went out into the hallway and thundered up behind Rowan, determined to find out what drama was going on with her.

"Where have you been?" I blurted out, barging into her fairy-light-lit room without bothering to knock. (Not nice, I know – but then I was still pretty wound up. Even if I was stupendously glad to see that she hadn't been abducted. Well, not bodily anyway. But what she said next made me wonder if her *brain* had been abducted and left a stupid great hole where it should have been…)

"What?" she asked me, her cheeks doing that pink hot-spot thing.

"Where have you been, Ro?" I repeated, trying to look stern, even though Rolf had just head-butted me in the knees as he squeezed his way into the room to see what all the excitement was about.

"What do you mean, 'Where have I been?' I've been at school, same as you!"

"Nuh-*uh!*"

OK, so "nuh-*uh*" isn't the smartest bit of cross-examining, but I had used up so much brainpower stressing out about Rowan all afternoon that I couldn't rely on my words to work.

Still, who was she kidding?

"Ro, if you were at school this afternoon, how come your teacher, Mrs Wilson, gave me a hard time, asking me why you weren't in her class? Hmm?"

Rowan's cheeks went as pinky-red as the roses on her white duvet. Her eyes were as wide as her mouth was open. She knew she'd been rumbled.

"But I ... I ... I *was* in her class today!" she stammered.

"What – but you just happened to be *invisible?*" I suggested sarcastically.

I mean, how dumb did she think I was? Or Mrs Wilson for that matter. Who could miss Rowan in a hurry? Even today, when she was dressed down again, she was still more noticeable than Harrods at Christmas, when the entire building is covered in white lightbulbs. It wasn't that Rowan was her usual colourful self today (hair scraped back and dressed in mostly black again, I noticed, except for the return of the red velvet mules). It was just that she was tinkling. Yeah – tinkling. Rolf had noticed it too; he was jerking his head round every time he heard it, as if he was expecting Colin or one of the other cats to emerge in their belled collars at any second.

"Where's that tinkling noise coming from?" I quizzed her.

Reluctantly, Rowan pulled up her school shirt and showed me. It was a belly chain made out of a fine strip of black leather, with teeny-tiny silver balls attached every few centimetres.

"Do you like it?" Rowan asked, batting her long, dark lashes at me appealingly.

(Right that second she reminded me of a goofy-but-sweet King Charles spaniel that me and the dogs often meet up in Ally Pally park at the week-end. I looked at Rolf and really wished he could talk; just so I could ask him if he agreed with me.)

My honest answer about the belly chain? Well, it would have looked nice on a beach in Brazil, worn with a bikini, and preferably if you were a tanned-tummied goddess. But if I was honest, under a school uniform, in a crumbly terraced house in Crouch End, north London, and on a white-as-cottage-cheese stomach it looked a bit strange.

Still, "strange" and "Rowan" kind of go hand-in-hand...

"It's ... nice!" I said irritably. "But what happened to you today at school, Ro?"

If she tried to tell me she was there again, I'd scream. Or grab her by her belly chain and shake her till she played "Jingle Bells".

"I... I..."

Suddenly Rowan seemed all small and pathetic, as she flopped down on to her bed. Against the backdrop of the multi-coloured fairy lights twinkling round most things that stand still in her room, Rowan – with her dark hair, pale skin and big brown eyes – looked like a forlorn little pixie. And I was the big, bad, bullying witch, even though here I was, her thirteen-year-old kid sister.

I wasn't going to give in, though. She'd made me too sick with worry all afternoon to back down. I took a leaf out of Mrs Wilson's book and narrowed my eyes at her. It soon did the trick. (Thank you, Mrs Wilson, even if I do think you're a miserable old bat.)

"Please don't tell on me but I was at Von's she had the afternoon off college and begged me to come round and hang out with her I know it was stupid I won't do it again please don't tell Dad Ally please please don't," blabbed Rowan in one breathless blur.

I'm not very good at confrontation. In fact, doing anything confrontational gives me the same twitchy thing as lying does. But while I'd got Rowan talking at last, I had to hit her with the stuff Billy had said.

"Ro," I began tentatively, feeling one shoulder go a bit juddery, "someone I know saw you on Saturday night up at Muswell Hill Broadway. Bil— I mean, he— I mean, this person saw you staggering about, like you were drunk. Or something."

"What? Billy saw me and thought I was *drunk*?! How *could* he?!" Rowan gasped.

Oh wow. I wish I hadn't started this now. And so much for me "subtly" keeping Billy's identity under cover.

"I wasn't drunk, Al!" whimpered Rowan.

Rolf immediately stopped searching for non-existent cats and their tinkling collars and started gently whining in sympathy.

"But, Billy said you were sort of ... *staggering* and stuff!" I tried to argue, feeling horrible now that Rowan looked so hurt.

"We were just being silly! Goofing around!" she whimpered again.

Whiiiinnnnnnne!!

"Shush, Rolf," I said soothingly, patting him on his big, hairy head.

"Chazza just kept pushing me off the pavement, for a laugh! Honest!" Rowan tried to explain in a high-pitched, pleading squeak.

Aaa-ooooooooooooowwww!

Right – enough was enough. Either Rowan was going to start crying or Rolf was going to start howling at the moon (or both) and my jangled nerves couldn't stand it.

I had to get back to normality. Even if that was a kitchen full of grumpy grannies, Jaffa Cakes and flapping pigeons.

"I'm going to make some tea. Do you want a cup?" I said softly, grabbing an agitated Rolf by the collar and hauling him out of the room.

"Yes, please," sniffed Rowan, managing a swift, wobbly smile.

"Jaffa Cake?" I added.

"Yes, please," nodded Rowan.

Well, in her delicate state, she'd never notice the odd peck-mark or two...

Chapter 13

TO SKIRT OR NOT TO SKIRT...

"What's wrong with your black cords?" Sandie whispered.

She had to whisper. Teachers don't really like you discussing what you're going to wear for your try-out Saturday job. In fact, they don't like to hear you discussing clothes when they're teaching you full stop. Funny, that...

"I dunno," I shrugged in reply, while looking down at my legs under the desk.

There were a couple of dusty paw-prints on my thigh, I noticed. Cat-sized.

By the way, it wasn't just me and Sandie that were doing the whispering. Everyone was beginning to witter away, seeing as Mr Horace was a bit distracted. He was tutting a lot and trying to get the TV to work, so that we could all enjoy the treat of *Maths is Fun! No – We're Not Just Paid To Say That!* or whatever. (Now, I'm no electrical engineer, but if I was brave enough – and if I cared enough – I might have been tempted to point out to Mr Horace that thumping a badly behaved TV repeatedly on its side with your fist is liable to cause even *more* damage to it.) Still, at least Mr Horace's mistreatment of the telly gave me a few seconds' cover to continue my conversation with Sandie.

"But they're really nice trousers. *And* they look smart enough without being ... y'know – *smart*," Sandie hissed helpfully.

"Yeah," I shrugged again, while spitting on my finger and rubbing away the paw-prints.

Dad had bought me these cords to wear to school a couple of months ago.

And *that* was the problem.

"It's just that they make me feel ... thirteen," I mumbled, knowing it was pathetic.

But just their association with school and the fact that they had this little "Age 12–13" tag sewn in the waistband made me come over all under age again. Not, by the way, that I assumed Mrs Merrill would be inspecting the inside of my trousers when I stepped into her shop in a couple of days time (I think that's an arrestable offence, actually). But, unlike my immaculate sister Linn, I find it very hard to stop my clothes from a) having a magnetic attraction to pet hairs and b) staying where I want them to. This means that socks slither down, tops ride up and tags ping out on a regular basis. And Mrs Merrill might be mad and wear a wig, but I'm pretty sure she can read OK – specially a sticky-out tag that says "Age 12–13".

"What about your combats?" Sandie suggested next.

"Too laid-back," I shook my head.

"Your jeans?"

"Too scruffy."

"Your purple velvet trousers?"

"Too clubby."

"What about a skirt"

"Too … skirty," I shuddered.

The thing about skirts is that I really like them. On other people. And on hangers in shops. It's like, I see a cute-looking skirt, so I'll try it on. And it'll look kind of OK, but within about half a second, I just really want to get into a pair of kecks again. I don't know why; maybe I'm just allergic to skirts.

"Well, why don't I come round tomorrow night and we'll do a dress rehearsal?" said Sandie.

I was just about to tell her that that was a fantastic idea, and that she should maybe bring around her new charcoal-grey trousers from TopShop, just in case they suited me, when we were rudely interrupted.

"What are you two doing tomorrow night?"

asked Kyra, slithering herself right across her desk behind us and joining in the conversation.

"Are you earwigging?" I teased her.

"Well, I wouldn't *have* to if you two *spoke* properly, instead of whispering," she grinned at me, not even attempting to lower her voice. "So what are we doing tomorrow evening, girls?"

I didn't mind that she'd invited herself. The more the merrier – and it would take my mind off my try-out on Saturday: i.e. distract me from barfing through sheer nerves.

"Dress rehearsal – I'm working out what to wear for my first day at the card shop."

First day … last day. Who knew how it was going to turn out? Oh God, I was starting to feel a bit sick already.

"Great – I'll bring some of my stuff, if you want to borrow something," said Kyra breezily. "But if I was you, the one thing I'd definitely wear is a pair of headphones and a Walkman. You are going to get *sooo* bored!"

She did one of her throaty cackles. It was so loud I wouldn't have been surprised if Linn had heard it reverberating over in the sixth-form block.

"Shush, he'll hear you, Kyra!" warned Sandie, her enormo-blue eyes wide and round as headlights.

"Who? Horse-arse?" she replied, with a "so-what?" expression on her face. "He's too busy faffing with the telly!"

"Not too busy to give you detention tonight, Kyra Davies!" came a booming male voice from the front of the class.

As Kyra sighed and grumpily slithered back into her seat, me and Sandie faced forward smartish and tried *very* hard to look like we didn't know her...

"Sorry..." I muttered, from the discomfort of one of the school loos.

"No worries," Kyra yawned from outside the cubicle somewhere.

I don't know why I felt the need to say sorry to her in the first place – Kyra hadn't got detention just 'cause she had been talking to me and Sandie (if that was the case, the whole class would have got detention, since everyone was blah-blahing quite happily while Mr Horace broke the TV some more). It's just that calling Mr Horace "Horse-arse" in a very loud, very sarky voice is kind of asking for it. And Kyra did that all by herself.

Reaching over for some loo roll, I saw that – surprise, surprise – there was none. (That's not including the full, soggy roll that was sitting in an ominous puddle on the floor...)

"Hey, Kyra, Sandie – can one of you do me a favour?" I called out to my mates. "Can you chuck me some loo paper under the door?"

"Sure!" I heard Sandie say. The other thing I heard was the flick-flicking of some magazine pages, so it looked like Kyra wasn't exactly joining in the hunt.

"None in here … uh – none in there either," Sandie kept up a running commentary as she banged open every free cubicle door. "Aww – yuck! How can anybody be so disgusting?"

While Sandie was playing loo inspector, I sat slouched where I was, with my feet on tiptoes to avoid the dubious puddle, grumbling to myself about how much hassle it was to go for a simple wee in our scuzzy school toilets.

Then, just as I was mulling over that (disgusting) thought, my eyes settled on something scribbled on the back of the cubicle door. It was right at the end of this really boring, long piece of graffiti that's been going for a couple of months; graffiti that had started out with someone writing *"Ellie F is a total muppet"*, then someone underneath added *"I know who you are, and YOU are the muppet!"*, then in completely different handwriting, there was *"No, you are the muppet, you big MUPPET!"*, and it went on and on and *on* like that.

But now there was a new addition to the slagging.

Who's getting it this time? I wondered, bending forward to make out the red-penned scrawl.

Then I wished I hadn't bothered.

"The biggest Muppit at Pallace Gates", wrote someone who couldn't write, *"is Rowen Love"*.

Unless a new girl with a ridiculously similar name – give or take the odd vowel – had started at our school, then it looked like my sister had just been voted this week's muppet.

Uh-oh…

Chapter 14

TARAMASALATA, ANYONE?

"Ro!" I called out, when I got home at lunchtime. "Ro! You home?"

It didn't look like it. Unless she'd transformed herself into a grumpy-looking, short, hairy dog carrying an old, curly-edged Odour-Eater between her clenched teeth.

"Winslet? Where's Rowan? Hmm?" I bent forward and asked, hoping our number two hound would turn into a search-and-rescue dog or anything else remotely useful for once. "Fetch! Fetch her, Winslet!"

Winslet gave me a withering look then bounded off up the stairs, in search of a dark and dusty corner to hide her latest treasure.

"What about you, Rolfy?" I said, ruffling the head of our number one hound, who'd just padded out of the living room, yawning, after an energetic morning shedding hairs all over the sofa.

He licked my hand, then, sensing there wasn't a sandwich in it yet, he tippetty-tapped his way over the polished (and scuffed) hall floor towards the kitchen.

"OK, I get the message," I mumbled, hanging up my blazer and following him through. "So, what do you fancy? Low-fat strawberry yogurt? Cottage cheese with chives? Taramasalata? Whatever that is?"

I was pointing to everything in the fridge that had those annoying "Property of Linn Love" Post-It notes stuck on. I mean, when is Linn going to give up doing that? She seems to think that it'll put me and Rowan off nicking any of her "special" stuff, but it just has totally the opposite effect.

"Is Rowan skiving again?" I asked Rolf, who was happily licking the gloopy taramasalata stuff off the finger I was holding out to him.

I knew, without anyone (any *dog*) answering, that she was. Skiving, I mean. But what was I going to do about it? If I told Dad, it would just be another big hassle for him to sort out, just when he could probably do with a break. If I told Grandma, she'd be really disappointed with Ro, and give her some big lecture. If I told Linn, it would just be more ammunition for her; she'd treat Rowan like she's (even more of) a goofball. If I told Tor, he'd just get quietly worried and ask if a visit to the zoo might make Rowan feel better.

OK, so I knew I wanted to try to help Rowan (of course I did – I had already spent a good few minutes that morning, doodling over the "Muppet" graffiti with Kyra's eyeliner pencil so that no-one else could read it. And if *that* isn't being a good sister I don't know what is (especially since it meant that I owed Kyra a new eyeliner pencil). I also knew that I wanted Rowan to get into as little trouble as possible, which meant sorting this out on my own...

Von's number is in the address book that lives beside the phone in the hall. Dad's got the number of all our friends in there, so that *if* he ever worries about where we are or what we're doing, he can reach us. Not that he's ever done it – it's more like an insurance policy, I guess.

While I listened to the phone ring, I could hear a whirring coming from upstairs, where one of Tor's small furballs was running a marathon in its metal wheel. The whirring was going as fast as the whirring in my mind – I was trying very quickly to think of the right thing to say, if anyone ever bothered to pick up the phone, that was.

After ten thousand rings and a seventeen-year wait, I was just about to give up and stick the receiver back down when the phone was finally answered.

"Hello?"

It was Von. And it was just a wild guess (fnar), but if she was answering the phone, then it meant she wasn't at college. Which meant Rowan was very probably there. Again.

"Von? It's Ally," I squeaked.

"Who?"

I've only known Von for like *two years*, and she has to ask me who I am. But then, when I say I know her, I use the term very loosely. Whenever Von comes round to our house, she's always pretty polite and everything to my dad and Grandma, and she's really nice to Tor (mainly 'cause he's as much of a space cadet as Rowan is, in his own way). But when it comes to me and Linn, forget it. Von doesn't think much of Linn at all – Rowan once told *me* that Von told *her* Linn's way too uptight and straight. And me? I think I'm just too boring for her to bother with. I'm thirteen, I don't have weird dress sense, I don't have any interesting character hang-ups (championship worrying doesn't count), and I have no random bits of me pierced or tattooed.

And you know something? It's kind of tough knowing that you rate really low in someone else's consciousness. Specially when I'm totally fasci-nated by Von. Who wouldn't be? She's totally like

Morticia Addams, except with black combats and a nose stud.

"Ally," I repeated my name. "Rowan's sister?"

"Oh yeah..." Von replied.

And then didn't say anything else.

"Uh, is she there?"

I heard the phone clunk down and could only suppose that Von had gone to get my missing sister. Or maybe I'd just bored her so much with my dull, thirteen-year-old normal-ness that she'd just dozed off on the spot or something.

"Ally?"

Good – it was Rowan.

"Ro!" I exclaimed, relieved that I'd tracked her down.

"What are you doing phoning here, Al?" said Rowan, sounding distinctly huffy around the edges.

Well, pardon me, I thought, feeling equally huffy. *I was only concerned*.

"Why aren't you here?" I said instead.

"Because I'm *here*!" said Rowan defensively.

This was turning out to be a stupid conversation. And she was making me feel stupid for trying to help.

"You didn't go into school this morning, did you?" I blurted out.

I didn't know that for sure – it was only a guess.

But Rowan didn't seem in a hurry to deny it.

"That's none of your business, Ally!" Rowan snapped.

I felt my face flush. Rowan didn't snap at me – ever.

"Ro, if Mrs Wilson or any of your other teachers ask me where you are, I'm not going to cover for you again!" I announced, feeling a bit shaky round the edges.

"Fine!" said Rowan, before slamming the phone down on me.

Right – that was it. I didn't care if my in-between, weirdo sister got into trouble.

And I had half a mind to go back into the school loos this afternoon and wipe off Kyra's eyeliner – so the world could see that Rowan Love really *was* a muppet, thank you very much...

Chapter 15

SYMPATHY AND SNAKES

I was totally miserable all afternoon after my fight with Rowan.

OK, so technically, it wasn't *really* a fight – more like a big, spiky huff – but it was as close as me and Rowan had ever got to a fight.

In fact, I was *so* miserable that right after school, Sandie did something that made me cry. (Before you go thinking that Sandie had a personality transplant and turned from being the sweetest mate anyone could have into Cruella De Vil, I'll explain…)

I was supposed to be going to Billy's house straight after school; he'd phoned the night before (Wednesday) asking me to come round and and help him with his Maths homework (tonight, Thursday). It just shows how bad Billy is at Maths, when he has to ask *me* – who got twenty-seven per cent in my last-but-one Maths test – to help *him*.

Anyway, come four o'clock and home-time, I was planning on just mumbling "bye" to Sandie and moping my way over to the W3 bus stop, where I could catch a bus that would take me over the hill, past Ally Pally, and on to Billy's place. But Sandie persuaded me to hang on for a couple of minutes, asking me to come over to the shops with her and wait while she went into the mini-supermarket for a magazine/some chewing gum/a dead mouse/some high-octane explosives or whatever else she'd told me that I hadn't heard (hadn't listened to, more like). So I was hovering in a generally miserable way when she came out and presented me with a chewy, marshmallowy snake sweet that was nearly as long as my arm.

"Thought you needed cheering up," she smiled, putting her head to one side and gazing sadly at me.

To be honest, I'd have preferred a Toblerone, or a Chunky Kit-Kat. But I was so touched by Sandie's thoughtfulness that I just stared stupidly at the snake as though it was the most special thing I'd ever been given in my life. Then she *really* did the wrong thing; she put her arm around me and said, "Don't worry, Ally Pally – it'll all be OK!"

And that's when I started blubbing.

That's the thing when you're feeling miserable and sorry for yourself, isn't it? All it takes is for one person be really nice and understanding and you end up doing an impression of Niagara Falls.

And, of course, right then – right when I'm having a soggy moment of weakness – over walk Salma and Jen.

"What's wrong?" asked Salma, as she and Jen stared hard at me, their expressions all alarmed and curious at the same time.

I mean, how could I tell them? I knew Sandie understood (as a best mate always does), but how could I stand there with a marshmallow snake in my hand and snot dripping out of my nose and tell Salma and Jen that this was all because I had a bit of a bust-up with my sister? It would sound *so* lame...

"She just tripped and hurt her arm," Sandie covered up for me. "She'll be OK – won't you, Ally?"

Good old dependable Sandie. I nodded a bit and rummaged through my pockets for something to mop up Niagara.

"Aww!" said Jen, beating me to it and handing me a white tissue she'd pulled from her bag.

I wished she hadn't bothered – from the blue ink-stain and unidentifiable crumbs and fluff attached to it, it had been in there for a long, *long* time. Still, it would have been rude to refuse it, so I parped my nose hard into it and hoped none of the crumbs and fluff would stick to my face.

"I don't think your sister's having too much luck this afternoon either," said Salma, gazing at me through her spookily long, dark eyelashes.

"Who, Linn?" I sniffed.

"No – Rowan," Salma replied. "We just saw her a couple of minutes ago by the water fountain, and she was having a really big argument or something with Lisa Dean and Tasha Franklin."

For a millisecond I was pleased – if Salma and Jen had seen Rowan, then it meant she'd come back to school in the afternoon, so even if I felt rotten, at least our bust-up made her think twice. And then my heart sank; what was Rowan arguing about? And what was she doing arguing with Lisa Dean and Tasha Franklin? They were only two of the toughest girls in Rowan's year; the kind of girls who think it's really funny to put stones in the middle of snowballs and spit chewing gum from the third floor stairwell just for the fun of seeing whose hair it lands in.

I'd kind of stopped crying as soon as Salma and Jen had turned up (embarrassment has a great drying-up effect), but hearing this stuff about Rowan really shook me out of blub-mode (panic too has a great drying-up effect).

"I'd better go and see what's going on," I muttered, starting to walk back in the direction of school.

"Nah – she's left already," said Jen. "We saw her running to catch the 144."

The 144 bus? The only time Rowan ever caught that was when she was going on one of her little after-school shopping trips to Wood Green. Was she going to splurge on something again? When we absolutely couldn't afford a single splurge?

Suddenly, a switch in my brain flipped from being worried about Rowan, to being mad with her again. This was turning into a bit of a habit...

I was *so* mad, I decided right there and then to walk up over the Palace to Billy's house. Stomping across the hill would help me to get rid of some aggression (i.e. I could spend twenty whole minutes picturing how I could *kill* my thoughtless sister) and save on the bus fare too.

Well, if one of the Love family was so busy chucking money away, then the least I could do was try to spend nothing.

Feeling virtuous and grumpy, I left Sandie and the others standing on the pavement while me and my snake stomped off...

"...and then it's just a case of multiplying *that*, by *that*," I explained, punching numbers into Billy's calculator.

"Uh-huh," I heard him mumble.

"Oh…" I muttered, blinking from the calculator to the page in the textbook and back again. "Er, maybe you're meant to *divide* it."

"Uh-huh," Billy mumbled again.

There I was, trying to make sense of stuff that made my head go twirly, and what was Billy doing? It took me a minute to twig, but the rustle of paper soon gave him away.

"Billy!" I yelped, turning round and catching him reading *Viz* instead of looking at the Maths questions I was trying to help him with. (Probably just as well, really, since I hadn't the teensiest clue what I was doing…)

"Oh! Sorry!" grinned Billy, as if *Viz* had just accidentally *materialized* in his hand.

"Look, I'm not here just for fun, you know!" I told him off.

But it wasn't true. Coming round to Billy's was always fun (apart from his stupid dog and his stuck-up mum, of course). Billy has this brilliant way of talking drivel that always made me laugh. *And* it's easy to wind him up and tease him, and I couldn't get away with that at home (Linn would tell me to get lost, Rowan wouldn't "get" it, and Tor's too sweet to wind up).

Even though I don't like her too much, it's quite good fun to wind Billy's mum up too. I mean, I know she used to be a friend of Mum's once upon a time (though goodness knows why), and I know she's been really nice to Dad and got him to come along to hers and Billy's dad's evening class (I can hardly bring myself to say *line-dancing* class – good grief) but she's such a snob, she really is.

It was like at teatime, she starts showing off about Billy's big sister Beth and how well she's doing in her study year out in France ('scuse me, but this Beth that she's so proud of is the same one that's hardly ever bothered to get in touch with her entire family since she went to university). Anyhow, I couldn't resist it: I had to ask, "Where is Beth again, Mrs Stevenson?" It's not like I don't know that Beth is in Paris (who could forget the capital city of France?), but I just love it when she puffs up like a proud pigeon and says, "She's in Par*ee*!" in this naff French accent. And when I did it tonight, Billy didn't let me down – he got caught in a snort of laughter *just* when he'd eaten a mouthful of bolognese and did this *excellent* tomatoey nose spray over his mum's blindingly white tablecloth.

"Hold on," Billy said now, pointing back down to the cartoon he'd been reading in *Viz* when he was supposed to be listening to me get his homework wrong. "I just want to finish this page…"

"Nope!" I replied, yanking the magazine off his lap. "You've got to concentrate on *this*!"

"Ooooh!" Billy gasped, holding his hands up in front of him and pretending to be scared of me. "You're *such* a bully, Ally Love!"

And that's when it hit me – not the fact that I will never, *ever* be any good at Maths, no matter *how* hard I try, but the thing about bullying.

Rowan acting tetchy recently... Rowan skiving school... Rowan and the chewing gum on her blazer... Rowan running that day when I heard someone yelling horrible stuff... Rowan looking all upset when I saw her with Von afterwards... Rowan looking gutted holding on to those broken heart-shaped sunglasses... Rowan and the graffiti... Rowan arguing in the playground this afternoon...

Were Lisa Dean and Tasha Franklin bullying my sister?

Chapter (16)

"G" IS FOR...

I didn't stay long at Billy's after that. Once that thing about bullying and Rowan had weasled its way into my head, I couldn't get it out.

Billy seemed sort of disappointed when I said I was going home. He even tried to distract me by doing this impersonation of his Maths teacher, Mr Murphy, but since I don't go to Billy's school and don't *know* Mr Murphy it was hard to be too excited by it. Specially since Billy's impersonation was just made up of Billy doing a stupid walk and talking in a voice that was Billy's, only a bit deeper.

When I got home, I peered round into the living room but, although the telly was on, there was no-one there – unless you count four cats (one that was Colin and three that weren't) and Winslet, who'd fallen asleep on the mat while chewing a toothbrush. It was too chewed up to make out whose toothbrush it was (well, it was safe to say it was Winslet's now...).

I could hear the gush of water coming from the

tap in the kitchen (and the gurgle and thud of water pipes juddering the length of the house because of it), so I walked through, catching sight of my dad at the sink.

"What are you doing?" I asked him, thinking it was pretty late to be tackling the dishes, especially since we all do them in a rota right after tea (I should have been on drying duty tonight, but I'd been round at Billy's watching him pebble-dash the table with bolognese).

"Oh, hi, Ally Pally!" my dad grinned, looking over his shoulder at me. "I didn't expect you back so soon. I thought you were Linn for a second – she's out somewhere or other tonight."

He was holding a blazer, I noticed. For a second, I wondered if it was mine, and then I realized I still had my uniform on (duh).

"I was just coming back down from putting Tor to bed when I spotted Rowan's jacket on the coat rack," he explained, holding the jacket up.

Uh-oh, I thought. *More chewing gum?*

"There's some sort of chalky marks on the back of it," Dad continued. "Dunno what she's been up to, but I just thought I'd sponge them off..."

"Where is Ro?" I asked him, feeling my thudding heart slide up from my chest and into my mouth.

Should I tell him? I fretted. *Should I just blurt out*

what I think? Or should I speak to Rowan first?

"She's gone to bed. Bad headache, she said."

My mouth was just about to open, ready to spill, when Dad spoke again.

"You don't think Rowan's stressing out about the money situation, do you?" he asked me.

I noticed that his short, dark, spiky hair was coming together like a point at the front. It looked funny – like an exclamation mark. Only his face spoilt it – all concerned and worried and tense.

"I don't think it's that..." I shook my head, as I wandered over to the sink and stood beside him.

At that second, a vision of Rowan flitted through my mind; a vision of Ro leaping on to the 144 to Wood Green in search of trinkets and baubles to cheer herself up after a long, hard afternoon being bullied by Lisa Dean and Tasha Franklin.

"'Cause you girls shouldn't worry yourselves," said Dad, staring at me with serious brown eyes that told me *he* was still busy doing any worrying that had to be done. "And it's lovely of you to try and get this Saturday job, Ally, but you don't have to do it. I'm sure we'll be out of this bad patch pretty soon..."

On the one hand I felt reassured by what he'd just said – but only the bit about my Saturday job. It just meant that he hadn't realized yet that I was, strictly speaking, too young to do it. But the "I'm sure we'll be out of this bad patch pretty soon…" stuff didn't exactly make me feel too fantastic.

Should I tell him? Should I not…? I mused at a million kilometres an hour.

"Dad, I, um, I—"

But I didn't get any further than that, thanks to a small, practically inaudible cry, followed by Rolf coming skittering into the kitchen anxiously, his four paws sliding over the lino in his haste to alert us to the fact that Tor was having a bad dream.

"Uh-oh," said Dad, staring upwards, as if he had X-ray vision that could pierce the kitchen roof and let him see straight into Tor's room up on the first floor.

"Here, I'll do that," I said, grabbing the jacket and the soggy sponge out of Dad's hands.

"Thanks, Ally Pally – better see how the little guy's doing," Dad smiled gratefully, bounding out of the kitchen and following Rolf into the hall.

I listened to six feet thundering up the stairs (two belonging to my dad, four belonging to Rolf) and then turned my attention to Rowan's blazer, holding it stretched out tight by the shoulders.

"G" was the first chalky letter.

The next was "E".

The one after was an "E" too.

Then "K", which all together spelt "GEEK".

OK, so if I'd had any doubts before I didn't have them now. 'Cause it sure wasn't the fairies that had scrawled that stuff on Rowan's jacket.

WHO NEEDS MOUSSE WHEN YOU'VE GOT MARMALADE?

I didn't get a chance to have a private talk with Dad for the rest of the evening, mainly 'cause poor little Tor was fretty and miserable and too scared to fall asleep in case his bad dream came back.

In the end, I went to bed. Dad – and Tor – eventually nodded off in front of some snoresville political programme (I think it was so dull that it zonked them out like a sleeping pill). Linn gently shook Dad awake when she got home, and he took Tor up to his room.

But Tor's bad dreams had started up the minute he got put back in his own bed, and the only thing that would calm him down was Dad lying down beside him till he fell asleep again. It worked OK, only Dad woke up at half past six in the morning on the floor of Tor's room, where he'd rolled at some point in the night. Tor, meanwhile, had tiptoed up to my room in the wee, small hours – I discovered him when the alarm went off, all curled up with Colin under the duvet at the bottom of the bed.

Now Dad was sitting at the kitchen table looking like he'd had a fight with a steamroller and lost.

"What exactly were you dreaming about last night, Tor?" I asked him, taking my place at the breakfast table with my brother, Dad and Linn.

"Dunno," shrugged Tor, quite happily, while biting the head off the toast bat he'd just carved.

"He can't remember," Linn continued, rolling her eyes at me.

All that drama and he'd totally forgotten it.

Dad made a little groaning noise and tried (and failed) to straighten his neck. But the hours of lying in a weird shape on a cold floor had taken their toll. It didn't look like this morning was a good time to talk to him either.

Plus, there wouldn't be time. We'd all have to leave for school soon, and I planned on breaking the habit of a lifetime and keeping Rowan company on the way there, so I could talk this bullying thing through with her.

(I had put my head around her bedroom door the night before, in the hope that she'd be awake. But her room had been in darkness – not the weeniest twinkle of a solitary fairy light – and Rowan was just a huddle under her rose-covered white duvet.)

"Where's Ro? Is she in the shower?" I asked anyone who cared to answer.

"No," Dad replied, grimacing and rubbing his neck with one hand. "She's off to the doctor's. She says she still got this headache and that she's been getting a lot of them lately."

"No wonder, since she sits in that stupid room of hers so much. That pink she painted her walls is enough to give *anyone* a migraine," interrupted Linn, as she licked some low-fat strawberry yoghurt (property of Linn Love) off her spoon.

I suddenly remembered that I'd eaten half of that yoghurt yesterday lunchtime, with a little help from Rolf, and now I was quite glad I had. I even quite hoped Rolf had left the odd doggy hair in it. Why did Linn always have to be so mean about Rowan?

"Anyway," Dad continued, shooting a bit of a tsk-tsk look Linn's way. "I told Rowan that she should go round to the surgery before school and try and get seen, or at least make an appointment for later."

She's getting those headaches because of the bullying! I've got to tell him, I thought, deciding that I'd wait till Linn had mooched off to school (after that last unsympathetic remark, I didn't want her knowing what was going on). Then I'd distract Tor by telling him I thought I could hear one of his stick insects whimpering or something, and he'd be off like a shot, leaving Dad to me.

Good plan.

Which – naturally – didn't work.

"Come on, Tor! We'll have to get going now; I've got to get round and open up the shop early today for a delivery of gear levers!" said Dad, rolling down the sleeves of his checked shirt as he got up from the table.

"Hold on – I'll help you out," Linn chipped in, getting to her feet too.

Rats – so much for getting Dad on his own.

I waved bye as Dad and Tor trundled out of the kitchen, then let my eyes fall on Miss Perfection, who was busy giving her perfection one final check in the mirror by the door, reaching up with her hands and smoothing down her already smooth, shiny, blondey hair.

Unconsciously copying her, I found myself running my fingers through my dull, brown hair, leaving a fine trail of toast crumbs and marmalade – which I wouldn't notice till I spotted my reflection in the school loos at breaktime...

"Why didn't you tell me?" I said into the mirror.

"I didn't notice!" Sandie protested, leaning in

and staring at my reflection.

How could she not notice that half my breakfast was in my hair? I mean, what are best friends for if it isn't to tell you when you're accidentally wearing toast and marmalade?

"Honestly, you can hardly see it..." Sandie tried to console me, as I carried on picking bits out.

"Yes you can!" grinned Kyra, leaning in from the other side. "Look! It's all over the place!"

I know Kyra was only being honest. But suddenly, I much preferred Sandie and her nice, comforting white lie.

"I forgot to put my brush in my bag this morning," I grumbled, pinging an especially big dollop of marmalade into the sink. "Could I borrow a brush or comb from one of you? It might get rid of this stuff quicker..."

"Get lost!" snorted Kyra. "I don't want *my* comb messed up with all that gloop!"

"There you go, Ally!" said Sandie, pulling out her Barbie hairbrush and passing it over to me.

Urgh. Barbie.

"You know, Kyra's right – it's not fair to mess up your brush. Look it's nearly all out, anyway!" I smiled at Sandie.

(And the translation of that is: "*Actually, I'd rather wander about with food in my hair than be seen by everyone in the school loos, using a brush with* Barbie *on it. And while I'm at it, why do your parents insist on buying you such totally corny stuff?!"*)

Then another face came into view behind me in the mirror.

"Rowan!" I squeaked, feeling stupidly surprised to see my own sister, at the school we both go to practically every day of our lives. (I say practically, to take into account weekends, holidays, and days when Rowan is skiving round at Von's...)

But I guess I was on edge with her; it was as if there was a big, unspoken secret between us. Actually, there *was* a big, unspoken secret between us, come to think of it.

I was just about to ask Rowan if she was all right and if she'd been to the doctor, when she spoke first.

"You know something, Ally, you *really* embarrassed me, yesterday!" she snapped at me, her brown eyes all dark in her whiter-than-white tense face. "I mean, phoning Von's like that, as if you were my mum or something!"

That wasn't a great thing to compare me to, since neither of us can hardly remember what our mum's voice is like *normally* never mind over the phone.

"Who do you think you are, ordering me back to school like that?" she snapped some more.

I didn't need to check in the mirror to know that my face was by now flushing prawn-pink. Normally, Rowan is such a funny little space cadet that I feel like *I'm her* big sister, and not the other way around. But here she was, telling me off worse than *Linn* ever had, and making me feel about three years old. *And* in front of my mates too.

I noticed that Rowan's hand was kind of shaking when she lifted it up and pointed her finger at me. God, she must have been *so* mad at me.

"Just leave me alone, OK, Ally?!"

OK, I'll leave you alone, I thought, trying hard not to go shaky myself. *I'll never care about you* or *worry about you again!*

For a second, I even imagined myself sneaking into her room and unscrewing one bulb from each of her string of fairy lights. (You only need to take one bulb out and *none* of them work. Sneaky, huh?)

"Wow!" gasped Kyra, as soon as Rowan had turned and flippety-flapped her way across the tiled floor and out of the loos. "I thought she was just weird! I didn't think she could do bitchy too!"

"Neither did I," I answered her, hoping my voice didn't sound as wobbly as I felt inside.

Sandie opened her mouth and closed it, then opened it again – stunned at seeing my kooky sister act like a complete dragon lady.

"Is Rowan all right?" asked Sandie, frowning so hard her eyebrows nearly met in the middle. "She doesn't look normal. I mean normal for *her*..."

It was true – once again, there was no mad hairdo, no wild clothes; only her little red embroidered mules made her stand out. Rowan looked (almost) like everyone else at school, and somehow, that didn't make sense.

"I don't really care," I shrugged, pretending to look in my bag for something that didn't exist.

(Translation: *I think I might cry, so I'm going to rummage around in my books for a minute until I get my tear ducts under control.*)

"Ally?!" a breathless voice suddenly blasted into my thoughts.

"I'm here!" I called out, raising my head and staring at Kellie, who'd just come barging through the door that lead out into the corridor.

"Thank goodness!" Kellie panted. "Chloe said she thought you were here!"

"Yeah, but why? What's up?" I asked her, with my heart squidging in and out in a panic.

"You've got to come quick – it's Rowan!"

I don't think I've ever moved so fast in my life.

I tell you, if I'd ever run that fast on a school sports day (fat chance), I'd have won a medal...

Chapter 18

HOW TO SHOCK BOYS, IN ONE EASY LESSON

If it hadn't been for the fact that Rowan was in the state she was in, it would have been quite funny.

A whole bunch of boys – some so startled that they hadn't done their flies up yet – were hovering about, stunned into stupidity at the sight of so many girls in their loos at once.

It had started with Lisa Dean and Tasha Franklin, who'd grabbed hold of Rowan about two seconds after she'd left me, and bundled her straight through the door with the *Boys* sign on it, straight past a load of flummoxed lads, and left her skidding in humiliation across the tiled floor.

Next, no sooner had Lisa and Tasha run out giggling, then I'd run in, followed by Kyra (who later told me she got quite a kick out of noseying about in there), Sandie (who hated it and was scared she'd pick up "boy germs", whatever *they* were), and Chloe and Kellie.

"She's in there!" said this one lad pointing towards a cubicle. "She just went in there and locked it!"

He didn't really need to tell me that – I could hear Rowan sniffling only too well. And over by the sinks, I could see the one red velvet shoe that she'd lost in the scuffle.

Poor Rowan; she was like Cinderella, huddled in the ashes. Although – and Sandie maybe had a point here – a bunch of ashes were probably a lot more hygienic than the smelly boys' toilets at Palace Gates school.

"Ro – it's me. Please open the door…" I said softly.

From behind the white cubicle door, the sniffling stopped. A bit.

"Go away!" said Rowan in a teeny-tiny voice.

"Please come out, Ro – Lisa and Tasha have gone now!"

At the mention of their names, Rowan did this sort of *whimper*, a bit like when Rolf goes to the vet and knows there's a needle with his name on waiting in the next room.

I looked around at my girlfriends, but they all pulled "uh-oh" faces and shrugged helplessly at me. Except for Kyra, who – bless her – started shooing all the boys out, even the ones who were a lot older than us.

"OK, Ro – you don't have to come out, but please open the door and let me come in," I tried to persuade her.

Me and the others all held our breath for a second, then heard a shuffle, followed by the screech of the lock being pulled back.

In the long, thin crack of the door, I could just make out Rowan's forlorn face – and quick as a flash, I slipped inside, before she changed her mind.

Rowan looked all crumpled and wet, but I think that was an optical illusion; she was huddled so far inside her blazer that it looked six sizes too big for her and she was mostly dry, apart from the big, fat tears scooting down her face and plopping off her jawline.

"Is it Lisa and Tasha?" I asked her, slithering my back down the door so that I ended up on my haunches in front of her. "Not just today, I mean – *all* of it."

Rowan nodded, and fluffy bits of brown hair started to come loose from the ponytail scrunchie at the nape of her neck.

"Is that why you've been acting so…"

I was going to say weird, but then that's Rowan's natural state, so I had to pick a better word.

"…*tense* about everything?"

She nodded again, and wiped her drippy nose with the back of her hand.

"Have they been giving you a really hard time?

Shouting at you and stuff?" I asked her, thinking of Monday, when I'd been on the way to my interview at Something Special and seen her running along the other side of the road.

"Yeah," she whispered. "It's 'cause of what I wear. They just go on and on and *on* at me, calling me names and stuff."

A soon as she said that, a thought walloped into my head.

"Those new sunglasses you had," I frowned at her, "did Lisa and Tasha break them?"

"Mmm-humm," she nodded shakily. "Tasha took them off me and Lisa stood on them. She said they were dumb."

Well, technically speaking, those purple, heart-shaped sunglasses *were* pretty dumb, but that was no reason to go standing on them. *I* think everything that presenter Donna Air wears is dumb, but you don't see *me* hanging about outside TV studios, waiting to try to stand on her pink crocodile-skin cowboy boots. O*r* chuck her into boys' toilets.

"And you've been skiving off round at Von's, just to get away from them?"

Rowan nodded hard, so that more droplets of salty tears splashed around.

I was going to ask her about the chewing gum and chalked nastiness on her blazer, and about the graffiti in the girls' loos, but there didn't seem any point in going over all that stuff and upsetting her even more than she was already upset.

"Ally, that's the bell!" came a voice from floor level somewhere. I knew – you can hardly miss something that loud, even when you are in the middle of a family crisis.

"I'd better stay here," I told Sandie, who was peeking up at me from the small gap between the tiles and the cubicle door.

Another face appeared, as Kyra joined Sandie on the floor.

"We'll tell Mr Matthews that your sister was sick, and you had to take her home," said Kyra, coming over all enterprising.

"Do you want me to tell the office that you're ill, Rowan?" Sandie blinked up at my sister.

Rowan nodded down at her, tears welling in her eyes again.

"Thanks, guys," I whispered. "I'll take her home after everyone's gone to class and it's quiet."

I could make out the shuffle of a few footsteps as Sandie, Kyra, Chloe and Kellie made their way out, and then apart from the distant hubbub of passing people in the corridor, there was silence … and Rowan's sniffling.

"We've got to tell someone, Rowan. We've got

to tell one of your teachers, and we've got to tell Dad!" I implored her.

"No!" she squeaked. "I can't tell Dad – he's too worried as it is! And I can't tell anyone at school! Li–Lisa an' Tasha said to me that if they got into trouble, they'd make things much, much worse for me!"

"But it's much worse already!" I tried to reason with her. "It was bad if they were just calling you names and stuff, but if they're breaking your things, and starting to shove you around..."

I was trying to sound like I knew what I was talking about, but inside my head was a big sign saying *Panic! Panic! Panic!* It's just that I knew what she meant – girls like Lisa and Tasha were seriously scary. Another thing I knew was that I didn't know what to do.

But I knew someone who would...

I don't know who designed the windows in the doors of the sixth-form block, but whoever it was was *really* tall.

I must have looked like a total moron, jumping up and down outside every classroom, desperately trying to peer in and catch a glimpse of Linn. All the while, Rowan was still locked away in her cubicle in the boys' toilets, going absolutely nowhere till Linn and I came back for her and took her home.

And that's where we were now, the three of us sitting in the living room, at eleven-thirty on a Friday morning, while everyone else was in school.

It was nice – well as nice as it can be when you've just found out that your sister's being tortured by some brain-dead meatheads. It was nice because Rowan was lying on the sofa with her head in Linn's lap, while Linn gently stroked her head – just like Mum used to do when we were little – and tried to keep Rolf from licking Ro's face in sympathy.

And let me tell you, that doesn't happen too often in our house (Linn and Rowan being so close, I mean. Rolf licks everyone's face all the time, especially after he's just eaten his very honky Dog-E-Chunks or whatever).

"And Von and Chazza," said Linn, "do they know what's going on with you?"

"Only a little bit," Rowan replied, blinking up at her. "I told them some stuff when it all first started up, but they both wanted to come down and speak to Lisa and Tasha about it and warn them off, and I just thought that would make things a thousand times worse for me, so I stopped telling them anything."

"So, you've been keeping this stuff all to yourself?" asked Linn.

"Uh-huh. And it's just made me feel so *tense* and everything, like I've got to be looking over my shoulder all the time," Rowan went on. "I never feel like I can just, y'know, relax. And that's … that's kind of why I got out of it last Saturday."

"How do you mean?" asked Linn, gazing down at her.

"Well, I was out with Von and Chazza and everyone…"

As Rowan spoke, Linn nodded down at her. Meanwhile, a thought was busy forming itself in my befuddled head.

"…and, y'see, there was this boy Joe there, and he didn't know I was only fifteen and that I don't really drink, and he said he was going to the bar, and did I want a beer and I just said yes!" explained Rowan, her hands flapping in mid-air as she babbled.

"So, *were* you drunk last Saturday when Billy saw you?" I asked her, as the realization finally dawned.

"I was … sort of, I suppose," said Rowan, turning her face sideways to look at me. "But I just wanted to escape for a while – stop worrying for a few hours. And so I ended up drinking a few beers!"

"*Did* you stop worrying?" Linn asked her in a very gentle, very un-Linn voice.

"Yeah, but then I felt absolutely terrible and ended up *barfing* on the pavement in front of all my friends, and I had to go back to Chazza's and try to sober up before I came home."

"So that's why you didn't get home till so late," I said, slotting the pieces of the mystery together.

"Yeah, and I had a horrible hangover the next day and then I ended up yelling at Dad, just when he's so miserable about money and everything, and I feel terrible, even though I've told him I'm sorry for shouting, and that's why I don't want him to know what's going on at school so please don't anyone tell him, please please Linn please Ally!"

She was off again, getting all her words in a big, panicky jumble.

"Well, we've got to tell Mr Bashir, Ro. We have to! Lisa and Tasha can't get away with—"

Rowan had slapped her hands over her face at the sound of our headmaster's name, and from somewhere underneath her hands, I could make out her saying, "They'll kill me!"

Linn looked over at me. I looked back. I didn't know what to say that could help.

"OK, don't worry, Ro. We'll work out another

way around this, I promise. Cross my heart and hope to die..."

Slowly, Rowan slithered her hands down her face and peered hopefully at Linn.

"Promise," Linn repeated. "Now, me and Ally are going to have to go back to school after lunch, but why don't you go to bed and try and have a sleep this afternoon? I'll explain you're ill to the office. And I'll try and work something out that doesn't get you in more trouble. Honest."

"She's all right," said Linn, coming back into the kitchen after she'd checked on Rowan. "I gave her the hot-water bottle and put her favourite picture of Johnny Depp beside her bed..."

"Good," I said, pushing over a sandwich I'd just made for Linn, in my effort to feel less helpless and a little bit more useful.

"Thanks," mumbled Linn, flopping down on to one of the wooden chairs.

"So..." I began. "What are we going to do to help Ro?"

"Well, first, we've got to work out a rota, so that one of us always walks her to and from school, so those two losers don't get a chance to get her on her own."

"And then?" I asked, feeling a wave of relief

wash over me as my Super-Star Sister (I've never said a bad word against her, honest) took control.

"And then," said Linn, "I haven't a clue, Ally…"

Chapter 19

THE DRESS REHEARSAL

Kyra, Sandie, Frankie and Eddie were all sitting on my bed, staring at me.

"Well?" I asked them, self-consciously giving them a twirl (and tripping over a row of trainers at the same time).

What I was trying to do – apart from fall over – was show them my current number-one choice of outfit for my try-out at the card shop the next day. I had on my black school-cords, my black school-shoes and one of my white school-shirts (i.e. I hadn't had to change very much – just undo my tie and chuck it over the chair in my room).

"What do you think?" I asked again, picking at the splodge of orange beaniness I had just spotted on one cuff.

"Nice!" smiled Sandie encouragingly.

"Boring," yawned Kyra, flopping back on to her elbows.

Eddie and Frankie didn't say anything. In fact, now that I was standing still and not doing anything interesting like twirling and stumbling, I seemed to have lost their attention altogether. Both of them were slowly closing their eyes and getting all zen-like while Kyra and Sandie got on with stroking one each. They were both purring so much that Dad must have had to put up the sound on the telly downstairs, just to drown them out.

"Why's it boring?" I asked Kyra defensively, even though I knew it was boring.

"It looks like it's your school uniform, just without the tie!" she snorted.

Urgh. She'd spotted it.

"Try my grey trousers!" said Sandie, taking them out of the plastic bag she'd brought round with her.

But even though I really liked Sandie's trousers, before the girls had come round tonight I'd already decided it was a bad idea to wear something I'd borrowed from one of them to the shop. I mean, what if I got the job? I couldn't wear Sandie's trousers every week, and I sure couldn't afford to get myself a pair the same...

Nope, I definitely had to come up with something from my own wardrobe. However cruddy that was.

"No, it's OK, Sandie – I'll just wear something of my own, even if it is *boring*," I replied, directing the last bit at Kyra.

"Oh, for goodness sake..." muttered Kyra, pushing herself off the bed. "Let me have a look through your stuff. You've got to have something better than that stupid school shirt."

I think Kyra was a bit huffy with me because I hadn't wanted to wear any of the tops she'd brought round. But honestly, was she listening to what I'd said? Did she understand that I was going to be selling old ladies birthday cards for their grandkids all day, not going *clubbing*? And I could never have worn one of those skin-tight things anyway, 1) because they were so humungously skin-tight that I didn't think I'd be able to *breathe* properly, and 2) I'd be so self-conscious, imagining that every customer who came in was staring at my chest and thinking, "Poor girl – is it a medical condition that's left her so flat-chested?".

Just as Kyra yanked open the nearest drawer and began to haul out all my clothes on to the floor, there was a knock at my bedroom door.

"Come in!" I called out, and saw Rowan's face peer round the door.

She looked more like Rowan today – she had her hair pulled into two fat, brown bunches, with giant sunflower hair-elastics holding them in place. I knew she hadn't worn them to school like that (she was still playing safe and dressing down), but at least if she was acting like her normal, weirdo self at home it was a good sign. Even though, as far as I knew, Linn hadn't come up with a plan to deal with the bullying yet, I think Rowan felt better just having told us both her deep, dark secret.

"Hi!" Rowan smiled round at us all. "Dad sent me up. He's doing some cheese on toast and wanted to know if any of you fancied some."

"Do you want some, Kyra, Sandie?" I asked my friends.

"Yep! Red sauce too, please!" said Kyra, still busy dragging out clothes.

"Yes, please!" nodded Sandie.

"Tomato sauce on yours too?" Rowan asked, as she hung on to the door and surveyed the room.

"If that's OK," Sandie replied, doing her usual ooh-I-don't-want-to-make-a-fuss! face. Like adding a splurt of tomato sauce would put my dad to too much trouble, I *don't* think.

"I'll have some too," I nodded, assuming that Rowan would disappear back downstairs now.

But instead, she hovered by the door, watching Kyra hold up a black long-sleeved T-shirt.

"Now *this* would look really good with your black trousers," said Kyra triumphantly. "All black is very plain, but *very* cool."

"What are you guys doing?" asked Rowan, her

eyes suddenly bright at the sight of something involving dressing up.

"I'm trying to decide what to wear at the shop tomorrow," I explained.

Rowan bit her lip and stared at the top Kyra was holding up, then stared at me.

"Hold on! I've got to show you what *I'm* wearing tomorrow, to this party I'm going to!"

And with that, she was gone. By the time she reappeared, a few minutes later, Kyra had me dressed in my all-black uniform, and was experimenting with pulling my hair up into a high ponytail. (She was pulling it so hard that it hurt; but I was too scared she'd think I was a wimp to moan about it.)

"Ta-daaaa!" announced Rowan, standing at the bedroom door with her arms outstretched.

She looked great, in Rowan kind of way. She was wearing the lilac butterfly T-shirt she'd bought the week before, and – since she was holding her arms so high – I caught a glimpse of her new, tinkly belly chain. I hadn't seen the skirt before – it was pink, fake suede with a sort of lacy effect round the bottom where holes had been punched out. I hadn't seen the bag she was holding before either: a really pretty, beaded number. One of those that are so small you could probably only fit a Lypsol and a pound coin for the bus in it. (I couldn't ever have one of those – I need a rucksack the size of an Arctic explorer's for all the rubbish *I* lug around with me.) At least I recognized what she was wearing on her feet – it was like those red velvet mules were super-glued to her feet.

"I won't have *these* in, of course, 'cause they don't really go," said Rowan, pointing at her sunflowers.

She was wearing clashing lilac, pink and red so far. What made her think that yellow wouldn't "go"? Especially since nothing else did...

"So what *are* you going to wear in your hair?" asked Sandie.

Thankfully, Kyra was keeping stum. I thought she might be her usual cheeky self and tell Rowan she should get checked out for colour blindness, but she didn't. Partly, I think it's because she still felt sorry for Rowan after seeing what had happened to her the day before, and actually – even though she's never said so – I think she kind of admires Rowan. Even though she always calls her my "weird sister", Kyra knows that Rowan's a bit of an outsider at school, and having felt like that herself often enough, I'm sure Kyra feels like they've got something in common.

"I've got these new butterfly clips. They're

covered in this sort of velvety stuff and they look so beautiful!" Rowan gushed, clapping her hands to her chest.

New.

New, new, new.

The word stuck in my head like it was a big, flashing neon sign.

"Ro? Rowan? Where are you?" Dad's voice drifted up from two flights below.

"Oh! I forgot!" gasped Rowan. "I'm supposed to be helping him with the cheese on toast!"

"Have you and the rest of your family never thought about buying her a *mirror*?" Kyra couldn't resist joking, once Rowan had closed the door and safely pattered off down the stairs.

"Ha, ha," I groaned, rolling my eyes up to the ceiling.

"Nah, she looked all right," Kyra smiled at me, to show she hadn't meant it. "She'd look great at a party – on Mars!"

Being mouthy – it's like a reflex with Kyra. But I'm getting used to it. Slowly.

"I really liked her skirt," Sandie chipped in. "Is it new?"

See? There was that "new" word again. And in our house, and in our financial circumstances, that was *not* a good word to hear.

"I don't know where she's getting the money for all this stuff," I blurted out. "I mean, I've never seen that bag either!"

"Maybe she's nicking it!" Kyra laughed. "Maybe Rowan's face is going to turn up on *Crimewatch* for shoplifting half the stores in Wood Green High Street!"

"*Kyra!*" I blasted out at her. "That's *not* funny! How can you make nasty jokes like that about my sister, after what she's been through?"

But you know something? Kyra had been right tonight when it came to my clothes. And now, it was crazy, but I had this horrible, tummy-wrenching feeling that she might just, maybe, *possibly* be right about this too...

Chapter 20

AND WHAT HAPPENS IF I PRESS THIS BUTTON HERE...?

It was going quite well. I'd only made three mistakes on the till (those machines make a terrible squealy noise when you press the wrong button), forgotten to give some woman her change (I had to chase her down the road to give her it back), and burnt out the element in the kettle when Mrs Merrill asked me to make us coffee (well, anyone can forget to put in water, can't they?).

OK, so it wasn't going *fantastically* well, but Mrs Merrill was really sweet to me about it. She just kept smiling and trilling away with her songs, in-between helping me sort out whatever mess I'd got into. And after turning to jelly and speaking in a wobbly voice to the first thousand customers, I'd finally started to relax a bit and even begun to enjoy my day at Something Special.

"Will you get paid for this?" Chloe asked, just a little bit *too* loudly, when her and Kellie came into the shop to see how I was doing.

"I don't know, I didn't ask," I hissed back, *willing* them to go away. (Suddenly I realized how bugged Linn must have felt last Saturday when me and Tor tried to say hello...)

"Even if it's just a trial day, I still think you should get paid!" Chloe said sniffily, as if she knew everything there was to know about shops, just 'cause her dad ran one. In case she'd forgotten, my dad ran his own shop *too*.

"Well ... whatever," I shrugged, trying to tidy up a totally tidy rack of cards and looking over Chloe and Kellie's shoulders to check that Mrs Merrill wasn't shooting me a dirty look for having my friends in.

"Does she know yet?" Kellie suddenly asked me. "That you're only thir—"

"What about *this* one? It's very funny!" I practically yelped, covering up what Kellie was about to say by thrusting a card under her nose.

"Huh?" said Kellie, frowning down at the *Sorry to hear you're under the weather!* message.

"*No*," I whispered to Kellie, "she *doesn't* know how old I am yet, and she *won't* know, unless one of my friends blurts it out!"

"Ahhh!" sighed Kellie, getting my point, thankfully. "Sorry!"

Chloe rolled her eyes at me, just to let me know

she understood what a goofball Kellie could be.

"Come on, Kel – let's go get a burger," said Chloe, steering her towards the door. "See you later, Ally!"

"See you!" I called after them as left, weak with relief that they'd finally gone.

Only I didn't feel relieved for long. There was Chloe and Kellie outside on the pavement, waving in at me through the big plate-glass window and pointing to someone else they'd just bumped into: Billy.

I widened my eyes at him as he grinned mischievously at me.

Go away! I mouthed silently at him.

Mrs Merrill didn't see all the commotion behind her; she was standing at the counter, her back to the window, tra-la-la-ing away while she studied some order-form thing.

Outside, Billy was busy puckering up his mouth, and had put one hand on his hip while the other one seemed to be stroking an imaginary hat or something. Except...

Omigod. He was stroking an imaginary *wig*. His rotten impersonations didn't stop at his Maths teacher; he was doing Mrs Merrill now.

Go away! I mouthed more urgently. *Now*!

Oh boy. I could really see how I'd wound up

Linn last week. I was so, so sorry. This was karma, paying me back for letting Tor dribble hamster food all over the carpet of the clothes shop and thinking it was quite funny...

Outside, I could now see that Billy, Chloe and Kellie were doubled up laughing. There was only one thing I could do (apart from praying Mrs Merrill wouldn't turn round), and that was to ignore them. I deliberately mussed up a whole row of cards – shovelling them together like a deck of cards – just to give myself the task of sorting them out.

A few minutes later, I dared to look round ... and saw no-one outside at the window. My shoulders sagged in relief. Chloe must have appealed to Billy's better nature (i.e. tempted his stomach with the news that they were going for a burger). At last, I was safe.

For about five minutes.

"Hi, Ally!" said Rowan brightly, as she and Tor stumbled into the shop, laden with bags of cat litter and hamster bedding. (Since I was busy today, Rowan had stepped into my much more sensible shoes and taken over Saturday Pet-Shop Duties with our little brother.)

"Um, hello..." I smiled at the two of them.

Mrs Merrill gave me a look – I didn't know

whether it was an annoyed look or a curious look, but I thought I'd better do something.

"Mrs Merrill," I began, deciding that she'd be less irritated with my visitors if she knew this lot were family and not school buddies. "This is my sister Rowan and this is my brother Tor."

"Ooh, hello!" simpered Mrs Merrill, smiling first at Rowan but saving the bulk of her beaming smile for Tor. "We've spoken on the phone, haven't we, young man?"

Tor nodded wordlessly. I noticed that his eyes were glued not to Mrs Merrill's face, but to her head.

"And what have you been up to? What's in that heavy looking bag of yours?"

"Litter," muttered Tor, still gazing at her head.

Oh, please, Tor, I said to myself, *please stop staring at her wig!*

"Litter?" tittered Mrs Merrill. "You're such a good boy that you've been picking up other people's rubbish?"

"No, *litter*," said Tor, not getting her joke. "For cats to poo in."

Mrs Merrill seemed delighted by his response and tittered away some more.

Rowan gave me a little smile and a wink, then wandered off to look at cards.

"Mrs Merrill was only teasing you, Tor," I explained, standing aside as a customer came through the door.

"Oh," Tor shrugged, staring up at me with his huge, brown eyes.

"So you've got a cat, have you, poppet?" Mrs Merrill beamed down at him, her blonde tower of fake curls teetering over him.

All of a sudden, Tor's eyes lit up and I knew that he was going to do what he never usually does much of – talk. There's only one subject that gets him yakking, and that's animals. And now that Mrs Merrill had unconsciously triggered the pet conversation, I knew the floodgates would open.

"I haven't got one cat, I've got *five*," he started babbling. "And their names are Colin and Frankie and Eddie and Derek and Fluffy. Colin only has three legs because—"

I hoped Mrs Merrill had a spare five hours, 'cause that was how long it was going to take to get through every single fluffy, scaly or feathered thing that lived in our house, as well as its individual history. Luckily for me – who knew it all inside out and back to front – the customer needed to be served.

" 'Scuse me!" I smiled at Mrs Merrill, as I slipped behind the counter and made for the till (with my fingers crossed that I wouldn't mess up this time).

"Ooh! Awwww! Really? Aw bless!" I heard Mrs Merrill comment after each pet's CV had been explained.

"Bye!" I said to the customer, as they left with their card *and* correct change (result!).

But then I noticed something.

Mrs Merrill was still smiling, but her smile was fading fast. Also, she didn't seem so entranced by the cuteness of my little brother. I followed her gaze, which was focused on something at the back of the shop.

Cricking my neck slightly, I bent over where I stood, to see what exactly Mrs Merrill could see.

Maybe she's nicking it! Maybe Rowan's face is going to turn up on Crimewatch *for shoplifting!* I heard Kyra's words from the night before ringing in my ears.

I'd been so wrapped up in work today that I'd conveniently put that whole, horrible conversation to the back of my mind. But it couldn't help springing forward now; not when I was watching Rowan stuff a birthday card into the pocket of her old, moth-eaten, leopard-print coat...

Chapter 21

FIRST-AID HOT CHOCOLATE

You know how some shops have those OPEN and CLOSED signs? Well, Mrs Merrill had another one. I was still standing, with my neck cricked, and Tor was still babbling on (about Mad Max, our thug of a hamster), when I saw Mrs Merrill step back, grab something from below the counter, and slap it on the door.

I caught a glimpse of it before she stuck it on – it was a white envelope with BACK IN 5 MINUTES! scrawled on it, and it already had a curly, old bit of Sellotape attached to the top.

As soon as she'd done that, Mrs Merrill flipped the Yale lock on the door. It looked like Something Special was most definitely shut.

"...and my stick insects all came from ... um..."

Tor was fading out now – now that he'd realized Mrs Merrill wasn't listening any more. And that she'd started to look very serious.

"Ally," she said to me, patting her wig just as Billy had imitated minutes before, "Ally, I think we need to go through to the back office for a chat. *All* of us. *Especially* your sister…"

The back office still had the metallic smell of burnt kettle hovering around, and that just made the atmosphere all the more brittle and horrible as Mrs Merrill started telling Rowan off for stealing the card.

Me and Tor stood speechless by the office door, as Rowan sobbed and Mrs Merrill ranted. It was miserable beyond words to have to hover there and listen to it all. Even the sight of Mrs Merrill's wig slipping to one side as she ranted didn't help.

Rowan was *so* in the wrong that I knew I couldn't stick up for her in any way, so all I did was stand with my face staring down at the floor, give Tor's hand a big, comforting squeeze, and wish this could all be over *soon*.

"…well, all I can say is that you're very, very lucky I'm not calling the police!" I heard Mrs Merrill say suddenly.

Oh, thank *goodness*…

I flicked my gaze around at Rowan, but I think she was sobbing too much to have heard. Right then, I felt I could spontaneously combust, I was so hot with the stress of it all. (I could just see the headlines in the local paper: *Crouch End Girl*

Spontaneously Combusts In Shoplifting Drama!
Wonder if there was a chance that story would
turn up in a newspaper wherever Mum was, and
get her hurrying back home to us?)

"Th – thank you!" I stuttered, speaking for both
of us.

"That's all right, Ally," Mrs Merrill nodded
majestically.

(If I'd been in the mood, I'd have said she
suddenly reminded me of the Queen Mother, only
with one of that big-boobed country singer Dolly
Parton's wigs on. But the only mood I was in was
to *kiss* Mrs Merrill, I was so grateful.)

"Rowan's really sorry, aren't you, Rowan?" I
prompted my sister.

But Rowan was *way* too crumpled and soggy to
respond.

"Well, maybe she is sorry and maybe she isn't,"
sighed Mrs Merrill, "but one thing's for sure – I
think you'd all better go now."

"Thank you, Mrs Merrill," I whispered, grabbing
my jacket and bag off the coat hook on the wall.

At the same time, I grabbed Rowan, who was
going to be dribbling runny mascara on the floor
soon, the way *she* was going.

"Thank you! And sorry!" I babbled to Mrs
Merrill, as I pushed Rowan in front of me, towards

the front of the shop.

"Bye, Ally. Bye, Tor, dear," Mrs Merrill replied straight-faced, as she held the door open for us and blatantly ignored my sister.

"Thanks..." I heard myself whisper, as the door closed behind us.

"Oh, Ally! What have I done!" snuffled Rowan, dragging her feet along the pavement.

You've just lost me my job, I thought, though I didn't say it out loud. Rowan was awash with guilt at the moment and me piling on more wouldn't make things any better.

And anyway, it wasn't like I was the goody-goody sister in all this – I *had* tried to get the job under false pretences, after all. And when I thought about it, it was probably for the best. I wasn't going to be fourteen for *ages*, so if I *had* ended up working in Something Special, I'd have spent every Saturday feeling sick, just *waiting* to be found out.

"What have I done?" I heard Rowan repeat under her breath.

Rowan was a mess, there was no doubting that. But what about poor Tor, who'd had to witness all the horribleness? I glanced down and saw that he was looking a little shell-shocked round the edges.

Now, Grandma had once told me some old

wives' tale about shock … something dopey about sugary tea or something. Well, *stuff* the tea – I knew of something better.

"Come on!" I said in my best schoolteacher voice, putting a hand behind the backs of both Rowan and Tor. "It's Saturday, and you've just been to the pet shop. And Tor – do you want to tell Rowan what we always do for a treat after we've been to the pet shop?"

"Shufda's!" squeaked Tor, a smile (thankfully) breaking out on his face.

"What for?!" I prompted him.

"Hot chocolate!" he positively grinned.

"Ally, I think I – hic! – I should maybe just go home…" Rowan whimpered some more.

The benefit of Rowan being as limp as a rag doll meant that I could totally ignore what she was saying and gently steer her through the door of the café and over to a formica table that was tucked nicely out of sight at the back.

Right then, I knew what was best for her, and that was to sit and get a hold of herself before we got back to the house. OK, so Dad was round at the bike shop, and Linn would be busy trying to sell over-priced clothes to women with too much money weighing them down, but Grandma was going to be there doing one of her "spring cleans", which happened about once a month, whether it was spring, summer, autumn or doodah. And I *had* to get Rowan looking less hysterical before we could face Grandma...

"Is she OK?" the bloke who ran Shufda's whispered to me, as he placed our steamy mugs in front of us.

I could understand why he was worried, considering Rowan was hugging a plastic carrier bag of hamster bedding like it was some kind of hay-scented comfort blanket.

"She's fine," I whispered back, trying to nod reassuringly.

"Mmm, this is nice..." Rowan murmured in a teeny-tiny voice, slightly calmer now that she'd sat for a couple of minutes and taken her first sip of hot chocolate.

She even started slackening her grip on the hamster bedding.

It was all right; she was starting to come out of it. I felt like I could – just about – ask her the dreaded question.

"Why did you do it, Ro?" I asked quietly, so no-one at the other tables, eating their eggs and bacon, could hear.

"I... I ... wanted to take a card to Carla's birthday party tonight – even if I couldn't afford to buy her a present," she whispered, keeping her mascara-smudged eyes fixed on her hot chocolate.

"But Dad would have given you money for a card, Rowan!" I said to her. "We're not so skint that he couldn't let you have *that* much!"

Then – uh-oh – something else occurred to me. I hoped there was enough money left over from the pet-shop shopping to pay for these hot chocolates ... or we were going to be in big, big trouble for the second time in ten minutes. *And* find ourselves banned from going near the shops in the Broadway ever again.

Billy calls Tor "Spook Kid", and right that second, he lived up to his nickname. Reading my mind (or seeing me staring at the three mugs in a panic), Tor rummaged in his pocket and took out a handful of coins. Phew...

Now that we weren't going to be arrested for drinking stolen hot chocolate, I could concentrate on Rowan again.

"Ro..." I began. "Um ... have you ... have you ever shoplifted before?"

Rowan darted her anxious, dark eyes at me, and I could see the splodges of red flood into her cheeks. She knew I was talking about the purple sunglasses. And the beaded bag. And the belly chain. And that little pink skirt. And possibly other stuff that I hadn't even seen yet...

For a second Rowan said nothing, then it all came rushing out in a big, rambly burble.

"Oh, Ally! I didn't mean to! But I've been so totally miserable with Lisa and Tasha always having a go at me that I – I guess I just wanted to cheer myself up, y'know, with pretty things, and I know that sounds stupid now but I wasn't really thinking straight 'cause I was so stressed out and well, we're so poor right now and I didn't dare ask Dad for any extra money so I – oh God! – so I stole some stuff and ... and I can't believe I did it and please don't tell Dad please!"

While my brain was busy getting in a tangle with all this latest information, Rowan seemed to notice Tor for the first time in ages.

"Oh, Tor!" she squeaked, getting all dewy-eyed again. "Poor Tor! You had to see all that! I'm *so* sorry!"

Tor suddenly found his head in a vice-like arm lock, as Rowan cuddled our little brother to death. I knew how bad she must have been feeling; she and Linn and I have this kind of pact about keeping bad stuff away from Tor, since he's just a little kid and everything. But even if she was feeling bad, I knew I was going to have to prise her arms away from him in a second, before his face went *blue*.

"S'okay!" Tor managed to say, as he wriggled free from her bear hug, all by himself.

"Are you angry with me for being such a stupid idiot of a sister?" Rowan blinked at him pleadingly.

Tor picked up a serviette from the table – one that was only slightly soggy with hot-chocolate spills – and dabbed at Rowan's dribbly nose.

"Those girls you said – are they bullying you?" he asked her, obviously having picked up on the Lisa and Tasha remark.

Rowan gave him a wordless nod.

"So you stole things because you were feeling bad?"

Rowan nodded again.

"Well, bullying is very, very bad, but so is stealing."

"I know," muttered Rowan.

"You have to promise *never* to do it again," he said simply.

"I will. I mean, I won't," said Rowan, giving him a wobbly smile.

"*Ever*."

"Never ever, cross my heart," whispered Rowan, doodling a finger over her leopard-print coat.

"Good girl."

Good grief.

I'd always thought that Tor would end up as a World-Wildlife-Fund scientist studying equatorial anteaters or stuff like that, but the way he was going today, he could start a job as an Agony Uncle in one of the magazines I read.

"So ... ready to go home now?" I asked Rowan, who was looking almost like her normal self, apart from the red-rimmed eyes and matching nose. But we could always say she was coming down with a cold, or bubonic plague or something.

"Yep, I'm ready," said Rowan, taking a deep breath.

"Sure you don't want to tell Grandma?" I asked tentatively. "At least about the bullying stuff, I mean?"

Rowan shook her head hard. "Oh no! She'll just tell Dad and I don't want to worry him! Anyway, Linn'll think of a plan..."

I nodded in agreement – and crossed my fingers *really* tight under the table.

Chapter 22

LINN'S CUNNING PLAN. AND MINE.

Despite everything (and despite Grandma and Dad being slightly suspicious of how polite and lovely all of us were being to each other) it was quite a nice weekend.

When we'd arrived home, I'd had to tell Grandma a bit of a white lie about the job. Feeling my left eyelid start doing one of those telltale twitches, I launched into some story about how I'd got it wrong; how the try-out with Mrs Merrill was only a couple of hours, not a whole day, and how I didn't think I'd got it anyway because I made lots of mistakes on the till and destroyed the shop kettle (at least *that* much was true).

Then Grandma – who was on her hands and knees doing something with bleach inside the cupboard under the sink – sat up straight, pinged at the fingers of her yellow rubber gloves and said to me straight, "Well, Ally, you weren't really old enough to be doing it anyway, were you?"

Urgh, so much for thinking no-one in my family had spotted that one.

"I know you were only trying to get a job to help your dad out, Ally, dear," she said, giving me a knowing look. "But I think it's worked out for the best, don't you?"

I nodded and started backing out of the kitchen. I felt a little unnerved, to tell you the truth, and I didn't want Mrs X-ray-eyes to see into my brain and suss out Rowan's secrets stored in there.

After that, me, Rowan and Tor took Winslet and Rolf for a long, long walk up around Highgate Woods (the dogs were deliriously happy about that, although the walk home got a bit much for Winslet's fun-size legs and Rowan and I had to take turns carrying her).

That evening, Rowan went out to her friend Carla's party, wearing – I noticed – the lilac butterfly T-shirt, but with some of her old stuff; not the pink skirt or bag or anything. (She also wasn't wearing her velvet mules, but that was because they were covered in mud. I *did* tell her they weren't going to be any good for stomping round a wood in, but she didn't listen...)

She came home really early from the party though. The next day, when me, Linn and Tor were playing Mousetrap with her (Tor's favourite game, though he does get a bit upset when the mouse gets trapped at the end), Rowan told us that she hadn't really been able to enjoy herself at the party, what with, y'know, *everything*.

Linn – who did, by now, know everything too, since I'd insisted Rowan told her, if no-one else – smiled a lot and was very nice to Rowan. But she still said nothing about a plan, and I didn't want to hassle her by asking about it.

So that was the weekend, which, by the way, turned out especially good when Dad announced he'd sold a whole family four bikes, and could pay off the bulk of the bills.

But now it was Monday morning, and it was not so wonderful. Me and Rowan were walking to school together, and both of us were stony silent. Rowan, 'cause I knew she was facing another day of dread, wondering what torturous little treats those creeps Lisa and Tasha had in store for her next; me, 'cause I knew *that* was what she was thinking. And, for once, I couldn't come up with a single thing that might cheer her up.

I lost sight of Rowan once we got to school and had to go into assembly. (You know how it is: you're meant to sit with your class. Who knows why.) For a second, I was distracted from worrying about Rowan as I filed my way into a row and saw

Kyra sitting right between Chloe and Jen. And – most peculiarly – it didn't look like Chloe wanted to kill her.

"How's your sister?" asked Sandie, as my other mates bent forward to listen, concern etched on all their faces.

"OK," I nodded quickly, seeing that Mr Bashir, the Headmaster, was striding up to the rostrum.

Everyone straightened up, before our Year Head – the mean-faced Mrs Fisher – gave us the evil eye.

"What's going on with *them*?" I whispered to Sandie, keeping my eyes front.

She knew what I meant. I mean, seeing Kyra sitting quite happily in amongst the rest of my mates was as unexpected as finding my mum at home, making the tea (I wish).

"Chloe says she thinks Kyra's OK, you know; after the way she helped out when your sister was chucked in the boys' loos," Sandie whispered back, in that way that's so quiet that only ultra-sonic radar and best friends can pick up.

Well, there was one good thing to come out of the misery Rowan had been through. Maybe I would be able to start inviting Kyra along to our Girls' Video Nights...

We couldn't whisper any more – Mr Bashir had started talking. To be honest, I think he's a pretty nice guy – a million times better than rotten teachers like Mrs Fisher – but I couldn't help going off into a dream when he was talking at assembly. Sometimes I wake up when he makes a joke or something (they're usually pretty bad, but pretty good for a teacher), and sometimes he does have the occasional interesting thing to say (like "There's going to be a school dance", or "The boiler isn't working so if the temperature drops too low we'll have to sent you all home early" or something just as fascinating).

But today, I really woke up. I mean, *really*. And it was all because Mr Bashir had started talking about … *bullying*. I listened to him as he went on about how he'd heard bullying was really bad at other schools in our area, and speaking about the heavy-duty punishments bullies get there. Then he said that he hadn't heard of any bullying lately at *our* school, but if he did, then he'd have to deal with people just as harshly as the other headteachers did.

I felt Sandie poke me in the leg with her finger, and I gave her a little nod in reply. What Mr Bashir was saying was brilliant; now he was even saying stuff about how people shouldn't be hassled because they're different, and all the time mentioning no-one in particular. I really, really wanted to look round the hall and see if I could see Lisa Dean or Tasha Franklin, but I didn't dare.

Please! I thought. *Please let them get the message, if they're not too brain-dead for it to sink in...*

Me and Rowan were just about to turn out of the gates and go home for lunch, when we heard Linn calling after us.

"Wait up!" she panted, leaving her friends behind and hurrying over to join us.

"Won't you be late for school dinners, Linnhe?" asked Rowan. "Won't you miss getting the best table?"

Linn waved back as her friends Mary and Nadia trotted off without her. "Nah, I thought I'd come home with you guys for a change," she shrugged.

Wow. All this stuff with Rowan really had changed things. Not only was Linn dodging out of school dinners with her mates to hang out with us, but she hadn't even got annoyed with Rowan for using her whole name.

"So, Rowan," said Linn, checking the road before we crossed. "How's it been going with Lisa and Tasha so far today?"

"OK, I suppose," replied Rowan, following Linn and me as we darted between the traffic. "I saw them a couple of times, but they just blanked me."

"That's pretty good, isn't it?" Linn smiled at her.

"Definitely better than getting shoved in a toilet," I joined in, trying to make Rowan laugh.

And she did, for about the first time in a *year*. (Well, OK, it was just over a week, but it *felt* more like a year.)

Linn shot me a pleased look.

"Hey, Linn," I said, about to hit my big sister with a question that had been floating round my head all morning. "Did you have something to do with what Mr Bashir said in assembly this morning?"

"Course I did!" she answered matter-of-factly. "I went to see him on Friday afternoon; told him exactly what was going on with Ro but said that she was too scared to get those two drongos into trouble. And so we came up with a plan for him to say that stuff today. Y'know, shaming them with-out naming them – at least that's what he called it."

"But why didn't you tell me you were going to do that?" asked Rowan, looking more than a little bit gobsmacked.

"Because knowing *you*, I thought you'd freak out," Linn explained. "I thought you'd be too worried and mortified to go to assembly if I told you."

That was true, I thought to myself. *Mind you, she could have let* me *in on the secret…*

But I sure wasn't going to be petty about it, not

when it seemed to have worked. I mean, it was early days, but if Lisa and Tasha had ignored Rowan this morning, specially after what they'd done to her last Friday, then it *must* be a good omen.

"Thanks, Linnhe!" Rowan blinked at her.

God, she wasn't going to cry again, was she?

"Hold on," said Linn, stopping where she was on the pavement.

Me and Rowan stopped too, and wondered what was going on.

"There, that's better!" grinned Linn, reaching round and pulling the scrunchie out of Rowan's plain ponytail and letting her hair tumble loose. "That looks more like you now! What about sticking in some of your stupid butterfly clips when we get home, so everyone recognizes you?"

Instead of making Rowan smile again, that last little comment of Linn's made her go all pancake flat for some reason.

"What's up?" I frowned at her.

"I just remembered ... those new clips, and all the other stuff that I ... I ... that I..."

"Stole?" I suggested.

OK, it was a bit blunt but someone had to say it if Rowan found it too difficult.

"Yeah, that," she nodded, steering herself around the word. "Well, they're all stuffed in a bag under my bed. What am I going to do with them? I can't wear any of it!"

OK, so far today, Linn had done an amazing job at helping Rowan out. But now it was my turn for a bright idea.

"Come on," I said marching towards the post office in the parade of shops.

"What are we doing?" asked Linn, following behind me.

"You can remember where all the bits came from? Everything you stole, I mean?" I turned and asked Rowan.

Wincing, she nodded.

"Then we are going to buy a whole pile of padded brown envelopes and stamps," I announced, "and then we're going to spend lunchtime packaging everything up and sending them back. With notes saying sorry."

Rowan looked a bit alarmed.

"You don't have to sign them, silly," I grinned at her. "We'll do it anonymously!"

"*That*," Linn beamed at me, "is the most *brilliant* idea, Ally!"

Well, there's a first time for everything, and Linn praising me like that sure was a first.

But don't get too excited. After Rowan's little drama, everything slowly got back to normal in the

Love household. Dad managed to pay the bills and we've gone back to being just slightly skint, instead of super-skint. Rowan's begun to wear her usual selection of bizarre clothes and hairstyles, and – thankfully – Lisa and Tasha don't do any more than throw her dirty looks these days. And after being the best, nicest, friendliest big sister anyone could have, Linn has gone back to being her usual grumpy self, slagging off Rowan's (rotten) attempts at cooking, and never praising me for a thing ever since.

Speaking of Linn, I've got to go – she'll be back in from her Saturday job soon and I'd better chase any random pets out of her room. I left the door open when I sneaked through and borrowed a pen to write all this stuff down, and someone hairy is bound to have taken advantage and sneaked on to her pristine white duvet for a snooze.

Uh-oh – too late... I can hear Linn stomping up the stairs. And now she's yelling at Winslet, telling her to drop her Wonderbra and drop it NOW!

And there they go – Winslet's claws are pattering down the stairs while Linn thunders after her, growling. (Linn, not Winslet, in case you were wondering.)

Ah, home sweet home...

* * *

PS And the moral of the story is … if you're being bullied, you've got to do *something* about it. Even if that just means imagining whoever's bullying you sitting with their knick-knacks round their ankles on the loo. There, feel better already?

PPS Hope Grandma never reads this: she'd be like, "Oh, Ally, do you *have* to be so disgusting?" And the answer is … yes!

Coming soon:

Friends, Freak-outs and Very Secret Secrets

"Maybe he isn't coming," Sandie suggested.

"He'll come. He *always* comes," I replied, keeping my eye on the silvery white plane cruising by overhead.

It was going to ... Santa Fe, I decided, settling for today's fantasy destination. I could be up there on that plane now, flicking through my *Rough Guide to New Mexico* – my dream boy (Alfie, natch) in the next seat – instead of sitting on a park bench getting splinters in my bum and a crick in my neck.

"Maybe he's forgotten," I heard Sandie continue.

"Billy won't forget. We do this every Sunday morning."

Yep – every Sunday, whether it's rain or shine, whether I'm tired or not, I trudge up to the bench me and Billy call home (around 11 a.m. on a Sunday, anyway), high up on the grassy banks of the park, with Ally Pally at my back and the high-rise pointy bits of central London off on the horizon in front of me.

By my side are Rolf and Winslet (the reason I *have* to come, rain or shine, tired or not). And either Billy will be here already, or he'll be on his way, to catch up and gossip with me, while his monstrously annoying little dog spends quality time driving *my* dogs mad.

OK, so Sandie doesn't usually join us, but she does know that's the routine. So how come – this one time when she'd tagged along – was she supposing that Billy wouldn't show?

"Maybe he's busy or something."

I stopped looking skyward and turned to look at my best friend instead.

"If he was busy, he'd have phoned," I said, wondering what she was getting at.

"Yeah, but maybe he's so busy with something that he hasn't noticed the time," she shrugged. "And that would be all right, because then it would just be the two of us and—"

"*Aaaaarrghhhhh!!!*"

Billy arrived with a roar and a thump, as he leapt over the back of the bench to join us.

Rolf and Winslet found this extremely exciting. There was a general scuffle of barking and hairy paws as they jostled for position, both of them desperate to clamber all over him and lick his face. I was also pleased to see Billy, but didn't feel the need to lick his face. Instead, I just grinned.

"Can't you just walk up and say hello, like a normal person?" I asked him.

"Why?" Billy replied, blinking at me from below the peak of his baseball cap.

Fair enough. There wasn't a rule book around that said Billy had to act normal if he didn't want to.

"Is that new?" I asked, tugging at the cap till it came down over his face.

Billy had about a million baseball caps. Looked like he'd just bought his millionth-and-*one*.

"Yep," he mumbled from behind it. "It's Nike. Got it yesterday. Hi, Sandie, by the way!"

He waved at her, although he couldn't see her. Well, not till I pulled the cap off and tried it on for myself.

Maybe it was the fact that I was nicking something from his master, or maybe it was just the way Billy's hair was sticking up that frightened him, but Precious the not-at-all-precious poodle went into yapping overload.

Yappitty-yappitty-yappitty-yap-yap-yap!

"I thought baseball caps were out of fashion now," said Sandie, over the top of the noise.

"Dunno," shrugged Billy. "Don't care. Shut up,

Precious! Go away! Go and play with Rolf and Winslet!"

"Since when have *you* cared about what's in fashion?" I laughed at Sandie.

I didn't mean it horribly, I just meant that she's the same as me when it comes to clothes and stuff – we like keeping up with what's in the magazines, but we don't exactly want to *shoot* ourselves if we can't afford the latest kitten-heeled *wellies* or whatever is "in". In fact, we are both guilty of sniggering quite a bit at some of the fashion junkies we see wandering around the shops on Saturday afternoons. You know, those people who look like they're trying so hard to be cutting edge with their clothes that they're just kind of *sad*.

Anyway, like I said, the remark about not caring about what's in fashion; I didn't mean it horribly. But Sandie seemed to take it that way.

"Are you saying I'm not trendy or something?" she blinked at me, her vast blue eyes extra-wide and full of hurt.

Uh-oh.

"No, of course not!" I protested.

Wow, she can be *so* touchy sometimes.

Yappitty-yappitty-yap-yap-yap-yap-yap-yap!

Turning away from Sandie, I yanked the baseball cap off my head and stuck it back on the bonce of its rightful owner – hoping that might shut Precious up.

It didn't.

Yip-yip-yippetty-yap-yap-yap-yap-yap!

"What's *wrong* with him?" I asked Billy, staring down at the barking ball of fluff in front of us.

"I think he just wants to play," Billy mumbled, straightening his cap, since I'd rammed it on sideways.

Hat sorted, he bent forward and scooped up Precious in both hands, turning the dog round to face my hairy hounds, who were now stretched out and panting on the grass.

As if he had the brain of a battery-operated toy, Precious now totally forgot us and started yapping directly at Rolf and Winslet. I wished for a second that he *was* battery-operated – that way there might be a volume control on him somewhere that I could turn down.

"So, how come you're here today, Sandie? Just desperate to see me?" Billy grinned mischievously.

From the other end of the bench, Sandie made a little tutting sound and blushed silently.

Here we go – the usual way my two best mates communicate, or *don't* communicate, to be more accurate. In front of Sandie, Billy gets cheekier and more show-offy than normal, and that makes

Sandie get shyer (and quieter) than normal. And that makes it really hard work for *me* – trying to keep a lid on Billy being silly and trying to drag Sandie into the conversation whether she likes it or not.

"Very funny, ha, ha," I said sarcastically. "Sandie stayed over last night, and just fancied hanging out for a while, didn't you, Sandie?"

"Mmmmm," Sandie nodded, keeping her gaze fixed on the three dogs playing (and, in grumpy Winslet's case, growling) in front of us.

"Yeah, my Grandma brought her boyfriend, Stanley, round to visit last night," I continued, keeping Billy up to date with the latest events in the world of Love. "It was pretty funny – I think he got a bit freaked out by Rowan's cooking—"

"No wonder!" grunted Billy.

"—and then, when Tor cut his pizza into the shape of a beard and moustache and tried to wear it, you should have seen his face! It was pretty funny, wasn't it, Sandie?"

"Yeah," nodded Sandie.

"And the poor guy – it turns out he's allergic to animals, and he'd taken this anti-histamine tablet to stop him sneezing and everything," I continued, turning my head to face Billy again, "but it didn't work – not against our zoo! He was snotting all over the place by the time they left, wasn't he, Sandie?"

I turned to face her.

"Uh-huh," was all I got for my efforts.

And so it went on.

Billy told us about football practice the day before, and demonstrated – in slow motion – how he scored the winning goal (see what I mean about the showing-off thing?) He told us about these three girls who hung around and watched, whistling at the lads and generally annoying them (a lie, I'm sure – I bet all the guys *loved* it). He even told us about the lad on his team who'd cleverly managed to stop a pass at goal by letting the ball collide with his *nose*, and how amazing it was that so much blood came out of it. (Apparently the girls disappeared pretty quick after that, looking a bit white-faced.)

The way Billy told it, with lots of acting out and exaggeration, it kind of made me laugh. Sandie? Well, Sandie didn't seem to manage much more than a limp smile here and there.

Maybe she wasn't feeling very well and just didn't want to say anything in front of Billy, I decided.

"Oh, and I forgot to tell you," said Billy, dragging my thoughts back to him.

"What?"

"Well, I saw Richie at football yesterday, and he said he wants to talk to you."

"Richie/Ricardo?" I asked, frowning. "Kyra's Richie/Ricardo?"

From what I'd seen of my mate Kyra's on-off boyfriend (currently *off*), he had all the charm of a doorknob. He might have tried to make himself sound more impressive by introducing himself as "Ricardo" to Kyra when they first met, but impressive, he was not. Big-headed, self-centred, slimy ... yep, all those words described him well. At least, that's how he came across to me. Billy (who knew him as Richie, like the rest of the world) thought he was kind of all right. Which made me think that Richie/Ricardo is one of those boys that can't handle girls as *people* – only things to snog.

"Yeah, Kyra's Richie!" Billy nodded at me.

"What does he want to talk to *me* for?" I asked, feeling myself go pink.

But Billy wasn't listening; he was watching the situation that had developed between our dogs...

"Winslet!" I shouted, seeing what was happening. "Put Precious down! *Now!*"

Grudgingly, Winslet opened her jaws, releasing the grip she had on the scruff of Precious's neck. She'd been determinedly stomping her four stubby legs in the direction of the nearest bin, dragging a whining Precious with her. I could be wrong, but it seemed to me like she was planning on flinging him inside it – maybe after one too many attempts to sniff her where the sun don't shine. Winslet may be a strange-looking dog (a cross between something big and hairy and something with sawn-off legs), but she does have her dignity.

"Hmm, maybe I should take him home," mused Billy, as Precious bounded into his arms, away from harm (i.e. Winslet).

"Hold on!" I said urgently. "You haven't told me what Richie/Ricardo wants to talk to me about yet!"

"Huh?" Billy frowned at me, as if he hadn't the faintest clue what I was on about.

Hopeless.

For a second, I felt like doing a Winslet and chucking *Billy* in the bin...

There's always something going on in

ALLY'S WORLD

Make sure you keep up with the gossip!

(4) FRiENDS, FREAK-OUTS and VERY SECRET SECRETS

OK, so I *did* have a best friend called Sandie, but I think she's been replaced by a Star-Trek type android. She still *looks* like Sandie, but since when did my *real* friend copy everything I do, and storm off in big huffs over nothing? I think the same thing's happened to Kyra's mum – the super-witch mum from hell Kyra's always moaning about actually seems super-*nice*. Have all my mates gone mad, or have I stumbled into Crouch End in a parallel universe...?!

Look out for loads more fab Ally's World books!

Find out more about Ally's World at

www.karenmccombie.com